NO ESCAPE

The man's shape was just a blur to Katie, and it seemed like he was moving in slow motion as she began squeezing the trigger as fast as her finger could move. The gun repeatedly fired, making a deafening sound and jumping wildly with each shot. The man stopped his forward charge, and started moving backward . . . right out through the door.

A quick thought passed through her mind that he had probably not expected a greeting like this from a refined and educated lady. But all such thoughts vanished when a hand holding a black gun suddenly reached through the front door and sprayed five shots into the room. Then Katie knew there was no place to hide. She would have to come face-to-face with a twisted killer ready to dispense his dose of deadly medicine. . . .

FINAL DIAGNOSIS

FINAL DIAGNOSIS

by

Roger C. Dunham, M.D.

A SIGNET BOOK

SIGNET
Published by the Penguin Group
Penguin Books USA Inc., 375 Hudson Street,
New York, New York 10014, U.S.A.
Penguin Books Ltd, 27 Wrights Lane,
London W8 5TZ, England
Penguin Books Australia Ltd, Ringwood,
Victoria, Australia
Penguin Books Canada Ltd, 10 Alcorn Avenue,
Toronto, Ontario, Canada M4V 3B2
Penguin Books (N.Z.) Ltd, 182–190 Wairau Road,
Auckland 10, New Zealand

Penguin Books Ltd, Registered Offices:
Harmondsworth, Middlesex, England

First published by Signet, an imprint of New American Library,
a division of Penguin Books USA Inc.

First Printing, March, 1993
10 9 8 7 6 5 4 3 2 1

 REGISTERED TRADEMARK—MARCA REGISTRADA

Printed in the United States of America

PUBLISHER'S NOTE
This is a work of fiction. Names, characters, places, and incidents either
are the product of the author's imagination or are used fictitiously, and any
resemblance to actual persons, living or dead, events, or locales is entirely
coincidental.

BOOKS ARE AVAILABLE AT QUANTITY DISCOUNTS WHEN USED TO PROMOTE
PRODUCTS OR SERVICES. FOR INFORMATION PLEASE WRITE TO PREMIUM MAR-
KETING DIVISION, PENGUIN BOOKS USA INC., 375 HUDSON STREET, NEW YORK,
NEW YORK 10014.

This novel is dedicated
to the memory of my classmate
Sigrid Anna Schulze, M.D.
U.C.L.A. School of Medicine, Class of 1975

Acknowledgments

My wife, Keiko, for her love and encouragement.
Stephen and Rochelle for their invaluable assistance.

Lois R. Johnson, L.A. County Superior Court
    Reporter
Peg Roberts, pilot, United States Army Air Force
Brig. General N. J. Roberts, Attorney at Law
The Professional Men and Women of the United
    States Coast Guard Aviation Service
Tom Campbell, Advisor, U.S.N. Seal Team, Vietnam
David DeVorre, Special Agent, Drug Enforcement
    Administration
Howard Orr, paramedic, Mobile Life Support
Melody O'Shock, Certified Respiratory Therapist
Richard Dodge, Far West Gun & Supply
Ralph Quijano, M.D., Obstetrics and Gynecology
Michael Richardson, M.D., Chairman, Dept. of
    Pathology, St. Francis Medical Center
Andy Binder, M.D., FACCP, Pulmonary and Critical
    Care Medicine
Paul Castillo, M.D., Family Practice and Emergency
    Medicine
Judy Sweigart, Certified Radiologic Technologist
Wendel Hans, Dynomotive USA
Jamie Riley

Chapter 1

Sunday, July 1
U.S.C./L.A. County Hospital
Prep Room
5:43 A.M.

"Two more bogeys on the horizon, closing fast!" Ray Fellows, M.D., hollered as he stared out the window.

"Oh God, no!" Joel Peck, M.D., wailed from the other side of the Prep Room as he walked across the blood-spattered floor to join Dr. Fellows at the window. After thirty hours without sleep and ten cups of bitter black caffeine, his hands were shaking and his eyes were puffy and red.

"Goddamn!" he groaned as he peered out at the lights of Los Angeles. "Here they come. They had to dump one more on us before the new crew arrives."

"A last-minute treat," Fellows said softly, the corners of his mustache sagging. "Another hour and we could have just punted it away."

"Look at those bastards accelerate. They must be hitting 80," Peck said, watching the lights move up the freeway. "Something must have really pissed them off."

"Five minutes more of peace and quiet. Fifty-five minutes of fun and games. Heard anything about the new interns?" Fellows asked.

"The guys at orientation last week said there's eight of them coming here—three females, one of whom is a knockout, and five males including somebody named Skeeters."

"Skeeters?"

"Skeeters. They say he graduated first in his class at Harvard."

"First in his class? Well, now, that's just what we need, more brains at the County Hospital."

The two physicians, white coats stained with Betadine antiseptic, blood spots, and secretions from almost every part of the human body, gazed out the dusty south window from the thirteenth floor of U.S.C./L.A. County Hospital, high above the lights of nighttime Los Angeles. The smiling faces on their plastic identification badges showed none of the trauma and battle scars from the past month on the Jail Ward. Their coat pockets were jammed with needles and syringes, tourniquets and reflex hammers, penlights and mutilated *Washington Manuals*. It had been a tough night—even by Jail Ward standards—fourteen admissions, but the end had been in sight, only an hour to go. And now another pair of red lights. . . .

Across the Prep Room, two deputy sheriffs, each with a 9mm Smith & Wesson in his holster, watched the doctors from the doorway. Neither officer asked what was happening outside the window; hundreds of night shifts on the Jail Ward had numbed them to the routine. With no change of expression on their stone faces, they both turned in unison and ambled toward the elevator door.

Five miles from the hospital, two pulsating red lights in tandem formation screamed along the fast lane of the Golden State Freeway in the direction of Los Angeles County Hospital. The Paramedic Rescue Ambulance, tailgated by a black-and-white California Highway Patrol car, squealed onto the curving off-ramp at Brooklyn Avenue, roared through the row of stop lights up State Street, and screeched to a halt at the emergency room entrance.

Five minutes later, in the silence of the darkened Jail Ward lobby, a single white light above the elevator door popped on, accompanied by the distant sound of an old, rusted bell. The two deputies, standing at opposite sides of the elevator door, stiffened and slid their hands toward their pistols.

Fellows and Peck heard a muffled thumping noise before the elevator doors opened. They had learned that it was best to stand away from the elevator, *well away* from the elevator, until the law enforcement people who delivered prisoners to the Jail Ward were able to control whatever violence may be coming from within. Fellows's mustache twitched as he clenched his teeth and waited.

The elevator doors rumbled open with the squeal of aged machinery. Within seconds a wheeled gurney bearing a fat, balding middle-aged man in four-point handcuff restraints was thrust out of the elevator by two red-faced highway patrolmen in the direction of the Prep Room. Close behind was another gurney carrying a curly-haired, bare-chested young man with blood covering the lower half of his face. The heavy smell of bourbon filled the room.

One of the highway patrolmen grimaced at the gathering of doctors and deputy sheriffs.

"This son of a bitch, Barragan, has already killed three people on the Pomona Freeway tonight," he said with disgust as he pushed the gurney past the doctors. "Drunken bastard left three more injured civilians sprawled out across the road and then proceeded to take down a goddamn half mile of fencing before he finally crashed his goddamn Sherman Tank Buick into the overpass."

The other highway patrolman shoved the younger prisoner into the Prep Room. "And then this stupid drunk, son of a bitch college puke in his beer-filled BMW managed to plow into almost everybody on the freeway before *he* stopped," he said.

"I'll take Barragan, you take the stupid, drunk son of a bitch college puke, okay?" Fellows muttered to Peck as they watched the deputy sheriffs transfer the two men to the Prep Room examining tables.

"Okay, let's get it over with," Peck said.

"And you can all go to hell!" Barragan slurred out as he began to thrash around on the table. "The accident wasn't my fault!"

"Of course it wasn't your fault, Mr. Barragan. Where do you hurt?" Fellows said matter-of-factly as he walked up to him and slapped a blood-pressure cuff around his right arm.

Barragan struggled to sit up, but the handcuffs on his ankles and wrists pulled tightly against the rings at the side of the exam table. "Goddamn it, let me go!" Barragan yelled. "You're treating me like a prisoner!"

"You *are* a prisoner, Mr. Barragan. A prisoner on the Jail Ward." Fellows jammed the stethoscope into his ears and began pumping up the cuff. "And I'm your doctor. Where do you hurt?" he repeated.

"I hurt all over." He twisted his head and looked up at Fellows. "You're too young to be a doctor! What kind of goddamn doctor are you?" He jerked his arms and legs against the restraints. "Let me out of here!"

"Your blood pressure is only 100 over 50," Fellows said as he released the air from the cuff. "Are you taking any medicine?"

"Just some nitro my doc gave me for when my chest

hurts." He turned his head again, stretching the rolls of red fat under his chin. "Lemme have some nitro, Doc, my chest hurts like hell."

"Your heart's tachying along, buddy. How much did you drink tonight?" Fellow asked as he inspected the bruises and bleeding cuts on the man's arms and legs.

"I only had a couple! I'm not drunk!" The folds of fat around Barragan's mouth twisted into an attempt at indignation. Fellows leaned over and inspected a large purple discoloration in the center of Barragan's chest. As he pushed lightly at the edge of the bruise, an area of skin overlying the bones below the left nipple popped up and Barragan screamed.

At the adjacent examining table, Dr. Peck's younger patient sat stiffly upright, eyes wide with fear. He pulled his legs against the cuffs that had been attached to his ankles at the end of the examining table. Using a wad of sterile gauze, he nervously blotted drops of blood that rolled across his chin.

"Can I get out of here soon?" he asked Peck as he sniffed and reached up to pinch his nostrils.

"Soon as I finish your exam, draw an alcohol level, and take an X ray of your nose, you'll be going down the hall to one of the holding beds. You'll stay there until they can transport you to L.A. County Jail in the next couple of hours." Peck thumped on his patient's chest and listened to his heart.

"But I'm innocent!" the man blubbered, tears forming in his eyes. "What are my parents going to say? I was just driving home after the frat party at USC when this terrible accident—"

"Listen," Peck said with strained patience as he took his stethoscope out of his ears, "you were injured in an accident, you have been arrested for driving under the influence, and until you either make bond or get your medical problems fixed, you will have to remain here. Just keep cool and—"

He was interrupted by a shout from Dr. Fellows. "Joel, we got a big problem over here. This guy's pressure's dropping and he has some anterior rib fractures. Can you call for three or four units of packed cells, get a chest surgeon up here stat, and get us a chest X ray? I need to draw a 'crit; his heart is taching at 140 now and his systolic is down to about 80."

"Okay, you got it." Peck turned away from his patient and walked quickly over to the ward telephone. "Is his IV opened up?" he called over his shoulder.

"Yeah, I got this one going with Ringer's lactate at 250 an hour. I'm going to start a 16-gauge second IV. This guy's really starting to lose it." Fellows worked quickly, sticking monitor leads across Barragan's chest and attaching wires to the bedside EKG monitor. Peck grabbed the telephone and hollered directions to the page operator, the lab, and the radiology department.

"Barragan! Can you hear me? Wake up!" Fellows yelled as the patient's eyes closed and his head rolled back and forth."

"Fuck you, you no good son of a . . ." Barragan's head stopped moving as his voice faded. The heart monitor showed a series of malignant-looking irregularities marching across the green screen. Fellows ran to the corner of the room and grabbed the red crash cart and defibrillator equipment.

"Joel! He's out! He must have some kind of a major bleed in his chest!"

Peck dropped the telephone and raced to the other side of the bed. "Christ! Nobody bleeds out that fast! You think he's ruptured his aorta?"

"Hell, I don't know! He's got a chest steering wheel injury with some broken ribs."

"Let's tap his pericardium!" Peck said. "Those units of blood we called for will take another five or ten minutes."

"Or more! And the X ray will take an hour. I've got to tap his pericardium now!" Fellows pulled a 4-inch cardiac needle from the crash cart and attached it to a syringe. After a quick wipe of alcohol across Barragan's chest, he inserted the needle between two ribs and pushed it straight down into his chest. The prisoner abruptly groaned and began wildly jerking his arms and legs while vomiting a yellow combination of beer and foul-smelling food.

"He's having a grand mal seizure!" Peck grabbed the intubation equipment as Fellows quickly pulled out the cardiac needle and squirted 10 milligrams of Valium into the IV line.

"Are the surgeons on their way?" Fellows asked frantically.

"They ought to be here in a couple of minutes. Let's get a trach tube into him! He's not breathing very good."

From the other side of the room, the college student watched the doctors' efforts with widening eyes as he absently dabbed his nose with the gauze.

"He's probably aspirated half his dinner already." Fellows turned on the suction machine and pulled chunks of food particles from the patient's mouth and throat. An endotracheal tube was quickly inserted through his mouth and into the windpipe as Fellows pumped 100 percent oxygen into the tube.

"We gotta try to tap his chest again!" Peck said. "He's going to arrest any second!"

The two deputy sheriffs, watching from outside the Prep Room, glanced at each other with a smirk. It was their secret joke, shared many times. *The prisoner couldn't arrest since he was already arrested!* The highway patrolman had taken care of *that* detail half an hour ago!

Peck inserted the thin cardiac needle 2 inches into the

front of Barragan's chest again and was immediately rewarded by a return of dark red blood that filled the syringe. "Jackpot! He does have a pericardial sack bleed. The surgeons are gonna have to crack him open pretty fast."

The cardiac monitor alarm suddenly blasted a loud buzz as the electronic screen displayed a pattern of wild cardiac activity.

"He's gone into V. fib!" Peck quickly pulled out the needle and grabbed the paddles from the top of the defibrillator box. "His blood pressure's gone! Charge it up!" he yelled as he placed the paddles on the front and left side of Barragan's chest. "Let me know when you're at 300 watt-seconds!"

Fellows pressed a large red button on the top of the defibrillator machine. "It's 100 and charging! Two hundred——250——300! Go!"

"Clear!" Peck pressed the two buttons on the back of the paddles and an electrical surge slammed through Barragan's chest. The air filled with the unmistakable odor of burned hair and flesh as the doctors lifted the paddles away and stared at the monitor.

"Nothing! Goddamn it! He didn't convert!" Peck yelled. Let me have 400!"

"Two hundred——300——350——stand by——400! Go!"

Peck hit the buttons. Electrical current crackled through Barragan's chest again, jolting him 3 inches up off the table. The interns stared at the monitor.

"Damn! Nothing again!" Peck yelled.

"I'll pump him!" Fellows said as he leaned over the patient and began rhythmically pumping on his chest. Blood seeped out from broken skin and covered Fellows's hands with a coagulating red film as the jagged edge of a fractured rib began working its way through the skin.

"Christ! He's bleeding all over me!" Fellows said. "Get me some gloves! I need some goddamn gloves! Start some Levophed in the IV! Where in holy hell are the surgeons?"

Chapter 2

"Can anybody here tell me the source of these statements?" Dillon Marsh, M.D., called out as he hit the blackboard with his wooden pointer.

The cluster of new interns sitting in the first three rows of the dilapidated classroom stared at the blackboard, blank-faced. Several shifted nervously in their chairs, starched white coats rustling, as they pondered the origin of the three sentences.

Dr. Marsh scowled at the group, drawing his bushy white eyebrows together as he waited for an answer.

"In seventeen years of instructing interns, I have never seen such a collection of *statues*!" He hit the board with his stick again. "Are there any *intelligent* doctors in this group? Goddamn it, where are the thinkers!"

The interns stared back at the tall, distinguished-looking man. Dillon Marsh had been watching interns struggle through their first years of direct patient care for most of his professional life. During previous work as the director of the sprawling Los Angeles County Hospital emergency room during the 1950s and 1960s, he had hammered out the same lesson over and over: lives depend on adequate physician knowledge and proper physician action. When the University of Southern California finally formalized an affiliation with the hospital, twenty-five years before, he had been elevated to a full professorship and given a choice of assignments at the medical school. Ignoring the coveted lecture circuit lavishly financed by every pharmaceutical company with an emergency medication to sell, and turning away from the clean lecture halls of the new medical campus, Marsh shocked everybody by choosing to supervise the interns on the Jail Ward.

"I repeat!" he roared, smashing the blackboard again with the pointer. "Is there anybody in this room who can tell me the source of these statements?"

Another ten seconds of silence passed. Abruptly, Dr. Marsh pointed his stick at a lean, blond-haired intern sitting in the third row.

"You! The one with a smile on your face! What is your name?"

"Steve Decker, sir!" The smile disappeared.

"Decker! Would you be so kind as to tell us the source of these statements?"

"I'm not sure, sir." Decker tried to look respectful as several of the interns turned to look at him.

"Can you read them?"

"Yes, sir!"

More silence as Decker studied the sentences.

"I am *delighted* that you can read them, Dr. Decker," Marsh said, his voice heavy with sarcasm. "After four years of college and four years of medical training, I *expect that you would be able to read them*! Would you kindly read aloud so that all of us may share in your understanding?"

"Yes, sir!" Decker could *feel* the smiles of the two female interns sitting to his right. " 'Tact, sympathy—' "

"Would you please stand so we may all hear what you say."

Decker's face reddened as he stepped away from his

chair and stood in the aisle. His clear blue eyes looked piercingly at Dr. Marsh, then turned back to the blackboard as he worked to control his anger at being forced to perform such a recitation. His voice boomed out across the lecture hall.

" 'Tact, sympathy, and understanding are expected of the physician, for the patient is no mere collection of symptoms, signs, disordered functions, damaged organs, and disturbed emotions. He is human, fearful, and hopeful, seeking relief, help, and reassurance. The true physician cares for people.' "

"And the source of this thesis, Dr. Decker?"

Decker stared at Dr. Marsh. "These statements were made by the Dean of the University of Southern California School of Medicine at the recent commencement exercises."

"Thank you, Dr. Decker!" Marsh's pointer hit the board with such force that the rubber tip flew across the room and bounced off the door. All heads turned in unison to watch the tip's trajectory as Dr. Marsh hollered, "That was a good guess, Dr. Decker, but you are wrong!" A large blue vein began to bulge in the center of Marsh's forehead. "You may sit down! Would anybody else care to make a guess?"

"I believe, sir, that—"

The jagged end of Dr. Marsh's broken pointer aimed directly at the source of the voice, sitting in the front row. "Please stand up, young man!"

A chubby intern with pink skin and a pained look of embarrassment rose hesitantly to his feet. "I believe—"

"Your name and specialty!"

"Blake Skeeters, sir."

"Dr. Skeeters?" Marsh's eyebrows arched inquisitively.

"Yes, sir." Skeeters adjusted his glasses and

shifted his feet. "I'm specializing in internal medicine. I believe, sir, that the statement is on the first page of our medicine textbook, *Harrison's Principles of Internal Medicine.*"

"Thank you, Dr. Skeeters. You are correct! Very good! Please be seated." Skeeters looked relieved and quickly sat down.

Dr. Marsh paced back and forth, waggling his pointer at the interns. "The statement on the first page of *Harrison's* is a classic definition of how you will be viewing your prisoner patients, and how you will be caring for them on the Jail Ward this month. All of you rotated through Medicine in your third year of medical school, but no one else besides Dr. Skeeters bothered to read the first page of *Harrison's*? Anyone else going to become an internist? Dr. Decker! Your plans?"

"Surgery, sir!" Steve Decker called out enthusiastically.

"Dr. Decker is going to be a surgeon!" Dr. Marsh announced. "Any other surgeons?"

A woman with a square chin and thick biceps shot her hand up. "Whiting, orthopedics, sir!" she called out in a crisp military voice.

"Good for you!" Dr. Marsh said as he looked down and studied his roster again. He pointed his stick at a blond female intern in the second row. "And what are you going to be? Dr. Levy, correct?"

"Yes, sir! Tyra Levy. I'm going to be a dermatologist."

"Good! A dermatologist! And do we have any psychiatrists here?"

Two men, both with full beards, popped their hands up.

Dr. Marsh scrutinized the men closely. "Good! Mawson and Newberry! Any other specialties?"

A red-haired man slowly raised his hand.

"You!" The pointer aimed again. "Eric O'Conner!"

"Yes, sir! Ob-gyn, sir!"

"Okay! Dr. Hill!"

A thin woman with a straggly brown ponytail shyly raised her hand. "Yes, sir. Family practice, sir!"

"Excellent! Obstetrics and gynecology, surgery, orthopedics, dermatology, family practice, psychiatry, and Dr. Skeeters is going to practice internal medicine! What a spectrum of talent we have!"

He paused and looked around the room. Finally, he took a deep breath and roared, "For the next month, all of you are going to be all of these things! You're going to give psychiatric consultations! You're going to suture lacerations! You may deliver a baby, and even, God forbid, a coke baby or two! You're going to give medicines, practice cardiology, perform lung function tests, cure rashes! You will be neurologists, ophthalmologists, and social workers!" His voice became soft as he added, "And each pair of you will do this together each night, without supervisors, without guidance, without your mothers, without anything or anyone to tell you the right from the wrong."

There was the rustling noise of starched white coats as the interns shifted anxiously in their seats.

Marsh continued. "You will have experiences, profound experiences, that will shape your entire career! You will endure staying up all night—not to pass a written examination but to save a life! You will save lives that may not seem worth saving, and you will feel pride in the accomplishment! Some of you, maybe one or two of you, will enjoy the Jail Ward so much that you will consider a career in penal medicine!"

The two female interns in the back row glanced at each other and smiled.

"And through it all, I want you to remember the

words of *Harrison's Textbook;* these patients are human and they are hopeful. As physicians, you will care for them!"

The group of eight interns crowded into the elevator as a seated black woman of immense proportions closed the door.

"Thirteen," Blake Skeeters said politely.

The woman sighed. It was such an imposition. She pushed 13 and promptly returned to her paperback romance novel. If she read quickly, she could get to the bottom of the next paragraph before the elevator reached the Jail Ward.

From the back of the elevator, Steve Decker checked out the seven other interns. At an even six feet, Decker was the tallest of the group, standing almost half a foot above the three female interns and that chunky internal medicine guy—what's his name, Skeeters?—in the front who had memorized *Harrison's* textbook. He surveyed what he could see of the three females: one gal, the thick one with a name tag that said Whiting, looked like a graduate from a Marine Corps Special Warfare Camp. The second one, Dr. Hill, had a nice shape but mousy brown hair that was tied up in a tight ponytail just below Decker's nose. The third, the blonde named Tyra Levy, was spectacularly beautiful with deep blue eyes, long and glossy blond hair, and a figure that would turn heads a block away. *One out of three, not bad,* he thought, *and a full month ahead to learn everything about her.*

Decker had jumped at the chance to include a month on the Jail Ward in his surgery internship year. During the intern registration two weeks before, all the doctors had been given the master plan for interns: you will rotate, they had said, from one specialty to the next, each one lasting one month, and you will gain an expanding spectrum of experiences from these rotations. The twelve monthly choices were selected by lottery and, for reasons that were unclear to most nonphysicians, almost twice as many interns wanted the Jail Ward each month as could be accommodated.

Decker was eagerly looking forward to jumping into the internship battle. Throughout the year the "Great White Mama," as the County Hospital was unaffectionately known, would be his "Mama," and he was ready to be nurtured and trained to the limit. He had had enough of biochemistry, physics, and biology lectures; now was the time for hands-on, real-life experiences.

The elevator door opened and the eight interns emerged into a brightly lighted sally port enclosed by steel walls and bars. Serving as a lobby area for the Jail Ward, the entrance channeled all who entered into a narrow corridor where their badges could be inspected by the deputy sheriff on duty. Steel bars surrounded the interns, and the distant sound of shouting male voices reverberated off the walls. At the end of the room, a barred, filthy window let in just enough smoggy light to establish that it was, in fact, daytime in Los Angeles.

"Form a line and the sergeant will give you your identification badges," a deputy sheriff instructed the young physicians.

Ten minutes later, the interns passed through metal detectors, two iron gates, and finally into an open area in front of an elevator. A deputy sheriff, looking like a stocky bulldog, with jowls that vibrated as he spoke, stepped in front of them and cleared his throat.

"I am Sergeant Grossman, and I am in charge of the deputy sheriffs on the Jail Ward." He turned himself slightly so they could see that he had three chevrons on his shoulders rather than just one or two like the other deputies.

Decker watched the jowl movement and quickly considered a surgical procedure that could help improve the man's looks.

"If you have any problems with prisoners or with the enforcement officers who stand watch here," he said, "I want to be informed immediately. This elevator is the prisoner elevator." He pointed at the doors behind him and continued, "It is absolutely off limits to all medical staff. The elevator is for prisoners, specially assigned orderlies, and for enforcement personnel only; it is guarded at all times by two deputies here and two more down on the first floor near the emergency room."

He turned and pointed to a locked door. "We call that room the Ladies' Room, and it's for female prisoners only. There is a female deputy inside the room at all times. The door is to remain locked; one of the guards will open it for your daily rounds or if any of the prisoners need any special treatment. Now follow me."

He led the interns away from the Ladies' Room and into an area with bright neon lights over two examining tables and several cabinets filled with medical equipment. Two orderlies were scrubbing blood from the stainless-steel table closest to the door; foamy streams of pink-tinged hydrogen peroxide flowed from the table to the floor and into a drain. Tyra Levy's eyes widened as she saw the stream of bubbling fluid approaching her feet. She quickly stepped back.

"This is the Prep Room, where you'll be caring for prisoners when they're admitted to the Jail Ward. Everything you'll need for all but major surgery is available here." He pointed to a tall, lanky male nurse with a neatly trimmed black beard, standing near the medicine cabinet. "This is Peter Martel, the head nurse on the Jail Ward. He will be helping you admit and take care of your patients in the Prep Room."

"What happened there?" Decker asked, pointing to the bloody fluid moving into the drain.

"A couple of prisoners involved in a motor vehicle accident were here earlier this morning. The one on this table apparently had a lot of bleeding," Grossman answered, looking annoyed at the question. "Now, follow me to the medical ward." He turned to walk out of the Prep Room.

"Pardon me, Sergeant Grossman?"

Grossman turned to look at Tyra Levy.

"I'm just curious, could you tell us what happened to the prisoners?"

"I told you—"

"No, I mean what happened after they were treated?"

"What she means, Sergeant, is how did the prisoners do? Like, are they alive?" Decker chimed in.

Sergeant Grossman stared at Decker for a few seconds then looked around at the group, speaking in measured tones. "Let me tell you people something. You are new to the Jail Ward, and you don't know what these prisoners are like. They will try to get you on their side. They will lie to you. They will tell you they are innocent. They want you to believe that they really didn't commit any crime, that they didn't hurt anybody. They will battle with us, and then try to get your sympathy when we have to knock them down. Well, let me tell you"—he waved his finger at the interns—"contrary to what you see on television, they are *all* guilty as far as I'm concerned, and I don't believe their lies. Any of you want to become a public defender for these guys? You want to be one, Doctor?" he glared at Decker.

Decker stared back, saying nothing.

"Sergeant Grossman, I'll take it from here," Dr. Marsh said as he walked up to the group of interns. "I think you've made your point. These people need to finish the orientation and get paired up for their night-call duties."

"Dr. Marsh, I was—"

Marsh held up his hand. "Thank you, Sergeant. You may return to your duties now." He gestured to the doctors. "Follow me."

The interns followed the Jail Ward director down the long hallway as Sergeant Grossman clamped his mouth shut and walked away. When they had moved out of the deputy's hearing range, Dr. Marsh stopped them and turned to speak.

"The prisoners brought to this ward are among the most dangerous people in Los Angeles County. The safe prisoners, the ones who don't try to shoot it out with the police or try to escape, are sitting quietly at the County Jail. You'll probably never see them. People like Sergeant Grossman get callous after years of battling the tough ones; it's easy to get hurt if you're not careful. The deputies are the people who will protect you. They consider these prisoner-patients guilty of their crimes, because most of them *are* guilty. However, as I've told you, you're not in the judging business, you're in the healing business."

"Sir, if I may ask one small question," Decker said. "Tyra and I were just wondering if the two prisoners who were brought in this morning survived. That's all we wanted to know."

"Yes, Decker, they survived although one of them is undergoing a thoracotomy right now. Now, let's finish up. In a few minutes each of you will be assigned

five or six patients to care for until they can be transferred to the County Jail."

The long central hallway stretched the full length
of the hospital's thirteenth floor, and small groups
of prisoners, all wearing light-blue hospital gowns,
milled about under the watchful gaze of the deputies. At regular intervals along both sides of the hallway, smaller corridors led into four-bed wards that
held the sicker prisoners, most of them lying in bed.
Several of the prisoners had plastic intravenous lines
stretching from bottles of clear fluid hanging over
their beds down into their veins.

At the end of the central corridor was the Cage.

Built to serve as a maximum-security enclosure, the
Cage jutted from the far wall, its steel bars looking
thicker to Skeeters than the bars he had seen elsewhere on the Jail Ward. Inside the Cage was a sink,
a metal commode, and a single bed attached to the
wall. The large swinging door, constructed of tightly
spaced vertical bars, was securely locked, Skeeters noticed as he narrowed his eyes and tried to see who
was inside.

Sitting on the floor in front of the bed was a thin
sickly young Caucasian man.

"This is the Cage," Dr. Marsh said as he pointed
to the enclosure, "and inside the Cage is William
MacFarland, also known as Biting Billy. Mr. MacFarland is thirty-one years old; he has AIDS with an asso-
ciated encephalopathy that keeps him in a borderline
psychotic state. He likes to bite. He will bite deputies,
he will bite other prisoners, and he will bite you if
you get near him. Sometimes, when he is frustrated
or bored, he will even bite himself."

MacFarland was rocking slowly back and forth on
his mattress. His lips were moving as he maintained a
steady conversation with himself. Every ten or fifteen

seconds, he gave a pleasant little laugh and waved his arms in the air.

"Why was he brought here, and how are we supposed to examine him?" Skeeters asked.

"Billy is a heroin addict, which is how he got his disease—from the dirty needles—and he is finishing a cold-turkey withdrawal that just about killed him at the County Jail. He'll be leaving here in a day or two, but one of you will be picking up his case. No physicians are to enter the Cage without at least three deputies going in first to properly restrain him. The deputies will tape his mouth shut, but he'll still try to bite you through the tape, so watch out."

Skeeters stood well back from the bars and stared at the prisoner. He felt his heart pounding and realized, with extreme annoyance, that his white coat was becoming saturated with sweat. The one thing in this world that struck a chill into Skeeters's soul was the thought of catching AIDS from a healthcare encounter. The gays caught it from careless sex, the addicts caught it from dirty needles, but to catch it from trying to *help* somebody . . .

He suppressed a shudder. As everybody said, the chances were infinitesimal, but when the likelihood of dying from a disease is 100 percent, it really gets your attention.

Taking the group back to the prisoner elevator, Dr. Marsh pulled a list of names from his pocket. "I'm going to pair you up now," he said. "All eight of you will be working during the daytime on weekdays, caring for your assigned prisoners, while each pair of you will rotate the nights. If your rotation comes up on a Saturday or Sunday, you'll be working a twenty-four-hour shift. If and when things get quiet at night, you can sleep in the Doctors' On-Call Room, across from the Prep Room."

As Decker listened, he mentally tossed around the alternatives of the different matches. Tyra Levy would be the top choice, the only choice. He entertained a quick and fleeting fantasy about spending every fourth night with her. Even on the Jail Ward, it would be nice.

"Okay, listen up, here's the list."

Decker leaned forward, trying to make out the words on the paper Dr. Marsh was holding.

"Levy and O'Conner!"

Damn! The carrot-top Gynie got her.

"Mawson and Whiting!"

Decker scowled. *Psychiatrist gone, with Miss Muscles.*

"Decker and Skeeters!"

Damn! Marsh did it to me! I got the brain!

"Newberry and Hill!" Dr. Marsh put away his list and told them to get acquainted.

Well, that's just great! Decker thought as he swallowed hard and gave a quick smile to answer Skeeters's pleasant upward glance. *God, is this going to be a month.*

Over the shrill scream of the paramedic siren, Andy Blum hollered from his shotgun seat, "Hang on, three more miles to go!" With its red lights flashing, the van accelerated down Santa Fe Avenue under the tight control of Willie Peach, a ten-year veteran paramedic of the Compton Fire Department. Willie had made more than 2,500 emergency calls in the heart of the Compton ghetto, and by his own count, he had personally saved the lives of 387 people.

Although Willie had lost count of the times he had been shot at while fulfilling the duties of a paramedic, this call had come as an "A" (minor) injury. Both he and Blum had agreed that as long as a "C" or "D" (major) injury was not waiting for them, it was safe enough to leave their heavy bullet-proof vests hanging inside the rescue van. Not completely safe, but safe enough.

Behind the two paramedics, Steve Decker and Blake Skeeters sat across from each other, facing the center of the van, both clutching the steel framing on the back of the front seats. It was their first night on the Jail Ward rotation and, as Dr. Marsh had explained that morning, it was important that each pair of interns "broaden their understanding of emergency medicine" by riding with a Rescue Unit for at least one night. A quick lottery with the other interns had yielded the first assignment to Decker and Skeeters.

Flashes of reflected red light lit up the dark interior every three or four seconds, and each time the van hit a pothole, the cylinders of high-pressure oxygen loudly clattered against their metallic bindings. The two men had their seat belts and shoulder straps securely fastened, and both were vigorously hyperventilating.

In spite of an occasional worry about 18-wheelers in cross-traffic collisions, Decker was having a great time. It was like a wild ride at the L.A. County Fair Fun Zone, complete with noise, speed, and excitement. The major difference, he thought, was the suspense of never knowing for sure if you were going to get killed or where the ride was going to take you. But that difference made it all that much more fun. He could see Skeeters's eyes, wide as saucers, looking through the front windshield over Willie's right shoulder, watching a series of near disasters as cars, trucks, and buses came straight at them each time they crossed the center divider line. Blake Skeeters obviously wasn't having any fun at all, and the sight of him made Decker want to laugh.

Skeeters swallowed deeply as he saw another pair
of headlights swerving around them. He felt streams
of sweat running down the side of his face, and every
time the white lights blinded his eyes, he found the
same thoughts racing through his mind. *I'm going to
throw up, I'm going to die, I don't belong here, my
wife is pregnant and I'll never see her again.* He felt
his fingers turning numb as he clenched his fists and
struggled to control his breathing.

"Why don't any of the cars on these side streets
slow down for us?" he hollered.

Willie grinned, large coffee-stained teeth gleaming
in the night, as he cranked the steering wheel back
and forth to maneuver around three low-rider cars
slowly cruising in formation. "Lots of reasons, Doc,"
he called over his shoulder. "They got their radios
going, they've been drinking, they're looking at their
girl instead of the road. Some of them think it's a
game—beat the paramedics, like beat the train to the
crossing. It seems kind of crazy, but you get used to
it after a while."

Willie jammed on the brakes while Blum triggered
a ten-second warbling shriek from the backup siren as
they squealed around a left turn against the red light
at the Rosecrans Boulevard intersection.

"One mile to go, almost there!" Blum called to the
men in the back. Andy Blum was Willie's opposite in
every way, and most of the men in the department
felt that was why they had worked so well together
for so many years. Peach was black and big, Blum
was pale and small. Willie was at ease with himself,
taking events are they came, while Andy was nervous
and rarely smiled. Known widely as the "Peach &
Plum" team, the two had been making emergency
calls together for more than six years, longer than any
other paramedic team in Los Angeles County.

"What's the call on this one?" Decker asked as the van approached a large apartment building.

"Some kind of possible injury to a woman," Blum answered. "Screams were heard and there was a report that somebody was bleeding. It's probably just a domestic dispute."

"That's all we have?" Decker asked. The previous calls had been much more exciting, involving a house fire and rescue, two children trapped in an overturned car, and a mysterious gas that had caused chest pains in about twenty people at a downtown garment warehouse. The last call had involved interviews with reporters from the *Los Angeles Times* and a picture had been taken of Decker examining one of the employees. *Going to have to check the morning paper,* he reminded himself, *see if the story got published.*

And now they have to go to a "domestic dispute"?

The radio blared out the twin tones of an emergency call, followed by a monotone female voice, "Rescue 405, do you copy?"

Blum turned up the volume and grabbed the microphone. "Four-oh-five, 10-4, copy previous transmission, on the run!"

"Second call at 2871 Rosecrans. Possible injury, female victim. See the lady, apartment 229."

"Ten-four, apartment 229," Blum answered. "ETA one minute. Black and white rolling?"

"Affirmative, two units advised, ETA about five minutes," the radio crackled back.

"Ten-four." Blum hung up the microphone and rotated the van's spotlight to shine on the graffiti-scarred side of a dark two-story apartment building. "Number 2871. There it is!" he exclaimed.

Peach slammed on the brakes, squealing to the curb, then reached over and turned off the siren and flashing red lights. It was better not to keep the overhead lights flashing if there was no traffic congestion, he knew. They attracted attention from the local population, leading to significant risks that the van would not be there when they returned. Blum grabbed the radio transceiver and the red-and-white drug box, while Peach picked up the defibrillator; the four men climbed out of the van and headed for the building.

There were no streetlights and, except for a dim glow through the bars across the front entrance, the building was dark. As the men crossed the dirt expanse in front of the apartment, their flashlights picked up the shimmering reflections of broken glass.

"Don't step on the glass," Blum cautioned.

"And don't step on the rusty needles," Peach added.

"Rusty needles? You're kidding, right?" Skeeters asked as they quickly moved up the concrete walkway.

"Nope," Blum replied, "one of our paramedics was taken to Martin Luther King ER last month with a needle that had poked through to the top of his foot. Took 'em an hour to dig the thing out and by the time they finished shooting him full of antibiotics, AZT, tetanus antibodies, and gamma globulin, he wasn't good for anybody for about two weeks."

Decker and Skeeters began to pick their steps carefully as they studied the ground ahead.

Blum pulled open an iron bar gate that hung from one hinge in front of the entrance. The men entered a dingy foyer and began climbing a long, narrow staircase. Halfway up the stairs, a thin black man with a grizzled beard lay sprawled across one of the steps, his head lolling back and forth. A can of Colt 45 was in his left hand, and three more empty cans had rolled down the stairs below him. When he heard the sounds of approaching footsteps, he tried to sit up straight and almost fell down the stairs.

Peach paused in front of him. "Hello, ol' buddy, any problems down the hall tonight?" he asked pleasantly.

"Jus' the same ol' thumpin' 'n' thrashin'," the man slurred, his eyes half open, his head propped at an angle against the banister support. "More screamin' than usual tonight, though, been goin' on for hours."

"Okay, we'll try to fix it for you," Peach said as they passed by.

Decker and Skeeters followed the two paramedics down a long, dark corridor. The only sound was the distant cry of a baby. The lighting was dim enough to require flashlights as they read the numbers on the doors, searching for the right apartment. A couple of doors creaked open, and they caught an occasional glimpse of intent eyes peering out at them.

"God, I hate this kind of call," Blum said nervously as they moved down the corridor. "Never know who's going to pop out a door."

Skeeters looked behind to make sure nobody was following. The hallway was empty all the way back to the staircase.

"Number 219 here, a few more to go—" Willie said, his light shining across the doors on the right.

"Don't hear anybody screaming," Decker observed.

"Here it is, 229," Willie said. He knocked on the door. They waited, listening. Inside, they heard a faint rustle, followed by silence. Peach rapped sharply on the door again with his flashlight.

"Somebody's in there," he said as they waited again.

"I think you're right. But I don't think they're going to answer the door," Blum said.

"Maybe it was a false alarm and maybe we should go," Skeeters said as he looked up and down the hallway.

"I don't think it's a false alarm," Peach said. "Andy, why don't you check the next apartment down there, 231, and I'll check 227." He looked at the interns. "Hang around here in case somebody decides to answer the door."

Decker and Skeeters waited while the paramedics proceeded in opposite directions. Willie loudly rapped his flashlight on the door of apartment 227, calling out for anybody to open the door. Decker turned to Skeeters and muttered, "This whole thing gives me the creeps. Where the hell are the police?"

"Maybe they're waiting for confirmation that there's been a crime," Skeeters said softly. He turned to see what had happened to Blum.

Andy Blum was carefully pushing open the unlatched door of apartment 231, shining his flashlight into the darkened interior. For a moment all Skeeters could see was the paramedic's left foot in the hallway. Suddenly Blum leaned back into the hall and hollered, "There's somebody on the floor here! Hurry!"

The three men ran down the hall as Blum entered and turned on the light. A young black woman was sprawled on the floor in the center of a disheveled living room. Her hair was matted with blood, and a red stain was spreading on the dirty wood floor under her head. She was breathing rapidly, with small pants, and her face was disfigured by a swelling beneath her left eye. Apart from her respiration, there was no movement.

"Check her pupils, Andy," Willie ordered, "and I'll get her blood pressure." He pulled a cuff from the equipment box.

Blum knelt next to the girl's head and pried open her eyelids. "It's hard to see her left eye with all the swelling, but it's open about 2 millimeters and reactive, same as the right. There's some roving eye move-

ments here." He began a methodical exploration
through her thick Afro to find the source of the blood.

"Blood pressure's 96 over 40, pulse is 126," Willie
said. "We better get the IV going—be careful, she
may have a fractured neck if she was hit hard
enough." He looked over at the interns, who were
pulling intravenous lines from the equipment box,
and said, "Let's run an 18-gauge Intracath and open
up a liter of Ringer's lactate."

"Here's where she's bleeding," Blum exclaimed,
peering into the depths of her thick hair. "She has a
laceration, about 5 centimeters along the left side
here. The bone around the cut feels pretty solid. Let
me have a couple of four by four's and we'll seal this
thing up with a little pressure."

"Skeeters, get some gloves on and hold pressure
on the head wound while I get the heart monitor on
and start her IV," Willie commanded. "Decker, see
if you can establish contact with the base station."
He handed Decker the Abcor radio. "You may need
to take this to that window at the end of the hall.
Just crank up the antenna there and you should be
able to reach them okay. By the way, tell 'em to get
the police out here—"

"Willie, I don't like the way she's breathing. I'd
feel a lot better if she had an airway in." Blum
probed around her neck. "Do you think she'll need
a cervical collar?"

Willie looked at the girl's head. "Yeah, put a collar
on her, then go for a nasotrach tube."

Decker walked down the hallway, hearing several
apartment doors click shut as he passed. When he
reached the window, he stood for a moment, trying
to remember the proper radio communication techniques he had heard earlier in the night. *Should be*

simple, he thought, *just call the base station and tell them what's going on.*

The radio was black and compact, no larger than a small suitcase. He carefully placed it on the floor, pulled up the antenna, and flipped on the master switch. A small meter jumped to life as several red lights on the front of the radio began to glow. The base station hospital was . . . Martin Luther King, right? He turned a couple of knobs to dial in the A-5 MLK code, and he picked up the microphone, holding it near his mouth as the speaker began to generate crackling static noises. He pushed down on the microphone key and blurted out, "Martin Luther King Hospital, this is Paramedic Unit 405 with an injured woman, can you hear me okay?"

There was a moment of silence, followed by, "King base, go ahead."

"Thank you. Wait a second, I'll get a paramedic to talk to you." *Great radio technique,* Decker thought, *but they really don't teach this sort of thing at medical school.* He stood up and stopped, frozen, as he stared at the open door of apartment 229.

The girl had just recently been injured, he thought. *A cut on her head with fresh blood reaching the floor just before they had arrived. Nobody had come out the apartment door.* He set the microphone down on top of the radio.

"Rescue 405, are you there?" the radio crackled.

Decker reached down and picked up the mike again. "Unit 405, I'm getting the paramedic—"

"Ten-four, standing by—"

Decker began to walk toward the open apartment door. He was five feet away when he heard the crash from within the apartment of a door being kicked open, followed by a roaring voice.

"Get away from the bitch, you bastards, get the hell away from her!"

Inside the apartment Skeeters jumped away so quickly he almost fell over the back of the equipment box. He rolled off to one side and stood up, backing toward the wall as he stared at the man. Willie stepped away from their patient and held out his right hand, "Easy, buddy," he said, "easy—it's cool, it's cool, we're away from her."

Standing in the frame of the bedroom door, a tall, fat black man had a slate-gray 9mm pistol clutched in his right hand. The gun's ugly black barrel waved back and forth as if searching for the right person to shoot. His face was covered with a three-day growth of wiry dark beard, and his eyes were narrowed, almost shut, with swollen eyelids. He was barefoot, clothed only in oil-stained jeans and a soiled white T-shirt stretched across an enormous belly. Enraged, he stared at Blum, still crouched over the woman's face.

Blum was furious with himself. He had spent the past four minutes trying to insert an endotracheal tube through her left nostril and down her throat into the windpipe, as he had done thousands of times. He had been working to advance it the final couple of inches, but had been repeatedly blocked by a thickened epiglottis. To add to the frustration, her rate of breathing was becoming increasingly erratic and, during the past minute, she had twice gasped and stopped breathing entirely for several seconds. He had thought the tube was in her lungs once, after she had first stopped breathing, but when he squeezed the Ambu-bag, her stomach had started to distend and there were no breath sounds in her lungs. He knew that if he could just move it a couple more times, with a little proper twisting and a little more insertion, he could get it into her lungs before she stopped breathing entirely.

"I said get away from the goddamn bitch!" he screamed.

Blum pulled the tube back slightly and tried to insert it again.

"Andy—the guy's serious! Get back—!" Peach hollered. At that instant the intruder's huge hand tightened around the pistol and fired a single shot.

Blum felt the impact high in his left chest and simultaneously heard the thunderous roar of the gunshot. It felt like someone had hit him with the full force of a baseball bat as he was thrown violently up and across the floor, settling 5 feet away from his patient. He tried to sit up, but his left arm wouldn't move. He looked down at his chest, unable to comprehend the spreading warmth of bright red blood soiling the front of his blue paramedic uniform. He looked at his right hand, still clutching the endotracheal tube. He found himself breathing fast and straining with the burning pain that felt like lava in the center of his chest. He coughed twice and tasted the rusty flavor of fresh blood. He felt a consuming fatigue spreading across his entire body. He lay his head down on the floor and tried to rest.

"Why did you shoot him?" Peach hollered. "You didn't have to shoot him, goddamn it!" He started walking across the room toward Blum, stopping only when the gunman hollered, "Get away from him or you're next! You!" He pointed the gun at Skeeters, who was standing against the wall, his face pale, his eyes wide with fear. "Both of you, get in the corner and get away from her. The goddamn bitch doesn't deserve anything from you. Get over in the corner and stay away from her!" He waved the gun back and forth again at Peach and Skeeters as they moved slowly to the far corner of the room. The gunman stepped over the woman's body and stared down at her.

Not until the last moment did he hear the footsteps coming from behind. Just as he turned his head toward the door, he saw the round steel canister on a direct trajectory to his face. When it hit, his head snapped back with a loud crunching sound of broken facial bones, his left cheek taking the direct impact of the fully loaded 30-pound fire extinguisher. Only a grunt escaped as he fell and sprawled across the floor, his right leg twitching violently. Willie and Skeeters hurried across the room to help Blum while Decker stomped his foot down on the gunman's right hand, still clutching the pistol.

"Blake! Bind his arms and legs together before he comes around! Use some of the EKG wire!" Decker yelled to Skeeters as he pulled the gun free. "I'll call the police again and get some more paramedics!"

Decker ran down the hallway, jamming the gun into the big pocket of his white coat. He noticed as he grabbed the microphone that his hand was shaking violently and his entire body was trembling. He hollered into the microphone, "Mayday! Mayday! Paramedic's been shot!"

Chapter 3

After the last dark shape with a gun disappeared, Steve Decker bolted upright in bed and stared at the clock.

Five minutes before the alarm goes off, less than an hour to get to the Jail Ward. His face was covered with sweat and his heart was pounding as the memory of the nocturnal gun battle faded from his mind. He looked around the room, trying to orient himself. The morning light filtered through the smog layer that hung over the San Gabriel Valley, spreading a dirty glow across the hardwood floor of his one-bedroom apartment.

"What a bitch," he muttered to no one in particular as he stretched expansively and swung his legs to the floor. The apartment, while small and sparsely furnished, had been adequate for his limited needs. He had moved in four years before, after being accepted at the University of Southern California School of Medicine, and after being awarded his degree, he had decided to remain until completing his surgical residency at L.A. County Hospital. The apartment was cheap, relatively quiet and, most important of all, was located next to the San Bernardino Freeway, providing ready access to the hospital, 10 miles away.

The thin white envelope that had announced his acceptance to medical school four years before had been a shock, considering his grade-point average at the time. His undergraduate years at San Diego State had been filled with social engagements and surfing; academic achievement was far down his list of priorities. With bursts of late-night energy, he had barely been able to maintain a high enough grade-point average to beat the substantial odds against acceptance to medical school. After the letter from USC arrived, his family had marveled at their son's good fortune as they prepared to remortgage their home to finance four years of postgraduate medical education. Now, *at last* (as his mother always liked to emphasize), the Decker heritage will be enriched by the first physician in its history.

He had surprised them all by abruptly putting medical school on hold and departing for a six-month trip to Europe.

The six months lasted for three years. He couldn't explain why he needed the time away to put his priorities in perspective. The previous sixteen years of continuous schoolwork compelled a powerful need for escape, away from more academic pressures, away from final exams and grade-point averages. He just wasn't ready for another eight to ten years of formal schooling, and if the truth be known, he wasn't sure if he would ever be ready.

He had spent most of his time in Europe working at various manual labor jobs. His letters back to his parents were brief and noncommittal—no promises, no return date. The letters made no mention to his parents of the passionate six months with Anne in Germany, nor was there a word of the near-marriage to beautiful Renee in La Couronne, France.

At the end of three years, he almost gave his mother a heart attack by appearing unannounced one morning at his San Diego home, adorned with a full

beard and carrying a cashier's check that represented
three years of earnings, for $62,000. Once his parents
were sure that the man at their doorstep was in fact
their son, and once all the frantic kissing and hugging
was over, he announced that he was ready to start
medical school.

He shaved his beard, he spent a final weekend with
his surfboard riding the waves at Swami's, and finally,
after storing the board in the darkest corner of his
parents' attic, he drove up the 405 freeway to Los
Angeles where, four years later, he graduated *cum
laude* from the University of Southern California
School of Medicine.

Decker stood up and smacked the top of his alarm
clock radio to prevent the 7:15 A.M. racket. His lean
body moved with the smooth agility of an athlete as
he began his morning ritual of calisthenics. Ten minutes later, he showered and dressed, opened the refrigerator, and pulled out a generous slice of cold
pizza. Closely inspecting it under the kitchen light, he
found that a part of the cheese was already sprouting
a thin patch of white mold.

Only two days and fungus already.

Decker grabbed a knife, nonchalantly scraped most
of the growth away, and in four bites devoured his
breakfast. He pulled out his car keys and five minutes
later, his shiny red 1984 Corvette rumbled into the
10-mile stretch of cars creeping down the San Bernardino Freeway toward Los Angeles.

Skeeters and Decker waited as Dr. Marsh bolted
the door shut behind them. The Ladies' Room, located at the opposite end from the Cage, was filled
with women mostly under the age of thirty, and the
air was heavy with perfume. As the three men walked
across the room, several prisoners sat up to scrutinize

their visitors. The women were wearing the standard-issue L.A. County Hospital gowns and most of their faces were plastered with substantial quantities of makeup.

The men passed a husky red-haired deputy sheriff with a badge pinned just above an immense left breast. Her pudgy face was deeply pockmarked from years of intractable pustular acne. A sturdy black nightstick hung ominously at her side as her narrow eyes watched the men pass by. *Like some kind of a gorilla,* Decker thought.

"Mornin', Dr. Marsh," she said, her voice sounding like gravel.

" 'Morning, Miss Kraus," Dr. Marsh rumbled as they passed.

"Hey, Doctor, ya need to do a pelvic exam?" one woman called. "I'd like to teach you how."

"Hold it down over there!" Kraus growled as she put her hand on her nightstick and glowered at the woman.

"Hey handsome, come on over to my bed," another hooted as laughter rippled across the room.

The doctors gathered around a rusted hospital bed in the far corner where a young black woman was curled up in the fetal position under several blankets. An intravenous line was connected to her left arm, and a bag of saline and antibiotics was suspended at the head of her bed. Her eyes were closed, her arms curled against her chest, and she was breathing with a slow regular rhythm.

"Dr. Skeeters, meet Miss Julia Jackson, otherwise known on the street as Trixie," Dr. Marsh said as he handed the chart to the intern. Scowling at her quiet form, he continued, "Trixie is twenty-three years old and works—that is worked—as a prostitute. To supplement her income, she became active selling coke, heroin, and various designer drugs to her clients. One week ago, she had a party with her friends at a shooting gallery."

"Shooting gallery?" Skeeters interrupted.

" 'Shooting,' as in to shoot up drugs," Dr. Marsh said, looking annoyed. "She and her friends gathered together to shoot up drugs."

"Oh," Skeeters said quietly.

"And so her friends, who are experts on the anatomy of arteries and veins, advised her that she could get a better rush if she injected the heroin directly into her jugular vein. She was further told that the left side of the neck is where the vein is located, and that the right side of the neck is the location of the artery, where you never, ever, want to inject heroin. Following this advice, she poked the needle into the left side of her neck, and it went, unfortunately, into her left common carotid artery. She then squirted 2 cc's of pure heroin directly into the left side of her brain."

"Christ!" Decker said.

"She immediately stroked out her left cerebral hemisphere with loss of all movement of her right arm and leg and with a total inability to speak. She also developed a large hematoma in her throat that compressed her trachea, causing an additional hypoxic encephalopathy. She is now completely aphasic, both expressive and receptive, fully unable to speak or to understand anything. She also developed a raging meningitis and is on triple antibiotics to cover what appears to be a mixture of staph and strep in her brain."

"Infectious Disease consult going on her?" Skeeters asked.

"Done. Herb Barcley on the ninth floor is following her. You'll be doing the general medical care."

"Why is she on the Jail Ward?" Decker asked.

Dr. Marsh looked pained. "Everyone with medical problems engaged in illegal behavior is brought to the Jail Ward. There was a small quantity of heroin crystals and drug paraphernalia in her room. After her friends thoughtfully called 911, the paramedics called the police and she was arrested for possession and intent to sell drugs. She'll never see Sybil Brand, however, and as soon as her white blood count and CAT scan are stable, she'll be transferred out of here for long-term rehab care."

"Pardon me, sir." Skeeters looked embarrassed again. "Who is Sybil Brand?"

"Sybil Brand Institute for Women, over on Eastern Avenue, just south of here," Dr. Marsh said as he glowered at the ignorance of the new intern. "It's where women, about 2,000 of them, convicted of various crimes, are incarcerated instead of being sent with the men to the County Jail. However, druggies who have pulled things like this"—he looked down at her and scowled—"don't ever end up doing any real time in jail, anyway. They just lie around for the rest of their lives, receiving expensive care, all compliments of the taxpayer."

Skeeters leaned over the bed and placed a hand on her right shoulder. "Can you hear me, Trixie?" he called into her ear.

She stirred with a groan and tried to turn herself on her back. Her right arm lay uselessly at her side, her hand contracted into a tight claw. Her eyes opened to narrow slits and she drooled down the side of her face to the pillow.

Skeeters straightened, beginning to bristle with anger. Ignorance, just plain ignorance, listening to "friends" telling you how to destroy half your brain with one quick squirt. One little injection to fulfill your need, and now look at what you've done. He shook his head.

"You can check her in detail later, Dr. Skeeters," Dr. Marsh said. "We have four more patients for you this morning. Also, both of you are on the call schedule to take all admissions this afternoon and tonight."

Three hours later, Steve Decker and Blake Skeeters stood in front of the Cage, looking at Biting Billy. Dr. Marsh had left the thirteenth floor a couple of hours before, and the interns had immersed themselves in the initial examination of their new patients. Decker had picked up the care of a wiry heroin addict named Hank Block with draining stab wounds everywhere inflicted by someone who took exception to his special price of China White. A prisoner named Jack Diamond, with brilliant purple hair and a mournful expression, had been assigned to Skeeters. The final prisoner assignment went to Decker: Biting Billy.

"He likes to bite," Decker said as he studied the man's chart.

"Even himself," Skeeters responded, watching the man rock himself back and forth in the corner of the cell. "What kind of workup has he had for his compromised mentation? Maybe he has multifocal leukoencephalopathy or a toxoplasmosis infestation—"

Decker felt a flash of irritation: *goddamn internist.* "You mean what workup for his being wacko?" He opened the radiology section of the chart. "He's probably just a schizo. He's had an EKG, which was normal, and carotid duplex studies, which were also normal. His blood studies are normal, except for his AZT anemia, and his Toxo and CMV screens aren't back yet. The guy doesn't have any surgical needs . . . what the hell am I supposed to do with him?"

"Probably the best thing is to ship him back to the County Jail as fast as he can go. Dr. Marsh said he is supposed to go back soon. It looks like he's finished with his heroin withdrawal." Skeeters turned to leave. "Good luck, Steve, I'm going to check over Mr. Diamond."

"The Purple Queen? Good luck with him. You don't want to trade him for Biting Billy, do you?"

Skeeters smiled. "I don't think trading is allowed, Steve, but I'd be happy to help you with any medical problems Mr. MacFarland may have."

"Thanks," Decker replied halfheartedly.

Skeeters walked off with a bounce in his step and Decker peered through the bars of the Cage at Billy. MacFarland was humming a happy tune as he rocked, his legs folded against his chest, his arms wrapped around his legs. Decker scanned through his chart again, then put it aside and called into the Cage, "Mr. MacFarland. Can you hear me?"

Billy stopped rocking, looked up at the ceiling for a few seconds, and started rocking again.

"Mr. MacFarland. I'm your new doctor. Can you hear me?" Decker tapped the bars with the chart.

Billy continued rocking and began humming again, interspersed with a variety of obscenities.

Decker put his hands into the pockets of his surgical greens and stared through the bars at the man. *Biting Billy was in a different world from everybody else,* he thought, *probably a happy little world with everybody humming songs.*

Decker took the patient's chart and slammed it against the bars as hard as he could.

Billy didn't blink.

Decker turned and walked briskly down the central corridor, past the crying Purple Queen being interviewed by Skeeters, to the duty officer's desk near the elevator. A tired-looking deputy sheriff with a wrinkled uniform looked up as he approached.

"What do you need, Doc?" he asked.

"I need to get into the Cage," Decker said.

"And why do you need to get into the Cage?"

"To see my patient, Biting Billy. Can I get a couple of you to unlock the door and hold him down?" Decker felt a flash of anger.

The deputy sheriff grunted and yawned as he turned to call over his shoulder, "Sergeant Grossman! There's a doc here who wants to see Billy!"

Sergeant Mel Grossman lumbered out of the holding area behind the front desk and approached Decker. "Whatdya wanna see Billy for?" he asked.

"He's my patient, for Christ sake. Can a couple of you guys hold him down so I can examine him?"

"He was supposed to go back to jail today or tomorrow . . ."

"Sergeant," Decker said forcefully, "I need to check him over and make sure he is damn well ready to leave. Now, if I could get some help for a few minutes, maybe I can clear him for the transfer before the end of this month."

Grossman held up his hand. "Easy, boy, you don't have to get all hot under the collar. Just settle down and we'll come and hold Billy for you."

"Thank you," Decker said with restrained sarcasm as he turned to walk back to MacFarland's cell.

He found himself grinding his teeth as he paced back and forth in front of the Cage. *Working with these deputies this month is going to be lots of fun.* After a five-minute delay, three deputy sheriffs ambled slowly in the direction of the Cage. One of them carried a roll of white surgical tape, and all three of them wore thick leather gloves. Decker reached into his pockets and pulled out a pair of sterile surgical gloves.

When the key was inserted into the lock, Billy

stopped humming and stared at the four men outside the Cage.

"Now, now, Billy, everything's okay. Take it easy now and the doctor is going to check you over," the deputy with the keys said soothingly. The three officers entered the Cage with Decker behind, pulling on his gloves and digging around his pockets for his stethoscope. As they approached Billy, he remained on the floor in the corner, frozen and unblinking, staring at the men. "Now, that's okay, Billy, don't move now, you're going to be okay . . . stand back, Doc." One of them motioned to Decker. "Sometimes this ain't that easy."

On a prearranged signal that Decker missed, the deputies suddenly jumped on top of William MacFarland.

"Look out! He's going to bite you!" one of the men yelled.

"Quick, tape his mouth!"

"Watch it! He's twisting his fuckin' head around! Strap his head down! Strap his legs down!"

The man thrashed in every direction, kicking and snapping his teeth until a large piece of tape was wrapped across his mouth and around the back of his neck. Two minutes later they had the man strapped to his bed in four-point restraints, his feet and hands secured by thick leather straps and tied to the frame.

They stood up and turned to Decker as one of them said, "There you go, Doc! I wouldn't advise you to check his tonsils." The three men chuckled as they departed the cell, leaving the door wide open.

Like goddamn veterinary medicine, Decker thought. He kneeled down next to the man's rack. No need for introductions and amenities, nothing to be gained by socializing. Might as well just stick to the job at hand.

"Mr. MacFarland, fighting won't help. Just hold still for a few minutes and let me check you over." Billy's eyes were wide open, his head covered with sweat, and his fingers methodically opened and closed. He was pale and scrawny, with the glassy look of uncontrolled psychosis and a constant writhing of his arms and legs. His hair was greasy and his entire body was covered with foul-smelling dirty sweat. Decker subconsciously pulled his gloves tighter and began mouth breathing before wrapping the blood-pressure cuff around the man's right arm.

"One hot dog, please," Skeeters said as he watched the massive woman across the counter reach into a vat filled with oil-covered gray wieners. He slid his tray farther down the counter and studied the mound of stale glazed donuts that loomed in front of him.

"Hey, Blake, save me a spot, I'll be right there," Decker called from the other side of the cafeteria where he was gathering a tray and some silverware. Five minutes later, in the corner of the crowded room, the two interns sat across from each other, staring at their lunch.

"Look at this food," Decker said, wiping the sweat from his forehead. "Jesus! And why do they put the cafeteria in the basement? It's like a goddamn oven down here. I feel like I've descended into hell."

"Think of it as a sauna," Skeeters replied as he chomped down on the end of his hot dog. "Biting Billy get his teeth into you?"

"Nope. They had him taped up tight. He sure is a crazy son of a bitch, thrashing continuously, trying to claw and bite. Funny thing about it was"—his voice dropped low—"funny thing was that he has fresh needle marks on him, down a vein on his left leg. And the tracks are on the back of the leg, like he was trying to hide them."

"On the back of his leg? Maybe somebody else was injecting him back at the County Jail. He *is* a heroin addict, isn't he?"

"Of course he is, but he's been on the Jail Ward for, what, a week or ten days now. Those tracks were fresh,

Blake, really fresh, like within the past couple of days. Now, how in the hell could he do that on the Jail Ward, since he's under observation. He has no access to drugs or needles, and he is supposed to be Looney Tunes."

"Maybe the lab drew blood there." Skeeters squirted another shot of mustard across the top of his hot dog as several beads of sweat ran down his forehead, across his cheeks, and dripped onto his plate.

"No way! The phlebotomists don't leave tracks—and they always go for the same hole, if it's a proven gusher. And even if they did leave tracks, they wouldn't be down the back of his leg for Chrissakes."

"Sounds like he's getting drugs from somebody—maybe from one of the other prisoners. With his AIDS diagnosis, he won't be getting them for very long."

Decker took a long drink from his Pepsi, watching Skeeters over the top of the cup. He slowly put the drink down. "That's another thing. I'm not even sure he has AIDS. I couldn't find any lab to confirm the diagnosis, nothing except the previous resident's note saying "HIV +."

Skeeters smiled. "Well, so your patient hasn't been confirmed to have AIDS, he is using drugs supplied by magic into the Cage, and he has some kind of encephalopathy that eliminates the ability to provide all historical information. This is a great mystery." Skeeters stopped chewing and thought for a moment. "You probably should go ahead and get some drug screens on his urine, and check the CD-4 level and P-24 antigens in his blood."

"I'll tell you, Blake, I am going to keep Biting Billy on the ward until I find out more about this underlying disease. If he's getting drugs from one of the prisoners, there's going to be hell to pay. And I really don't think he's all that crazy."

"No, probably not," Skeeters replied. "He just thrashes around trying to bite everything in sight, he tries to claw you when you get close, he spits at you if you're too far away, and he pees in his bed." Skeeters smiled. "Good thing he's not really crazy."

"Very funny. I just have a feeling he's not as crazy as he seems. By the way, anything new on Andy Blum?" Decker asked. "Is he still under intensive care at Martin Luther King Hospital?"

"He was this morning. I called over to check on him. He's got a chest tube in on the left and they say the bullet missed the axillary nerve plexis in his shoulder by about 1 centimeter."

"Lucky bastard," Decker said. "He'll probably be back on the job in another month or so."

"Soon as he's out of the Unit, let's try to see him at King. Maybe send him some flowers, too. The nurse there said that his paramedic buddies were in the process of transferring him to the Huntington Hospital in Pasadena, soon as he's stable."

"Sounds like a good idea to me. Maybe we can see him this weekend, if we can get away." Decker changed the subject. "How was your Purple Queen? What were you saying to him? He was crying pretty hard."

"Poor Jack Diamond. He's gay, and although he seems to be a reasonable enough person, he's so emotional that nobody wants to have anything to do with him. They moved his bed out into the central corridor, where nobody has to interact too closely with him. He resents being kicked out of the regular sleeping area by the other prisoners, and so he just sits there next to his bed in the center of the hallway, crying and crying. I couldn't even get a decent history about his problems, he was sobbing so much." He popped the final piece of hot dog into his mouth. "Apparently somebody back at the County Jail kicked him pretty hard last week, and he fractured his hip. It was a compound fracture; unfortunately, it became infected, and now he has a slowly healing osteomyelitis."

"That explains 30 pounds of cast sticking up in the air. But what about his hair? Why is it purple?"

"It's not purple. That's a wig he's wearing to cover his thinning gray stubble. And he's very sensitive about the wig—you should have heard him when I removed it. He's really not a bad guy, even though he is on the unstable side. He just likes purple because he says it cheers him up."

Decker smiled. "Well, I think the Purple Queen does have the potential to provide a great learning experience. You should submit to the *New England Journal of Medicine* a photograph of him sprawled out in that old wooden wheelchair, his right leg sticking up in the air, his purple hair flowing across his shoulders, and his mouth open with sobs, with the statement under the picture: Name That Diagnosis! Anybody who says 'hip fracture with osteomyelitis' gets a free subscription for one year—wait a minute, what do we have here?" Decker sat up straight as Tyra Levy entered the cafeteria line.

"Suddenly the sauna is looking better," Skeeters said, glancing in her direction.

"Quick, move these trays, maybe she'll join us!"

The men quickly cleared the table next to them, then hunched over their trays, concentrating on their lunch. Tyra picked up her tray, paid the cashier, and looked around the cafeteria. A moment later, she walked over to an empty table 20 feet away and sat down, her back facing Skeeters and Decker.

"Damn!" Decker looked frustrated.

"Guess you could just stroll over and join her," Skeeters said, "since she probably didn't see us here."

"Don't want to be too overt," Decker said as he calculated his chances. He looked back at Skeeters. "You're married, aren't you?"

"Been married to Barbara just over a year now. She put me through my last year of medical school, back in

Boston. In fact," he said, beaming, "our first kid is due in about three months. How 'bout yourself? Are you from California?"

"Of course," Decker answered, "from San Diego, where the ladies are tan and beautiful. At least that's the way they were before medical school. Haven't had much time to reassess during the past four years, though." Decker looked in Tyra Levy's direction again. "Who are those people sitting next to her?"

"I don't know," Skeeters said, looking across the room.

A young man wearing surgical greens sat down across the table from Tyra and was promptly joined by a female resident who sat next to him. A moment later, Tyra began talking to them as they ate their lunch.

Decker stood up. "All she can say is no, right?"

"She could say a lot more than that, Steve. Don't forget, we're on call for the Jail Ward admissions—don't rev up any late-afternoon dates."

Decker walked confidently up to her table with a big smile on his face and pointed at the empty seat next to her. "Hello, Tyra, anybody sitting here? Mind if I join you?"

Tyra looked up and smiled back. "Nobody yet, have a seat. You're Steve Decker, aren't you?"

"Yes I am, I . . ."

"Let me introduce George Wroblewski"—she gestured to the man in surgical greens—"and Katie Shields. They're both pediatric residents at the Peds Pavilion next door and George and I were in medical school together. This is Steve Decker, surgical resident with us on the Jail Ward." She looked back at Decker. "Steve helped me get a straight answer from the guy who runs the deputy sheriffs up on the Jail Ward. I never had a chance to thank you, but I did appreciate it."

"You're quite welcome, Tyra. That Sergeant Grossman is going to be tough to deal with this month."

Katie Shields looked at Decker and said, "I heard about him last year from a couple of the interns up on the Jail Ward. They said he had a tendency toward brutality with the prisoners, and you definitely don't want to cross him. I'm just glad there's no pediatric cases on that ward."

"Not until they start arresting the kiddies," Decker said. "How's it going for you?" He looked back at Tyra. "Are you surviving?" *God, she's beautiful!* he thought.

"After last night, I don't know. I got into a bit of a battle with that nurse—Peter something?—about the meds he was supposed to be giving a couple of the injured prisoners. And then things got really wild, at about 3 A.M., when they brought in a pack of drunks who had been on a Rambo trip with the police. They had enough ethanol analgesics aboard that they were having no pain at all."

"Did you get any sleep?" Steve asked sympathetically.

"Bits and pieces, like every ten or fifteen minutes when I listened to someone's heartbeat."

Decker brightened and smiled again. "You do that, too? Doze off when you're listening to their heartbeat?"

"Can't help it. The methodical whispering sound of respirations mingled with—"

"—the soft thumping of a beating heart," Decker said, "and the humming of the blood—"

"Wait a minute"—Katie began to laugh as she held up her hands—"you Jail Ward characters are really getting weird."

At that instant, Shields and Wroblewski were paged over their beepers by the Pediatrics Ward operator for an incoming premature delivery emergency. They both grabbed their hot dogs, stood up and said good-bye, and quickly departed in the direction of the Pediatric Pavilion.

"I don't know if I could do surgery on those 9-inch human beings," Steve said to Tyra between bites.

"That's why I'm going into dermatology," Tyra said.

"The skin looks the same, whether it's enclosing 5 pounds of human or 500. Also, there's less stress—not too many dermatologic code blues."

"You're right, although I think we'll be seeing a little stress this month. Where are you from, Tyra?"

"Billings, Montana, where everything moves about one tenth the speed of Los Angeles. When I finish this year, I'll be going back to Montana for the derm residency. I don't think I could handle three years down here. I like a little slower pace."

Decker popped the last piece of hot dog into his mouth and pushed his tray aside. "Tyra, would you like to go out to dinner with me this Saturday? Maybe get away from this place to somewhere we can get some really good food?"

Tyra smiled and gently shook her head. "I'm sorry, Steve, I can't. I'm engaged to a fellow—Tom Bradshaw— we're going to get married after I finish my internship. That's really nice of you to ask me, though."

"I'm happy for you but I'm sad for me." Decker smiled. "Congratulations to both of you—"

"Thank you very much."

"If I can help with anything this month, just ask." The warbling noise of Decker's beeper abruptly interrupted the conversation. He turned up the volume control of the beeper and cocked his head to the left to listen. A rasping mechanical voice screeched, "Red blanket in Jail Ward! Red blanket in Jail Ward! Dr. Skeeters! Dr. Decker! Red blanket in Jail Ward!"

"Damn!" Decker said as he stood up. He saw Skeeters running out of the cafeteria in the direction of the central elevator. "See you later, Tyra," he said as he turned away and followed Skeeters's departing figure.

The exam table nearest the door of the Prep Room was covered with vomit and blood. Eric Knight, a six-foot-four-inch, red-haired prison inmate from the Los Angeles

County Jail, was thrashing violently against the leather straps that secured his arms and legs to the steel table. The red blanket that had been tossed across his seizing body, a signal from the emergency room to all who had medical interests that he was seriously unstable, had been kicked across the room by the flailing patient upon his arrival. A male nurse was rigging bottles of intravenous fluids on the coiled rods above the bed as three deputies stood nearby, watching.

Decker and Skeeters walked into the brightly lit Prep Room just as Eric Knight snarled and broke loose from the leather strap securing his right arm. Both doctors jumped back against the wall as the deputy reacted like he had been shot. "Grab his arm!" the nurse yelled as one of the deputies reached for the man's sweating biceps. Knight grimaced and closed his thick hand into a fist that swung upward, flattening the deputy's nose with a sickening crunching sound. Decker and Skeeters moved farther away, toward the corner of the room, as six more deputies poured in and launched into a flurry of policehold and pressure-point activities that quickly allowed a firm reattachment of a thick new strap around his arm.

"You're going to regret this, Knight!" the deputy with blood streaming from his nose said as he held a fistful of tissues to his face. "Your ass is gone, you son of a bitch!"

"Get down to the ER, David," an older deputy ordered as the men stepped away from their prisoner. "Get your face x-rayed and do something about all that blood. Gentlemen"—he looked at the two interns standing in the corner—"you may examine your patient. If this bastard even twitches, I want you to personally let me know."

Knight grunted and turned his head back and forth, his eyes scanning the room with a crazed look. Every few seconds his arms and legs thrashed upward against the straps as he strained and groaned. A stream of white foaming mucus drooled from the left side of his mouth and down the side of his neck. The physicians stepped up to the table.

Skeeters leaned over Knight and said, "Can you hear me, Mr. Knight? Why are you here?" He waited for a response as Knight's head continued to flop back and forth. Then he straightened up and looked at the male nurse standing a few feet away. "You're Peter, aren't you? Obviously, he's not going to tell me anything at all. You know anything about his problems?"

"I'm Peter Martel," the nurse answered. "Best we know is that he was transferred from the L.A. County Jail, having some kind of toxic reaction, according to ol' Doc Barner over there at the dispensary. When he got here, he was put on red blanket status in the ER when he started foaming and thrashing around."

"Okay," Skeeters said as he absently tapped the side of the exam table with his reflex hammer. "Okay. . . . Let's figure out what the toxic reaction is."

The exam was thorough and efficient as Skeeters carefully covered every inch of the man's body for the next fifteen minutes. Not until he turned him on his side did Skeeters find a 3-inch laceration on the back of his right thigh, high and inside where it was concealed to all but the most detailed search. It was a ragged cut with a fiery zone of yellow encrusted tissue around it, and red streaks extended up the lymphatic vessels. A combination of clotted pus and blood had collected at one corner of the wound.

"Look at this, Steve," Skeeters said, pointing to the back of his patient's leg.

Decker scrutinized the wound under the operating spotlight hanging down from the ceiling. "A surgeon's nightmare," he said as he examined the area of inflammation. "How the hell would he get something like this?"

"Unusual place for a stab wound," Skeeters replied,

"and it's at least a week old. Do they just let these things fester like this over at the jail infirmary?"

"I sure as hell hope not, although I did hear something about a State Department of Health investigation into substandard medical conditions there. I can't believe they would let anything like this go. He must have just not let anybody know about it." He studied the inflamed skin. "That's really crazy since it must hurt like hell," he added.

"Well," Skeeters said, "you can't suture an infected mess like this. We'll have to clean it and drain it and start some intravenous antibiotics."

"First we have to figure out how to flip him over on his stomach. He's so stiff. Let's get seven or eight deputies over here." Decker looked at Skeeters. "What's wrong with his brain? Any sign of a head injury?"

"Nope. There wasn't any focal neurological injury that I could find. His reflexes are a little hyperactive, but he's pretty rigid and it's hard to test his strength. I think he's probably septic from the bacteria seeping out of this wound, but I don't know what his baseline mental function is."

"Maybe he's just been crazy like this all his life. He's a goddamn addict too. Look at these needle marks tattooed over every vein in his body. Took me ten minutes to start an IV."

Skeeters looked at the wound again. "This thing doesn't bother me as much as the stiffness. It's almost like strychnine poisoning. Look at his face!"

Knight's face had become rigid, his lips pulled back, showing his teeth like a gnarling animal.

"Well, my diagnosis is that he's psycho, a real wacko," Decker said.

"Pretty crazy all right." Skeeters studied the man's face as he considered the possibilities. "Maybe risus sardonicus," he said.

Decker looked at the intern. " 'Risus' what?"

"I think maybe we're looking at risus sardonicus, or, to translate loosely, 'laughing derisively' . . . at us."

"Huh?"

"Lockjaw, Steve, he's got a *Clostridium tetani* infection."

"Tetanus? You're kidding!"

"Well, I may be wrong, but it'll take two or three days to get the cultures back, and we can't wait that long." He looked at the nurse. "Peter, would you give him 10,000 units of Hyper-Tet intramuscularly, stat, then hang penicillin G 4.8 million units q six hours by IV piggyback. Also, he needs to be placed in a quiet room down at the far end of the hall."

Thirty minutes later, the interns had finished their cleaning and debridement of Eric Knight's wound, and the deputies placed him on a gurney for transport. Skeeters pulled out his list of patients—the Purple Queen, Trixie, the Knight—like a list of characters from a Batman comic book.

He could see the pattern. Three patients now, a night of admitting—how many more? Six? Ten? And the next three days of trying to take care of them all before the next on-call night when anything could come through the elevator door.

He could have ten or fifteen patients in the morning—how could he ever keep them straight? As a medical student at Harvard, Skeeters had only been responsible for two or maybe three patients at a time. He had excelled at knowing every detail about those patients and about their diseases, and he had been excited during rounds each morning at the prospect of being "pimped" by the senior residents about the most obscure medical facts they could ask him. The other medical students had always dreaded this pimping process; who could always know everything about every disease?

But Dr. Skeeters would shock them with his detailed

answers, volumes of details extracted from journals and medical textbooks. He had a genius IQ and a photographic memory.

He had always been an A student, from the gifted special classes at Winchester High School, through the four years at prestigious Amherst College in Massachusetts. Intellectual challenge was his substitute for sports and the pursuit of women; neither had encroached on his academic schedule before Harvard Medical School. His parents, both tenured professors in Boston, had given him little advice during his adolescence. Their one and only lesson in life, repeated hundreds of times, was: "Study hard, achieve academic excellence, and the world will be at your beckoning."

But what was beckoning now was the Purple Queen, Trixie, and Knight, and maybe ten more tonight. Skeeters scratched his head. He'd need a change in strategy, that's all. Just a simple change in strategy. Bring them in and get them out would be the agenda for the month. Do it like Dr. Marsh wants it done, "care for them, they are human and hopeful." And make damn sure nobody dies because you hurried too much and made a mistake.

By 7:30 P.M., Decker and Skeeters had seen seven new patients on the Jail Ward. There was the drunk attorney who had crashed his Mercedes and who had posted bond before they could even finish taping the bandages across his forehead. There was the hallucinating motorcyclist who went vertical with his Yamaha FZR 1000 into the pepper trees at the side of the Ventura Freeway. There was the fast-food robber who was bitten by a customer's German shepherd when his escape route coincided with the dog's tail.

And then there were the four gang members with bullet wounds received during the evening's running gun battle down Crenshaw Boulevard. Although Decker later reflected that he should have figured out which youth belonged to which gang on the basis of their headband colors, it didn't occur to him until one of the deputies took him aside and informed him that the reason they were doing weird things with their fingers was because opposing gang members had been placed side by side in the Prep Room. Those signals are gang signals, Dr. Decker (how can you be so dumb?), and it would be better to try to keep members of the same gang next to each other while trying to keep members of different gangs apart from each other. However, one of the four died before the first unit of blood could be infused, and the other three were whisked away by the surgeons with advancing blood loss and shock, their colored headbands in the trash can and their hand signals temporarily at rest.

An hour later, there was an actual lull in Jail Ward activity, and Decker decided to check on Biting Billy one more time before trying to sneak down to grab a quick snack in the cafeteria. He felt good, his enthusiasm bolstered by the surgical problems he had been caring for as he walked down the central corridor to the Cage. In spite of early indications to the contrary, it was becoming clear that this was going to be a great month. Even Skeeters was starting to seem reasonable. He stopped in front of the bars and peered into the dark corner where Biting Billy liked to assume the fetal position.

The Cage was empty.

Decker stood frozen, staring at the wall where Biting Billy's huddled form was supposed to be. His mind raced ahead, scrambling through a jumble of thoughts. The door to the Cage is shut. Where the hell is he? How could he be gone? The man is psychotic and vicious, he has AIDS maybe, and he sure as hell was not ready to go back to the County Jail yet.

Decker turned and quickly walked down the corridor to the wall phone outside the Prep Room.

"Radiology, this is Dr. Decker on the Jail Ward. Do you have a William MacFarland down there for a CAT scan of the brain?"

After being placed on hold for five minutes, he finally had his answer. William MacFarland had not been in radiology all day, his CAT scan was scheduled for the next week, and just why would a man be in radiology for a routine CAT scan at ten o'clock at night?

Decker hung up and scowled at the telephone.

"Ya looking for the prisoner MacFarland?" a voice called out from behind the deputy's desk.

"Yes, I am," Decker said as he looked at the officer slouching in his chair.

"Well, son, I got his chart right here where they left it when he was processed back to the County Jail this afternoon."

"The County Jail! Who said he could leave here this afternoon!"

"He was cleared to go, Doc."

"I'm his doctor, and I didn't give him any clearance to leave! This is a hospital, and doctors are supposed to admit patients and doctors are supposed to discharge patients. Who gave the order for his discharge?"

"Well, somebody gave him clearance. Let me check his order sheet here," the deputy said while he thumbed through the pages at the top of the chart.

"I thought a doctor's order was required for the transfer of a patient."

"Jes' hold on now, son, there's got to be an order

here somewhere—ah, here it is." He held out the page for Decker's inspection.

At the opposite end of the Jail Ward, Skeeters pressed the telephone receiver against his ear.

"Yes, sir, Dr. Barner? I'm sorry to bother you at home, sir, but I need to ask you about this patient you sent us today. This is Blake Skeeters, medical intern at the Jail Ward at the County Hospital."

Dr. George Barner struggled to think clearly. He had already finished his two traditional after-dinner Old Grand-Dad on the rocks, and had settled back on the living room couch to begin his traditional two-hour session of vegetation.

"Dr. Scooters"—his voice boomed out as he stood up and tried to remember why this doctor was calling—"what can I help you with?"

"Yes, sir. Uh—it's *'Skeeters.'* I wanted to ask you about Mr. Eric Knight who came to the Jail Ward today."

The haze cleared as Dr. Barner tried to visualize Eric Knight. "Ah, yes, Knight, the one with the infected cut on his leg. Shoulda been able to fix it in the dispensary if he had come in sooner. What would you like t'know?" he slurred.

"It looked as if the laceration was about a week old, and I wondered if you could tell me, sir, what antibiotics he was on and whether he received any tetanus immune globulin."

"Ya mean a tetanus shot?"

"No, sir, a Hyper-Tet shot." Skeeters hesitated. "The shot with the tetanus antibodies, not the tetanus toxoid."

"Ah . . ." Barner's mind struggled. "No, I don't think he's had any tetanus shots."

"Okay, sir. Uh—can you tell me if he had any cultures taken or if he was on any antibiotics?" Skeeters winced as he realized the question was insulting. Of course they did a culture.

"Hell no, he didn't get any antibiotics," Barner roared. "And no culture either. He just showed us the cut today. That's why I sent him over to you guys."

"All right, sir," Skeeters said, trying to sound reasonable and certain his quota of questions had been exceeded. "We'll take care of it and get him back to you when he's better."

"Fine, fine, and thank you, Dr. Skooters."

"Oh—sorry, sir, one more question, if I may—"

"Yes?" Barner's voice was getting louder.

"Any idea how he received the wound?"

"No idea at all, Doctor. He just brought it in. By the time we saw the injury, it was already seriously infected. It was so infected and he was so toxic that we had to send him over, there was no choice."

"Thank you, sir, and good night."

Skeeters hung up the telephone and slowly walked down the central corridor. *It doesn't make any sense,* he thought, *no matter how you look at it. A self-induced injury? You could die from an injury like that, especially if you wait long enough while it festers.*

It just doesn't make any sense at all. . . .

Decker was furious. He had spent the better part of an hour examining and writing up an extended on-service note about William MacFarland, at considerable personal risk. He had, therefore, been established as the patient's physician. *This means,* Decker fumed to himself, *that I determine the medicine he gets, the food he is allowed, the activity permitted, and, goddamn it, I determine the day and time he may be discharged from medical care. The psychotic bastard is crazy as hell, and nowhere is there a decent diagnosis about his underlying disease. Hell, there isn't even a CAT scan on the guy's brain anywhere in the chart.*

And, to top it all off, what is Dr. Dillon Marsh doing discharging him from the Jail Ward!

He stormed into the Prep Room, kicked the base of the nearest exam table, and walked back out to the deputy's desk.

"Where can I find Dr. Marsh's phone number?" he fired, his voice shaking with anger.

"Well, now, son, that's just not available to the interns," the deputy drawled. "If there's an emergency, we can call him."

"Good." Decker straightened his shoulders and stuck out his chin. "I'd like to declare an emergency."

"Sorry, Doc. A patient being transferred to the County Jail is not an emergency. Especially when he's been transferred by Dr. Marsh himself." The man smiled, knowing that there was no way that this smartass intern was going to obtain a single digit of Dr. Marsh's telephone number.

"What's your name, Sheriff?"

He stiffened in his chair. "I'm not the sheriff. There's only one sheriff in Los Angeles County and it ain't me. I'm a *deputy* sheriff. Like my name tag says, Doctor, Deputy Simpson."

"Who's in charge of you—who's your superior?"

Simpson stood up and glared at the intern. "Sergeant Mel Grossman is in charge. Do you want to talk to him? He's going to be pissed to be called at night."

"What is his number?" Decker held out his hand.

*   *   *

The two physicians walked briskly side by side down the center of the huge first-floor corridor in the direction of the cafeteria. At six minutes to eleven, Decker and Skeeters knew they were almost out of time to pick up a late-evening snack at the doctors' cafeteria. So far, they had seen a total of fourteen patients on the Jail Ward. Four prisoners had been admitted to the ward and nine had been triaged to the harassed interns in other specialty areas of the hospital, each prisoner handcuffed and strapped to his gurney, a deputy sheriff at his side. One prisoner had died—actually, he was already dead on arrival to the Jail Ward, his inferior vena cava having been penetrated by a 9mm hollow-tipped slug, complements of the city of Los Angeles, for his having attempted to extract a fully-loaded Beretta from the firm grip of a city policeman.

On the floor in front of them stretched 4-inch wide bands of multi colored lines, each one leading to a different part of the hospital. Prior to the lines being painted on the linoleum several years before, patients had regularly got lost trying to follow directions, regardless of how clearly the directions were given. Now, with the lines, all that was necessary was "Follow that pink line, sir." The biggest hazard was colliding with another patient walking in the opposite direction concentrating on his colored line.

"So, did you reach Sergeant Grossman?" Skeeters asked.

"Did I ever," Decker answered. "He about blew my head off just for asking about Dr. Marsh's phone number. Simpson was right, he really did get pissed off." Decker grinned. "I hope I screwed up his whole evening. However, Grossman did say I would be permitted to see Marsh tomorrow morning in his office at 8 A.M. Like he's working as his secretary or something. How's Knight getting along?"

"I really think he does have tetanus. The guy's symptoms are damn near classic for it. I'm just going to keep pouring in the penicillin, hope the Hyper-Tet is doing its job, and then we'll just have to see what happens. I called the doc running the dispensary at the County Jail—not much help."

"Well, how did he get the laceration?"

"The guy didn't know. And he didn't know how long he had it, either. I don't think they keep very close track of their prisoners at the jail." Skeeters looked at his watch. "We better hurry if we want any food."

A minute later, they arrived at the doors of the doctors' cafeteria. A morbidly fat woman with a soiled L.A. County Hospital uniform was locking the entrance door. Decker stepped up to her and tapped her on the shoulder.

" 'Scuse me, ma'am, we'd like to just grab a quick sandwich," he said.

"Sorry," she said as she turned her immense body to face the doctors. Her voice was deep and masculine, and Skeeters noticed that she had a bristle of a mustache. Her face looked remarkably similar to a pig, with a large bulbous nose and small eyes set close together.

"The cafeteria closes at 11 P.M. You'll have to get your sandwiches tomorrow morning."

Decker and Skeeters both looked at their watches. "It's 10:56, we have four minutes to go," Skeeters protested.

"That's 10:56 by your watches."

The interns stared at her.

"What are you doing, playing some kind of game with us?" Decker said heatedly, waving his arms in the air. "This is Dr. Skeeters," he jerked his thumb in the direction of the other intern, "and I am Dr. Decker, and we're going to be up all night on the Jail Ward. This is the doctors' cafeteria, we're here well before closing time, and—"

"Easy, Steve," Skeeters said, "we can get pizza delivered to the floor."

"I'll be damned if I'm going to accept this—this"— he looked at her—"this 'woman' shutting down the cafeteria early. Lady, we're going to get a sandwich here and you damn well better step aside!"

She backed up against the shut door and shrieked, "You touch me and you'll spend the first ten years of your practice paying off the lawsuit. This cafeteria is closed, and if you don't like it, you can file an employee's grievance!"

"We're not employees!" Decker hollered.

They were interrupted by a soft female voice. "You're Steve Decker, aren't you?"

Katie Shields walked out the cafeteria's exit door. She was wearing hospital on-call greens, and she was holding a cafeteria tray filled with a stack of sandwiches. Glossy black hair covered her shoulders and her dark eyes glanced at the cafeteria employee. "They've been trying to fire this . . . Godzilla for years, but she kept filing union suits until they finally just gave up. They say she has an attorney in every pocket."

The woman crossed her obese arms and glowered stone-faced at the interns as she blocked the entrance.

Katie smiled at the men. "I have some extra sandwiches, if you want any."

Five minutes later, the two interns were back in the elevator on their way to the thirteenth floor, each holding three sandwiches and a soft drink.

Skeeters looked at Decker and asked, "How could anybody so beautiful and so nice . . . work as an intern in a place as ugly as this?"

"After fixating on that—'Godzilla' thing for five minutes, she was like something out of a dream—damn nice of her to let us have these," Decker said as he waved a sandwich. "I think she's a senior pediatrics resident and she spends most her time down the hill, at the Pediatric Pavilion."

"And now we owe her a dinner."

"I think I owe her my career, since I was about ready to level that bulldozer in front of the cafeteria door."

The Jail Ward was quiet as they passed a nodding Deputy Simpson at the night watch desk. Sounds of snoring rumbled up and down the corridor, the Prep Room was darkened, and the lights of Los Angeles glimmered through the dusty barred windows. An occasional faint gurgle noise reverberated from the coffeepot outside the equipment room.

"Looks like maybe we're going to have a nice quiet night," Skeeters said. "I'm going to finish these sandwiches, check on Knight, and then try to get some sleep."

"Sounds like a good plan," Decker said. He walked down the central corridor to the Cage again and looked through the bars at the darkened empty bed. *Biting Billy was now back at the County Jail*, he thought, *a threat to everyone there and probably deteriorating further from whatever it was that was infecting his brain.*

He finished his roast beef sandwich and walked to the men's room at the far side of the doctors' sleeping area. The single stall in the room was unoccupied. If there ever could be a peaceful and quiet time on the Jail Ward rotation, this was it.

Ten seconds later, the silence was pierced by the warbling squealing screech of his beeper's emergency call, followed by the rasping voice, "Red blanket in Jail Ward! Red blanket in Jail Ward! Dr. Skeeters! Dr. Decker! Red blanket in Jail Ward!"

Chapter 4

"Come in and have a seat, Dr. Decker."

"Thank you, sir," Steve answered politely as he walked into the office toward the oversized leather chair in front of Dr. Marsh's desk.

The room, a stunning contrast to the stark surroundings throughout the rest of the hospital, was luxuriously furnished with an expensive mahogany desk, exquisite medical antiques displayed on marble stands, and two large Oriental area rugs of crimson and gold. Decker was still wearing his faded surgical greens from the night before, and he hesitated briefly before sitting. *It would not be helpful to the conversation if the rich leather seat was stained with prisoner secretions from the night before.*

"Let's get right to the point, Dr. Decker." Marsh's voice was surprisingly gentle, in contrast to his eyes, which seemed to burn holes through the intern. "Sergeant Grossman told me you had a problem. How can I help you?"

Decker sat stiffly in his chair. "It's about my patient, Biting Billy—that is, Mr. MacFarland. He was transferred back to the County Jail yesterday before I had a chance to finish working him up for his encephalopathy."

"Yes, that's correct."

Decker hesitated, surprised at the lack of any defense for the transfer. "Well, sir, I always thought it was the responsibility of the doctor doing the work on the case to arrange for such transfers and discharges."

"That *is* correct, and Mr. MacFarland was transferred as directed by his intern. Of course, I approved the transfer since it was proper that he return to the County Jail."

"You didn't transfer him?"

"No, as you have said, it is up to the doctor on the case to order a transfer."

"But, sir, I am—or that is, I *was* his intern, and I didn't order the transfer!" Decker protested.

"Dr. Decker,"—Marsh placed his hands flat on his desk and spoke as if to a child—"you were certainly his doctor, but you picked up the case in the middle of the transferring process. His workup for the encephalopathy seemed quite complete to me; Mr. MacFarland is a paranoid schizophrenic and will always be a danger to everyone around him. The sooner he left the Jail Ward, the better for all of us. Dr. Joel Peck was his intern last month, and if you had checked the order sheet from two or three days ago, you would have found his order to transfer him to the jail. Did you see the order sheet?"

"Dr. Peck ordered him to be transferred?" Decker began to feel acutely embarrassed. *How could he have missed an order such as that?*

Dr. Marsh stood up and smiled. "I'm sure that Doc Barner over at the County Jail infirmary would have called us if he was still having any problems. I like your style, Dr. Decker, and I think you're going to have an excellent month on the Jail Ward. Is there anything else I can help you with?"

It was a dismissal, and all Steve could do was apologize and leave the room, feeling stupid.

* * *

The Pediatric Pavilion, known as "Peds" by the residents in training, was a two-minute walk down the hill from the mammoth main hospital. Located at the base of the hill, Peds was a comparatively small building that held only fifty beds for the tiny patients who required admission (although seventy children could be admitted if they were busy, which was almost always the case). As Katie Shields told herself each morning as she walked past the towering concrete building that loomed above her on the hill, Peds was a "nice little hospital," perfect for the training of physicians who would like to see everything in their quest to excel at practicing pediatric medicine.

When she arrived on the clinical ward to start her twenty-four-hour on-call shift that Friday, it was immediately apparent that it had been a very bad night. Not only was every bed in the hospital filled, three children with leukemia had almost simultaneously gone into a bacterial sepsis that rendered them unstable and at great risk of dying from infection. If that wasn't enough, a highly contagious virus that generated diarrhea of remarkable proportions spread throughout the wards, resulting in at least five hours spent just trying to start intravenous lines into threadlike veins to allow fluid replacement in the dehydrated babies.

The two interns, supervised by their tall and anorectic pediatric resident, George Stilt, looked like they had just crawled out of a torture chamber that morning. They mumbled out the stories of having been up all night drawing cultures from every secretion they could find from each septic child, checking chest X rays, supporting dropping blood pressures with vasoconstrictors, all done while trying to admit another four more infants and two children to the overflowing wards.

In summary, it had been a typical night in the Pediatric Pavilion.

Katie had wanted to be a pediatrician long before she had even entered medical school. She had always felt linked to children in some mysterious way, from the days of baby-sitting in junior high school to the volunteer work as a wide-eyed, sixteen-year-old at Hawthorne Hospital emergency room near Los Angeles. At just over five feet three inches, Dr. Shields was a beautiful clear-skinned woman with soft, full curves that filled her hospital greens and had brought exciting fantasies to the college men who were lucky enough to find themselves in her classes. In spite of her remarkable dark-eyed beauty, she had dated only rarely until after her sophomore year at UCLA; most men either presumed that she was already steadily locked up with *someone* or they developed severe difficulty talking in complete and coherent sentences when they were in her presence.

Without much effort, she was able to out-compete approximately 4,000 other premedical students trying to enter the UCLA School of Medicine, and four years later, she walked out of Royce Hall with an M.D. degree. She promptly chose her internship at the Pediatric Pavilion next to the Great White Mama and now, in her third year of pediatric training, she had only a little more than eleven months to go before she could start her own pediatric practice.

Dr. Stilt and his interns finished their morning report and dragged off to finish working on the mountain of paperwork that gave stark testimony to the difficulty of controlling leukemic white blood cells proliferating out of control. Katie and her two interns gathered up the charts of their eighteen children and began the long process of moving from one bed to the next, examining each child and planning future care strategies.

They had seen four children when the pediatric emergency room nurse delivered Baby Guan Ng to the examining room.

"Dr. Shields, this is a *stat*," the central scheduling nurse had told her on the telephone, marking the case as the equivalent of a red blanket up on the hill. Katie assigned the case to her intern, Dr. George Wroblewski, and the two physicians quickly left the pediatric wards and walked into the examining room.

"What is the problem?" Katie asked the nurse as Wroblewski looked over the infant. She was a chubby but nearly comatose six-month-old baby girl with purple blotches scattered across her skin and three neatly aligned red circles across the lower half of her abdomen.

"It's hard to say for sure, we really couldn't get the story," the nurse said. "The mother is Vietnamese and can't speak a word of English—she's outside in the waiting room. We're trying to get a translator down from the White Mama but that may take another hour or two. I thought we might not have that much time with this one." She looked at the baby, who was lying still, eyes half closed, breathing in rapid pants, arms held out as if in submission. The nurse turned the baby on her side, poked a thermometer into her bottom, and wrapped a tiny blood pressure cuff around her left arm.

"Look at these petechiae," Wroblewski said as he pointed to a cluster of red specks on the skin between the purple blotches. "The kid's probably got no platelets." He placed his hand on the retracted abdomen. "Feels hot as hell." He studied the inflamed circles on her stomach. "Looks like she's been abused, too, look at these burns. What have they been doing to her?"

"Let's get the intravenous equipment in here stat," Katie said to the nurse. "I think this little gal will soon be going into shock if she isn't already. We've got to get an IV line into her right away, and let's get a stat CBC, and type and cross for 10 units of platelets. Give me a needle and a couple of red and purple top tubes, and let's get the admission blood studies as fast as we can. Need some blood cultures and clotting studies too," she added.

"Temperature is 105 degrees, blood pressure is 95 over 40, pulse weak and tachy," the nurse said as she pulled the stethoscope from her ears and left the room to gather the equipment and arrange for the transfusion.

Wroblewski quickly examined her. "Lungs are clear, heart is going like a bat outta hell, abdomen is quiet, oropharynx is calm, no nuchal rigidity and she moves all four," he said as he took an ophthalmoscope from the wall. "Let me take a look into her eyes." He leaned over in front of her face, light shining into the pupils. "A couple of flame hemorrhages on the right, the left is clear."

"So what have we got, and what are you going to do?" Katie asked her intern.

"Okay—" Wroblewski thought for a moment. "Sepsis—"

"Good!"

"Thanks." He smiled and immediately looked serious again. "Sepsis probably from meningococcemia with thrombocytopenia and shock, without meningitis."

"Excellent!"

"If this is meningococcal disease, it's called fulminate meningococcemia."

"Perfect!" Katie said. "How contagious is it?"

The intern thought for a moment. "Minimal . . . spread by carriers, usually, and not by patients."

"Correct!" Katie smiled at the intern. "You're batting 100 percent so far! The disease is also called?"

"Huh?"

"What syndrome is it also called?"

"Oh—uh—Waterhors, or Waterhouse-Frederic syndrome. Bad prognosis."

"Right, almost, Waterhouse-Friderichsen syndrome and *extremely* bad prognosis. Let's carry this baby into the intensive care unit where we can talk about penicillin and steroids while we're hooking her up to arterial lines and getting a couple of cutdown IV's going."

"Okay," he said as he carefully picked up the baby. "But what are these round burns on her abdomen?" he asked.

"Those are coin burns, George," Katie said. "It means the family cares about this little girl."

"The family cares about her? They care about her by *burning* her?"

"Old Southeast Asia tradition. She had a high fever, and so they tried to burn it out of her. They heated silver coins and placed them on her abdomen; according to tradition, it burns the fever out."

"Jesus, it sure would take your mind off whatever was causing you the fever in the first place. Helluva tradition." He held the baby girl firmly against his chest as they walked out of the examining room and down the hall toward the ICU.

Thirty minutes later, every medicine ever known to be useful for Waterhouse-Friderichsen syndrome was infusing into the veins of Guan Ng. As she left the unit, Katie sent her intern and the finally arrived Vietnamese translator to the waiting room to discuss the problems with the baby's mother.

"Dr. Shields! Telephone!" the ward clerk called out from behind a stack of charts.

"Thanks!" she answered as she picked up the telephone in the Doctors' Transcribing Room. "This is Dr. Shields."

"Good morning, Dr. Shields, this is Dr. Decker."

"Dr. Decker? Oh, from the Jail Ward." Her voice lowered and softened imperceptibly, "Good morning . . . Steve."

The Jail Ward was filled with a bedlam of shouting voices, prisoners being shuttled up and down the central corridor, and white-coated interns talking with their pa-

tients or furiously writing admission notes on the green
sheets of the L.A. County Hospital charts. Tyra Levy
and her fellow intern, O'Conner, were struggling with a
disoriented man on an exam table in the Prep Room while
Dr. Marsh, looking like a white-haired commanding officer, supervised from a distance. Steve Decker was
hunched over the telephone outside the Prep Room, while
the door leading to the female prisoners in the Ladies'
Room was being unlocked by one of the deputy sheriffs
for Blake Skeeters.

The Decker and Skeeters team would be responsible, until the night shift took over at 5 P.M., for
every fourth patient who arrived on the Jail Ward.
Each intern faced a continuous threat of being dis-
rupted by the arrival of a new patient, always abruptly
announced by the grating loudspeaker voice of the
Jail Ward clerk, Gerald Brodie, who sat at his
desk near the elevator door. All Skeeters wanted
to do was complete the rounds on his patients
before his name was blasted out over the loudspeaker.

It was apparent to Skeeters that Julia Jackson was
in very bad shape. For three days she had been curled
up like a baby, nasogastric tube draining yellow high-
protein fluid in one end while the Foley catheter
drained yellow urine out the other. Her right arm and
leg were becoming further cramped into contractures,
and in spite of an egg-crate mattress and frequent
turning by the nurse's aid, she was beginning to develop early breakdown of the skin across her right hip.
Every four hours the nurse hung another bottle of
antibiotics that drained into a vein in her left arm,
which as far as Skeeters could tell, appeared to be the
last usable vein in her entire body. Twice a day, the
physical therapist tried to straighten out the con-

tractures and adjust the numerous splints that resisted further cramping.

"Trixie?" Skeeters called out softly as he placed his hand on her left shoulder. "Trixie, can you hear me?"

Her eyelids lifted slightly as her eyes tried to focus on Skeeters's face. Her left hand opened and Skeeters let her grip his fingers. Although she had been in a near coma for more than a week, he could see from her delicate facial features that she had previously been quite attractive and probably in considerable demand in her chosen line of work. For this girl, he reflected, with no education and uncertain intelligence, prostitution must have been one of the most viable options to earn a substantial income. He pulled out his stethoscope and listened to the rattling noises within her chest.

In the central corridor of the Jail Ward, Decker said good-bye to Katie and hung up the telephone. As he walked past the ward clerk's desk, the nasal voice of Gerald Brodie whined out, "You're next up, Dr. Decker." Steve stopped to look at the man, sitting in front of his microphone with eager anticipation, his beady eyes, his narrow pointed nose, and his matching chin all aimed at the intern.

"Thank you, Gerry," he said pleasantly. In just three days of duty as Jail Ward clerk, Brodie had become widely known by prisoners and interns alike as the Jail Ward Razor-Faced Scoundrel. Finding a sadistic pleasure in torturing interns with announcements of new prisoner-doctor assignments, he reveled in delegating misery. The worse the prisoner, the happier Gerald Brodie was to proclaim over the speaker system which intern would get the prisoner. Steve could almost tell what would be waiting for him in the

Prep Room simply by listening to the inflections in Brodie's voice.

Decker had just finished transferring another prisoner from the Jail Ward back to the County Jail, when Brodie's whining voice echoed up and down the corridors, "Dr. Decker to the Prep Room! Dr. Decker to the Prep Room!" The voice sounded just enthusiastic enough to be worrisome.

The prisoner sitting on the end of the examining table was a thin, pale, middle-aged man with snow-white hair that looked like it had been arranged by a hurricane. His hands were handcuffed behind his back and his feet were wrapped together with a black leather strap that had Long Beach Police Dept. stamped on the side. His thin chest was enclosed by a filthy open-neck shirt that was covered with grease and bloodstains. He wore jeans that had been white at one time but that were now almost black with dirt and oil.

"Good morning, sir, I'm Dr. Decker, what problem are you having?" Decker asked.

"I'm Dr. Decker, what problem are you having?" the man answered.

Steve glanced at Peter, who was quietly tending to his nursing duties on the other side of the room. Raised eyebrows and a shrug of the shoulders was provided in return.

"What is your name, sir?"

"Fuck."

"Fuck? What kind of a name is that?"

"Fuck shit!"

"Okay—" Steve hesitated. "Could you tell me where you hurt?"

"Fuck shit!"

Steve's face began to redden as he took a deep

breath and let it out slowly. "All right, did you come from the County Jail?"

"Fuck shit!"

"You really like those words, don't you? Okay, I'm going to check you over now and then we'll get you on your way," Steve said. As his hand touched the top of the man's scalp, the patient abruptly jerked away and hollered, "Fuck shit!" at the top of his lungs.

"He's from Long Beach," Sergeant Grossman said from the door, as if that was some kind of helpful announcement. "They found him throwing rocks into store windows along the waterfront and kicking the glass into the street. The LBPD arrested him on a drunk and disorderly charge, but he started tearing up the Memorial ER when they tried to fix his knee. Here's his lab from Long Beach."

Decker took the sheet of paper and looked over the numbers. "All normal, alcohol level zero. What's his name? It sounds like he has a British accent."

"Who knows? You've heard his limited vocabulary and there was no ID on him."

"Okay, would you send in a couple of your people to hold him down so I can examine him? Peter, give him 50 milligrams of Thorazine I.M. and stand by to give him some more."

Ten minutes later, as three deputies held the patient's right leg tightly against the examining table, Steve injected 2 cc's of Xylocaine anesthesia into the wound, pulled out several pieces of glass from a gaping knee wound, and began to suture the laceration shut. The sedative effects of Thorazine seemed to work in reverse; the man became increasingly agitated as Decker tried to place a few interrupted sutures across the opening. Long streams of threats and obscenities spewed from his mouth as he thrashed wildly, jerking his secured arms against the restraints.

When his thrashing bent the needle during Decker's third attempt to place the final suture, Steve hollered out with exasperation, "Hold his knee tight or we'll never get this finished!"

"Fuck shit!" the man frothed.

"Anything I can do to help, Steve?" Blake Skeeters walked up and asked from the other side of the examining table.

"You can start by stuffing a big rag into this derelict's mouth so I can get this last suture tied!"

Skeeters walked up to the head of the table. "No bruises on his head?"

"No, just a torn-up knee!"

"Fuck shit!"

"What's this behind his ear?"

"Huh?" Decker asked.

"It's a Scope patch! Here, let me peel it off."

Decker secured the last suture as Skeeters carefully pulled off the tiny round patch from behind the man's right ear. "A Scope patch, what the hell—" Decker said.

"Skin-colored little devil, hard to see. Probably was out sailing, or going to go sailing, trying to prevent seasickness. That scopolamine can trigger a full psychosis, sometimes." He tossed the patch into the wastebasket. "See ya later, I got to go check on Knight," he said as he left the Prep Room and walked down the corridor.

For the first time since his admission, Eric Knight was able to sit up and drink some fluids. His bed had been left in the center of the corridor, across from the Purple Queen's bed, where they could keep a closer eye on his condition. The patient had two intravenous lines dripping fluids and antibiotics into his veins, and a portable cardiac monitor next to his bed emitted a beeping sound with each heartbeat. Skeeters dragged a chair to the bedside and sat down as he opened Knight's chart.

"Looking better, today, Eric, how's it going?" Skeeters asked.

Knight yawned, his hairy arms dragging the intravenous tubing out of the sheets. "Okay, Doc. When do I get these tubes out of my arms?"

"Soon as you take in more fluids, probably today sometime, since your fever is down and it looks like you're going to kick this thing. Do you know what happened to you?"

"Hell no, I don't know what happened."

Skeeters moved his chair a couple of inches farther from the prisoner's bed as he remembered Knight's fist flattening the nose of a deputy sheriff in the Prep Room. "All I remember was this cut on my leg," Knight continued, "on the back of my leg, and the next thing I know, here I am. When do I get some food?"

"Later today, we'll start you on a full liquid diet—"

"Liquid hell, when do I get some *food*?"

"Later today, if all goes well."

"Shit, might as well send me back to the County Jail, where at least they have some real food."

Skeeters turned off the beeping sound from the heart monitor and leaned toward the bed, speaking softly. "Mr. Knight, you should be dead right now, and if it wasn't for some very specific immunotherapy, you would be dead right now, from tetanus. You understand tetanus, Mr. Knight, like lockjaw, seizures, and no breathing? I'll do everything I can to move you safely out of here, but I'm not going to start filling your stomach until I am sure your system can handle it. Do you understand what I am saying?"

Knight lay back and looked at the ceiling for a minute, then turned to look at the chubby intern. "Sorry, Doc, I tend to get a little excited. That's why I'm in jail. You're not shit'n me about the lock-jaw bit?"

"That's what it was. How did you get the cut on the back of your leg?"

"Uh—I don't remember, and if you don't mind, Doc, I really don't want to talk about it. Just fix me up and get me out of here."

He was lying, Skeeters was sure of it. *No point in pushing too hard with the questions*, he thought, *and it really doesn't matter since the laceration was repaired, the tetanus was treated, and—the guy might flatten my nose if I rev him up too much. However, just one more little question wouldn't hurt.*

"Mr. Knight, did somebody do this to you, or did—"

"Okay," Knight interrupted loudly, "that's enough. You saved my life and I appreciate that. You're a great doctor and I appreciate that. However, I think you ask too many goddamn questions, Dr. Skeeters. And I don't have any more answers. Now, leave me alone for Christ's sake."

The prisoner crossed his arms and rolled on his side, facing away from the intern. Skeeters stared at the white gauze bandage on the back of the man's leg for ten seconds, then slowly straightened up and walked away.

Two hours later, Professor Malcolm VanDeemer from the Organic Chemistry Department of Cal State Long Beach was handed fresh flowers and a clean change of clothing by his wife at the entrance of the Jail Ward. After changing from his prison clothes and combing his white hair neatly into place, he thanked Dr. Decker for fixing his lacerated knee and for saving his mind from the ravages of transderm scopolamine. After shaking hands with every deputy sheriff in sight and apologizing profusely for any trouble he might have caused, Professor VanDeemer left for home.

Katie Shields knew that Baby Guan Ng was dying when the respirator switched to the automatic mode.

The Sechrist ventilator, a complex piece of machinery connected to plastic tubing that coursed through the baby's mouth and down into her tiny lungs, had been triggered for five hours by her gasping efforts. Each time the machine sensed another attempt to take a breath, the pressure manometer needles twitched, a yellow light flicked on, and it pumped another surge of oxygen down her windpipe. By two o'clock, the twitching of the manometer needle had become progressively weaker and the respiratory rate indicator showed a decreasing breathing rate. Finally, at exactly 3:32, Baby Guan Ng stopped triggering the machine. Without delay, and without causing even a single missed breath, a small red light popped on simultaneously with the buzzing of the apnea alarm, and the machine took over the full load of breathing.

"I think she's bleeding internally," George Wroblewski said as he pointed at the heart rate indicator. "Look at the pulse rate. It's all the way up to 175."

"She's either bleeding or going into septic shock," Katie Shields answered from the other side of the baby.

She was beginning to feel the aching frustration of having done everything to reverse the deterioration of the baby, and so far there had been no measurable success. Dr. Barnwell, the soft-spoken chief of pediatrics, had reviewed the case and had nothing more to offer. The frail Vietnamese mother, trapped in this building filled with strangers who spoke not a word of her native tongue, sat quietly in the corner of the waiting room, clutching her hands in a combination of anxiety and prayer to her unseen God.

Shields glanced at the face of her intern, a craggy, rugged face with kind eyes, and knew he was going to lose this one, the first loss in his emerging pediatric career.

For the first time since starting the Jail Ward rotation, both Decker and Skeeters were each assigned a new patient at almost the same time. The ward had been a zoo of new prisoners all afternoon, keeping the eight interns working nonstop as they tried to manage the torrent of patients. Although each pair of doctors was supposed to pick up new patients in an orderly rotation, the crush of humanity was enough to keep everybody continuously running.

When Mary Marcy arrived on the thirteenth floor, Decker was assigned the case. He arrived in the Prep Room a couple of minutes later, expecting to see another criminal-looking type and was surprised to see an enormous Caucasian woman sitting on the end of the exam table, talking angrily with two female deputies. She was pointing her finger at one of them, cursing for all the injustices in her world while the deputy stared back, stone-faced. As her finger waggled, rolls of loose fat jiggled along the underside of her arm. She was wearing a huge, brightly colored dress that looked like a circus tent. Under the bottom flap of the tent, her morbidly obese legs were covered with thick and wormy purple veins that protruded from hairy skin. Slabs of fat from her thighs had rolled off each side of the table and her buttocks had spread out over several square feet of table area.

As Decker walked past the Prep Room nurse, Peter mumbled under his breath, "You're gonna love this."

"Good afternoon, ma'am, what problem are you having?" Decker said pleasantly.

"You can tell these bitch cops to—"

"Shut your face, Marcy, we'll do the talking here," one of the female deputies, the one with the thin lips, interrupted. "This is Mrs. Marcy," she told Decker, "and she is a suspect in a narcotics case—"

"You be *lyin'*!" Mrs. Marcy wailed. "I didn't ever get involved in no narcotics, you bitch cop!"

"I told you to shut your face, Marcy!" Thin Lips said. "One more time, just one more little squeak, and you're off to solitary for two weeks after the doctor examines you." She paused, straightening her shoulders and adjusting her uniform, "Now, as I was saying, Mrs. Marcy is a suspect in a narcotics case, and we have reason to believe she is concealing contraband on her person." She looked at Marcy and wrinkled her nose. "It is not physically possible for the deputies at the County Jail to examine her properly, so here she is, for your examination."

Decker surveyed the patient. "She needs a complete examination?"

"Complete." Thin Lips's lips became thinner.

"Pelvic exam?" he asked quietly.

"Pelvic, rectal, under the arms, under the breasts, in the hair, in the mouth, in the ears, and in the folds of fat across her stomach." Thin Lips was having fun. She sniffed and added, "And in the folds of fat that surround her butt."

Decker looked at the patient again as he briefly wondered why he had decided to become a doctor. "Why doesn't she have handcuffs on?"

"They wouldn't fit."

"Oh." He raised his voice, "Peter! Get her gown off and set her up for a pelvic!"

"I want a female nurse!" Marcy shrieked.

"Button that lip, Marcy!" the deputy sheriff growled.

"I want a female doctor!" she wailed even louder.

And that was when Skeeters and his new patient, Robert Lamb, arrived in the Prep Room.

"Just hop up on that examining table, Mr. Lamb," Skeeters said, "and I'll check you over."

Lamb was a muscular thirty-three-year-old man with jet black skin and a happy expression on his face. He jumped up on the end of the second exam table 5 feet to the right of Mrs. Marcy and sat upright, ready for inspection. Marcy's eyes widened with horror as she hollered, "Nobody's gonna examine me with this Negro man in the same room!"

Thin Lips glared at her and said, "I really don't think he's interested in you. You're not exactly a sex object, honey."

Lamb glanced at Marcy and back at Skeeters as he waited for his examination to begin. Marcy narrowed her eyes to slitlike openings then wrinkled her face in a defiant expression to the deputy that resembled a humanoid prune. Decker struggled to maintain his professional demeanor.

"Peter"—he called again—"let's get some curtains between the prisoners, and then stand by to help with the pelvic."

As Peter slowly dragged the portable curtain across the Prep Room with all the enthusiasm of a man on his way to an interment, Skeeters held Lamb's abdominal X rays up to the light.

"What is this in your abdomen?" he asked.

Lamb looked at Skeeters and smiled happily. "That be a razor blade, boss. In my stomach!"

"Thank you, Mr. Lamb. It does look very much like a razor blade, and it does appear to be in your stomach. Would you care to share with me *why* there might be a razor blade in your stomach?"

"I swallowed it!"

Skeeters pondered the response for a moment. "I see," he said as he studied Lamb's happy face. "Would you therefore, care to share with me, Mr. Lamb, why you would want to swallow a razor blade?"

"He was trying to fend off iron deficiency," Decker said from behind the curtain. "Mrs. Marcy, can't you get your legs any wider apart than this?"

"They're as wide as they go!" She screamed, beginning to sound hysterical. "This be very embarrassing, you know?"

Skeeters took a deep breath and let it out slowly. "Were you trying to commit suicide, Mr. Lamb?"

"Sho-nuff! Ah was trying to do myself in!"

"Mrs. Marcy, this is a very severe case of hemorrhoids!"

"Don't touch 'em! They be very sensitive!"

"Mr. Lamb, have you wanted to commit suicide for a long time, or did you just recently decide to do this?" Skeeters was beginning to feel an aching tiredness spreading through his bones.

Robert Lamb looked confused. "Why, I was just depressed a couple of months ago, that is, a couple of weeks ago. Why do it matter when I started up bein' depressed? The fact is, boss, that I am depressed and here I've gone and tried to commit soo-inside!"

"The difference, Mr. Lamb, is that if you have been depressed for a long time, I'll have to send you over to the House for the Criminally Suicidally Insane. Also known as the psycho ward."

"What if I be soo-insidal for just a short time? Then

can I stay here? So we can wait for the razor blade to move on through and to watch me so you can be sure I won't bleed to death?"

"Mrs. Marcy, you have fungus under your breasts!" Decker held his breath for a moment and then began mouth breathing. In spite of his efforts, he caught a whiff of a sour musty odor and felt a deep urge to gag. "Don't you ever wash this area?"

"Dermatomycosis!" Skeeters called out from the other side of the curtain before she could answer.

"Thank you, Dr. Skeeters. Mrs. Marcy, you have a severe case of dermatomycosis, inferior to your mammary tissue. How often do you wash?"

"I wash once a week! I'm a very clean lady! I jus' keep sweatin' and I guess the fungus jus' likes to grow!"

"Okay, I'm going to put Nizoral ointment under your breasts." Peter followed the cue and handed Decker a large tube of ointment from the medicine cabinet. "Hold up your right breast and I'll put on the ointment!"

She clutched her right breast and heaved in an upward direction.

"Higher. Can't you get it any higher?"

"I'm doin' the best I can!" Marcy howled as she tugged on the mountain of tissue that covered the right side of her chest.

"Have you had any signs of bleeding since you swallowed the razor?" Skeeters said.

"No bleeding yet, boss, but it may start at any time!" A lopsided smile filled with crooked yellow teeth lit up his face.

"Very good, Mrs. Marcy, now hold up your left breast!"

Five minutes later, Mary Marcy was led away by her guards, free of dermatomycosis and certified to have no orifice concealing contraband. Decker, feeling depressed, left to finish a stack of paperwork at the dictating station, while Skeeters sat at the table in the corner of the Prep Room to write Robert Lamb's admission orders to the Jail Ward. He had just finished ordering cascara suppositories and milk of magnesia, when Dr. Dillon Marsh walked up behind his chair.

"Are you admitting this man, Dr. Skeeters?" he asked, white eyebrows drawn together.

Skeeters turned his chair around and looked up at the Jail Ward director. "Yes, sir, I think it would be safer to watch him for a couple of days."

"And what is his medical problem?"

"He swallowed a razor blade—suicide attempt. Do you want to see the X ray?"

"No, I've already seen it. What treatment plan do you have?"

Well now, why are you asking me what problem he has, if you already looked at his X ray? "Black and white dynamite, sir, that is, Cascara and milk of magnesia. We'll be straining his stool and I expect the razor should pass in a day or two."

"What is his underlying problem, Doctor?"

Skeeters stood up and faced the director. This was the first time he had been quizzed about an admission, and something in Dr. Marsh's voice warned of impending danger.

"The razor was swallowed as a suicide gesture, sir, and so I believe his problem must be some kind of endogenous depression."

Marsh's eyebrows drew closer together. "Did he look depressed to you, Dr. Skeeters?"

Skeeters felt his heart beginning to pound. "No, sir, he did not seem to look very depressed. In fact, he looked unusually happy—"

"Like somebody ready to go on a vacation, right?"

"Yes, sir, very much like that."

"Like maybe a three-day R & R from the County Jail?"

Skeeters thought for a minute. "Dr. Marsh, that razor is in his stomach, and there is some concern that a gastric or enteric laceration could occur."

"You are correct on the point of the razor, it *is* in his stomach. However, it is surrounded by about a quarter-inch of tape, sealing up the cutting edge of his mucosal lining."

"Tape?" Skeeters's mouth dropped open.

"Tape, radiolucent tape. The radiopaque razor shows up on the X ray, the radiolucent tape is invisible on the X ray. Like swallowing a big pill. An R & R pill. No depression, no danger to the enteric mucosa, just three days of vacation on the Jail Ward. If he's not sent back to the County Jail in the next hour or so, we'll see a swarm of patients with razors in their stomachs by midnight. They do this sort of thing about once a year, and Mr. Lamb is their trial balloon."

"I'll send him back," Skeeters said, as he neatly tore the admission order sheet in half. "I should have picked up on his affect discrepancy. Should I confront him with this, sir?"

"No, Dr. Skeeters, he'll just deny it."

"Thank you, sir."

Skeeters walked across the Prep Room to his patient. *The last thing Steve and I need tonight is a swarm of new patients with razor blades in their stomachs.* Robert Lamb was quickly changing from his County prisoner blues into the Jail Ward patient gown and his face lit up when he saw his intern approach.

"Hello, Dr. Skeeters. No pain so far."

"Good, Mr. Lamb. I've just talked with the director of the Jail Ward, and we both feel that with this razor blade in your stomach, you must have been depressed long enough to warrant an immediate transfer to the House for the Criminally Suicidally Insane."

"The House for the Insane?"

"The House for the Criminally Suicidally Insane. There's no other way. You won't be able to stay here, not with this degree of depression. The House will be perfect for you. There are many other people with mental problems there, although regrettably most of them are *violent* mental problems—"

Lamb's eyes opened wide, his pupils dilating. "Jeez, boss, I don't need to go there, do I? I'm not insane, I'm just—"

"No question about it. You've got to be insane to swallow razor blades."

Lamb's forehead glistened with sweat. "Doc, please, no. I want to stay here."

Skeeters hesitated, looking thoughtful. "You can't stay here with your kind of depression, but we could send you back to the County Jail, although I may get into trouble for doing that."

"I won't tell nobody, Doc. You're all right, man, I really 'preciate it. Ya cleared up my mind completely, I'm gonna stay away from those razors—that's really crazy, swallowing razors! Ah'm gonna tell all the other guys about the House for the Criminally Soo-insidally insane!"

"Good for you, Mr. Lamb. I'll change the orders and send you right back to the County Jail." Skeeters left the room as Robert Lamb continued to praise his doctor to anybody who would listen.

An hour later, Steve Decker felt a surge of elation as he walked out the side entrance of the hospital and followed the stone path in the direction of the Residents' Parking Structure. *It couldn't be better,* he thought, as he looked at his watch. *Not a bad day on the Jail Ward (at least nobody died), already showered and changed into decent clothes, and now just a quick drive down to the Pediatric Pavilion to pick up Katie at six o'clock sharp.*

He entered the parking lot and passed the young guard strolling down the row of cars, eyes dull and glazed, rent-a-cop insignia emblazoned on his left shoulder. The hundreds of cars belonging to the resident doctors working at U.S.C./L.A. County Hospital were packed tightly together in the drab and dimly lit six-story concrete structure as their owners toiled inside the adjacent hospital building. Since most of the physicians enrolled in the residency program were in varying degrees of dire financial straits from the draining years of medical school, the cars were mostly old and run-down, looking like relics from a seedy used-car lot.

The glistening red Corvette at the end of the far row of cars was the notable exception.

Decker looked at the polished red paint and the smooth curving body covering the wide-track rear wheels, and felt the same thrill he had felt six years ago when he had first seen the car in the showroom window. He loved his Corvette, maintaining it for 76,000 miles in flawless condition, meticulously caring for every square inch to prevent any traces of corrosion or deterioration. He had parked it in the corner spot, at just the right angle to protect it from the swinging doors of nearby cars with mindless drivers— seven years without a scratch, not bad.

He pulled out a small electronic transmitter from his pocket, punched the button, and heard the satisfying "Bleep!" sound as he disabled the car's alarm circuits. He quickly made the usual survey around his machine, like a pilot preflighting his aircraft, inspecting the tires and searching for any alterations since the last inspection early that morning. As he sank into the low bucket seat and strapped on his seatbelt, he savored the thought of the sweet acceleration down the freeway. *Like an F-18, just before launch.* He reached down, placed the key into the ignition, and with a quick flip of his wrist, he brought the engine to life.

Five minutes later, right on schedule, he gunned the beefed-up 5700 cc L-83 engine up the driveway to the front entrance of the Pediatric Pavilion, his wide rear wheels emitting just the briefest hint of a squeal. Clusters of white-coated pediatric residents and interns, with stethoscopes dangling out of their pockets, were exiting the building, their day of work completed.

There was still more than an hour before sunset— Decker knew she would be standing outside the front door, looking for him. He slowly cruised past the entrance, mentally rehearsing how he would stop the car at her wave, jump out smoothly and open the passenger door to gallantly provide her entrance to his sleek machine.

Katie Shields was nowhere to be seen.

He slowly circled around the first row of cars in the parking lot and cruised past the entrance again, carefully searching for any sign of his date. Nobody was standing near the entrance, nobody waved. He spotted several pediatricians studying his car as they left the building, certainly admiring the flawless lines, he thought, and probably wishing the car was theirs.

After parking and arming the car's alarm circuits, he walked through the front entrance of the pavilion and headed for the central circular desk. A wall of noise surrounded him as a crowd of women, most of them holding crying babies, clamored for attention from a thin, frizzy-haired woman standing behind the desk. Decker mentally gave thanks that he had moved away from the general anarchy of pediatrics after the third year of medical school. A pediatrics specialty had never really been in the running for him, especially when contrasted to the quiet, almost military-like, organization of the surgical theater. A theater where the *surgeon* was the star. He scanned the room for Katie, glanced back at the woman behind the desk, who now appeared to be in the early stages of a nervous breakdown, and finally turned to explore the first pediatric ward he could find.

On ward 3A, he found cartoons of Bugs Bunny and Yosemite Sam on the walls and a middle-aged nurse standing in the nursing station, reading a chart.

"Dr. Katie Shields anywhere around here, or is there any way I can page her?" Decker asked.

"Dr. Shields? Last time I saw her, she was on her way to the ICU. One of the babies was having some problems."

He was given directions to the pediatric intensive care unit, and five minutes later, another nurse told him that Dr. Shields had gone down to the M room in the basement. The elevator, running measurably faster than its counterpart up on the hill, delivered him with minimum clanking noises to a darkened, deserted underground corridor filled with laundry carts and discarded boxes. He looked up and down the corridor and sniffed. There was the unmistakable odor of formaldehyde mixed with the sweet-musty fragrance of mold.

Most hospitals have an M room, or equivalent, usually stashed far from where any visitors might inadvertently enter. Serving as a temporary morgue, they are refrigerated and are available to receive the final carrion products of disease, pending instructions that identify the pathologist or the mortician as the next recipient of choice.

He found the door to the room, marked appropriately with a large black M and the red letters that warned the uninitiated not to enter. At the instant he reached for the doorknob, the heavy door swung wide open.

"Steve!" Katie Shields exclaimed as Decker jumped back. She looked upset, her eyes were moist and her black hair was in disarray over her white coat. "I'm sorry I couldn't meet you upstairs. We just lost a real bad case, a Vietnamese baby." Decker caught a quick glimpse of the body of a lifeless, deeply purple baby lying on a stainless-steel examining table behind her as the door was pulled shut and they walked to the elevator.

He reached out and touched her shoulder. "I'm sorry—" He felt uncharacteristically awkward and out of place, unable to think of anything proper to say.

"Katie, would you rather go out another night?" he said as he punched the button for the first floor. "This is a bad afternoon for you. We could get together some other time."

She smiled at him, her dark eyes looking beautiful in the muted elevator light. "Thanks, Steve, that's really nice. I think dinner tonight would be the perfect respite—I need to get away from here for a few hours. Especially after today."

They left the elevator, passed through the crowd standing around the receptionist's desk, and headed for the front door. The woman behind the desk was hollering, alternately in English and Spanish, as she tried to get everyone to start *nicely* taking a number from a number-dispensing machine near her desk.

"My car is right over there"—he pointed toward the last row of cars—"it's the red—"

"Oh, Steve, let me just drop my coat off in my car before we go. I can't believe I almost wore my white coat to dinner!"

"I'm sure the waiter would have been very impressed," Decker said, as they diverted toward a white Ford Mustang in the front row of cars. She pulled off her coat, tossed it across the front seat of the dusty car, and carefully locked the door again.

Decker found himself enjoying the simple act of watching her as she transformed from a pediatric physician to a softer and more relaxed woman, preparing for an enjoyable evening. Oblivious to his admiring gaze, she pulled out a clip that was holding the back of her hair, and with a toss of her head, it gently fell across her shoulders. Without the white coat, Decker noticed, her slender waist and the soft breasts that filled her blouse were much better appreciated.

She is a survivor, he thought as he took her hand and escorted her toward his Corvette. His peripheral vision caught the new bounce in her step, the increasingly feminine movements of her body. He had watched the Death of Femininity, as he called it, occur to so many women physicians these past years that he had almost come to expect it. Refreshing, to have one who has escaped the plague. . . . He unlocked the passenger door to his car and acknowledged the sweet praise of his perfection machine.

He took her to Lawry's Restaurant for a prime rib dinner—*that should take her mind off Baby Guan Ng,* he thought—and her mood did improve as she began to talk more, with increased spirit in her voice. After dinner, they drove the short distance to Westwood and walked hand in hand for more than an hour along the crowded streets, admiring the products in the shops catering to the nearby UCLA student body.

They avoided the subject of the baby throughout the evening and not until two hour later, after driving out Santa Monica Boulevard to the ocean, did she bring it up again. They had strolled down the Santa

Monica Pier and sat on a wooden bench that faced the dark glistening swells of the nighttime Pacific Ocean. He put his arms around her, pulling her close to him as they watched the movement of the water below.

"You're really sweet, Steve. I just wanted you to know how much I appreciate it," she said softly.

"After today, I think you needed a break," Decker said.

"It really hurt to lose that one. And from a bug that can be nailed so easily if we only had a chance to see her sooner."

Decker held her tightly. "The mother didn't know— she just didn't know."

"That's what makes it so terrible, the innocence and the ignorance of it all, the trust in Asian remedies when that little baby girl needed Western antibiotics so badly. And it can happen again in that family, exactly the same way, if another infant is sick. It takes generations to break the cycle." She felt the sting of tears filling her eyes. "God, I hate to lose a baby!" she said with emotion.

Decker looked out at the water, remaining silent while she continued.

"When I was nine years old, my baby sister died. Sweet Sherry, my father used to call her— She *was* sweet, unlike the hellion I used to be at that age. She was only two years old when they finally figured out that the bruising and the fatigue was from acute lymphocytic leukemia. They used archaic chemotherapy and every other trick they could think of, but in less than a month, she was dead. My parents had stayed with her in the hospital during the final week, while my older brother remained at home and took care of me.

"When my parents came home, we didn't even

know she had died—we didn't know until I saw the look on my father's face. I will never forget the way he looked; it was like a face of stone. He said nothing to us, not a word. That night, after my brother and I had gone to bed, I heard him cleaning out the little nursery he had built for Sherry. He took the crib, her toys, all of her clothes, everything, he took it all away that night, and we never talked about her again. She simply seemed to have just disappeared from the face of the earth.

"There was some kind of a ceremony, a funeral of sorts, while my brother and I were in school, but my parents never mentioned it to us. I didn't even know where her grave was until three or four years ago when I researched it through the County Bureau of Records.

"The night my father cleaned out her room, when I was listening to him from my bed, was the night I decided to become a pediatrician. I had never thought much about being a doctor, but that night I knew I would become a *pediatrician*. I wanted to have the chance to save other children from this kind of tragedy, and to try to save families from feeling such a terrible loss. Funny thing was, my grades in school turned to A's after that, while my brother's dropped to D's and F's—he barely made it through high school. When I was going to medical school, he was a hippie somewhere in Oregon—none of us have heard from him for about ten years."

She looked up at him, studying his face in the dim light of the pier. "I'm sorry to tell such a sad story on such a beautiful night—"

He stroked her cheek and gave her a gentle kiss. "It was a good story, because you became a pediatrician. Have you seen many children with leukemia since you started your residency?"

She looked back at the water. "About thirty now," she said. "And, since we've figured out a better chemotherapy program, almost every one of them has been put into remission. Some of them have had their disease shut down for over five years and we're even beginning to talk of a cure." She laughed. "And if it wasn't for Sweet Sherry, I'd probably be a fat housewife with ten kids, sitting around eating bonbons!"

They walked to his car and he drove her back to the Pediatric Pavilion, eliciting a promise from her that she stay overnight in the on-call room instead of trying to drive home at such a late hour. He escorted her up the front steps to the building and gave her a good-night kiss.

"Good night, Katie, I'll call you soon."

"Good night, Steve, and thank you again for a wonderful evening."

He drove down the San Bernardino Freeway to his apartment, where he showered and climbed into bed. He stared at the darkened ceiling, thinking. She was beautiful, she was kind, and she was sensitive—she had everything he had ever looked for in a woman. *Dangerous thinking,* he thought, *for a man who is a confirmed bachelor. But then, she did say I was sweet—*

He reached over to his telephone and a minute later she was on the line.

"I told you I'd call you soon!" he said. "Good night again, it was wonderful to be with you—"

"Now that I know you're home safely, I can go to sleep. Good night, Steve."

Chapter 5

The Corvette smoothly followed the curving freeway into Pasadena as Decker restrained himself from exceeding the posted 45 miles-per-hour speed limit. The 8-mile Pasadena Freeway was the first in California, built in 1940 when cars did not easily achieve speeds above 50 miles per hour. The California Highway Patrol, recognizing the difficulty chasing down each driver exceeding the speed limit—since *everyone* exceeded the speed limit—had developed a system of radar-triggered photographs that allowed for mass-production fines, neatly collected courtesy of the U.S. Postal Service. Anyone cranking their speed above the posted limits would soon receive greetings from the state of California in an envelope containing the fine, the speed at the time of the radar picture, and a remarkably clear photograph of the license plate and the owner's happy face.

In the passenger seat, Blake Skeeters tried to look at Decker's road map without taking his eyes off the curves of the freeway ahead. His stomach had tightened into a knot of cramping pain that was fluctuating in perfect synchrony with the winding turns in the road. They had only been traveling along the freeway for five minutes and he was already nauseated and nearly ready to lose the sandwich and the rest of the lunch that his wife had prepared for him that morning.

If they were going to continue using this path as a freeway, he thought as he suppressed a surging belch, *the least they could do is straighten the miserable thing out.* Finally, in the distance, a large green sign proclaimed that the Orange Grove overpass was approaching.

"There it is, next exit," Skeeters said with relief as he pointed to the narrow and steep uphill off-ramp ahead. They left the freeway and headed north, toward Huntington Memorial Hospital.

"The Huntington Heaven, that's what they call it." Decker grinned. "Good thing Blum transferred here— the word is that he was dying over at Martin Luther King. They had him in some kind of a twelve-bed ward, surrounded by the Crips and the Bloods."

"The county paid for the transfer?" Skeeters asked.

"Are you kidding? His friends at the Compton Fire Station paid cold cash for it. Felt sorry for the poor bastard, I guess."

Ten minutes later, they walked into Andy Blum's dimly lit room on the fourth floor. It was a private room and Blum's bed was near the window at the far end. He was sound asleep, his casted left arm supported by a collection of bars and chains that held it in a fixed position, pointing straight at the ceiling. He had dark circles under his eyes, and he looked older and more shrunken than Decker had remembered. Colored helium balloons were attached to various points on his bed, and the wall behind his head were covered with a colorful montage of get-well cards. A glossy full-color photograph of a negligee-clad Playmate of the Month was stretched across the wall at the foot of his bed.

"Andy?" Decker whispered. "Andy, you getting along okay?"

Blum's eyes popped open and his head jerked to the left as he looked around.

"Hello!" he said, blinking a couple of times. "Hello!" he repeated as a look of recognition spread across his face. "The interns!" His narrow face broke into a smile.

"Yep!" Decker said, handing him a get-well card as Skeeters poked a small bouquet of flowers into a cup of water. "How the hell are you doing?" Decker said.

"We just stopped by to see if you were getting along okay," Skeeters added.

"Well, that's real nice of you guys," he said. "I'm doing just fine, going to get out of here in two or three days." His voice dropped low. "You should see the nurses here, they're gorgeous! Every one a beauty queen! Except the one on the graveyard shift—I thought I was having a nightmare the first time she walked into the room!"

"While Willie Peach is out working the streets, you're gettin' massages from Pasadena Rose Queens!" Decker said, grinning broadly. He pointed to the cast enclosing Blum's left arm. "How'd the surgery go? They get the bullet out okay?"

"Yeah, you won't believe this, but they didn't need to! It bounced off my third rib on this side and angled up through my shoulder, just missing the—something—bundle?"

"Neurovascular bundle?" Skeeters said.

"Right! Just missing the neurovascular bundle and spinning its way up against my arm bone, the humerus here, and out the back! The police found it sitting on the other side of the room, just *sitting* there in the corner. Ortho guy over at King fixed up the crack in the bone, everything's healing just fine, and I'm almost ready to get out of here." He frowned. "Doc said if it was a millimeter higher, I'd have been stuck with a dead arm for the rest of my life."

"Jesus—" Decker murmured.

"Have you heard anything about the girl we were working on? Did she come out of the coma okay?" Skeeters asked.

"Yeah, Willie said she had a cerebral contusion of some kind, but she should be okay. She has amnesia about the whole thing, so she won't be much help against the guy who was whacking her around. The DA's office is going to be calling all of us for depositions against him sometime soon. By the way, how's things on the Jail Ward?"

"Going just fine," Skeeters answered. "Seen a lot of cases since that night. Only another three weeks to go and we'll be through with the rotation."

"And off to a brighter world—" Decker added.

Blum struggled to sit upright, his left arm hitting the crossbar as he moved. "Damn! That hurt!" he grunted as he shifted around again, trying to get comfortable. "Still kind of sensitive under my arm where that bullet thrashed around next to the bone. By the way, there's some guy, a resident in medicine here, who was on the Jail Ward last month. He transferred here to finish his residency training for the final two years. Guy named"—he thought for a moment—"guy named Pick or Pack or something like that."

"Peck? Joel Peck?" Decker asked.

"Yeah, that's it. He's on a neurology rotation and the ortho guy called him to consult on the nerves going down my left arm. He had some great stories to tell about the Jail Ward while he checked out my nerves. Seemed like a nice guy—do you know him?"

"Never met him, just heard his name last week," Decker said, recalling the conversation with Dr. Marsh.

Skeeters looked at his watch. "We got to be going, Andy, got to get back to the Jail Ward for the afternoon rounds. Sure glad to see you're doing so well."

Everybody repeated their wishes for good luck and good health, and the two interns left the room. In the lobby of the hospital, Decker abruptly asked Skeeters to wait for a moment while he made a quick call. Two minutes later, he left the telephone booth and joined Skeeters again as they walked to his car.

"Damn. He doesn't answer his beeper. They say he's probably off call today since he was up all night," Decker said. "Told the operator to have him give me a call."

"Who? That guy Peck? Who is he anyway?"

"He's the guy who was taking care of Biting Billy before I picked up the case."

"Oh," Skeeters said as he paused to think. "He's the one who transferred him back to the County Jail?"

"Yup." Decker popped a stick of gum into his mouth and began chewing furiously. "I've been trying to find the chart for a week now, but it's lost in the bowels of the County's basement—probably gone forever. I need to ask him a few questions about the transfer. He really screwed me up with that case, and I want to find out why."

"Dr. Decker to Prep Room! Dr. Decker to Prep Room!"

The effect of Brodie's nasal voice echoing up and down the central corridor was like fingernails scraping across a blackboard. Steve's skin prickled with the sheer irritation of the sound as he leaned over and, once again, plunged the 21-gauge needle into the arm of Charlie Hall. The patient, a thirty-two-year-old black man, was a living textbook example of the entire spectrum of STD (Sexually Transmitted Disease), and if it hadn't been for the sepsis from his inflamed prostate, he would have been roaming the streets again, looking for his next conquest.

The good news for Charlie, by some miracle of Mother Nature, was that he did not show any evidence of AIDS. The bad news for Decker was that Charlie, by virtue of a drug habit that spanned more than twenty years, did not appear to have any veins. This was even more of a problem now, since Decker was up for the next patient of the morning and Brodie's voice sounded ominously happy.

"Jesus, Doc, ya gonna get it this time?" Charlie asked as Decker probed the needle around under the skin, searching for any sign of blood.

"Charlie, where the hell are your veins? How does blood get back to your heart?"

"Doctor Decker to Prep Room! Dr. Decker to Prep Room!"

"Where is that weird voice be comin' from?" Charlie asked, looking up and down the corridor. "Sounds like a frog in mating season!"

"You got mating season on the brain, Charlie. That be Brodie, and some day before I leave the Jail Ward, I'm going to kill him!" Decker said as he pulled the needle back out of Charlie's arm."

"Let me get it for you, Doc, and you can go find out what's going on in that there Prep Room."

Decker handed him a fresh Vacu-tainer with needle and vacuum tube attached. He quickly scanned up and down the corridor, looking for Dr. Marsh. "Go to it, Charlie," he said, "but hurry. If anybody sees this, I'm hung out to dry."

Five seconds later, the needle was deep into the forearm of Charlie Hall, and a gush of dark red blood came swirling into the tube.

"Amazing!" Decker said as Charlie grinned from ear to ear.

From the look of Homer Stark writhing about on the Prep Room examining table, it was clear that there were only two or three possible diagnoses—few conditions in human experience cause so much excruciating pain that one cannot lie still. He was a forty-four-year-old Caucasian man of medium build with short-cropped brown hair and a pockmarked face that was severely contorted in pain. He was naked above the waist and was wearing the blue prison denims that confirmed his permanent residency status at the Los Angeles County Jail. Peter Martel was taping an intravenous line to his left forearm as a deputy sheriff gripped the arm tightly.

"What's the story here?" Decker said as the man rolled back and forth.

"Transferred from the County Jail," the nurse said as he ran a final strip of tape across the tubing, "with bright red blood in his urine and severe back pain. Came on right after breakfast. Thinks he passed a kidney stone five or ten years ago. Want him to get a shot of Demerol?"

"Go ahead and draw up 75 milligrams of Demerol with 25 milligrams of Vistaril, but don't give it to him until I check him over."

Martel left for the Medication Room as Decker helped Stark move to a semireclined position. The patient was drenched with sweat as he rolled back and forth across the examining table.

Decker leaned over the table and said, "I'm Dr. Decker. Have you ever had any pain like this before?"

"Only once before, back in '84, when I passed a stone," he groaned. "Doc, can you give me something for the pain, I can't stand it anymore!"

"Hang on, we'll give you something in a minute. Where does it hurt the most?"

"On the right side, in the middle of my back." He groaned again and shifted around on the table. "Soon as it started, I began to pee blood. Had the same thing in '84, put out blood for a week!"

"Are you sure it was a stone back then? Did the doctor tell you what kind of a stone it was?"

"The stone came out when I was taking a pee, dropped into the urinal at the County Jail and disappeared down one of the holes in the urinal. Never could get it back again. They took some X rays of my kidneys and said everything looked normal. Just told me not to drink milk anymore. Doc, please, give me something for the pain!"

Decker asked him a few more questions and quickly examined him. When Decker thumped his fist gently against Stark's right mid-back area, directly over his right kidney, the patient let out a loud cry of pain.

"I'm sorry, had to do that . . ."

"Doctor, I have the Demerol here," Peter Martel said as he returned to the Prep Room. "The bottle emptied out at 60 milligrams, couldn't find any more, do you want me to just give him this or do you want to wait until the pharmacy gives us another 15 milligrams?"

"The bottle is empty?" Decker stared at the nurse. "Why isn't there a backup bottle or a spare bottle? This man needs 75 milligrams of Demerol."

"We've been using an unusually large amount of the Demerol today—I've already given about ten or fifteen shots, with the pancreatitis patient and that guy with multiple fractures." He shrugged.

"Doc, give me something, give me *anything* for the pain!" Stark cried out.

"How about morphine sulfate?" Decker asked the nurse. "We have any morphine?"

"Nope, that bottle is empty too, I just checked. I have a stat call to the pharmacy for both drugs, but we'll just have to wait for them to get here."

"How long does that take?"

"Anywhere from fifteen minutes to two hours, depending on how busy they are. Today"—Martel cocked his head and rolled his eyes up to look at the ceiling—"today, I would say it will be about half an hour."

"Well, that's just unacceptable! I'm going to have a talk with the pharmacist about this problem. Go ahead with the 60 of Demerol, and do you have the full 25 of Vistaril?"

"Yes, sir, 60 of Demerol and 25 of Vistaril, ready to go."

"Okay, give it to him, then crank up his intravenous rate to 200 cc's per hour, strain his urine for stones, get another urinalysis in a couple of hours with a culture, and get him down for a stat IVP."

"Will do," the nurse said.

"Doc," Stark called out, "what's an IVP?"

"An IVP is an intravenous pyelogram, which means an X ray picture will be taken of your abdomen after you are given an injection of contrast material in a vein. The contrast collects in your kidneys, making them light up when the X ray is taken. If there is a stone, we should be able to see it."

At the end of the long central corridor that ran the length of the thirteenth floor, Jack Diamond reclined against the back of his wooden wheelchair, in his usual position. His right leg was propped high into the air, his purple wig was perfectly balanced on his head, and his mascara and eye shadow were flawlessly in place. Skeeters sat at his side, the patient's chart open in front of him.

"How are you feeling, Mr. Diamond?" he asked.

"Pretty good now, Doctor," he answered as he wiped his nose with the back of his hand. He sniffed and wiped his nose again.

"Here's some tissues," Skeeters said as he placed a Kleenex box on his lap.

"Thank you, Dr. Skeeters. I appreciate your being so nice to me."

"You're a nice person, Mr. Diamond. According to the orthopedic surgeon, you should be able to get out of here in another week or so."

Tears began to form in Diamond's eyes as he envisioned himself returning to the County Jail. It wasn't so much that he had been kicked by one of the prisoners there, or even that the assault had resulted in a fractured hip. It was the humiliation of going back to where there was no respect from anyone! So he was a transvestite, so what? It was an error of nature that he followed the softer and sweeter pathway in life; it certainly was not his fault. Why wasn't there some kind of support group at the jail, like a transvestite support group? They had support groups for everyone else—for those with AIDS, for the war veterans, for the divorced, for the elderly—for everyone except transvestites!

He blew his nose and dabbed his lipstick with the tissue Dr. Skeeters had so kindly given him. If only he hadn't written all those bad checks on that shopping spree six months ago—the judge couldn't understand that it was one of those things you just can't control, especially when there was such a blockbuster sale of lingerie. Six months in jail for just that one teeny-weeny mistake! It was so unfair!

"We're going to start the second phase of physical therapy tomorrow, Mr. Diamond," Skeeters said. "The therapist will start slow-walking activity so you can begin to build up the strength of your right leg. The muscles on that side are a lot weaker with these past two weeks of sitting around. The cast holding your knee in place comes off tomorrow morning and, hopefully, you will be able to start weight-bearing soon. Do you have any questions?"

He's so nice, Diamond thought. "No questions, Doctor, thank you for your help." He reached out to shake Skeeters's hand. "Dr. Skeeters, there is one thing I wanted to mention, if you have a moment."

"Yes?"

"Sitting out here in the corridor like this, I have a chance to watch what happens on the Jail Ward. There are a lot of doctors, and a lot of inmates, and all of them seem to be getting along okay."

Skeeters looked at him questioningly. "Is anybody giving you any problems?" he asked.

"Well, the doctors are just fine. And the other inmates leave me alone." *Actually, they ignore me,* he thought. "But, I wanted to say something about the deputy sheriffs, that is, about one deputy sheriff."

"Is one of them being tough on you?"

"No. I'm sorry to take so much time with this, but it isn't something you can just come out and say. I don't want you to think I'm a stoolie or anything like that."

"Go ahead, Mr. Diamond. I'll just keep it between us."

His voice dropped to a whisper. "It's okay if you talk to the doctors about this, but I think you should know that one deputy, the big one in charge, is dangerous."

"The one in charge? Sergeant Grossman?"

"Yes, Sergeant Grossman. He's very dangerous."

Skeeters looked down the corridor and back at his

patient. "Sergeant Grossman is dangerous to whom?
To the prisoners?"

"Yes, and to the interns and nurses." He sat up
in his wheelchair. "He's very dangerous to everyone.
That's all I'm going to say. Just watch out for him—
don't cross him."

Skeeters stood up. "Thank you, Mr. Diamond. I'll
watch out for him."

He said good-bye and walked down the corridor in
the general direction of his next patient. One of the
newer deputies passed him, walking in the opposite
direction; they both nodded a quick greeting. *There
were deputies everywhere, and they always seemed to
have everything under control,* Skeeters thought. Grossman was an imposing figure, to be sure, all 200-plus
pounds and 6 feet 4 inches of him, and he could see
why a prisoner might consider him dangerous. Skeeters filed the warning in the back of his mind—he only
had one month in his entire career to spend on the
Jail Ward, and he wasn't going to start worrying about
which deputy sheriff may be dangerous under what
circumstance. He would just take care of his patients
as they came in, and that should be good enough for
anybody.

As he passed the Medication Room, he heard
"Blake!" hissed out from the partially closed door. He
turned, pushed the door open, and walked inside. The
room was a brightly lit walk-in closet-sized area filled
from the floor to the ceiling with cupboards and draw-
ers. A green Formica counter wrapped around the
entire room, and various packages of different colored
pills were scattered haphazardly on its surface. Steve
Decker was standing in front of a large white metal
cabinet that was wide open.

"Welcome to the Medication Room," Decker said.
"Ever been here before?"

"Steve, what are you doing in here?" Skeeters asked.

"They didn't show it to us on our initial tour. I think it's supposed to stay locked at all times, but here it is wide open."

"I don't think we're supposed to be in here, Steve." Skeeters looked around nervously.

"Settle down, Blake," Decker said. "Nobody's going to sweat a couple of docs in or out of the Med Room."

"Okay," Skeeters said as he jammed his hands into the pocket of his greens. "So why are we here?"

"I was trying to get some Demerol or morphine for a patient of mine, a guy with a kidney stone. Peter Martel said we've run out of both drugs, and so I thought I would just take a look." He looked at the cupboards lining the walls. "The narc cabinet must be here somewhere."

"Probably have some system for signing them in and out, since they're controlled substances," Skeeters said as he looked around. "Back at Harvard, we had two nurses who had to sign the narcotics count, one nurse from the oncoming shift and the other nurse who was leaving her shift. And there was one key for the narc cabinet. If one of the nurses became drifty and accidentally took the key home, they had to call in the emergency key squad and replace all the locks."

"That's fine, Blake, and they probably do the same thing here, but where the hell is the morphine?"

"Probably in this cabinet," Skeeters said as he pointed to a white drawer below the shelf with a large keyhole in the middle. Decker reached down and pulled on the handle.

"Damn! It's locked!"

"We could always ask Peter to open the cabinet for us . . ."

"Right! Peter, we were jus' a little suspicious of your accounting of the downers and uppers, could you loan us your friendly key and let us take a quick look to see if you're lying to us or not?"

Skeeters's face flushed, and for the first time since they had started working on the Jail Ward, Decker realized that he had angered his fellow intern.

"Frankly, I think you're too suspicious, Steve. I think we should clear out of here and leave the morphine accounting to the registered nurses. Why don't you just ask Peter to expedite the delivery of more morphine from the Central Pharmacy so your man with the stone can get some relief?"

"I already did that," Decker said quietly, almost apologetically as they turned to leave the room. "But it takes them a long time."

Down the long hallway, in the darkened area near the elevator, Deputy Sheriff Donald Gobel looked up from his duty desk as the two interns closed the door to the Medication Room behind them. His lips tightened as he put his pencil down and considered the security implications of doctors entering the Medication Room. The rules were clear: the door is to remain locked at all times. He glanced at his log book on the corner of his desk, and made a mental note to remind the nurses to follow the posted security regulations in the future. *The rules are supposed to be followed,* he thought as he opened the book and noted his observations. With so many prisoners walking around on the Jail Ward, there must not be even the smallest opportunity for impropriety.

Conversation among the clerks and interns in the Medical Records room came to a halt as Decker leaned across the counter and began to holler.

"What do you mean it's not here? This is the fourth

time I've been to Medical Records! I need to find the guy's chart!"

"Doctor, Mr. MacFarland's chart is just going through the routing after discharge," the medical records clerk said in a whining "who do you think you are?" tone of voice. Her pale, pinched face stared at him with the open hostility of a practiced bureaucrat. *These interns are such a pain*, she thought, *always demanding this and that. If they would only try to cooperate with the system once in a while instead of yelling and screaming.*

"The charts have to clear seven different social agencies before they get here, you know, and sometimes it takes weeks," she said. "You'll just have to wait."

Decker shot back, "You keep giving me the runaround. Do you want me to come back there and start looking for the record? Biting Billy—that is, William MacFarland was just transferred back to the County Jail from where he came. What is the big deal about 'social agencies'?

"Even if the chart *was* here, Doctor"—her voice dripped with sarcasm—*"which it isn't,* you would have to search through the 2,000 active charts we take care of every single day. Now, don't you have something more important to do?"

Decker turned and stormed out of the room. Five minutes later, he was standing at the X-ray distribution desk in the radiology department on the first floor, facing a woman who looked like the medical record clerk's identical twin. Her drawn white face and hostile expression radiated a battle lost before started.

"Good morning, ma'am," Decker said sweetly. "How are you doing today?"

"Fine." Her expression looked like it was fixed in formaldehyde.

"Good." Decker smiled and leaned against the counter. "One of my patients on the Jail Ward, a Mr. Homer Stark, had a stat IVP done this morning. Could I see the X rays?"

"Medical record number?"

"Ah, yes, of course, I have it right here." He smiled pleasantly again, pulled a 3 by 5 card from his shirt pocket and read the number to her. The hospital system could not function without numbers.

She turned and disappeared into a room filled with shelves holding thousands of brown X-ray folders. Two minutes later, she returned empty-handed.

"Your film on Stark?"

"Yes?"

"Homer Stark?"

"Yes."

"Medical record number—"

"There's only one Homer Stark in the whole damn hospital who had an IVP—"

"You don't have to swear, young man!" she interrupted.

Decker stared at the woman for five seconds, then slowly leaned against the counter again and smiled. "I'm sorry, ma'am, you're correct, it *is* Mr. Homer Stark, medical record number"—he looked at his card—"MR003895968306, yes, that is the one. May I see his film?"

"We don't have it."

"Ahh . . . you don't have it." Decker felt his smile beginning to dissolve. "You don't have it," he repeated. "The patient had his films taken over an hour ago and you don't have it. Would you like to guess as to when you might have it? He's suffering with severe pain from his kidney stone, and he needs—".

"We don't have it, Doctor. Come back in an hour or two and we might have it then."

As Decker stiffened, he noticed that her eyes were unusually black and beady. Like a rat. He slowly lifted his right hand high above his head, watching the two black eyes carefully tracking the movement. He held his hand as high as he could for one full second, and with all the force he could muster, he slammed his open hand flat against the wooden countertop with a crash that vibrated the entire room. The woman let out a scream and jumped back as two other interns waiting for their X rays suddenly remembered important tasks elsewhere and fled the room.

"I want to see that goddamn IVP film now!" Decker hollered at the top of his lungs. "Now! I want that goddamn film in my hands now!"

The clerk nervously patted the sides of her clothes and said she certainly would look again for the film. The instant her thin figure vanished through the door, Decker walked around the counter and through another door with "X-ray Developing Room" emblazoned on the front. Inside the room, five machines were grinding out X rays with a steaming hissing sound as radiology technicians scurried about, collecting films, stamping them with the date, and assembling them into manila envelopes.

"Where would the IVP films be that were taken about an hour ago?" he hollered over the noise to a technician.

"Developer number 5!" a young black girl called out.

Decker moved to the fifth developer and looked at a stack of X rays that was accumulating at the far end of the machine. The upper right-hand corner of each film had patient nameplate information, and within two minutes of rapid scanning, Decker had Stark's

IVP X rays in his hand. He walked quickly across the room to an X-ray viewing box and jammed the first film against the white glass.

"Those films don't have dates stamped on them yet!" a shrill voice exclaimed as the radiology clerk reached around Decker and wrenched the film out of the viewing box.

"*You* again!" Decker hollered. With speed that even impressed himself, he ripped the film from the clerk's hand and jammed it back into the viewing glass.

"I can't allow these films to be seen until they have the date on them!" she screeched again.

"Put the date on them after I've seen them!" Decker bellowed as he scanned the nephrogram phase and tried to trace the course of the contrast moving down the ureters to the bladder. She tried to move around him to get at the film again, but his right elbow made a solid barrier in front of her rat eyes.

"Stand back!" Decker ordered.

"These films are not official films until they have the date on them!" she yelled as she tried to move around to his left side. Decker's left elbow quickly popped up in front of her face, blocking further progress.

"Stand back!" he sternly ordered again.

She cycled back and forth behind him, trying to grab each film, while he methodically fought off her advances. The difficult part, Decker found, was replacing each X ray on the lighted viewing box with a new one from the folder without letting her grab the films from his hand. As Decker moved his elbows up and down, frustrating her efforts to stop him, the pair took on movements like dancers performing an intricate two-step, in perfect time with the rhythmic sounds of the developing machines.

"Well, that does it!" she finally screamed at the top of her lungs. "I'm just going to call Security!"

She huffed her way to the wall telephone on the other side of the room as Decker continued to study the remaining films in the folder. The X rays showed the white contrast simultaneously lighting up both kidneys and collecting to flow down the thin ureter tubes to the bladder. Careful examination of the ureters showed no evidence of stones or any other kind of obstruction, and the final films demonstrated a normal lower urinary system. Decker could hear the woman bellowing into the telephone as he held the last film in front of the light. He glanced away from the X ray and was surprised at the intensity of rage in her contorted face as she reported the sheer arrogance and impudence of this intern to the security forces.

He completed his review, put the films back into the folder, mouthed "thank you!" in the direction of her furious face, and left the room. A minute later, as he exited the main doors of the radiology department, two young security guards with ill-fitting uniforms and expressions of importance rushed past him and charged in the general direction of the Developing Room.

Decker left the elevator on the thirteenth floor, walked past the duty deputy sheriff at his desk and into the Prep Room. The area was uncharacteristically silent and the two exam tables were empty. Peter Martel was seated on a high stool at the far corner of the room, his back hunched as he sorted through a tray of biopsy equipment.

"Peter, did Stark get his morphine?"

"Sure did, about ten minutes ago, feeling much better now." Peter Martel looked up from his tray and smiled. "The Demerol I gave him just didn't touch him—the guy was about blacking out from the pain—

but the morphine sulfate worked pretty fast. He's in bed now, down the hall on the left side, a urine container and a stack of coffee filters at his side. Should be putting the water out pretty quickly, the way he's getting the IV fluids. See anything on his IVP?"

"Just a couple of kidneys making urine. No sign of any stone on the films, although he may have a radiolucent one somewhere that just doesn't show up." Decker looked closely at the nurse. "Hell of a thing, not having any morphine—"

"Sorry about that," Peter said nonchalantly as he loaded the final group of biopsy instruments into a plastic bag. "The stuff just gets used up like crazy around here, with all the trauma and all."

"I guess it does." Decker dropped the subject and abruptly asked, "How long have you been working here, Peter?"

"About three years now. Spent several years in the minor trauma section of the ER, but was transferred here and have been on the Jail Ward ever since. Just enough variety here to keep it interesting, but will be going on my first vacation in another couple of months."

"You've worked here three years without a vacation?" Decker asked incredulously.

"Well, an extended weekend here and there, but no real vacations . . . it's been fun!" Peter smiled again, his black, neatly trimmed beard and mustache parting to show straight white teeth. "Only problem is a bit of a burnout from time to time, but a week or two away from it all should take care of that."

Decker thanked him for his help and walked down the corridor in search of his patient. A couple of minutes later, he called Skeeters away from an inspection of Diamond's intravenous line, and the two men moved to a quiet corner of the Jail Ward.

"How's the Purple Queen doing?" Decker asked as he leaned back against the wall.

"Mr. Diamond's doing fine," Skeeters answered. "His hip is healing and, with the physical therapy, he should be ready to leave in another week or two. Funny thing is, sitting out here in the middle of the corridor, he doesn't miss a thing. The guy's like an owl," he said with a smile, "an owl with purple feathers, watching the varmints scurrying around the thirteenth floor. He tells me that Sergeant Grossman is dangerous, whatever that means."

"Probably means, don't cross him. He *is* pretty nasty looking—" Decker said.

"Especially with all those pockmarks across his face."

"Especially with all the pockmarks. I don't think he has any fond sentiments for me either."

"I'm just avoiding the guy, especially since he's about twice as big as I am. Or at least, twice as tall. You finally get the morphine sulfate for your kidney stone patient?"

"Yeah, Peter finally came through. His IVP was negative, and he's feeling much better now. Gonna spend the afternoon trying to flush out the stone. Also, he has a cut on his finger—just happened to notice it, the guy didn't show it to me—so I have to clean that up, make sure we don't end up with another tetanus infection."

"Since he has a cut, you might want to get a witnessed urine on the guy. Wasn't the blood in the urine the only objective finding?"

Decker looked at the other intern, his face blank, for five seconds. Skeeters smiled and asked, "The gears are turning?"

"Jesus, you don't think . . . No, he didn't put blood in his urine. Why would he put blood in his urine?"

"Steve, I just got reamed by Dr. Marsh for a fake stomach laceration. Like Marsh told me, there's a lot to be said for a few days' R & R on the Jail Ward."

"Or a few days of morphine. Son of a bitch! See you later."

Homer Stark was lying back on his bed feeling good. The other three beds in the room were empty, and the surroundings were blessedly quiet and serene. Such an improvement from the County Jail—his ears were still ringing from the past months of continuous bedlam. He smiled contentedly and placed his hands behind his head. The morphine had given him a warm, floating, peaceful sensation with just a trace of euphoria. Precisely the right amount of euphoria, he decided. *What a good feeling,* he thought, as he struggled to stay awake. *It had been a hell of a morning, especially the X ray part, but now, just lie back and recuperate.*

"How are you feeling, Mr. Stark?"

The voice jolted him awake. He groaned and tried to turn on his side, tangling the plastic intravenous line around his left arm. He looked up and saw Dr. Decker standing over him.

"Feeling better, Doc," he said. "I don't think the stone has passed yet; it still hurts a lot."

"Able to put out any urine yet?"

"Just that urine down in X ray, after the IVP. Still looked pretty bloody, strained it, and no stone yet."

"Why don't you go ahead and give me another sample, so we can check more closely for any stones or blood."

"Okay, I can probably get you some in the next five or ten minutes."

"Good!" Decker exclaimed. "I'll just pull up a chair and wait."

"Oh, that's okay, Doc. I'll call you when I've finished. I have trouble peeing whenever anyone is watching, terrible time in public restrooms. Like my bladder—it just locks up on me."

"That can be a problem," Decker sympathized as he reached over and turned the intravenous control knob up to 300 cc's per hour, almost wide open. "I think you'll be able to put some out before too long."

Fifteen minutes later, Stark was still lying back on his bed, with Decker sitting on a nearby chair watching him. "Feel like you gotta go yet?" Decker asked.

"Nope, not yet. Like I said, it's hard to go when somebody is watching."

"Yes, but I'm your doctor, so it's okay."

"Just don't think I can do it, Doc."

Decker stood up and walked over to the corridor. He poked his head around the corner and looked toward the Prep Room. "Peter!" he called.

"What's up?" Peter called back.

"Lasix 80 milligrams in an IV syringe, could you bring it down here right away?"

"It's on its way."

Decker injected the Lasix into Stark's intravenous line and informed him that the medicine would soon be working. Stark replied that nothing would work when his bladder developed one of its "locking up" problems.

"Lasix frequently works like a key to open the lock," Decker said as he sat down again at the bedside to wait. A few minutes later, Stark began to sweat profusely and to move restlessly on his bed.

Finally Stark moaned and said, "Doc, I think my bladder is filling up, but I just can't go with you sitting here. Could you come back in two or three minutes? Or maybe you could put in a catheter?"

"A catheter would help, but it always causes blood to show up in the urine."

"But I already *have* blood in my urine!"

Decker smiled patiently. "I know, I just don't want to put more blood in your urine."

"Oh—"

After fifteen more minutes of sweating restlessness, and another 80 milligrams of intravenous Lasix, Homer Stark finally stood up, let out a howl of pain, grabbed the urine container, and voided the largest quantity of urine ever produced at one time on the Jail Ward. A urine dipstick test quickly confirmed the absence of blood, the intravenous line was promptly removed, and before Stark could even begin to think about his fate, two deputies were at the door to escort him back to the County Jail.

As he was marched to the elevator door, Decker presented him with a pack of small Band-Aids for the cut on his finger, with instructions to keep it dry and clean.

"Thank you, Dr. Decker," Stark said sarcastically as he was led away.

"And thank you, Mr. Stark."

Chapter 6

Avoiding the patients tracking the colored lines streaming down the center of the main corridor, Skeeters and Decker walked toward the entrance of the hospital. Wearing fresh surgical greens that were, remarkably, not stained with blood or any other patient fluids, both interns were looking forward to a lunch hour away from the hospital. Friday had been a good day for both of them, so far, their workload limited to making rounds on an unusually small number of patients and treating, in rotation with the other interns, prisoners with relatively minor conditions.

"We have until one o'clock, right?" Decker asked as they rounded a corner and circumvented a crowd of people waiting to see relatives in the emergency room.

"Yep, around one. Brodie gets riled if we're not all there by a few minutes after the hour," Skeeters said.

"But Brodie doesn't count—the pin-faced little bastard."

"But Dr. Marsh does, and Pin-face—uh—Brodie reports to Dr. Marsh."

"What's that slimo's problem?"

"Brodie? I figure his childhood years were complicated by regular beatings from his parents, his playmates, and his teachers." Skeeters smiled. "Regular beatings from everyone."

"The way he twists the knife, an intern must have joined in somewhere along the line," Decker said. "Well, I'm going to follow the orange line that leads in the general direction of the Pediatric Pavilion—"

"And to your sweetheart."

Decker smiled. "Ah, yes. And you give my regards to your sweetheart."

Ten minutes later, a dilapidated Volkswagen Bug rumbled up the Golden State Freeway in the direction of Griffith Park, with Barbara Skeeters behind the wheel. Her husband stretched out expansively beside her, marveling at the pleasures of fresh air and the company of his beautiful lady. She followed the freeway signs to the Dodger Stadium exit and drove into the park, finally pulling up to a shaded area of grass, away from the other picnickers. They spread out Barbara's quilted blanket and soon they were devouring the sandwiches she had prepared that morning.

At six months of pregnancy, Barbara Skeeters was beginning to feel the imbalance of her changing center of gravity. More than for most women, pregnancy fit Barbara well. She was attractive, with long brown hair, clear white skin, and kind eyes, but her beauty, now enclosed by the flowered maternity dress, seemed almost enhanced by the slow change of her soft figure. Barbara Skeeters looked like she was made to have children.

She had met Blake Skeeters in the medical library during his third year at Harvard Medical School—he had wanted to find information about anthrax spores, and she happened to be working in the section that handled biological toxins. She had helped him on two more occasions, and late one afternoon he asked her if she might consider joining him on a little picnic adventure at the Cape, with good food included. She had agreed that a picnic on the Cape sounded like a fine idea.

They began dating frequently, spending quiet evenings just holding hands and talking or taking long walks along the deserted beaches south of Boston. Three months later, during a weekend filled with some of the most violent thunderstorms the area had seen for years, they both simultaneously lost their virginity in a small rented beach cabin at Martha's Vineyard. They agreed that it was a *remarkable* experience, especially with the flashes of lightning and claps of thunder, and one month after that memorable night, they were engaged. Just before he started his fourth year of medical school, Blake Skeeters and Barbara Hobson were finally married in a small and formal downtown Boston church ceremony, attended just by close friends and family.

She glanced at her husband who was, at that moment, trying to pour milk into the two glasses that had been carefully placed on the grass by the blanket. He was not particularly good-looking, a little overweight and just a bit too short, and yet he was everything she had ever wanted in a man. He was kind and he was smart, and he treated her with the attention and caring that brought her more happiness than she had ever known.

His work at the hospital was a constant concern to her. It was wearing him down—in just two weeks, he had dark areas under both eyes that were bigger than she had seen even during the intense work of his fourth year at Harvard. She tried to understand his need for this. As he had told her so many times over breakfast in their tiny Boston apartment, the time at L.A. County Hospital was for experience, a critical year to learn how to properly manage patients with complex medical problems. The affiliation of the hospital with the University of Southern California made it uniquely able to blend the vast array of clinical experiences with quality lectures from the professors who write the textbooks. And if his performance while gaining these experiences was good enough, the doors would be open for the choice residencies at UCLA, Stanford, UC San Diego, or wherever he and Barbara wanted to go. The matter was settled long before they dragged their luggage to the airport. The intellectual foundation had been established at Harvard, but the clinical experience was to be found in California.

But she was never able to fully escape the guilt of her feelings—even when she tried to rationalize that they were only feelings and, therefore, not under her direct control. For when Barbara looked at the brown, dry hills that bordered the park and when she saw the hot slabs of concrete that enclosed what was known as the Los Angeles River, she felt a deep and almost painful nostalgia for the rich green countryside of springtime Massachusetts. She took the glass of milk he offered and toasted with him the precious time they had together in the park. It did not matter what his reasons were to expand his medical training so far away from everything she had known—she was deeply in love with the man and she would go anywhere in the world to be with him.

The cafeteria in the Pediatric Pavilion was a noisy place, and Decker could hardly hear Katie Shields over the clattering of trays and background conversations. He was beginning to regret having arranged coming here for lunch, and he made a mental note to go somewhere else next time so at least he could hear what she was saying.

He looked down at his Pediatric Pavilion cafeteria tray. The lunch meal consisted of meat loaf with gravy that looked like a thick lump of pure cholesterol—however, if you didn't like that, you could have a hot dog instead. He had selected the meat loaf with grease and she had selected the hot dog.

"I was asking, how's everything on the Jail Ward?" Katie said loudly, trying to be heard over the noise. She was wearing white slacks, a pink blouse, and a white resident's coat with a pediatric stethoscope and notepad jammed in her pocket. Her dark hair was neatly arranged behind her ears, and her dark eyes looked questioningly at Decker.

"It's going fine, halfway through now!" Decker answered as he poured catsup over his gravy and stabbed the corner of his meat loaf with his fork. "Had a patient a couple of days ago with a kidney stone that disappeared when the flow of blood from his cut finger was stopped."

"Blood from his finger?" She thought about that for a moment, then said, "Ah, the old malingerer trick! How did you figure it out?"

"Actually, Skeeters put me on to it. I then filled the guy with substantial parenteral volume and diuresed him under direct observation. Presto! Lots of urine, no blood, no stone, cured!"

"That's one thing we don't see very often in pediatrics—neither stones nor malingerers. Any idea why he was doing it?"

"I guess for some R & R from the County Jail. Also, for some morphine or whatever he can get for his 'pain.' " Decker doused a piece of meat loaf with more catsup. "We've been having a problem keeping enough morphine and Demerol on the ward. I don't know where the hell it's going, but we always seem to be short."

She took a sip of milk and looked at him. "Anybody trying to figure it out?"

"I talked to the head nurse, a guy named Peter Martel. He just says the stuff gets used up fast with all the trauma. He's probably right, with eight different interns ordering narcotics for everything that comes through there. It's hard to keep track of what's going where. The medicine cabinet is locked, and I don't know where they keep the logs. They need to do a better job keeping it on hand, though—they're always running out."

Their attention was diverted by George Wroblewski, waving from the other side of the cafeteria. Katie waved back and a moment later he arrived breathlessly at their table.

"Katie, I'm glad I found you! The Highway Patrol put in a call to the Pavilion a few minutes ago for a pediatrician to join with a surgeon and ob-gynie at the site of a pile-up on the Santa Ana Freeway, about 10 miles away. It was a hell of a crash, with a tanker and four or five cars, right in front of the old Firestone building. Apparently they've taken care of most of the injured, but some people are trapped in their cars, including some lady who's going into labor."

"How far along is she?" Katie asked.

"I don't know. That's all the information they had. The tanker is leaking, they stopped traffic in both directions, and they're sending a chopper. The MAST Unit that usually handles these things is tied up on the west side, and so they're sending one of the Coast Guard Dolphin choppers, in about—" he checked his watch—"it should be here any second. We got an OB gal—somebody named Leslie Chin—here already, and a couple of surgeons are trying to break loose from the OR up on the hill. I'm tied up with a couple cases in ER, and the dispatcher said they wanted a senior peds resident at the landing zone, stat."

As the two residents stood up, Katie looked at

Decker and asked, "If the surgeons don't make it, do you want to come with us? We'll probably be going right away."

"Absolutely. I thought you'd never ask. Can I get a couple of surgical trays with some drugs and operative equipment?"

Decker quickly considered calling the Jail Ward to tell them he'd be late, and dismissed the idea just as quickly. He was caught up on his workload and he was seventh to be called during the afternoon for any admissions. With any luck at all, there'd only be four or five prisoners admitted before he could get back.

"We have a surgical kit and a jar filled with sterile instruments in the Peds ER. Let's grab it along with an incubator, and the paramedics will have the rest."

Leslie Chin, a Chinese obstetrician from the OB-GYN building a short distance away, arrived at the landing sight first, carrying a large black bag and holding a pink stethoscope. She was soon joined by Katie and Decker, and the three physicians stood at the corner of a large, square asphalt landing pad with an encircled "H" in the center. They scanned the brown sky for the helicopter.

"Here it comes!" Decker said a minute later, pointing to a helicopter that was circumventing the main structure of the County Hospital. As the three watched, an H-65 Aerospatiale Dolphin helicopter, with black "U.S. Coast Guard" spelled out across its orange sides, thundered into the area with a pulsating roar and circled the landing area. After the pilot and copilot completed their scan to fix the positions of the various wires and telephone poles, the helicopter finally descended, the wind from the four fat main rotor blades whipping at the clothing of the three physicians. A large door on the starboard side slid open, and a Coast Guard sailor leaned out and waved for the doctors to board the aircraft.

"Where are the surgeons?" Katie yelled over the engine noise.

Decker and Chin looked toward the main hospital for any sign of the approaching white coats.

"They're not going to make it," Chin answered a moment later. "We can't wait any longer. That lady is supposed to be in active labor."

"I'll take care of whatever needs to be done!" Decker said, his voice carrying more confidence than he felt. "We have to go!"

With the enlisted man's help, the three doctors were soon strapped onto steel seats in the cramped compartment, the portable incubator was placed on the deck, and the door was slammed shut. After a thumbs-up signal to the pilot, the engine revved up to a roar again, and just as Decker wondered if the vibrations were going to shake them apart, the helicopter lifted vertically off the pad. A thousand feet above ground level, the aircraft tilted forward and thundered toward the Santa Ana Freeway.

At three minutes to one, Barbara Skeeters dropped her husband off at the main entrance to L.A. County Hospital. He gave her a kiss and, as he waved good-bye from the top of the steps to the building, they both noticed a large orange helicopter climbing above the Pediatric Pavilion and heading south.

Skeeters admitted only one patient to the Jail Ward that afternoon, but the case caused even Gerald Brodie to flee from his desk in terror.

One half hour prior to Spike Bond's arrival on the Jail Ward, the deputies had christened the new prisoner "Choo-Choo" for two reasons. First, the thirty-three-year-old black man was the biggest human being ever seen by anyone in the Rampart Division of the

Los Angeles Police Department, a division that, everyone agreed, saw more big human beings than almost any other group of police in the country. Second, it had become well established during the course of the day that when Choo-Choo started moving in whichever direction he chose, a tremendous amount of force was required to slow him down or to otherwise deter him from his objective. As he was escorted in chains from the elevator by four policemen, it was apparent that the 7-foot 1-inch 300-pound Spike "Choo-Choo" Bond was an awesome spectacle of solid bone and muscle.

There was no physical reason for Choo-Choo to be admitted to the hospital. There was not a mark on him, unless you counted the minor abrasions on his massive wrists when he had snapped apart a pair of handcuffs an hour before, or the bruises on his arms and legs from the chains that surrounded his body. Choo-Choo was admitted to the Jail Ward because he was suffering from advanced psychotic paranoid schizophrenia. Earlier that day, he had murdered—by strangulation, with his bare hands—three men and one woman. He had also seriously injured three of the six police officers who had tried unsuccessfully to wrestle him to the sidewalk. He was basically a nice guy, his mother would later tell the press, if people would just try to understand his problems. Spike Bond had serious psychiatric problems, everyone agreed.

The only thing that had prevented him from being shot several times by the enraged police, all of whom had no interest in his underlying psychiatric state, was his tendency to shield himself with innocent bystanders. He was particularly skilled at wrapping his huge arms around the chests of people who were trying to escape and clutching them like human shields. It had in fact become clear to the frustrated police, after twenty minutes of maneuvering on the sidewalk in front of Roddy's Bar and Grill, that nobody would be able to safely fire a shot without endangering the hostages held tightly in Choo-Choo's bearlike grip.

In the midst of all the excitement, the officer in charge of the detachment decided to light up Choo-Choo with a Taser.

For such an innocent-looking device, appearing as nothing more impressive than a flashlight, the Taser is a weapon that gets one's attention. Powered by a pair of 9-volt batteries and using fewer than 3 watts of energy, the device fires two tiny darts. The top dart travels straight out, whereas the bottom dart angles down slightly. The farther away the dart recipient is at the time the Taser is fired, the wider apart the darts are when they attach to his skin. As it worked out, Choo-Choo was standing exactly 10 feet away from the Taser at the time it was fired, and the two darts attached themselves to his back precisely 1 foot apart.

The result of 50,000 volts applied across 1 foot of Choo-Choo's skin was immediate and predictable.

The two hostages he was gripping were immediately released, Choo-Choo performed an unusual involuntary maneuver, something that was a cross between a back flip and a grand mal seizure, the net result of which was that he promptly became horizontal on the sidewalk. As his two hostages ran for their lives, half the Rampart Police Department descended on Choo-Choo with enough sets of chain and leather straps to secure a herd of wild horses. Before he could even think about sitting up and trying to grab more hostages, he was wrapped in chains, secured with leather straps around every extremity, and loaded by several of the stronger police officers into a paddy wagon.

The pinched face of Gerald Brodie lit up with excitement as he watched Choo-Choo being dragged from the elevator. This was the choice prisoner of the year.

"Dr. Skeeters to Prep Room! Dr. Skeeters to Prep Room!" he hollered into the microphone, sounding like he had just won the California lottery. At hearing the announcement, Choo-Choo immediately diverted his course in the direction of Brodie, causing the ward clerk to jump away from his desk and run down the corridor, his eyes wide open with fear.

"He's not going to the Prep Room, he's going to the Cage, you dumb shit!" one of the deputy sheriffs holding Choo-Choo's chains hollered after him as four more deputies helped direct the prisoner away from Brodie's desk and down the central hallway. Choo-Choo's half-closed eyes began to open as he felt himself being moved—*against his will*—toward a cage at the far end of a long corridor. His head turned to the left and he saw cloth partitions down the hall, hiding something. He felt himself filling with rage. He knew there was something behind the curtain, crouched there—waiting for him to get close—waiting until he was vulnerable. He growled once and all the deputies simultaneously tightened their grip on his arms. This infuriated him further, but he would wait until exactly the right time, until he was next to those curtains.

Mrs. VonStoffer from Beverly Hills was lying peacefully in the bed behind the partitions, recovering from her most recent phenobarbital, Valium, and alcohol overdose. She had been assigned to Tyra Levy and her primary medical treatment was a quick peek through the partitions from time to time to ensure the patient was still breathing. She was elegantly dressed in satin negligee when the Beverly Hills Police Department had chauffeured her to the Jail Ward one hour before, and Tyra hadn't yet had the time to move her stuporous figure into the standard hospital gown.

She was not a dangerous prisoner, since all the woman had done was accidently shoot herself in the foot with her Beretta Jetfire pistol while trying to murder her attorney husband during a Dom Pérignon state of drunken confusion that morning. The .25 caliber hole in her foot had been repaired in the emergency room, and now her mind was gradually recovering from the sedating effects of the drugs she had ingested. In the meantime, it had been decided to leave her behind the partitions in the central hallway—it wouldn't have been right to put her in the Ladies' Room and she certainly couldn't stay with the men. Only an hour or two more, Tyra knew, and her patient would have recovered enough to leave the hospital.

When Choo-Choo and the five deputy sheriffs reached the cluster of partitions, the prisoner let out a roar and furiously struck out with his left hand, pulling a clattering cluster of chains high into the air and ripping apart two leather straps that had secured his wrists. Two of the deputies were slammed to the ground and the partitions were cartwheeled down the corridor like toys. Mrs. VonStoffer looked up at the bloodshot eyes of the huge man above her and immediately screamed at the top of her lungs as she crossed her hands across her chest to conceal her partially exposed breasts.

Choo-Choo stared down at her and hesitated for a moment, his mind trying to comprehend. All hell then broke loose as Choo-Choo's arms and legs thrashed wildly at the woman, while teams of deputy sheriffs jumped on the prisoner, trying to hold him down, striking at his arms with nightsticks, pushing and sliding his contorting body in the direction of the Cage. Mrs. VonStoffer lost the contents of her bladder as her bed was kicked and jolted from the fracas in front of her. She put her fingers in her ears to drown out the grunting and yelling. She squeezed her eyes tightly shut and tried to *discreetly* slide off the far side of the bed, away from the attacking King Kong, while the expanding stain from her bladder created new patterns on her negligee.

Blake Skeeters stood flat against the corridor wall, watching the battle move in his direction. *I'm having a nightmare,* he thought. *There is no question that this is my patient—the sound of Brodie's voice left no question at all.* He edged along the wall, trying to ease away from the cluster of prisoner and guards, watching the battling men pass in front of him. With some final grunting and yelling, the huge man was finally shoved into the Cage, chains and all, and the door was slammed shut.

"His name is Choo-Choo Bond and he's all yours!" Mel Grossman said to Skeeters as he pocketed the keys. "I wouldn't suggest you go inside the Cage." He grinned, his yellow teeth looking vicious in the dim light. "If you do, we're not about to go in after you."

Skeeters walked slowly to the Cage to look at his new patient. Choo-Choo was running back and forth across the 10-foot enclosure, chains from various parts of his body clattering on the concrete floor. Skeeters winced as Bond crashed into the bars at one end of the Cage. The prisoner's eyes were glazed and his nose was bleeding, leaving a trail of red down his chest and onto the floor. The entire structure vibrated from each impact; he would slam into the bars, rebound, turn around, and charge in the opposite direction— *like a locomotive,* Skeeters thought. *Maybe I can give him some sedatives, but how am I ever going to administer the medicine?*

* * *

The helicopter flight lasted only ten minutes before the doctors heard the noise of the rotor blades changing tone as the craft tilted forward to descend to the freeway. The crackle of Unicom radio transmissions from the Highway Patrol filled the cabin as the pilot was directed to a landing on the freeway, safely away from the twisted cars and ruptured tanker truck.

Decker looked at Katie, strapped into her aluminum seat, her body vibrating with the shaking of the helicopter's powerful engine. Her dark hair was casually spread across her right shoulder as she sat high in her seat, straining to see the ground below them. She glanced back into the cabin and immediately caught him watching her. There was a quick flush as she smiled self-consciously before turning away to look out the window again.

The wheels had barely touched the freeway's surface before the sliding door was yanked open and a youthful blond-haired paramedic with ADAM stenciled above his left breast pocket stuck his head into the compartment.

"We have two trapped civilians in the red car under the tanker," he yelled, out of breath. "It's a woman and her son! The tanker's leaking—fuel oil of some kind—and we can't cut them out because of the explosion risk. The lady in there is seven months' pregnant and having contractions." He looked at the physicians. "One of you is a surgeon?"

"Right here." Decker popped his hand up.

"Good," the paramedic said. "The people are bleeding pretty badly." He hesitated as he tried to catch his breath. "They're both bleeding real bad, and I think the kid is going into shock."

"How old is the boy?" Katie asked.

"He's just a kid—his legs are trapped under the

dashboard, and we couldn't stop the bleeding," the paramedic answered.

"Let's go!" Decker said as they grabbed their bags and ran onto the freeway. The traffic had been stopped in both directions by two barricades of Highway Patrol cars, red and blue lights flashing. A crowd of several hundred people watched from the top of a noise-abatement masonry running along the sides of the freeway, and two news helicopters clattered noisily overhead. As Decker looked around, it appeared that there were six other cars involved in the accident, scattered about the freeway with various degrees of damage. Two of the cars, looking like bottom-of-the-line compact cars, were completely flattened into ugly masses of steel. The cars all appeared to be empty, their occupants apparently already taken to the hospital—or to the morgue, Decker guessed.

A huge double-trailer tanker truck had jackknifed on its side, and the battered nose of an old red Buick poked out from underneath. Five fire engines stood at a respectable distance from the truck, with over-cab nozzles spraying out an arc of white fire-retardant foam across the pavement near the tanker. Fuel oil covered the entire area around the truck and car, and an oily sheen was turning the foam black as it spread across the freeway. Decker felt his throat tighten as the stench of the oil enveloped them. Two men were working to attach large hoses to the front of the tanker trailer for transfer of the fuel.

"There's not enough time for the lady and her kid to wait for the fuel to be removed!" Adam hollered to the doctors. "The windows of the car are broken, and I think two of you can get in through the back window—we can run in fluids or oxygen, or whatever you need. The doors are jammed shut! One of our medics just climbed out—he's started IV lines with

Ringer's lactate in both patients. The lady's in active labor, don't know how far along."

"How far apart are the contractions?" Leslie Chin asked as she pulled out packets of obstetrics equipment from her bag.

"Only a minute or two—she's in a lot of pain and it's hard to tell. Also, she doesn't speak any English."

"The keys to the car are turned off?" Decker asked.

"The ignition area is partially crushed—we can't turn the key off and we can't disconnect the battery. There's a risk of explosion if they're left on—we're all just going to have to take the chance."

Decker looked through the back window into the dark interior of the car. "Can you hear me?" he called out. The doctors listened carefully, but the only response was a quiet moan. He repeated the question again, but all they could hear was the dripping sounds of fuel oil on top of the car.

"Let's get in there," Leslie Chin said as she handed the other two doctors her bag of instruments. "Let me have these after I get in—I've got enough here for a full C-section if necessary." She climbed on the trunk of the car and squeezed through the back window, twisting herself to avoid the sharp fragments of glass that protruded from the edges of the frame.

"Steve," she called from the dark interior, "you're next. Katie, I'll give you a five-minute warning if we have a viable baby on its way."

"Okay, Leslie, I'll be ready," Katie answered.

Decker squeezed through the window and dropped onto the backseat next to Chin. As he tried to position himself, his foot slipped on a pool of blood on the floor, and he fell back onto the tarp spread across the backseat. All of the windows had been broken from the crushing weight of the tanker across the top of the car, and shards of glass were lying everywhere, leaving a carpet of glimmering fragments. The cramped interior was dark and the air was filled with the thick odor of petroleum. The obstetrician was leaning over the front seat, shining a flashlight and trying to speak to a Spanish woman about thirty years old. Her head lolled back and forth and she kept moaning, *"Viene el bebe!"*

"Hablas ingles?" Chin asked.

"No," the lady answered. *"Hablo espanol solmente."*

"Great!" Chin grimaced. "And I had to take Latin and German during my premed years."

"I took French," Decker said disgustedly. "Never have met any patient from France." He moved across the backseat to the right side of the car, where a dark-haired boy of only six or seven years of age was lying, his eyes closed, breathing rapidly with shallow pants. An intravenous line had been dropped through the side window and was connected to his right arm. Decker ripped open the boy's shirt and placed the stethoscope on his chest, listening carefully to the various sounds of air movement and heartbeats.

"Can you hear me?" he called. There was no response. He could feel his own heart pounding as he measured the boy's blood pressure and shined a flashlight into his eyes and across his body. He stuck his head out the broken window on the right side.

"Adam, are you out there?" he yelled.

"Right here, Doc, whatdya need?"

"He's in shock with a blood pressure of 80 over 50, he has a right-sided pneumothorax, and he's pumping blood from a bleeder on his leg. He may also have some abdominal internal bleeding. He probably has a cerebral contusion from the looks of the hematoma on the front of his head. It looks like his feet are trapped under the dashboard, but we have a chance to pull him out if I can drop the back of the seat down. We need oxygen at 6 liters per minute through nasal cannula for both of them. Start running a liter of Albumisol into the boy's IV, hand me some pliers and a screwdriver, and pass in a strap that I can tie around his chest."

"Okay, coming right up!" Adam answered. "How's the lady?"

"We got a fetal distress problem here," Chin said calmly from the other side of the car. "Her membrane is broken, and she's got meconium coming out. We gotta deliver this baby now."

"No way we can get the mother out?"

"Her legs are wedged under the steering wheel—"

"Okay, Leslie, let me get the bleeding stopped here real quick, and I'll give you a hand."

"It's gonna have to be a C-section. No way to get her legs apart enough for a normal delivery."

He stuck his head back outside the window on the right side. "Katie, we're gonna do a section on her in a minute or two—the baby's putting out meconium."

Katie Shields grimaced. She had grown to hate the word. From the bowels of the baby, the black-green stuff was like a warning flag from Mother Nature that a serious fetal distress problem was developing. She had seen it when the cord was around the neck, when the mother couldn't deliver normally and fetal hypoxia was developing, and she had seen it prior to the delivery of babies who couldn't thrive or who had grave congenital diseases. Meconium always meant problems.

"Okay, Steve, I'm ready for it." She began to mentally prepare for the complex infant resuscitation procedure.

Decker felt like he was going to choke on the oil fumes. He coughed twice and called out for Adam to get a decent light into the car as fast as possible and to be sure it was already turned on and tightly screwed into its socket before it was brought close to the car. All they needed was a tiny spark—

Two minutes later, while Chin held the flashlight and Decker tied the sutures, the pumping bleeders on the boy's legs were tied off and a final careful inspection revealed no further blood loss. The oxygen helped him breathe better, and as they finished the work, he was starting to make small groans and move his arms.

"Steve, I'll be damned if I can deliver this lady's baby with her legs trapped like this in the sitting position. How long would it take for—damn! Look at that!" She pointed to the area between the woman's legs where more meconium was accumulating. "How long would it take for the back of the seat to be dropped flat?"

"Let me check real quick."

"Don't spark anything!"

"Right!"

As Chin checked her patient's oxygen supply and measured her blood pressure again, Decker grabbed the pliers and a screwdriver, and shined his flashlight along the base of the driver seat. Dark red blood, with irregular clots floating about, was forming a pool. Three screws on the latching mechanism were quickly removed, and the seat immediately dropped back flat and level with the backseat. A 200-watt light with a wire guard around the bulb was passed into the car and hooked into the cloth overhead, bathing them in brilliant white light.

"You good with bleeders?" Chin asked Decker, her eyes narrowed.

"Damn right I am," Decker answered without hesitation.

"Good. We're sure as hell not going to use a cautery here. Let's get it done."

Chin and Decker pulled on their sterile gloves and the plastic seal around a tray of surgical equipment was opened. Three cc's of morphine were injected into her intravenous line, the protuberant abdomen was exposed, and a cup of Betadine was splashed across the skin.

"Going to give her any anesthesia?" Decker asked.

"Can't give her any systemically—pressure's too low. We'll lose her and the baby. I'll run in some Xylocaine local anesthesia as we move along with the operation."

Several injections of Xylocaine were placed across her abdomen, and in less than five seconds, Chin cut a deep horizontal incision just below her umbilicus. Working rapidly, the two doctors began the process of cutting and spreading the skin and underlying tissue. It was the fastest operating technique Decker had ever seen, as he furiously tied off every vein and artery that looked like it could produce more than a drop of blood. The uterus was quickly exposed and opened with scissors to expose the baby's head. A tiny blood-covered premature baby girl was finally lifted from her abdomen. The cord was clamped and cut, and an oxygen mask was slapped across the baby's face as she was handed out the back window to Katie's outstreched arms. She immediately turned and ran with the baby to the helicopter. Thirty seconds later, they were off the ground and en route to the Pediatric Pavilion.

Fifteen minutes later, as Decker and Chin were closing the final outer layer of abdominal skin, they were both startled to hear a weak voice.

"Is my mommy going to be okay?"

Decker quickly turned around and stared at the boy. He had turned around in the front seat, and his swollen eyes had opened and were fixed on the suture line across his mother's abdomen.

"I think she's got a chance—what's your name?" Decker said.

"Joaquin," the boy said.

He placed his hand on the boy's shoulder. "I think she's going to be okay, Joaquin. We've got some more work to do—"

"Is my mommy's baby okay?" Joaquin interrupted.

Decker hesitated and glanced out the broken back window. "I'm not sure—I know everything possible is being done for your baby sister. She's in the best of hands right now. The very best of hands."

The hotel room had been a last-minute decision.

Decker and Chin had returned to the County Hospital with Joaquin and his mother late in the afternoon, transported by a couple of paramedic rescue vans driven by paramedics who loved high speed, red lights, and sirens. Both patients were safely handed off to the senior resident of the emergency room, and Decker had elevatored upstairs to the thirteenth floor for a shower and a final check of his Jail Ward patients. Skeeters was gone, lost somewhere in the bowels of the hospital looking for an X ray, but there was a remarkable new patient with chains and a bloody chest storming back and forth across the Cage. To Decker's relief, nobody had apparently missed his presence. Only Brodie had noticed the oil and blood on his surgical greens, wrinkling his pointed nose with unspoken disapproval.

He had called Katie and spoken briefly with her. The baby girl they had delivered was safe in an incubator, and most of the pediatric interns were betting that she would survive. Katie had sounded tired, but she eagerly accepted his invitation to dinner that evening.

He picked her up at the front of the Pediatric Pavilion in his Corvette and took her to the Downtown Grill in Los Angeles, where they both ordered the specialty of the house: New York steak. He told her of how they were able to extract the two victims from the car, out through the back window with vigorous manipulation of their pinned legs, and of the paramedic ride back to deliver the two patients safely to the hospital.

While chewing on foot-long celery sticks and juicy radishes, they observed that the waiters bore a startling resemblance to homeless men from the New York subway system. As the meat was finally thrown in front of them by a grizzled man who vaguely resembled Arafat, Katie Shields told him of the fate of Baby Arguelles.

At first she had thought it was a stillborn baby with no chance of revival. She wasn't breathing, her face had been covered with meconium, and her mouth and trachea were clogged with the thick black stuff. She had made abrupt twitching movements with her fingers and gave a little gasp; her Apgar performance score in the first minute was only two, abysmally low but leaving some hope. Working with the paramedics as the helicopter thundered across the sky, she tried to pump pure oxygen into the baby's lungs with a face mask and Ambu bag interspersed with mouth-to-mouth resuscitation. After an agonizingly long delay, she finally responded with additional tiny gasps and increasing movements of her dark blue fingers.

Katie suctioned more meconium from her windpipe and pumped in more oxygen, and as her little blue arms and legs slowly started to turn pink, her movements became more vigorous. After five more minutes of resuscitation, Baby Arguelles had finally let out a little cry that had seemed to protest the insults from nature, machinery, and medicine upon her small body. A cheer went up from the paramedics as the infant was wrapped in a blanket and placed inside the incubator and delivered to the Neonatal Intensive Care Unit.

Katie took another bite of the steak and looked at Decker. "This is delicious." She smiled and added, "Thank you."

"You're welcome," Decker answered with a smile in return.

"You did a real nice job with that delivery."

"Just placed a couple of sutures and zipped some bleeders shut, on request; Leslie Chin deserves all the credit. She told me what to do and I did it—just like back in medical school, except for the oil fumes and glass—"

"And 20 tons of tanker truck hanging over your head. We were all pretty lucky."

They toasted their good luck and jointly decided a more elegant victory celebration would be appropriate. Fifteen minutes later, they walked into the Bonaventure Lounge, thirty-five stories above the heart of Los Angeles, and after Decker provided for a quick exchange of currency to the maitre d', they were seated in front of a window that viewed almost 50 miles of city lights below. A bottle of the finest Moët & Chandon was uncorked and the two physicians cheered the survival of the Arguelles family. They fell silent as they watched the long streams of headlights and taillights moving along the Harbor and Hollywood freeways.

As he looked out the window, Decker felt the glow of the champagne beginning to spread through his body. In the distance, he could see the towering column of vertical orange lights that was the central structure of Los Angeles County Hospital. The Great

White Mama, now just a tiny tower in the distance—
and the thirteenth floor only one of the minuscule
orange specks. *It looks so peaceful,* he thought, *from
the top of the Bonaventure Hotel.*

Katie placed her head against his shoulder, and he
felt the warmth of her body next to him. He gently
put his arm around her shoulders and pulled her close,
feeling her press up against him.

She turned her head slightly and whispered softly
into his right ear, "There's too many people here."

The mist from the champagne abruptly cleared from
Decker's mind as his eyes opened and he felt his heart
beginning to pound. *There's too many people here.*

It had caught him totally by surprise. Twenty-eight
years old, man of the world, man of romance, and
he hadn't even thought about a conquest tonight. He
mentally kicked himself. The basics were in place, but
he hadn't even thought about the ending.

"You're right," he whispered to her. "Back in a
moment."

Decker stood up and headed for the maitre d's
desk, feeling like everyone in the room was watching
him.

"Could I borrow your telephone?" he asked a prissy-
looking blonde behind the front desk. "I need to make
a quick call down to the lobby."

The blonde smiled tightly. "I'm sorry, this telephone is for hotel lounge reservations only. There is
a house phone up the steps there." She pointed up a
long corridor filled with a line of people waiting to get
into the lounge.

"Thanks," Decker said as he squeezed past a cluster
of fat men and women—*doesn't anybody ever go on
a diet around here?*—and finally made it to the telephone. An unusually fat woman with thick lips and
thicker red lipstick was standing near the telephone,

looking angry. He edged past her and picked up the telephone. A moment later, he had the Bonaventure reservations woman on the telephone.

"How many persons and how many nights, sir?"

"Two people, for tonight, please. It will be under the name of Steve Decker."

A couple of minutes later, the reservations were made and he walked back down the corridor toward the lounge. If he stood on his toes, he could just see her, still sitting in front of the window sipping her champagne. Good. Now all he needed was the key. He turned around and walked quickly to the elevator.

Compressed to the back of the glass-walled elevator by nine other people who crowded in behind him, he endured six stops and three "isn't it breathtaking?" before the doors finally opened at the main lobby. An Oriental clerk at the reservations desk confirmed that Dr. Decker did indeed have reservations for tonight, taking note that the room was "one of their best," on the thirty-second floor.

As he was handed a plastic magnetic key, he informed the clerk that, no, he did not need help with his luggage. But thank you for asking.

By the time he had gathered Katie up from the Bonaventure Lounge and they took a breathtaking ride to the thirty-second floor, Decker was exhausted. They closed their room's door behind them, and as Decker carefully latched the chain, Katie admired the expansive room and the sweeping view of the city that matched those in the lounge.

"Too many lights in here," he said as he walked around the room and turned off all but one small light in the corner. He stopped by the radio and flipped a couple switches, filling the room with soft music.

"Perfect," she said as he walked over to her and took her hand. They silently looked out the window

at the lights of the city below, and after a moment,
he placed his arm around her and gently turned her
face to him. She could feel her breath quickening as
he gently caressed her arm and slowly leaned toward
her, lightly touching her lips with his. As they kissed,
she could feel the hot tip of his tongue, exploring and
penetrating. She felt a sharp surge of desire as he
pulled her firmly against him.

"You feel so good . . ." Decker said softly as he
took a deep breath.

"This *is* very nice . . ."

"And not too many people . . ."

"Just the right amount . . ."

They kissed again as he reached down to her back
and lowered the zipper on her dress. Pulling the straps
off her shoulders, he allowed the silky material to fall
away with a soft rustle. She unbuttoned his shirt while
he released her bra and allowed the dark, lacy material to fall to the floor. Her white breasts, free from
their confinement, were firm with erect pink nipples,
eager for his touch and for his lips.

As his shirt was thrown to the floor, she stroked
the hair on his chest and massaged his flat, muscular
abdomen, finally lowering her hands down to his belt.
A moment later, as he stood naked before her, she
grasped his hardness in her warm hands and felt his
hot, throbbing pulse.

"Such a *big* problem you have," she said. "I don't
know what we can do about it."

"There must be something . . ."

He placed his hand under the elastic band of her
panties and slid them down; she gracefully stepped away
from them. His caressing hand moved slowly down between her legs, finding her hot and moist, ready for
him. His hand brought the moisture up to her nipples,
where he leaned over and tasted her, sucking on the

eager erections as she moaned with pleasure and continued to stroke his hardness. He lifted her into his arms and carried her to the king-sized bed.

In the dim light Decker realized that she was the most beautiful woman he had ever seen. She was perfection, from her sensitive face with wide and dark eyes, down to her magnificent breasts, to her narrow waist, the silky black triangle, and her smooth, slender legs.

"Let me make you wet," she said as he lay back and she moved her lips down across his chest and abdomen, kissing him while her hands held his hardness, as if to control his desire. She gently kissed him on the soft tip, tasting the single clear drop of moisture before caressing him with her tongue and taking him deeply into her mouth. Her tongue stroked back and forth across him, tasting more moisture and bringing him more pleasure.

"Don't make me come, honey, I need you now," Decker said as she pulled away and lay back for him. He reached down and entered her with his fingers as she opened her legs to allow him to stimulate her.

Decker moved on top of her as she rotated her pelvis up to allow him to join with her. She wrapped her legs around him as he entered her slowly, the ancient rhythm of love growing in strength and energy as they rode together to ever increasing heights of passion. He fought to wait for her, and soon they were both fully enveloped in a molten hot fire.

Not until long after she had gone to sleep in his arms, did he realize he had—for the first time in his life—made love to a woman without saying that he loved her. He held her, thinking, as he watched her beautiful and peaceful face in the faint light. He felt warm, content, and completely fulfilled as he slowly relaxed, closed his eyes, and fell asleep.

Chapter 7

Rusty Esch was an ugly, simple boy, everybody knew that.

Throughout his nineteen years of life, his moonlike face and fuzzy red hair had prevented him from achieving meaningful social development. His lack of intelligence had further resulted in a mediocre high school performance that produced a remarkably long series of one academic disaster after another. Most of his free time was spent wandering about the streets, looking at trees and staring at the faces of people who passed by; homework was low on his priority list, somewhere just below his pastime of blowing up snails with firecrackers. When his high school graduation day had finally arrived, both he and his parents were amazed that he was actually awarded a diploma, since his grades in all his subjects except Gym and Shop were abysmal.

His high school diploma was also held in high regard because it allowed him to obtain a job as a pharmacist aid at L.A. County Hospital.

For Rusty Esch, it was a good thing that the job requirements for pharmacist aid were not difficult. Although he had received one of the lowest grades his high school chemistry department had ever awarded, he did complete three weeks of classes and fulfilled the county's pharmacy requirement of "experience with high school chemistry." It was also a good thing the competition for the job was not intense; although three other applicants had passed the civil service exam, Esch was the only one without multiple felony convictions.

After being hired, the job requirements further defined that the employee was required to show up to work on time, to wear a clean white coat, and to have his name badge prominently displayed at all times on the left front pocket. Simple requirements, no problem for Rusty on all three counts. Finally, the pharmacist aid must follow the pharmacist's directions so that the correct drugs will be delivered at the correct time to the correct wards throughout the hospital. This could have been a problem except for the fact that Rusty was able to read and to walk, and not much more than that was required for success.

The routine was simple. He would pick up the medicines from the satellite pharmacy on the eighth floor and deliver them to the hospital wards. The call from the Jail Ward usually came once a day, and for Esch, it was the best part of every day. He loved the authority of calling "thirteenth floor!" to the elevator operator, because he knew almost nobody else would be allowed to enter the floor that held prisoners. And then, even more fun, he reveled in pushing his cart of medicines toward the locked barriers in front of the Jail Ward and authoritatively flashing his badge to the sheriff's deputy. While others might be blocked from passing through the barriers, Rusty always found the deputies ready to open the barred gates for him.

After several months of diligent work, he had been advanced from probationary status to a permanent position with the pharmacy. Now he was allowed to wear a beeper, the speaker volume of which he always left on high—he loved to watch heads turn to look at him

every time the beeper fired off. Now he was allowed
to deliver not just antibiotics but also narcotics and
other controlled drugs to the Jail Ward. Now he was
accompanied by a uniformed armed guard to ensure
there were no drug diversions. And finally, he no
longer needed to drag himself to the little eighth-floor
satellite pharmacy to pick up drugs, since only the
main pharmacy on the first floor could dispense controlled medicine.

The pharmacists invariably loaded his cart with the
same drugs: eight boxes, each packed to the maximum
with fifty small glass vials standing in neat rows and
each containing a clear solution of what looked like
water to Esch. He would then be handed a sealed
envelope with an accounting of the drugs and a large
red "C" (for Controlled) emblazoned on the front.

That Monday morning, he left his guard standing
next to the elevator, just outside the entrance to the
Jail Ward, and he was given clearance to push his cart
down the central corridor to the Medicine Room.
Peter Martel, as usual, was waiting for him.

"Mornin', Rusty," the nurse said as he transferred
the medicines from the cart to the medicine counter.

"Mornin', Peter," Esch answered. He looked with
admiration at Peter Martel. He liked the nurse, always
working so hard to help his patients with their
problems.

"Got all the medicine you need, just like you ordered." He opened the manila envelope and handed
it to the nurse.

"Good, nice job." Martel studied the list of narcotics, checking off each section after inspecting the
boxes.

"Sure is a lot of medicine here," Esch observed.

"Sure is . . ."

"What do you use all this stuff for, anyway?" Esch

looked at the neat rows of glass vials that filled the boxes.

Martel glanced up from his inventory list and stared at Esch. "This is used to help the patients, Esch."

Esch thought he could detect irritation in the nurse's voice. "I was just noticing . . . I just noticed that there sure are a lot of those little vials. What *is* the medicine, anyway?"

The nurse's reply was quick and firm. "I don't think a pharmacist aid needs to concern himself with how much or how little of this or that medicine is needed on the Jail Ward."

"You're right, I'm sorry." Esch was confused. He glanced quickly at Martel. All he had wanted to do was just interact a little with the nurse, just a little friendly talk. The nurses on the other floors had no problems with innocent talk. He found himself wishing that Martel would hurry up and finish logging in the medicines so that he could leave.

The nurse finally checked off the last box and signed the form, confirming that the medicine was the same that had been sent from the pharmacy. He handed the papers back to Esch and glared at the man's homely face.

"We'll take proper care of dispensing these medicines. Your job is to get them here, okay?" he asked.

"Okay, sure, I'm sorry." He turned his empty cart and quickly pushed it back up the central corridor in the direction of the elevator.

The interns stood side by side in front of the Cage, watching Spike Bond.

The giant man was furiously pacing back and forth, his black hairy chest still carrying the matted coagulum of heme from his collisions with the bars. He was barefoot and his soiled black jeans showed patches of bloody residue from the injuries of the past three days. But he was now being more careful, Decker and Skeeters noticed. Now the only time he actually came in contact with the bars was when he sensed the approach of someone who annoyed him.

Almost everyone annoyed Choo-Choo.

Dr. Blackmore, a psychiatrist, a humble man with a tiny pointed beard, was an excellent case in point. Skeeters had called the consult within ten minutes of the admission. When the psychiatrist had come close to the Cage to conduct his first psychoanalysis session, pencil in hand, Choo-Choo stormed across the Cage, crashed against the bars, reached outside and grabbed the poor man's neck in his huge claws. Only the immediate action of a squad of shouting sheriff deputies with swinging nightsticks had prevented the prisoner from adding another strangulation victim to Choo-Choo's list of crimes. As a result, the prisoner had new bruised and bloody areas on his arms and hands, and the psychiatrist had gained a firsthand understanding about the realities of paranoid psychosis.

"The guy doesn't know when to stop walking, does he?" Decker said as they watched him snort and swat at a fly buzzing around his head, never slowing his pace.

"Actually, he does stop from time to time," Skeeters answered, "when he has to use the toilet or when a tray of food is slid under the bars. He seems to become almost human then, although his eating style would not be an inspiration to Miss Manners. She also would probably take exception to his habit of throwing the food tray back though the bars when he's finished—sure makes a lot of noise."

"Goddamn animal . . ." Decker looked down at the stubby intern. "What are you going to do with him? Have you been able to examine him?"

"Are you kidding? If I even get close to the bars, it's strangulation time. The psych consult did jot a few notes before his departure, suggesting that Choo-Choo's problem is some kind of cyclothymia with a good dose of full-blown manic depressive disorder, without the depression part, combined with a paranoid schizophrenic psychosis . . ."

"In other words, he's wacko."

"Right, but in a dangerous way. He doesn't know his hallucinations from reality, if there is any reality for him. Also, it looks like he'll be here for a few weeks before they formally get things rolling along for a trial." Skeeters looked depressed.

"A few weeks? Jesus, did Dr. Freud or Quackmore or whatever his name is give you any treatment clues?"

"The psych guy? He's still shaking from being attacked and he hasn't come back. Probably gone to see *his* psychiatrist." Skeeters smiled at the thought. "He did suggest a sedative to settle him down some, but we haven't been able to get any medicine into him—nobody wants to hand him any pills, and we can't get close enough for a Thorazine shot."

Decker brightened. "Can you sneak in when he's asleep? Sneak in real quick and zap him in the butt?"

"You probably could," Skeeters said with a grimace, "but you'd better have your will made out first. He only sleeps for ten-minute intervals, and anytime he hears a sound—like a key in the Cage's lock—he trips off into a psychotic rage. And then there would be the problem of escaping from the Cage after the zap—"

"Right, right, right," Decker said quickly. "Sorry, bad idea."

"I was thinking of working out some way to spike his food with Thorazine powder or syrup. Since he does eat the food, that may be the best way to get the medicine into him."

"Steve, Blake, could I talk to you for a second?" The interns turned around as Tyra Levy walked up to them. Decker was startled at her appearance—her white coat was wrinkled and heavily stained, her hair was in disarray, and the skin under both of her eyes was showing the beginnings of dark circles.

"Hi, Tyra, how's it going?" Decker asked. "Is everything okay?"

"Actually, Steve, everything is not so good right now. Along with everything else, I'm having a problem with Peter Martel. Have you guys been getting along okay with him?"

"No big problems—" Skeeters started.

"Getting along okay but some questions about medications," Decker said. "He does things a little differently that we did back at UCLA, and we always seem to be running out of narcotics."

"There's the problem," Tyra said. "I can't find out what's going on with the analgesics I'm giving the three guys I have with the head injuries from the DUI crash a few days ago. I was in the Medication Room to get some Narcan for that lady, Mrs. VonStoffer, and he got all excited that I was in the room. That was bad enough, but when I asked if I could review the morphine doses on those guys, he completely tripped off the line. He started yelling at me to get out of *his* Medication Room and then he almost threw the Narcan at me. I think there's something wrong with the guy."

"I think you're right, Tyra. The guy's all screwed up for some reason, and Blake and I were thinking of talking to Dr. Marsh about it," Decker said.

"Good. This month is bad enough without having

a hardnose like him walking around here. Let me know what Marsh says, okay?"

"No problem, Tyra, do you want to come up there with us?"

"No, thanks anyway. I have enough things to worry about." She turned to walk away.

"Tyra?" Decker called after her.

"Yes, Steve?" She stopped and faced the intern again.

"Tyra, you really don't look very good, and—"

"Thanks a lot. I needed that, it helps . . ."

Decker straightened his shoulders. "Tyra, you look like hell, are you getting any sleep?"

She looked him in the eye. "As a matter of fact, I haven't been getting much if any sleep, lately. I've ordered a few Restoril from the Central Pharmacy and they're delivering it up here later this afternoon."

"Good, that should help. Get some sleep tonight and let us worry about Peter Martel, okay?"

She thanked him as Gerald Brodie's whining voice bounced off the walls, notifying every prisoner on the ward that Dr. Decker's presence at the central corridor telephone was required "immediately." Decker turned and walked briskly down the corridor. *It had to be Katie—nobody else would call me here,* he thought, his pace quickening. After the night at the Bonaventure, she had been on his mind continuously. His Jail Ward rounds over the weekend had taken twice as long as they should have. He couldn't concentrate, he had trouble sleeping.

"Hello, this is Steve . . ."

"Dr. Decker? Is this Dr. Decker?" The man's voice was loud and harsh.

Decker's body stiffened with embarrassment, and his expression soured as he answered gruffly, "Yes, this is Dr. Decker."

"Good! That fellow—what's his name? Brodie? That fellow Brodie said you're next up for an admission. This is Dr. Barner, over at the County Jail."

Decker glared at Brodie's narrow face as he held the telephone a couple of inches away from his ear.

"What can I help you with?" Decker asked.

"There's a fellow here named Theodore Hallbrook!"

"Yes?" the intern answered with increasing irritation.

"Well, this fellow Hallbrook cut his arm. And don't ask me how he did it because I don't know. But he cut his arm this morning, and I started to sew it up."

"Yes?" Real *surgeons don't 'sew' for Christ's sake, they suture.*

"Well, I gave him some Xylocaine, for anesthesia . . .

"Yes?" *I know what Xylocaine is for, goddamn it.*

". . . and after a few minutes, he started twitchin' and chompin' down with his jaw! His pulse rate's starting to go up now and he seems to be getting a little warm. What I'm worried about is that he's having some kind of reaction. A reaction to the Xylocaine."

Decker hesitated. Xylocaine stings when injected, he had seen it a thousand times, but usually it doesn't cause any serious reactions.

"How's he doing now?" he asked. "Does he have a rash or any problems breathing?"

"No, no rash, just some twitching and his jaw keeps clamping down, like he's trying to bite something." After a moment of silence, he added, "It's real weird and I've never seen anything like this before."

"Did you finish suturing him?"

"Nope. Wanted to call you first."

"Okay, why don't you finish putting him together, and if he continues to twitch or anything else, go ahead and send him over. I'll take it from there."

"Okay, will do. I'll finish the job. Sure do appreciate the advice from you new interns, fresh out of medical school. I'll let you know if there's any problem."

Decker hung up the telephone and shook his head. "Chomping of the jaw while being sewed shut," *Christ. When are they going to get somebody who knows what he's doing over there?*

Two minutes later, Gerald Brodie looked up from his desk and watched two deputies push a gurney holding an obese man to the Prep Room.

"Santiago Gonzalez, from County Jail!" one of the deputies called out as he passed by.

Brodie almost knocked over his microphone with excitement as he hollered, "Dr. Decker! Dr. Decker! Patient in the Prep Room! Patient in the Prep Room!" *God, he loved this job!*

After a careful history and examination, Decker was sure that Gonzalez's problem was a dissecting abdominal aorta. He had seen it three times before, during the surgical rotations in the third year of medical school, and he recalled the severe pain that was often followed by a disastrous drop in blood pressure from a rupture of the huge blood vessel. He ordered Peter to give him an injection of 8 milligrams of morphine sulfate, and he arranged for an abdominal CAT scan as well as a stat vascular surgery consult. Ten minutes later, a team of men in rumpled surgical greens surrounded the man and agreed with Decker's diagnosis. Get the CAT scan as fast as possible, they advised, and after starting another large-bore IV line, they recommended that Decker type and cross his blood for 10 units of packed red blood cells—just in case his aorta ruptured.

Decker nodded and wrote the order. He looked back at his patient, absently tapping his pen on the patient's clipboard. It would be fun to join the surgical team for some real honest-to-God surgery.

"Also," the surgeon concluded, "you better give him some analgesia. He's having a hell of a lot of pain."

"I already—" Decker started to answer, but the surgeons had already turned to leave the room. He looked down at his patient, who was moaning and holding his stomach as he rocked back and forth on the table. He walked back to the patient's bedside and leaned over, speaking softly into the man's ear.

"Mr. Gonzalez, did the shot help the pain?"

The man's face was covered with a fine sheen of dirty sweat. He stopped breathing for a moment and slowly let out another low moan. His closed eyes opened to narrow slits that focused on Decker.

"Señor, that shot wasn't nothing. What are you doing, playing a joke on me?"

Decker stared at the man. "What do you mean?"

"What I mean, *Doctor*"—he spit the word out as Decker backed away—"what I mean is, that shot didn't have shit in it. My gut is hurting like hell and you haven't done a damn thing for me. What kind of doctor are you?" He closed his eyes and began moaning again.

Decker looked at Peter on the other side of the room, stacking sterile surgical kits into the equipment cabinets. He reached over and picked up the clipboard with Gonzalez's medical record, searching for the record of injections. Morphine sulfate, 8 milligrams intramuscular, there it was right on the sheet, given fifteen minutes ago.

"Mr. Gonzales, I'm going to give you another 8 milligrams of morphine, and you—"

"Eight milligrams! You gave me 8 milligrams? That would have been just right for this bastard of a pain"—he patted his abdomen—"but there wasn't no 8 milligrams in that shot!" He reached out and pulled

Decker close. "Doc," he whispered, "I know morphine. I know narcotics. I know downers and uppers, I know what they feel like, man. I been doing them for years, I know exactly what they feel like. That shot I got, that 'morphine,' Doc, there wasn't 'even one milligram of anything in it. There wasn't nothing in it." His voice faded into another moan. "There wasn't nothin' for my pain, nothin.' "

Blake Skeeters considered the alternatives as he watched the frenetic activities of Choo-Choo. He had no idea what he was looking for, and he was beginning to feel silly just sitting there in front of the Cage, watching the bizarre behavior. But Spike Bond was his responsibility for at least two more weeks, and he had to work out something to ensure he received proper medical care. Since he couldn't physically examine him, he was resigned to just watching, for now at least, until some kind of game plan entered his mind.

Skeeters had seen his first mentally ill patient, a sweet little elderly lady, back at Cambridge during his second year at Harvard Medical School. The psychiatry professor had introduced them, they had smiled at each other, and together they entered the consultation room for the interview. Sitting across the table from him, she had looked like *the classic grandmother,* normal in all respects. Until she began to speak about the bugs.

As Skeeters took notes and listened carefully from the other side of the table, she had described her insect problem. There were bugs everywhere, all over her skin, crawling out of her ears, out of her mouth, and even out of "down there below," she said blushing, "in the private place." She had kept repeating,

"I know it sounds silly . . ." as she rambled on about the insects that cursed her life.

He had been startled to realize that there was something morbidly frightening about not just what she was saying, but to an even greater extent, about the way she spoke. Perhaps it was the inflection, the flat monotone of her voice, or maybe it was the look in her eyes. Whatever it was, it gave Skeeters a chill that ran from the base of his spine to the rising hairs on the back of his neck.

She had been psychotic for thirty years, her record had said. Skeeters, still a medical student and a novice apprentice of psychiatry, had tried to reason with her about reality. After an exhaustive hour of working to convince her how unreasonable it was to perceive bugs crawling across every part of her body, he finally accepted the basic truth that, for her at least, the bugs really were there.

Not much point in arguing about that.

"If you check under your bed each night for the man you know isn't there," the psychiatry professor had said, "you have a neurosis. If you check under your bed and see the man who isn't there, that's a psychosis. And if you're caring for a psychotic, do not attempt to argue about what is seen under the bed." His final admonition had boomed across the lecture hall. "Psychiatrists are medical doctors before they are anything else. Ensure there is no medical condition causing the symptoms, and then treat the psychosis!"

His gaze returned to Choo-Choo. *How am I going to properly evaluate for a medical condition if I can't even examine him? Maybe I should try to treat the psychosis first . . .*

Okay, he thought, *Choo-Choo is mentally ill and so let's start with the basics. Psychosis requires an antipsychotic drug. Simple. A phenothiazine of some kind,* like the Thorazine he had been thinking about. *Manic behavior requires the consideration of a trial of Lithium. Why did the psych Doc want to use a sedative? Probably became a little demented himself after his close call in the clutches of Choo-Choo. Okay, ignore Dr. Blackmore, use some Thorazine, just the right amount in the food. Try about 50 milligrams, maybe 100, enough to do the job. But what am I going to tell the psychiatrist?*

"I have Mr. Bond's noon sedative, some Klonopin," the voice behind him said. Skeeters stood up and turned around to face Peter Martel, who was holding a small paper cup with a tiny blue pill inside. "Dr. Blackmore called to ask about his behavior; I told him that he was still somewhat anxious, and so he upped the dose to 1 milligram. The half milligram he was given this morning didn't seem to do much for him."

Skeeters felt a flush of anger. *Still somewhat anxious!* The patient was a total manic-depressive psychotic, for Christ's sake. He tried to control himself as he glared at the nurse.

"Thank you, Peter, but wouldn't you think that Mr. Bond is a bit more than 'somewhat anxious'?" he said, looking down at the pill resting in the center of the small paper cup.

"He looks anxious to me." Martel watched the prisoner pacing back and forth.

"Well, he looks psychotic to me. I think we'll hold off the sedative for now. Would you please bring me a 4-ounce bottle of Thorazine syrup?"

Peter Martel stood still, looking at Skeeters. "Dr. Blackmore ordered him to receive Klonopin at noon."

"Thank you, I am changing the order."

"You're going to countermand the order on the chart?" Martel looked down at the intern, his face expressionless, his eyes narrowed. "Dr. Blackmore is one of the senior psychiatry residents, and he—"

"Mr. Martel," Skeeters interrupted as he straightened his shoulders and glared back at the nurse. The time had come to set the record straight. "This patient has one primary care doctor, and I am that doctor. Dr. Blackmore was here at my request, to appropriately advise as to what may be done to improve the problem at hand. When a consultant advises, I may or I may not follow the advisement. Dr. Blackmore will be moving into the background on this case."

Skeeters picked up the chart and scrawled new orders with swirls of nearly indecipherable hieroglyphics. "Now, please, Mr. Martel, the Thorazine." He ripped off the order sheet, handed it to the nurse, and walked down the hallway to the telephone, where he called the Department of Psychiatry.

Five minutes later, Dr. Blackmore had one less patient to follow at L.A. County Hospital.

On his way back to the Cage, Skeeters stopped by the Jail Ward refrigerator and picked up a quart of orange juice, a plastic drinking cup, and a bag of ice. As he passed by the Medicine Room, Martel handed him, in silent protest, a bottle of fresh Thorazine with a measuring tablespoon.

"Mr. Bond, can you hear me?" Skeeters called through the bars as he peered into the Cage.

In mid-stride, Choo-Choo jolted to a stop at the sound of his name. Standing frozen, he slowly rotated his head and stared through the bars at his physician. His black face was shining with sweat and bloody residue, his breathing was heavy from exertion. His eyes, swollen and glassy, locked on the intern's face and stared.

"Okay, Mr. Bond, I have a nice cold drink for you. Come and get it while it's fresh!" Skeeters filled the cup with the ice cubes, opened the bottle of Thorazine syrup, and poured a tablespoon of the medicine over the ice. *One tablespoon,* he thought, *at 10 milligrams per 5 cc's, would probably be on the short side for somebody as big as Choo-Choo. Better to give him 2 tablespoons.* He poured the second tablespoon of Thorazine over the ice and swirled it into the cup. He glanced up at the Cage and saw Choo-Choo continuing to stare at him. A chill, the psychosis chill, ran up his back like electricity as he suppressed a shudder. He rapidly poured 3 additional tablespoons of Thorazine into the cup and filled it with juice.

"Here is your fresh orange juice, Mr. Bond! Would you like some?" Choo-Choo watched him for another five seconds before snorting and resuming his repetitive pacing across the Cage. Skeeters walked up to the side of the Cage and held the cup inside the bars.

"Mr. Bond, you must be getting thirsty, and this orange juice is cold and fresh," he called out, carefully watching the man, bracing to jump backward if there was any movement in his direction—Dr. Blackmore had been in almost the same position the day before.

He finally sighed and placed the cup on the floor inside the bars and pulled up his seat in front of the Cage.

Five minutes later, as he completed the first paragraph of Choo-Choo's admission note, Skeeters looked up to see Decker standing in front of him.

"Blake, we got a problem," Decker said quietly. "Break away from your psychotic friend for a minute, I gotta talk to you."

Skeeters stuck his pen back into his pocket and walked down the corridor with Decker to a small storage room near the far end of the Jail Ward. Decker closed the door behind them as Skeeters sat down on the edge of a wooden crate in the corner of the room.

"What's going on, Steve?" Skeeters asked as the door was locked.

"Remember last week when I couldn't get any morphine for that patient I had with a kidney stone? We looked around the Medication Room for the narcotics record—"

"Right, and found everything locked up. Did you get the medicine for your patient?"

"Yes, finally, but it's happening again. Now, Martel is giving narcotics, but the patients aren't getting them."

"You mean Martel is diverting—"

"Goddamn right he's diverting them. He's either using them or he's selling them. He sure as hell isn't giving them to our patients." Decker told him about his patient with the aneurysm and the shortages of morphine and Demerol. "There's just no way all of these things would be coincidental, and they all point back to the same guy, either acting on his own or with others in the unit. He has always been the nurse on duty when these problems occur. The thing is, we only have two more weeks on the Jail Ward, and I'm not sure how big a stink we should make."

"How long has Martel been working here?" Skeeters asked.

"That's another thing! The guy has worked at the County Hospital for about ten years, and he's been on the Jail Ward for three years . . ."

"So?"

"Three years without a vacation!"

"Holy Christ," Skeeters said softly. "Three years and no vacation? His mind must be fried by now."

"Or affected by the drugs. Never have seen him looking like he was under any kind of influence, though. It doesn't make sense that a guy wouldn't take a single vacation in three years. I just think he's trying to hide something in the medication books he doesn't want any of the other nurses to see."

The room became silent as the interns considered the alternatives.

"If we're wrong, we'll be nailed to the wall by Marsh," Decker finally said.

"Even if we're right, we'll probably still be nailed to the wall by Marsh," Skeeters replied glumly. "He's not going to like any disruptions in the operation of his Jail Ward. Also, under that nursing look, Martel looks pretty rough to me. He might come after us if he thinks we're watching him too closely."

"Come after us?" Decker smiled. "The guy's only a nurse, probably with a drug habit left over from the seventies. He's not some kind of South Central Los Angeles drug lord . . ."

"I *know* that." Skeeters looked at the floor, deep in thought. Finally, he said, "Let's just pass on what we know to Dr. Marsh and let him deal with it."

"Blake, I thought you might say that. I set up an appointment for us to see Marsh in his office later this afternoon.

"Good," Skeeters said. "It's the right thing to do. If the guy is taking drugs, the faster Marsh can get him out of here and off to a rehab center, the better off the Jail Ward will be. Anyhow, we shouldn't let this thing become bigger than it already is. Too many other things to think about."

"That's for sure," Decker said. "Like that call I had an hour ago from the County Jail, from ol' Doc Barner. I couldn't believe it . . . he tried to dump some guy in this direction, somebody named Hallbrook, who twitched a couple of times while he was fixing him up."

"Twitched? He tried to send him over here from the jail because he twitched?"

"Yup, his jaw started twitching while Barner was—get this—'sewing' him up."

Skeeters's eyes widened imperceptibly. "What had he given him before he started twitching?" he asked.

"Given him?"

"Yeah, did he give him anything, like Xylocaine?"

"Of course he did. He was suturing the guy."

"Steve, did he have a fever? Was the guy spiking a fever?"

Decker began to feel uncomfortable. "Yes, Barner did say that he was starting to have a little fever. Why is that so important?"

"Maybe you'd better check back with Barner again," Skeeters said quietly. "There may be a problem for that guy—Hallbrook? He may have a problem with malignant hyperthermia."

"Malignant hyperthermia? What the hell is malignant hyperthermia?"

The secretary had a face like a moose and a voice like a chain-smoking Army sergeant. "Go right in, Dr. Marsh is expecting you," she growled as she pointed at the door behind her. Decker and Skeeters followed her directions and entered the palatial office, seven minutes late for their appointment. For the first time, Decker noticed a huge tapestry on the back wall, stretching from the ceiling to the floor with a 6-foot black caduceus. The twin coiled snakes each had dark ruby-red eyes that seemed to fixate on him as he crossed the room.

"You're late!"

Dr. Marsh's voice boomed out from behind his desk at the other end of the room as the interns walked cautiously across the expensive carpets. His tall and imposing figure was standing at attention, white eyebrows drawn together and harsh lines across his face

reflecting anger. His jaw, square and solid, was firmly
set as he watched the two men approach. "Yes, sir,"
Decker answered quietly as they slid into leather
chairs and looked back across the desk at the piercing
gaze. "We were having some problems with a prisoner
on the ward."

"Problems, Dr. Decker?" the director asked. He
looked at Skeeters. "This isn't the prisoner the psychiatrist, Dr. Blackmore was involved with, is it, Dr.
Skeeters?"

"No, sir," Skeeters said as he shifted uncomfortably
in his chair. "This was a different prisoner, over at
the County Jail . . ."

"Good."

"Sir, if I may ask, did the psychiatrist himself give
you a call about Mr. Bond?"

"No, the Chief of Psychiatry at L.A. County called
me, and not too happy at all about one of his top
residents being told to back off a case, especially a
high profile case like that one. You had a problem
with his use of benzodiazepines, Dr. Skeeters?"

Skeeters swallowed and glanced at Decker. This
wasn't supposed to be an inquisition. "Yes, sir, to be
frank, I did have a problem with the use of benzodiazepines in a psychotic manic patient. I felt an antipsychotic drug would be more appropriate."

"Did it ever cross your mind to talk it over with the
psychiatry resident before countermanding his order?"

"Yes, sir, I did. However, the psychiatry resident
didn't . . ." Skeeters hesitated. "He didn't consider it
to be worth *his* while to discuss the matter with *me*
before ordering a drug that seemed controversial at
best. I thought his behavior was arrogant, and besides,
sir, Mr. Bond especially didn't take a liking to him
and almost strangled him to death—"

"I read the deputy sheriff's report."

"And so, since Dr. Blackmore didn't seem to be helping, and since he didn't talk to me about his plans, and since his life seemed to be in danger near Choo-Choo, that is near Mr. Bond, I decided to allow him to spend his time in more meaningful and safer ways. Sir."

Dr. Marsh's face broke into a broad smile. "Good for you, Dr. Skeeters. I like my interns to run the show like that when they're caring for their patients. When you invite a consult to see a patient, you may also invite him to leave the patient. That is what I told the Chief of Psychiatry." He turned to Decker. "Don't you agree, Dr. Decker?"

"Yes, sir. I agree completely," Decker said quickly as he sat up in his chair.

"Good. I consider the issue to be resolved." Dr. Marsh's face resumed its granite appearance as he looked over the two interns. "Now, why did you ask for this meeting, Dr. Decker? Is there a problem on the Jail Ward?"

Decker quickly considered the best way to start. Dr. Marsh always seemed to be in a bad mood—stern and uncompromising, always cracking the whip. And that smile . . . like the grin of an alligator. Best not to set him off, especially now that Blake had apparently done the right thing with that psychiatrist problem. Probably a good idea to mention Blake's name right in the beginning.

"Dr. Marsh, Blake and I have been concerned regarding medicines on the Jail Ward."

"Medicines? What kind of medicines?" His face suddenly looked cold.

"Well, sir, Blake and I have frequently noticed that our patients are not receiving enough narcotics to help them with their pain. There have been several instances when medicines ordered have not been as forthcoming as they should be. And it usually—that is, always—it seems to occur when a certain nurse is . . ."

"What nurse?"

"Peter Martel, sir," Skeeters said as Decker glanced at him and nodded in agreement. "Whenever Peter Martel is on duty is when the problem seems to occur."

"How many cases?"

"Three at least, sir, and probably several others," Decker said. "Tyra Levy has had some problems too. Martel refused to allow her to review the narcotics record on her patients when she was getting Narcan to reverse the drug overdose problems in that Beverly Hills patient, Mrs. VonStoffer."

Dr. Marsh looked surprised. "He wouldn't allow her to review the narcotics record on her patients?"

"Yes, sir."

The room became silent as both interns paused, waiting for his response. Dr. Marsh rocked his chair back and scrutinized the doctors. His face was blank, without emotion, and his hands were folded in his lap. Skeeters found himself nervously studying the tiny caduceus figure sprayed across Marsh's tie as the silence continued.

"Gentlemen, where is your proof?" Marsh finally asked in a voice so quiet that Skeeters barely heard him.

Decker piped up with the answer. "Our proof, sir, is in the close observation of the analgesic treatment our patients have received when narcotics have been ordered." He described the cases and clarified Peter Martel's role in each case. Marsh listened intently, then finally leaned forward in his chair, smiled, and placed his hands on the mahogany desk.

"Every once in a while, a nurse with some kind of drug problem gets into the system," he said. "Sometimes a nurse who likes to deal in drugs may be hired into the hospital work force. The personnel department tries to screen the applicants, but some of them always seem to make it in. This is a serious problem for the patients on the Jail Ward, and I appreciate your bringing it to my attention."

"Thank you, sir," both interns said in unison.

"I think we should move ahead and determine if there is, in fact, a problem here. I will need facts, times, drug names, and dosages. I will also need the names of anyone else you may feel could be involved. This may take the combined efforts of several interns, over the next two or three months. When we have enough specific information, I'll contact the Drug Enforcement Administration and let them take it from there. And when this nurse is prosecuted," Marsh continued, "and he will be prosecuted if he is guilty of what you are suspecting, I will guarantee you that he will never return to this hospital again."

"Sir, why don't you go ahead and have the police launch an investigation?" Skeeters began.

"At this point, there isn't enough information yet to convict anybody of anything, and I'm not about to destroy a professional career on the basis of unsubstantiated accusations." He smiled again, and Skeeters noticed the glint of a tiny gold filling on his left upper incisor tooth. "Also, if Martel suspects that anything is going on, the facts of this case will disappear and the Jail Ward will be stuck with him."

"Do you want us to conduct an investigation?" Decker asked. "While we're admitting patients to the Jail Ward?"

Dr. Marsh abruptly stood up and scowled at Decker. "I didn't say conduct an investigation!" he said, his voice rising. "You are doctors, not policemen. I said gather information so that an investigation can be conducted by the proper authorities. You don't have to do anything except keep this whole matter to yourself and bring me information about further narcotic problems as they may arise. Don't tell any of the other interns, don't talk to the deputy sheriffs, don't even tell your families!"

A buzzer on the corner of his desk emitted an annoying squeal and Dr. Marsh reached down and picked up the telephone.

"Yes?" he said, listening. "Yes, he's here." He looked at Decker. "Yes . . . yes . . . let them know he's on his way." He hung up the telephone and scowled at Decker. "Someone named Hallbrook was just admitted from the County Jail as a red blanket, with seizures and high fever. You better get down there." As the interns stood up, he added, "Just be sure you bring me all the information you come across. If we have a bad nurse, I want to get him off the Jail Ward, and I want him brought to justice."

"Yes, sir, we understand," Decker answered as they turned to leave the room.

Inside the elevator, Decker turned to Skeeters. "Tell me everything you know about malignant hyperthermia. I'm in over my head on this Hallbrook case. Problem with a fever, right?"

"Right. Weird disease, unknown cause, triggered by general anesthesia induction if the patient has the genetics for it. Can be triggered by local anesthetics also."

"Great, high fever but no infection?" Decker said.

"Like I said, weird disease. Some kind of defect in storage of calcium in cells causes a chemical reaction that generates heat."

"Heat?"

"Lots of heat, all through the body, unbelievably high fevers."

The elevator door opened to the Jail Ward, and the interns could hear shouting from the Prep Room. As they ran from the elevator, Decker called out to Skeeters, "All that yelling, bad sign . . ."

"Very bad sign," Skeeters answered.

The Prep Room was filled with deputies, nurses, and interns, and everyone seemed to be shouting at the same time. On the exam table closest to the door was a large Caucasian man, stripped to his waist, displaying a chest covered with a thick mat of curly black hair. At that moment he was fully enveloped in a grand mal seizure. His eyes were rolled up and his eyelids were violently twitching open and shut, his head was repeatedly slamming against the surface of the examination table, his arms and legs were jerking in a repetitive series of spasms, and his pants were showing the spreading stain of urine incontinence.

The sheriff deputies were trying to secure his arms and legs to the table, Dr. O'Conner was trying to start an intravenous line in his right arm, while his partner, Tyra Levy, was working to insert an intracath into the antecubital vein in his left arm. Peter Martel was leaning over the center of the crowd, hanging a bottle of saline on the hook above the table.

Levy looked up at Decker and Skeeters. "Does this guy belong to you?" she hollered over the noise. "If he does, he's all yours as soon as I start this line."

She pushed the needle into the man's vein, and a steady stream of dark red blood flowed off his bouncing arm onto her shoes. "Damn! Peter! Let me have that line!" She grabbed the tubing from the nurse and connected it to the end of the needle. "Barner," she continued, "sent him over when his temperature hit 103 degrees. He was 104 degrees downstairs in the ER, so they threw a red blanket on him and sent him on up with full red-blanket honors. Can you believe that? A 104-degree temperature and they threw a blanket on him! Started having grand mal seizures in the elevator and had two more after he arrived here."

"I can't get this backup line into his vein, with him bouncing all over the place!" O'Conner yelled as he pulled a long needle out of the man's left arm.

"Let me have that needle," Decker said. "I'll take the case from here." He looked around for the nurse. "Peter! Five hundred milligrams of phenobarb, intravenous, stat! Somebody get the bag and prepare to intubate! Tyra! Jam the tongue guard between his teeth before he bites off his tongue." He glared at the sheriff deputies fighting to secure Hallbrook's legs in restraints. "Forget his damn legs and clear out of here. Peter, grab a vial of Dilantin. We're going to have to start it soon; don't run it in faster than 50 milligrams per minute!" He put his hand on the man's arm. "Jesus Christ, he's hot as hell!"

Levy placed a strip of tape to secure her intravenous line to Hallbrook's left arm as she took a rubber tongue guard from the shelf and looked into his mouth. The man's face was purple and contorted with the spasms of the continuous seizures. His teeth were grinding with violent clenching movements, and blood was beginning to seep out from between his lips.

Levy sensed a sudden urge of nausea in her stomach as a roaring sound began to fill her ears. Her chest felt tight as she struggled to take a deep breath . . . it was a strangling sensation, a terrible feeling like she was being choked. *I can't breathe!* she thought. She placed her hand around the front of her neck as the roar became louder and a smothering weight began to press down on her head and shoulders. She dropped the tongue guard to the floor and backed away from the table as she began to feel light-headed. The walls of the room looked distorted, and O'Conner's face, looking at her with alarm, began to look hideously deformed. She backed up against the Prep Room's second exam table and closed her eyes.

"Tyra, are you okay?" O'Conner asked as he leaned over her.

"What's going on with Tyra?" Decker asked as he squirted the phenobarbital-filled syringe into Hall-brook's vein.

"I think all the excitement might be getting to her," O'Conner said. "She had a couple of prisoners die yesterday. I think she'll be okay—I'll get her into the Doctor's On-Call Room."

Skeeters pulled a wooden tongue depressor and a roll of surgical tape from his pocket. Ten seconds later, the end of the depressor was completely enclosed in the protective tape. Just as he managed to wedge it between the teeth of the patient's thrashing head, the grand mal seizure abruptly halted and Hall-brook quietly settled back on the table, devoid of any movements apart from shallow panting-like respirations.

"I told you to leave his legs alone!" Decker yelled at the two deputies, who were continuing to work straps around the prisoner's ankles. The deputies ignored him and continued, provocatively slowly, to secure his legs to the side of the table. Finally, as they buckled his legs down and ambled casually from the room, one of them called back, "Theodore Hallbrook is a rapist and a menace to society. We like to keep him well secured. And we take our orders from Sergeant Grossman, not from you."

Decker ignored them and picked up an ophthalmoscope. "What is going on with this guy?" he mumbled as he peered through the pupils at the man's retinas. "Fever and seizures, maybe he has some kind of meningitis . . ."

"I'm going to check his temperature again," Skeeters said as he stuck an electrical thermistor device under the man's lacerated tongue. At the side of the table, the digital temperature display showed the standard 888 display for five seconds, then began to make a beeping sound as it demonstrated Hallbrook's temperature. "It's 102 degrees . . . now 103 and equilibrating . . . 104 . . ." Skeeters called out. He studied the display as it calibrated itself and flashed the temperatures of the warming thermistor. "It's 105 and still equilibrating!" he said.

"His pupils are round and reactive to light, the disc margins look okay—no pressure in his brain," Decker said. "His neck is supple, no rigidity. Here's the laceration on his shoulder that Barner was suturing, looks clean to me." He moved down to the man's chest. "Clear chest, no pneumonia, heart sounds okay and without murmurs."

"He's up to 106, Steve! He's got it . . . no question!"

"Abdomen's benign, no distension, no—"

"Steve! Forget his abdomen! You're not going to find anything causing the fever! This has got to be malignant hyperthermia! The Xylocaine Barner gave him fired it off. He needs 70 milligrams of Dantrium immediately!" Skeeters said.

Decker looked at Skeeters. "Dantrium?" he asked, feeling stupid. "What is Dantrium?" His surgical rotations during medical school had always dealt with a fever in a logical manner: you check the lungs for infection, you check the urine for infection, and then you give Tylenol suppositories and antibiotics until the problem is resolved.

"Dantrium . . . good stuff, ties up calcium release from the sarcoplasmic reticulum," Skeeters said. "Works to reverse the hypermetabolic process of malignant hyperthermia."

Decker felt himself developing a pounding headache. A loud 3-second tone from the thermistor rang out as the display locked in on the final temperature.

"Temperature 107! Holy shit!" Decker exclaimed. "The guy's going to fry his brain. I should have had him brought over here when Barner first called."

"Don't worry about that, Steve, just get Martel to give him some dantrolene sodium, and a couple of amps of bicarb with some Lasix," Skeeters said. "I'll start packing him in ice and try to cool off his intravenous bottle. We'll fill him with ice water—that should cool him off. We've still got a chance."

Rusty Esch had the Dantrium on the Jail Ward within five minutes of the call, and thirty seconds later, Decker had it flowing into the patient's veins. Skeeters placed a rectal probe into Hallbrook for continuous temperature monitoring while O'Conner bathed the comatose man with ice water. Adjacent to the temperature display module, an electrocardiogram monitor showed a series of heart complexes marching across a green screen like perfectly formed waves moving across a verdant sea.

"Why is he still in a coma?" Decker asked no one in general. "He should be coming out of it by now. It's already been ten minutes since he was seizing."

"The phenobarb and postictal state is probably keeping him under," Skeeters answered. "You didn't find any focal neurologic signs suggesting a stroke or anything like that, did you?"

"Nope, just totally zonkered. No reflexes, no nothing."

"Well, we have him covered for hyperthermia. He's been drenched with ice water, both bags of intravenous fluids are packed in ice and almost frozen, he's had his Dantrium and Lasix, and I just squirted an amp of bicarb into him. Still breathing okay, getting 8 liters of oxygen. Should see the temperature drop to 103 or 104 soon."

"I'll crank out another temperature on him," Decker said as he reached over and pushed the reset button on the front of the temperature display module.

"Blood pressure's dropped to 95 over 50 and heart rate's climbing to 186 now," O'Conner said as he unwrapped the blood pressure cuff from Hallbrook's left arm. "He's starting to get some noises in his chest— I think his lungs are filling up with fluids!"

"I'm going to intubate him now," Skeeters said, grabbing an endotracheal tube from the red crash cart that had been placed near the table. "He needs a better airway and he's probably got some pulmonary edema."

The temperature display module equilibrated and emitted another three-second tone. The three interns turned to look at the digital display as 108 degrees flashed on the screen.

"Jesus!" Decker hollered. "We're going to lose this guy!"

"I'm going to douse him in alcohol and set up a fan. It will evaporate more quickly than the ice water, and maybe we can cool him better," O'Conner said as he pulled a gallon jug of denatured alcohol from the bottom shelf of the medicine cabinet. As Skeeters shined an intubation light into the back of Hallbrook's mouth to allow for the insertion of the tube down the trachea, O'Conner spread towels across his lower chest and abdomen and began pouring the alcohol onto the cloth.

"You don't have to drown him in that stuff, Eric. He's starting to twitch again. I think he's going to have another seizure," Decker called out as Hallbrook's right hand and arm started to develop jerking movements.

"Probably a Jacksonian march to a full-blown grand

mal seizure," Skeeters said. "Better give him another 500 milligrams phenobarbital, quick!"

"I'll get a fan blowing across the alcohol," O'Conner said as he left the room to search for a fan.

"Here you go," Martel said as he handed Decker another ampule of the medicine. Thirty seconds later after it flushed into Hallbrook's veins, the jerking movements stopped.

"He's intubated," Skeeters announced after connecting the tube that projected from his mouth to a plastic respiration bag. "I'll set this up for pure oxygen," he said as he attached the oxygen line from the wall to the intubation tubing disappearing into the depths of the patient's lungs. He wrinkled his nose at the alcohol fumes that saturated the air. "Smells like a winery in here. I'll check his pressure again."

The cardiac monitor began buzzing as the regular beeping sound of the patient's heart rhythm changed to a chaotic noise of an irregular heartbeat.

"His heart's throwing out a run of PVC's," Decker said, looking at the green screen. The smooth wave pattern was replaced by irregular spikes of disordered electrical activity.

"His pressure's down to 55 over 30! He's going to drop out any second!" Skeeters hollered.

Suddenly the cardiac monitor blared out a loud buzzing sound as the electrical heart pattern changed to a thin, wavering phosphorescent streak stretching across the center of the green screen.

"He's in V. Fib!" Decker yelled as he thumped his fist against the patient's chest. "Code Blue! Code Blue!"

Across the hallway, in the intern's sleeping quarters, Tyra Levy stirred, feeling like she had been drugged. Her head continued to spin, and she had a vague recollection of a nightmare, but she couldn't remember the details. The door was closed and the room darkened. She lifted the corner of the moist towel and looked around at the other beds, all empty. The pressure in her head seemed to be building again as she forced herself to lie still.

O'Conner appeared at the doorway of the Prep Room, a large fan in his right hand. He dropped the fan and ran to the defibrillator standing in the corner of the room. "Pump him while I charge this thing up!"

"I'm pumping him," Decker called out while Skeeters drew up an ampule of Adrenalin and injected it directly into Hallbrook's vein.

"Get the saline gauze pads on his chest. This thing's gonna have 400 watt-seconds in about five seconds—it's charging . . . charging . . . 300 . . . ready to go!" O'Conner said as he moved the defibrillator to the side of the exam table. "Stand back! Stand back!"

As Decker dropped a couple of saline-soaked pads on Hallbrook and moved a safe distance away, O'Conner slapped the two electrical paddles on the pads, one just to the right of the sternum and the other on the side of the chest, just as the textbook says. "Stand clear!"

As his thumbs pressed down on the red buttons extending from the back of the electrical paddles, Skeeters felt the burning in his nose from the alcohol fumes. He suddenly opened his eyes wide, took a deep breath, and hollered "No-o-o-o-o-o-o!" at the instant the defibrillating machine fired the high voltage across Hallbrook's chest.

The results were immediate.

With a muffled whoosh, Theodore Hallbrook's body ignited into an orange flash that quickly spread up to his face and down across his chest and abdomen. The fire ignited his pants and spread down toward his feet, emitting a thick black smoke that simultaneously acti-

vated the three smoke detectors in the ceiling of the
room. His hair melted across his chest, forming a
paste of burning tissue that dissolved the electrocar-
diographic chest leads and fed flames up the wires
toward the heart monitor. The blue-yellow flames lin-
gered at the edge of his mouth just long enough to
melt the plastic tube extending from his teeth. A second later, as a stream of pure oxygen poured from
the tube, the flames flashed to a blinding white flare.
The oxygen and plastic burned furiously; his lips
melted back as the fire raced down his windpipe and
into his lungs. A geyser of hot flames suddenly shot
out of his mouth, straight up almost to the ceiling.

In the room across the hall, Tyra Levy became
aware of a terrible odor. She pulled the towel from
her face again and slowly sat up on the edge of the
bed, trying to focus her eyes. It was a sweet, heavy
smell, a horrible smell, and she could feel a gagging
sensation rumbling across her abdomen. She stood up
and staggered toward the door. Through the window
that looked in the direction of the Prep Room, she
saw Decker and O'Conner running down the corridor,
shouting at the deputies.

She opened the door and saw black smoke rolling
out the upper half of the opening to the Prep Room.
Down the hallway, men were yelling for a fire extinguisher and interns were pulling a fire hose from the
wall. Feeling as though she was in a trance, her mind
not connected to her body, she moved to the Prep
Room door.

She leaned forward and looked inside.

Her eyes widened in horror as she saw flames and
smoke billowing out of a man lying on the exam table.
His face! My God, his face! She clutched the door
frame as she stared at his face. A satanic grin was
spreading across a face that was undulating with a

bubbling dissolution, a face that was alive with heat and fire. A face that emitted a white torch roaring straight up from it's mouth, straight up to the ceiling. Skeeters was at the far wall, beyond what was left of the man's head, frantically turning the green oxygen knob. As he shut the valve, the torch rapidly disappeared from the patient's mouth. Seconds later, Decker and O'Conner barged past her and into the Prep Room, where they doused Theodore Hallbrook's body with a roaring white cloud of carbon dioxide.

She turned away from the door and walked toward the elevator on the other side of the watch commanders' station. The nausea was replaced by a heaviness in the pit of her stomach. She shook her head and tried to clear the vertigo. She felt a deep and aching fatigue as she reached up with a shaking hand and pushed the elevator button.

As she waited, she knew it was time to go home.

Skeeters left the conference room on the fourteenth floor and returned to the Jail Ward. They had all attended the meeting except Tyra Levy, who really hadn't been much involved with "the incident" (as everyone was calling it), and they had all made their statements for the fire department, Dr. Marsh, and the Sheriff's Department.

Theodore Hallbrook was dead—a terrible death, all agreed—and the probable cause of his death was sent to the coroner's office as death by malignant hyperthermia. The coroner, after informal telephone conversations with the interns, was kind enough to concede that the fire had occurred after the man's death and so had little meaning beyond that of any cremation event—the fact that the cremation occurred so quickly after death was unusual, but of no significance as far as the official record was concerned.

As he walked by the Prep Room, Skeeters glanced at Hallbrook's exam table. It was clean and looked ready for the next patient. Although the air held a trace of an odor—*like a sweet burning tire*—there appeared to be no other residue from the violent events of five hours before, and no physical traces of the prisoner's remains. Skeeters was impressed with the efficiency of the Jail Ward orderlies. He continued down the central corridor and found Jack Diamond, purple wig nicely covering his sadly depleted scalp, ready with a word of sympathy. An outstretched hand, a sincere expression of encouragement, and a wish for "good luck on the next case," all gratefully accepted by the intern.

On the floor in front of the bars that enclosed the Cage was an empty cup.

Skeeters quickly peered into the Cage. Choo-Choo was flat on his back, sound asleep on the cot attached to the wall, his chest rhythmically expanding and contracting with his labored respirations, looking as peaceful as 317 pounds of human can look. He was snoring loudly, making a rumbling hissing sound that Skeeters noticed was remarkably similar to that of a slow-moving locomotive. He picked up Bond's chart from the chair and sat down to begin writing the remaining details of Choo-Choo's admission summary.

Steve Decker rode the elevator past the Jail Ward and down to the first floor. Five minutes later, he was outside the behemoth building and leaving a trail of rubber that stretched from the parking structure halfway up Zonal Avenue to the Mission Avenue intersection. Accelerating up the on-ramp to the freeway, every car ahead was like an obstruction. He powered his Corvette around the slowed traffic and finally roared into the Diamond Lane on the left side of the freeway. The lane was clear of cars as he slammed his foot down on the accelerator, pulling all of his 205 horsepower engine to life as he flashed past the bumper-to-bumper traffic that stretched to the horizon. Although his car did not comply with the "three people" rule that allowed for legal Diamond Lane transit—the Corvette only had two seats—and although hundreds of cars creeping along in the lanes outside the Diamond Lane blasted their horns in protest at the lone driver violator of the rule, Decker reached the Rosemead off-ramp in ten minutes without being observed by any California Highway patrolmen.

He squealed into his parking space, slammed his door shut, and walked into his apartment, locking the deadbolt behind him. He didn't bother to turn on the lights as he pulled a six-pack of Coors from the refrigerator and a package of Garcia y Vega cigars from his bedroom shelf. After dropping into the oversized chair that consumed a quarter of the small living room, he clenched the cigar between his front teeth as he flared a match to the other end. A cloud of gray smoke rose to form a layer of smoke that floated across the room. He snapped the top of the first can of beer and drained it in twenty seconds flat. The glow of the thick cigar brightened again in the dark as he drew in deeply. A flawless smoke ring rose slowly from his mouth and floated across the center of the cloud as he snapped the top of another can of beer. He chugged half the can down and stared into the gloom.

Two weeks into his medical career and everything was already a disaster. He grimaced as he recalled Hallbrook's face shooting the hot flames from his mouth. A nightmare, that was what it had been. What was it Dr. Marsh had said? "Your patient Hallbrook has just arrived with a high fever . . ." *Goddamn it all to hell!* "*Your* patient Hallbrook . . ." *Ol' Barner had given me all I needed to know over the telephone,*

*for Christ's sake. He had said the guy was twitching
after the Xylocaine, he had told me that the guy was
developing a fever. He had told me everything but the
fucking diagnosis! I was supposed to know the diagnosis . . . that is why he called me! So Hallbrook was a
rapist. He didn't deserve to die like that. Nobody deserves to die like that.*

He puffed on his cigar again. *I killed him,* he
thought. *I killed him just as sure as if I had injected
potassium chloride into that vein instead of phenobarbital. All I had to do to save the bastard was to have
told Barner to stop "sewing" him and to ship his ass on
over so we could control his malignant hyperthermia.
Control it with Dantrium . . . That's all I had to do.
Instead of mocking Barner's terminology—mocking
Barner while he was calling for help. Goddamn it!*

His head was beginning to develop the distinctive
buzzing sensation of alcohol penetrating the cells.
Skeeters had almost saved the day, almost but not
quite.

It was supposed to be so simple! Finish medical
school, take a residency, learn surgery, learn how to
do it right. Decker shook his head. Now the buzz was
getting strong. He had trouble focusing on the smoke,
trouble making sense out of it all . . .

He heard a distant ringing sound. He staggered
across the room and answered the telephone on the
third ring. Her voice was soft and sweet . . . she was
concerned, she hadn't heard from him.

"It's been a very bad day," he said, smashing out
the cigar inside an empty plate.

"Everybody has bad days, especially during the intern year," she responded.

"This was as bad as they get, Katie. This was worse
than as bad as they get—"

"Have you had dinner yet?"

"No, unless you call a couple of beers dinner. A couple or tree." He was having trouble enunciating.

"You need to eat, Steve. Everything will seem better if you get some food into you." She hesitated. "I'm off call tonight, and I just happen to have a special talent with New York steaks."

Through the haze he felt a surge of desire at the thought of having her in his apartment, close to him. It seemed like years since they had been together at the Bonaventure. "That would be nice," he said. "In fact, that would be great . . ."

"Good. I have to stop at the market, but I'll be there as soon as I can," she said.

They said good-bye and he looked in the direction of his refrigerator. The room was just a little out of focus as he tried to think. The pizza . . . the pizza was gone. There was some milk, and maybe an apple or two. *No problem, can get something real quick at the market across the street for a salad. Gotta clean up the apartment, the place is a mess. Maybe I can get rid of the cigar smoke, she won't like that. Put a fan in front of the window, blow it outside.* He wandered around the apartment trying to pick up clothes—every time he picked up one garment, another hit the floor. He finally sighed and dropped everything into a pile in the corner, pulled off his surgical greens, and stepped into the shower, turning the water up to hottest temperature he could stand.

Tyra Levy paced back and forth across her apartment and wondered if she was going to have a nervous breakdown before the end of her month on Jail Ward. She could not get the sight of that man—whatever his name was, she couldn't remember—out of her mind. Her nostrils flared as the terrible smell of his burning flesh seemed to penetrate her again, and her hands shook at the thought of the oxygen fire roaring out of his mouth as his face melted away.

Barely halfway through the month, and all of this has happened. It is moving too fast here, much too fast. She thought about Montana, the quiet rolling plains and the soft rustling of the grass in the afternoon breeze. The quiet, the peace, she needed it back again. She had taken a long hot shower, trying to wash it off, to scrub it off, to rid herself of the smell and the memory. She had called Tom, looking for solace, for comfort, and they had an argument. She had turned the television on and then immediately turned it off again, preferring the silence of her apartment.

She took the bottle of Restoril—the beautiful pink and red capsules—from her medicine cabinet and she washed one down with a glass of water. A minute later, she took a second pill; they were only 15 milligrams, and she had been needing a larger amount for most of the past week to get to sleep. She pulled the covers back from her bed and climbed between the sheets. She stared at the ceiling for five minutes, and returned to the bathroom to retrieve the Restoril. She placed the bottle of capsules on the nightstand, within arm's reach, and pulled the covers over her again.

She wanted to have the medicine ready, just in case she woke up in the middle of the night.

Chapter 8

"Dr. Skeeters, does Julia Jackson belong to you?" the deputy sheriff asked as he walked into the Prep Room.

Blake looked up from his work on the buttocks of Jeb Gist. The man had been brought in from the County Jail a half hour before with a 4-inch infected red pustule bulging from the right cheek of his buttocks.

"Yes, she does," Skeeters said from behind his white mask as he placed a scalpel blade back on the sterile tray. "Is she having some kind of problem?"

"Deputy Kraus says you should come and take a look at her."

"Okay, I'll be right there," Skeeters said. "Can it wait until I finish opening this furuncle?"

"Kraus said you should come right on over and take a look at her."

Skeeters sighed, pulled off his sterile gloves, removed his mask, and told Jeb Gist that the lancing of his boil would have to wait until he examined Julia Jackson.

"Well, hurry it up, Doc," Gist said with irritation. "My butt's been hurting for five days now."

The deputy unlocked the door and let Skeeters into the Ladies' Room. Unlike the previous times Skeeters had entered the area, the female prisoners were silent and there was no sound except the usual beeping noises from a couple of heart monitors. Deputy Kraus was standing in the center of the room with her arms crossed. Her pockmarked pudgy face looked stone cold in the gray light, and her pig eyes stared straight ahead. She ignored the intern as he crossed the room.

Skeeters knew before he reached her bed that Julia Jackson was dead. Although she was in the same position she had been in earlier that day, curled up on her left side in the fetal position, she was smaller and more shrunken. Her black hair and skin had become *lifeless*, and her thin muscles had lost the small movements that were a part of living. Her left eye, the good one that had been spared from the injection of heroin, was closed, while the glazed cornea of the blinded right eye stared straight ahead. A clear plastic tube, filled with yellow nutrients, emerged from her left nostril and connected to a pump at the bedside. A faint hum confirmed that the pump was still pushing Ensure Plus down into her stomach. Above the bed, a plastic bottle with the red letters MS stamped on the side was dripping saline and the concentrated morphine sulfate into her vein.

Feeling the watchful eyes of the other prisoners, Skeeters pulled out his stethoscope and knelt down next to the bed. *She is dead,* he thought, *but I'd better make sure.* He placed the diaphragm of the stethoscope under her hospital gown near the center of her left breast and listened carefully for a full ten seconds. Nothing. He moved it farther up to the top of her chest and listened again. Silence. He placed his hand on her neck, over her right carotid artery—the one that had escaped the heroin injection. No pulsations. He gently opened her left eyelid and aimed his penlight at the cornea. No pupillary response. He reached up and turned off the nutritional pump, shut off the morphine intravenous line, then stood and carefully pulled the sheet to cover Julia Jackson's head.

A faint gasp came from one of the prisoners on the other side of the room.

Skeeters blinked and felt a stinging sensation in his eyes. After being awarded his M.D. degree, this had been his very first patient. He had known she was going to die, he had known it for more than a week, and he had done everything he could to protect her from pain and suffering. He had even tried to make it easier for her—once it was clear that her chances for decent survival were virtually zero—with the morphine that allowed her a better rest without discomfort. Because he had seen her each day, the medicine had been boosted in small increments, as he had been taught in medical school, to ease the smallest distress and to prevent even a single unnecessary day of torment. He had been concerned this morning, since she had become so much more lethargic, that the dose was being increased too fast to be ethically proper. As a precaution, and to reassure himself that 4 milligrams of the drug every three hours was not too much for her, that he was not overdosing his patient, a morphine level had been ordered that morning with the routine blood tests that analyzed her internal chemistry.

And yet this final event hit him with an unexpected brutality that brought to the surface a frustration he had felt since he had seen his first death as a medical student. He felt himself clenching his teeth . . . *it was so final and absolute.* He looked down at the mound in the center of the bed. The shell of her body lying under the sheet is now nothing more than exactly that: a shell, a memory, no coming back to experience further events of life.

He tried to gather his thoughts as he brought his emotions under control. Before death, every problem a patient experiences has some kind of a solution that a conscientious and thinking physician has a chance of finding. From a tiny splinter under the skin to the rehabilitation needs for those most severely damaged, there is a solution. But at death there is no solution, just a terrible, irreversible finality.

He walked past Kraus, still standing with an expression of detached indifference, and let himself out of the Ladies' Room. He carried Julia Jackson's chart into the small dictating room off the main corridor and sat down to write his concluding progress note. He kept it brief, noting the lack of pulse and respiration and establishing the exact time of her declared death. As he turned to the order sheet near the front of the chart—the morgue would have to be notified—he paused to see if her lab from that morning had been filed into her record. The chemistry panel opened before him, and he reviewed the long string of numbers that documented that her multiple organ systems had been relentlessly moving into the advancing failure seen with the approach of death.

At the bottom of the page, just below the liver enzymes, was the morphine level from that morning. Skeeters eyes opened wide as he followed the dotted line to the printed result. He moved the chart to a better light and stared at the page.

MORPHINE SULFATE
  . . THERAPEUTIC RANGE: 20–100 ugm/liter.
  . . TEST RESULT: <1 ugm/liter (NON-DETECTABLE)

Non-detectable! Skeeters began to hyperventilate. Peter Martel had been stealing the vital narcotics from his dying patient, like some kind of parasite. The son of a bitch, stealing from Julia Jackson the chance to die without suffering. The quick thought of physical violence against the nurse entered his mind . . . and was quickly suppressed.

He left the dictating room and walked up to Gerald Brodie's desk in the central hallway.

"You have Julia Jackson's chart?" Brodie asked, his nose pointing at the intern. "I heard she just died. The sheriffs want to move her body out to make room for the next one."

"Here's her chart," Skeeters said quietly as he gently laid the stack of pages on the ward clerk's desk. "You may now go ahead and move her out"—his voice felt hoarse—"so there is room for the next one."

As he entered the Prep Room to finish working on Jeb Gist's furuncle, Brodie called out in his nasal voice, "Thank you, Dr. Skeeters."

Martel was standing there waiting for him. Skeeters felt his heart pounding as he walked around the exam table and pulled on another pair of sterile gloves. *Control, nothing to be gained by losing control now,* he thought. He forced his mind to ignore Martel and to concentrate on the surgical problem in front of him.

There would be plenty of time for Martel later.

He worked quickly to clean out the remainder of the pus from Gist's buttocks as the nurse assisted from the other side of the table. The patient swore and complained bitterly about his discomfort during the procedure; Skeeters sympathized with him and injected additional boosts of Xylocaine anesthesia into the area. Within a couple of minutes, the lesion was clean, hydrogen peroxide was flushed through the infected tissue, and iodoform gauze was packed into the underlying space.

"Peter, would you clean this with saline, cover the lesion with Polysporin ointment, and place some packing over the furuncle? Before taping the dressing in

place, cover the skin with adequate Benzoin and dry
it real good. Okay?" He forced himself to look at the
nurse.

"Sure, no problem," Martel said nonchalantly as he
looked around the Prep Room for a bottle of saline.

"Good. I'm going to check on Bond."

Skeeters left the Prep Room and walked down the
central corridor, past the Medication Room entrance.
The door leading into the room was slightly ajar and
the room was dark. Skeeters hesitated and continued
past the door, another 20 yards down the hall. Jack
Diamond, his leg propped up in its usual position,
spotted the intern and gave a little wave. Skeeters
responded with a quick move of his hand and turned
toward the Medication Room again. As he approached
the entrance, he quickly stepped inside.

Skeeters had never liked covert operations, at least
not when he was involved in the operation. However,
he rationalized, this was not exactly clandestine, but
something perfectly proper being done without a lot
of fanfare. Besides, prowling about the Medication
Room was not improper per se; it was just not common for a doctor to be in a dark room, shining a
penlight around, and snooping through medication
logbooks.

He thought about locking the door. No, if the nurse
did come, a locked door would escalate this whole
thing to a much more ominous level. He knew Dr.
Marsh would approve—*he has commissioned us to
gather information*—and Steve Decker would not only
approve but would probably be holding the door for
him. Peter Martel was the only real danger, but he
was occupied for about another five minutes. Skeeters
hoped no deputy sheriffs would pass by.

The medication logbooks, several three-ring bind-
ers, were stacked on the main counter over the refrig-

erator. His penlight shined over the names of each until he found the one with "Female Prisoners" on the cover. He opened it and his light quickly spotted Julia Jackson, the seventeenth prisoner. The list of medications was long, including antibiotics, lotions for her skin, multivitamins, and special nutritional supplements. There was no mention of narcotics and certainly nothing about morphine sulfate.

"What the hell, I think it should be done anyway."

Skeeters jumped at the sound, slammed the medication book shut, turned off his flashlight, and jammed it into his pocket. He crouched down, waiting for the door to fly open.

"Hell, yes! We're going to do it and they better watch out."

Skeeters crept to the door, still open a half inch, and peered out into the hallway. Mel Grossman, looking twice as large as usual, and another deputy were walking down the corridor directly toward the Medication Room. Skeeters backed away from the door. Their voices grew louder as they approached; five seconds later, they had passed the room without so much as a sideways glance. Skeeters let out a sigh of relief.

The light shined around the room again. There it was. The Narcotics Book, a red binder with the black lettering "NARCOTICS" on its side was on top of the refrigerator. Within ten seconds Skeeters had the book open to Julia Jackson's page. The light scanned the information and quickly settled on the area of morphine administration.

Five days before, on July 14, the medicine had been started. Correct, that was about when he had started the morphine. There were daily notes that reflected his orders to slowly boost the dosage over the next three days until the final order last Tuesday. There it was in black script. Tuesday July 16: *Morphine Sul-*

*fate, Four Milligrams per hour, by Intravenous Piggy-
back.* And there was the total, all added up properly,
268 milligrams over the past sixty-seven hours. Signed
and countersigned, at 4 milligrams per hour.

He shut the book and was out of the Medication
Room thirty seconds before Peter Martel finished his
work taping up the buttocks of Jeb Gist.

"This sure beats hell out of the doctors' cafeteria,"
Decker said as he took a huge bite of his pizza and
looked around the interns' sleeping quarters.

"Sure does," Skeeters mumbled. "Don't have to
look at dead weenies, either."

Decker smiled. "Dead weenies and stale buns . . ."

"Yup."

The two interns looked at each other from across
the small table as they chewed large chunks of Domi-
no's Pizza, brought to the Jail Ward by a delivery boy
five minutes before. They had learned early in the
month that big bites and fast chewing improved the
chances of finishing the food before the next case
came crashing out of the elevator.

Skeeters swallowed a section of pizza crust and felt
a scraping pain as it passed down the back of his
throat. He was developing a cold and could feel a
tired, aching sensation spreading throughout his body.
His throat was sore, his nose was clogged, and he had
that early feeling that his brain was becoming filled
with sludge.

He popped another piece of pizza into his mouth,
this one with a clump of mozzarella cheese hanging
from a slice of green pepper. It was not surprising that
he had picked up a virus, considering all the people
he was in close contact with on the Jail Ward. At least
the more serious infectious diseases, the blockbusting

viruses that could stop a career, were either very rare or required considerable effort to acquire.

Barbara had induced a promise, back when he had first announced that he would be applying to the County Hospital, that he would never, ever perform mouth-to-mouth resuscitation on any patients who stopped breathing for any reason. She had insisted on the promise with unusual determination. No particular disease was mentioned, but they both knew the one she feared the most. He gave her the promise she desired, and the matter was dropped.

"This has been a pisser of a month. How's your load so far?" Skeeters asked.

Decker snorted. "A 'good start' on the Jail Ward is anything less than ten patients before midnight. So far, I've seen three and sent three back to County Jail. The place is like a turnstile tonight. You'd think their infirmary could take care of some of these guys. How's your man Choo-Choo doing?"

"Ah . . . Choo-Choo." Skeeters smiled. Everybody always wanted to know how Choo-Choo was doing. Nobody had ever asked how Julia Jackson was doing, or how Jack Diamond's infected fracture was doing. Something about Spike Bond just seemed to pique people's attention. Skeeters swallowed another piece of pizza.

"Choo-Choo is doing fine. He's taking his medicine and he's even starting to talk a little."

"Really? What's he saying?" Decker leaned forward with interest and jammed another bite of pizza into his mouth.

"Well, I can *hand* him his cup of Thorazine now and he takes it."

"But what does he say?"

" 'Uh-h-h'!"

" 'Uh-h-h'?"

"Yup, 'uh-h-h.' He says it real weird-like. He kind of hunches his shoulders and grunts it out with a rumbling kind of sound. First time he said it, I jumped about three feet. Scared the hell out of me."

"Tried to choke you yet?"

"Nope. Hasn't tried to choke anyone since the psychiatrist disappeared and I snuck some Thorazine into his system. In fact, he's been real nice to me so far. Another week or so, and I think he'll become real civil-like."

"Yeah, and probably offer you some Thorazine just to be sociable." Decker's voice dropped to just above a whisper after gulping down the last piece of pizza. He leaned forward over the table again and quietly asked, "Anything new on Martel the Cartel?"

Skeeters stopped chewing, glanced at the shut door, and put his section of pizza back into the cardboard box. He looked down at the box for a moment, then stared hard at Decker. "The addict bastard took medicine from Julia Jackson. He let her die in pain. I'm really pissed about this, Steve. The guy has no compassion, he doesn't care who suffers so long as he can take the drugs . . . for whatever he's doing with them."

Decker pulled out a small black three-ring binder from his coat pocket and laid it on the table. "Put it in here, put everything in here and we'll nail him. Simple as that. I've already documented what I've got, ten pages so far. Just write the Trixie story—"

"Julia Jackson, Steve," Skeeters interrupted.

"Sorry, put Jackson's story in here, we'll get a couple more events and lay it all down on Dr. Marsh in another week or so. I think we can get him if we bring together enough data on the slimo."

"Okay," Skeeters said as he picked up his section

of pizza again. "We may also want to interview the drug tech that brings the stuff in."

"That funny-looking little red-haired guy? The one who brings the narcotics to the Jail Ward?"

"He's the one. Saw the name Esch on his coat. Rusty Esch or something like that. He and Martel were going at it, right outside the Medication Room. Heard Esch say something about the supply of some drug and Martel told him to 'close your fuckin mouth' or something to that effect. They were really ticked off at each other—clammed right up when I came by, though, so I never was sure what they were talking about."

"I'll set it up to talk with him early next week," Decker said. "Christ, he delivers the narcotics direct to the Medication Room; he must know something about how much is used and where it goes!"

"Have you heard of any of the other interns having any problems with narcotics not getting to their patients? This can't just be happening to us." Skeeters stood up and washed his hands at the sink in the corner of the room.

"Nope, they all just seem happy to be on the Jail Ward, no problems with medications."

"All except Tyra," Skeeters answered as he dried his hands and tossed the paper towel into the wastebasket. "I heard she caught one of the deputy sheriffs with some Hycomine syrup. When she was on call last time, she spotted the guy chugging a full bottle of the stuff."

"So? The guy probably had a cough. Nothing illegal about that."

"Nothing except that U.S.C./L.A. County Medical Center was the only name on the bottle, he didn't know who his doctor was, he didn't have a prescription for the stuff, and hydrocodone is a controlled substance."

Decker leaned forward. "What did she do?"

"She reached out and grabbed the bottle from him."

"Holy shit! She *took* it from him?"

"Took it and wouldn't give it back, saying she was going to report the incident to the hospital Pharmacy Committee, and that she was going to have the docs on that committee track down how he got the drug in the first place. Grossman tried to get her to report it to Dr. Marsh, but she stashed the bottle in her locker and said that the incident would be on the agenda of the next Pharmacy Committee meeting."

"Gutsy gal. That must have really pissed off the deputies," Decker said, grinning at the thought.

"To say the least. On top of that, she's been getting a little strung out, battling with Martel, dealing with that Hallbrook fire, and I heard she's having some problems with her fiancé."

"That Hallbrook thing is something I've tried to forget about. I really don't want to even think about what happened to Hallbrook." Decker stood up and kicked his chair up against the table. "Let me tell you, that just about finished me off, I damn near quit the whole internship that night. I screwed up, the rapist bastard died—"

"Okay, Steve, okay!" Skeeters held his hands up as Decker stopped. "Okay, you screwed up, and you learned about malignant hyperthermia, right? Tell me how many surgeons who are *graduating* from this place have ever heard of malignant hyperthermia? How many? I'll tell you, none. Not a damn one, unless he has *seen* it! And that's the whole point of this place—you see things and you learn from them. The next time you see somebody twitch and spike a fever while going under, you'll stop the surgery, you'll give Dantrium, and you'll impress the whole hospital."

A knock at the door was followed by a deputy's voice calling for Dr. Decker. Manuel Garcia, with cuts from multiple lacerations, was en route by paramedic ambulance from South Central Los Angeles to the Jail Ward. Dr. Decker was up for the next patient. "Should be here any minute," the deputy said as he opened the door and looked at the interns, "gonna have to be ready for this one." The officer, a short man with a large red birthmark covering the right side of his face, watched Decker jam the notebook back into his pocket.

"What's his problem?" Decker asked.

"Bleeding, bleeding bad."

"Any idea why he is bleeding?"

"Somebody cut him up pretty bad, and he's been drinking. S'all I know, Doc."

"Thank you." *Worse than useless,* Decker thought as he watched the man slowly amble back to his watch station. He walked across the hallway to the Prep Room and looked out the window for the twin red lights that would announce Garcia's arrival.

Skeeters wandered down the central hall in the direction of the Cage. Another 50 milligrams of Thorazine had been given to Choo-Choo an hour before, and his mind should be feeling the effects of the medicine by now, he reasoned.

Thirty feet away, Skeeters could see the massive shape of his patient moving back and forth across the Cage. Although he appeared to be moving slower and less aggressively, he was still breathing hard and his back and chest were covered with sweat. The intern pulled up a chair at his observation post in front of the bars and sat down to watch a few minutes of Spike Bond. The drinking cup had been tossed in the general direction of the bars; Skeeters carefully reached into the Cage and pulled it out. Skeeters looked down into the cup; it was completely empty—no orange juice, no ice. And no Thorazine.

It was apparent that Choo-Choo was undergoing a significant change for the better. Skeeters reached into his pocket, pulled out a pen and notepad, and began to scribble a swirl of observations about his patient. Choo-Choo wasn't crashing into the bars every time he reached the Cage limits—that was very significant. He was now holding his head high, both eyes alertly looking around instead of lowering his head to an angle that allowed his skull to act like a battering ram. He wasn't making grunting noises as he walked, and he had stopped wheezing. He was no longer bleeding, and the cuts on his arms and legs were beginning to heal. After ten minutes of scrutiny and furious writing, Skeeters finally put down his pen and paper and stood up.

On only 450 milligrams of Thorazine per day, or about ten times the dose required to put Skeeters completely under the table, Choo-Choo was almost beginning to look human.

At the other end of the Jail Ward, Decker was having a major problem. Manuel Garcia had arrived as programmed, but his progress from the prisoner elevator to the Prep Room had been abruptly halted by Sergeant Mel Grossman. The prisoner was sitting upright in the middle of the gurney, swathed in blood-soaked bandages from the paramedics, his eyes darting around at the collection of deputies around him, his hands securely handcuffed to the D rings at his side. Standing next to the gurney, Grossman was leaning forward, his jaw thrust out, his face inches from Garcia's nose.

"Garcia, why don't you just shut the fuck up!" Grossman snarled.

"Thank you for the advice, Officer." Garcia sounded almost happy, speaking with a buoyant tone in his voice. "But there are more considerations to the problem than I think you understand, and—"

"I don't want to hear more considerations, I just want you to shut your mouth. The arresting deputies tell me you don't know how to stop talking. You are arrested and what you say doesn't count."

"I don't have any problem with talking, Sergeant, I was just trying to explain that those people in the store made a mistake before I went through the glass, and that they just didn't understand the underlying situation, since I wasn't trying to *steal* anything, but they suspected me of the worst, without even giving me any chance to—"

"Shut the fuck up!" Grossman's face was getting red as he gripped the prisoner's jaw with his hands, squeezing until Garcia's lips puckered out.

"That's very painful, Sergeant," he squeaked out, "and it makes it difficult to carry on a conversation."

Decker stepped forward from the Prep Room and held up his hand. "This man is bleeding, Sergeant, and I think we should get him into the Prep Room for some suturing."

Grossman squeezed Garcia's jaw tighter until the prisoner let out a howl of pain and tried to pull his head away. Grossman turned and looked at Decker.

"Doctor, why don't you just go back into the Prep Room and wait for us to get this prisoner under control?"

Decker felt his heart beginning to pound. "I'm not going into the Prep Room or anywhere else right now, Grossman, and I think the handcuffs on this man have him under adequate control."

Garcia's puckered lips tried to move as the man worked to speak again. Grossman released the prisoner's face with a push and walked over to Decker.

"Who do you think you are, mister?" he said, glaring at the doctor. "You're not in charge of prisoner control, you're in charge of medical care. When we have an obnoxious prisoner, we're going to properly control him before he's yours. Is that difficult for you to understand, or should I get Dr. Marsh down here to explain it to you?"

Decker stared back at the sergeant. "You can get anyone you want down here, Grossman. This man is actively bleeding while he's sitting on that gurney, and while you are trying to get him under control!" Decker said angrily. "If you wait for him to stop talking, it'll be when he goes into a coma from hypovolemic shock. Are you waiting for him to bleed out before we can stop the problem? That's the dumbest damn thing I've ever heard of!"

The three other deputies standing near the prisoner looked eagerly at Grossman. They loved to watch this sort of thing. If there was one thing about Grossman they knew for sure, he would not take crap from any punk intern, especially this one who showed so little respect.

"I've been on this ward for sixteen years, mister," Grossman growled, "and I'm not going to put up with this shit. You're out of your league, Decker, 'way out of your league." He advanced a couple of steps toward the intern as Decker stood his ground. "This matter is going up to the director—"

"Good! Do it!" Decker said. "This is a Jail Ward and a hospital ward! The guy's bleeding! Go ahead and call Marsh!"

Grossman took another step toward the intern, his hands flexing into fists. The men stared at each other as Grossman dropped his voice to barely a whisper. "Okay, I am going to do just that, Decker. You don't know who you're up against." The deputy turned around and stormed away.

Forty-five minutes later, after listening to a long run of continuous verbiage from Manuel Garcia, Decker finally secured the last of seventy-two sutures that held the man together. Moving out of earshot, he sat down and wrote his report for the County Jail Dispensary, including the recommendation that they consider a therapeutic dose of Lithium for control of Garcia's manic-depressive disorder.

By three o'clock in the morning, Decker and Skeeters were numb. There had been no time for sleep as they treated the surge of patients continuously arriving from the streets of Los Angeles and from the County Jail. There was the wiry little pimp with a draining infection oozing pus from the right side of his neck. There was the pale red-headed burglar with glass fragments imbedded in the palm of his left hand. There was the gay 300-pound black artist with swollen and bleeding hemorrhoids. There was the bony alcoholic with a body infested with the burrows of hundreds of scabies mites . . . each scratched and clawed open and seeping dark pus. And there was the group of motorcyclists, admitted from Hollywood's Central Jail, each with the characteristic sallow complexion of advancing viral hepatitis from the friendly sharing of one particularly contaminated needle.

At 3:15, just as it appeared that both men would have a chance for a couple of hours' sleep, Kekoa Puuho from Hawaii was delivered to the Jail Ward by the Los Angeles International Airport Police. Aloha Airlines, Flight 577, had delivered him across the Pacific earlier that evening, complete with a plastic pouch holding 14 ounces of cocaine wrapped around his midsection. He could have easily left the airport without problems if he hadn't developed severe paroxysms of intractable coughing during the last hour of flight. When the cough had produced solid plugs of green mucus mixed with strings of blood, the woman seated next to him had taken exception to his presence. To placate her and to settle his cough, he had downed 4 tablespoons of Tussi-Organidin with Codeine along with two servings of Jack Daniel's.

He was able to leave the airplane without serious problems, but by the time he had managed to plant his unsteady feet on the airport's moving sidewalk, his mind was accelerating into a cloudy twilight zone. He held on to the moving handrail until he reached the end of the sidewalk; the stationary carpet dumped him flat on his face. He still might have crawled off to a waiting taxi if it hadn't been for the group of elderly Japanese on the sidewalk behind him. In less than five seconds, eight people had fallen onto him in a pile of thrashing arms and legs punctuated by loud groaning sounds. As the Airport Police rushed to help the tourists, Kekoa Puuho was found at the bottom of the pile, with white powder spread across his face and chest like someone had hit him with a bag of flour. A final cloud of white dust dropped across his shoes as he quickly staggered to his feet.

It was one of the quickest and slickest arrests the Airport Police had ever made. And if he hadn't coughed up a pint of blood in the backseat of the police car, the Jail Ward interns might have been spared Puuho's early-morning intrusion.

Skeeters was next up for the case, and as he walked into the Prep Room, it was apparent that Kekoa Puuho was a walking medical end-stage disaster. His body, a scarecrow structure of bones and anemic flesh, was perched quietly on the end of the exam table. His blue prisoner uniform was draped over chicken-wing shoulders that sagged out from below his thin neck. His legs, like a couple of twigs protruding from the end of his cotton pants, were mottled and blue, and his toenails were heavily infested with fungi that curled them skyward in a gnarled deformity. His eyes were glassy and unfocused, but he was turning his head back and forth with an unusual amount of curiosity at his surroundings. When he saw Skeeters, his eyes brightened and he asked, "You're my fucking doctor?"

"I'm your doctor," Skeeters answered, his fatigue temporarily suppressed as he surveyed the ruins of his new patient.

"Hell of a way for me to lose weight!" Puuho exclaimed as his thin lips parted to reveal crooked brown teeth with heavy deposits of black tartar protruding from his inflamed gums.

"*What* is a hell of a way to lose weight?" Skeeters asked. *Three o'clock in the morning, we're going to discuss diet.*

"Whatever it is that's making me lose weight!"

"What have you got?" *Just tell me what your diagnosis is,* Skeeters thought. *Gotta get some sleep . . .*

"I don't know what the fuck I got, Doc, besides nausea. But I've lost 43 pounds in the last six months. Ain't that a diet for you!" The gums and teeth were displayed again.

"Helluva diet," Skeeters mumbled as his mind scrambled to assemble the long string of questions that would review the 200 or 300 causes of weight loss.

Decker had been asleep in the interns' quarters for thirty-five minutes by the time Blake Skeeters finished his workup and quietly opened the door to the room. He dragged himself to his bed on the other side of the room and slowly kicked off his shoes. He winced at the creaking sound of old springs as he sat on the edge of the bed and finally lay back, flat on the sheet. He turned on his side, snuggled up to his pillow, and reached down to pull the blanket over his shoulders. He closed his eyes and curled up in a tight ball. Sleep, even an hour or two, would be so sweet . . .

"Damn! Goddamn it! Jesus Christ!" Skeeters hollered at the top of his lungs. "Oh, God!"

Decker bolted from the bed and turned on the overhead light. "What is it? What's going on?"

"I've stuck myself! I stuck myself in my leg!"

"You stuck yourself with a needle?"

Skeeters was standing at the side of his bed, staring at an expanding blood stain spreading across his right thigh. "Something's stuck my leg, Steve . . . it's still in there!" His hand reached into the pocket of his green pants and pulled out a 10-cc syringe with a bloody needle attached to the end.

"It's one of the medication injection needles. The cap must have come off in your pocket," Decker said. "Was it a clean needle? Oh, shit, look at your leg. You must have hit one of the subcutaneous veins." He ran to the bathroom and grabbed a fistful of paper towels as Skeeters stared at the blood soaking into his green trousers.

"Quick, drop 'em down. We'll put some pressure on it and stop the bleeder."

In a couple of minutes, the bleeding was controlled and the two interns examined the needle under the desk lamp. The thin, shiny stainless-steel hollow needle ended with a sharp point that held a drop of blood across the beveled hole.

"That's my blood," Skeeters said glumly as he looked at the needle.

"*Your* blood isn't the problem," Decker said quietly. "Look at this. There's blood in the inside of the syringe—this is a used needle . . . like contaminated."

Skeeters felt himself sweating as he began to breathe faster. A roar filled his ears as he slumped back in his chair and stared at the wall. "Contaminated? Oh, my God . . ." he said softly. "I've been drawing blood and giving my patients analgesics all night . . ."

"You're giving the prisoners shots? Why are you giving the shots? The nurse should be doing it."

"Can't trust the nurses, Steve. Not since Julia Jackson. Can't trust anybody around here to give the medication. So I just started doing it myself. Didn't want to make a big deal out of it."

Decker's distant voice sounded strange, like something from another world. "Whose blood did you draw tonight, Blake? Who did you give any shots to? Any idea whose needle this might have been?"

"Could have been anybody's," Skeeters said. "I drew blood on at least seven or eight people—the gay guy with hemorrhoids, the pimp with his draining ulcers, about half of that jaundiced gang of—"

"Which half?"

"I don't know! I was helping you with your half, remember?"

"They all looked the same to me," Decker said. "What about that last patient, the one from the airport, the Mahoo?"

"Mahoo?"

"Sorry, Hawaiian for homosexual, the Hawaiian gay guy?"

"Kekoa Puuho. The guy has been wasting away, by 43 pounds, from some kind of chronic disease . . ."

"Jesus, Blake. A gay guy with weight loss would have to have—"

"AIDS," Skeeters said in a flat monotone.

"AIDS is right at the top of the list. Or maybe malaria or syphilis. And I guess cancer is possible."

"I drew his blood, of course. Been using syringes ever since we ran out of Vacutainers yesterday. Puuho was the last one of the night. Also gave him a shot of Compazine for his nausea."

Decker pulled on his surgical greens and jammed his stethoscope into his pocket. "We'll figure out which prisoner it was later. Let's get you down to the emergency room. The minor trauma section has a protocol of some kind for needle sticks; the nurses are doing it to themselves all the time."

"Dr. Skeeters, right? Intern on the Jail Ward?" the emergency room resident gave the intern a quick looking-over.

"That's right, Blake Skeeters." He shifted his weight uncomfortably on the exam table and looked back at the resident. The emergency room physician looked like the identical twin of Charles Manson, serial killer. His head was a mass of hair, from his thick beard to the swirls of dark brown fur that covered the rest of his head. A pair of bright eyes looked out from beneath the dense patches of brown hair that formed his bushy eyebrows.

"I'm Fred Sanderson. Nice to meetcha and sorry about your problem," he said casually as he shook Skeeters's hand. "Contaminated needle stick? Where did it get you?"

"Right here, in my leg." Skeeters pointed to the discoloration that had darkened the right thigh of his surgical green pants. The blood had turned a black color, looking almost evil in the dim light of the emergency room. Skeeters felt a deepening sense of hopelessness. "Had it in my pocket and it poked through the material into my leg when I went to bed."

"Any idea whose needle it was?"

"It could have been any one of the several people, no way to tell for sure. I normally clip off the needle after I give a shot or draw blood, but somehow I didn't do it to this one."

"It's tough when you get into a rush. I know what it's like up there sometimes. I was on the Jail Ward last year, and it can be a real bitch. When was your last tetanus shot?"

"About ten years ago, I think."

"Have you completed the Hepatitis B vaccine program for interns?"

"Nope, just got the first shot last week."

"Had any recent tests for syphilis?"

"Nope."

"Any recent AIDS testing, HIV serology?"

"Nope."

"Ever get a transfusion, use drugs, have sex with a man, have unprotected sex with a prostitute?"

Skeeters's face reddened. "Oh, hell, yes I do all of those things, every day. And my pregnant wife does the same. We both share our needles, and when our baby is born—"

"Hey, take it easy, buddy. I'm sorry." Sanderson held up his hand. "I know this isn't easy. I just have to ask these questions to fill out the paperwork on this thing."

"The hell with the paperwork," Skeeters said with irritation. "Listen, I'm as straight as they come. I've had no exposure to anything, nor has my wife. Just tell me the bottom line: what do we do now?"

"Okay . ." Sanderson's voice softened. "We're going to take some blood. We're going to run an HIV test for AIDS, we're going to test you for syphilis, for Hepatitis B, and for Hepatitis C. I'm going to give you Hypertet for tetanus, I'm going to give you AZT, zidovudine, for AIDS, I'm going to give you Hepatitis B immune globulin for Hepatitis B, and just for the hell of it, I'll give you additional gamma globulin for anything else that may have gone into you. You'll have enough antibodies to hit everything but AIDS. We can even give you an antibiotic for staph, strep, or syphilis, if you'd like, but it isn't absolutely necessary."

"So I'll be safe from everything except AIDS . . ."

"That's right."

"Shit," Skeeters said, immediately regretting the epithet. *Never used to talk like that,* he thought.

"You should run an HIV test on anyone you admitted last night, anyone you used a needle on. If they're all negative, your chances of having been exposed to the virus will be about zip."

"And if any is positive?" The statement hung in the air as the thought of Barbara ran through his mind.

"If the tests are positive or even if they're negative, we'll need to see you back at the lab every couple of weeks or so to test you for seroconversion."

Seroconversion. Nice clean word, Skeeters thought. *Sounds like some kind of religion, not a death sentence that includes five or ten years of torture.*

Twenty minutes later, Skeeters was back on the Jail Ward, his arms sore from the multiple injections and his right thigh bandaged at the site of the puncture wound. Decker was fast asleep again in the interns' quarters, and the Prep Room area was deserted except for the duty deputy, who looked like he was ready to slide off his chair in a narcoleptic slumber.

Skeeters checked his watch. Five fifteen in the morning. Plenty of time. He collected nine Human Immunodeficiency Virus Test Consent Forms and began walking around the quiet Jail Ward, pen in hand, waking the prisoners one at a time.

*   *   *

Slowly climbing the stairs to his apartment, Skeeters wondered for the thousandth time why they had rented an apartment on the second floor. Twenty-two dollars less per month had seemed such an important factor, especially when they had seen how little was left after their move from Massachusetts. But it was becoming obvious that the savings wasn't worth the repeated long hikes up the steel staircase, especially for pregnant ladies like Barbara, and for anyone else who has gone thirty-six hours without sleep.

He swung the front door open and walked into the apartment. "Hi, honey, I'm home," he called out.

She was standing at the sink in the kitchen, rinsing the utensils she had used to prepare their dinner. A bright pink apron covered the front of her dress, her maternal bulge pushing out with a soft rise at the lower half of her abdomen. At the sound of his voice, her face lit up and she called out a welcome as she dried her hands.

When he walked into the kitchen, she knew immediately that something was wrong. The skin around his eyes was puffy from lack of sleep, as it had been so many times this month, and his shoulders were sagging as if he was carrying a great weight. She had seen him like this before in the last year of medical school, each time he put in an "all-nighter," and she knew he would recover rapidly after a few hours of deep sleep.

But his eyes . . . his eyes gave it away. He scarcely glanced at her as she gave him a fleeting peck of a kiss, and he looked away as she searched his face for an answer.

"Blake? What's wrong, honey?" She felt the bite of fear as he stepped back, took a deep breath and rubbed his bloodshot eyes. Finally, he looked at her face and reached over to gently stroke her forehead.

"Honey, it's been a very bad night. It's been an

awful night on the Jail Ward. We're going to have to talk."

With a screech of tires, Decker powered his Corvette into the long expansive driveway and roared up to a parking spot near the huge front door of Dr. Dillon Marsh's home.

It was a typical summer day in southern California, hazy and cloudy in the morning, slowly warming to the afternoon "burn-off" that allowed filtered sunlight to remove the chill from the air. Neither Decker nor Katie had tried to talk over the noise of the wind as they had crossed Los Angeles and accelerated up Pacific Coast Highway to the home tucked away in the Malibu mountain range. The return address had been scripted, in swirls of ornamental gold, across the back of the engraved invitation each Jail Ward intern had received two weeks before. Decker set the brake and they both climbed out of the car, pausing briefly to admire the panorama of the dark blue Pacific Ocean.

"My God, what a view!" Katie exclaimed as she studied a cluster of sailboats beating their way against the wind a mile off the coast. "Too nice a day to be socializing with the director of the Jail Ward. Why is he holding this little affair?"

"Nobody is quite sure," Decker said, standing at her side. "I heard he has a bash like this every month with the interns on the Jail Ward. Even gets a couple of emergency room docs to cover the thirteenth floor for the afternoon so nobody misses the event. Probably wants to impress us with the good life of doctors who make careers out of Penal Medicine, although there is some kind of rumor going around that he was partial heir, via multiple relatives, to the Hughes estate."

"Hughes? They had money?"

"Hughes, like in *Howard*. Like in *Spruce Goose,* like in enough money from his brother's, or sister's, or whatever the relationship is, inheritance to build nice homes."

Katie smiled. "A little fanatic about it all, don't you think?" she said.

Decker pushed the button on his security transmitter to lock and arm his car. "Definitely. Heard about a guy who missed it last year and couldn't get signed off for the month he had completed on the Jail Ward. Screwed up his residency plans and everything, only given credit for eleven out of twelve months as an intern."

"Well, in that case, I'm glad we're here," she said. "Although I can think of better ways—"

"Lots of better ways . . ."

"—to spend a Saturday afternoon."

Their attention was diverted by the sound of a car rumbling up the quiet street in the direction of the house. A battered dark blue Volkswagen Bug with out-of-state license plates finally came into view and turned into the driveway. A cloud of smoke belched out of the exhaust pipe as the protesting engine struggled painfully up the hill. The car finally squealed to a stop a couple of feet behind the shining Corvette, and Skeeters and Barbara climbed out.

"Blake Skeeters and Barbara Skeeters and little one"—Decker gestured toward Barbara's maternal bulge—"I'd like you to meet my friend, Katie Shields."

The ladies smiled and politely greeted each other as Decker gave Skeeters, who looked like he was entering the final stages of complete exhaustion, a firm pat on the shoulder. His smile was little more than a wince, and his pained expression looked as if he was suffering from severe internal distress. His cherubic face had lost its pleasant and happy appearance, his eyes were swollen and red, and his hands were cold and tremulous.

Dillon Marsh opened the massive front door before they could ring the doorbell and boomed out a welcome to his four guests. Walking with a commanding air of authority, *presidential,* Decker thought, he escorted them into a foyer of inlaid white Italian marble. The room was two stories high, with an immense crystal chandelier hanging 10 feet above their heads.

As they continued ahead, down two marble steps into one end of the huge sunken living room, they waved a greeting to other Jail Ward interns who were standing with drinks in hand or meandering about the room. Several expensive Oriental rugs covered the polished hardwood floor. The rich reds and golds matched the colorful 8-foot Chinese tapestries hanging on the walls. Heavily padded white Italian leather sofas and glistening contemporary tables of thick beveled glass were carefully positioned, and shiny modern art statues were strategically evident throughout the room, each on its own marble pedestal. The east wall of the room held an enormous stone fireplace with a roaring log fire; a pair of large paintings on either side depicted sleek Montecito polo ponies, ready for competition.

"Jesus," Decker said softly, "can you believe this?"

Dr. Marsh stood in front of the fireplace and welcomed them all with words of gracious hospitality, even smiling from time to time. They were free to "roam the house" and to "partake of the feast" laid out on the long white table near the pool and fountain. They were invited on this fine day in July so they may enjoy themselves in an atmosphere of relaxation. And, most significant of all, Dr. Marsh was personally pleased that they were all so kind as to take the time to come and visit his "humble residence on the hill."

"Give me a break . . ." Decker mumbled.

"Now, Steve, be nice," Katie said sweetly. "Barbara and I are going to explore this place while you boys chat, okay?"

"Okay with me. Don't get lost," Decker said as the two women enthusiastically departed down one of the halls that led from the living room. He turned to Skeeters and said, "You look like shit, my friend. Did you get any sleep last night?"

"Not much," Skeeters answered.

"How's your leg doing, healing up okay?"

"Seems okay."

"What can I get you to drink? Maybe a good cold brew will make you feel better."

"I don't drink, Steve, especially at times like this. But thank you anyway."

"A Coke? Or 7UP?"

"Maybe a Pepsi, but not right now."

Decker looked at him for a few seconds and finally asked, "Did you tell Barbara?"

Skeeters winced. "Soon as I got home yesterday."

"How'd she take it?"

"Bad, very bad." He was quiet for a moment, then added, "Remember I told you she had me promise not to resuscitate anyone mouth-to-mouth?"

"Sure, and you just told her you'd use an Ambu bag like we always do, right?"

"No, I just told her I wouldn't do it, that I'd be careful. I told her not to worry. And now this needle thing has her scared silly . . . and me too. We can't touch each other, we can't even look at each other. She's worried that our new baby will get it, that I will get it, hell, she's worried that we'll all get it. She's worried that we're all going to die of AIDS."

"Did you send off blood from everyone you saw Thursday night?"

"I came up with nine prisoners, total, that I could have conceivably given shots to or drawn blood from. All of them, except one, gave the okay for all the tests, including AIDS."

"Except one?" Decker asked angrily. "Who refused?"

"The worst of them all—the guy from Hawaii, Kekoa Puuho."

"The gay guy? The guy who's lost all that weight? You gotta be kidding!"

"He's been refusing the AIDS test for over a year now, he says, apparently worried that he has the disease. He just doesn't want to know."

"Well, just tell him you won't let him know the results!"

"I told him that already," Skeeters said. "He still refused, and he said if we do the test on him, he'll sue us all, individually, collectively, and every other way. He has all kinds of legal friends back on Oahu and he knows we can't do the test if he doesn't sign the consent."

"The miserable son of a bitch!"

Skeeters looked unhappy.

"Can I get you men something to drink?" Dr. Marsh walked up to them, his expression one of beaming congeniality.

"Scotch on the rocks for me," Decker said.

"Chivas Regal okay?"

"That would be excellent."

"And what can I get for you?" Marsh turned to Skeeters.

"Pepsi would be fine, thank you, sir," Skeeters replied.

"Okay, be right back." He smiled and headed for the bar in the corner of the living room where a man was serving drinks.

"What's the story on this guy Marsh?" Decker asked. Has he got a family, a wife, or anybody?"

"Word is, he's a bachelor and he is an ardent fan of Genghis Khan." Skeeters's puffy face winced out a smile.

"Genghis Khan?" Decker's jaw dropped.

"That's what they say. He's supposed to have a huge painting of Mr. Khan, in genuine Mongol warrior garb, hanging in front of a spotlight in his study, and a whole collection of suits of armor, complete with an authentic 3-foot saber that is over eight hundred years old. A couple of the senior residents were telling me last week that he believes he's a reincarnated Genghis Khan."

"You're kidding!"

"Here you are, gentlemen, scotch and Pepsi," Dr. Marsh said as he walked up and handed them their drinks.

"Thank you, sir," they both said respectfully.

"You're quite welcome." He looked closely at the interns. "Say, would either of you happen to know where Tyra Levy might be this afternoon? Did one of her patients have a problem?"

"I don't know, sir. She told me a couple of days ago that she'd be here, she was coming with her fiancé," Decker said.

"Okay, maybe she'll show up a little later. Why don't you browse around my home, make yourselves comfortable, and fill up on some of the good food I have outside on the deck. There's food enough for an army." He looked down at his drink, swirled the ice around in tight circles, and looked up at Decker. "Hear you and Mel Grossman got into it a bit back on the ward. You work everything out okay?"

"Yes, sir, I think we both reached an agreement

of sorts. He gets a little aggressive on the prisoners sometimes."

"Yes, yes, he does, but most of the time there's a need for it. If he goes overboard with anything, Decker, come to me; I'll take care of it. Don't try to settle it yourself, okay?"

"Yes, sir, and thank you, sir," Decker answered politely as Marsh turned to join the other guests. A moment later, their ladies arrived, gushing about the "fantastic" painting of a famous warrior, with an authentic sword "at least five feet long!" perched just under the painting. Wouldn't they just love to take a tour with them and see all the exciting things?

Beulah Priest hated to work on the B-2 level of the Medical Center. The first basement level was bad enough, but B-2 was so far underground that it was like working in a dungeon. Just knowing that she was so deep underground gave her the willies. The dead quiet of the long dark corridors, the gloomy glow of the dim neon lights covered with decades of dust, the cold stone walls with glistening beads of water slipping through the cracks, all of it put together kept her in a state of continuous low-level creeping fear. But she put in her eight hours every day, she took the ancient elevators back up to the first floor when her shift was finished, and she gave thanks to God that she made a good salary, especially when there was so much unemployment around these days.

After five years on B-2, Beulah knew her job. There were the storage carts and there were the laundry carts. The storage carts were filled with medical supplies from whatever level was printed on the side of the cart. Most of the time they just sat in various corners, gathering dust and waiting for somebody to load them back into the elevator. The storage carts were almost never much of a problem, since it was rare that anybody in the hospital called down for needed supplies.

The laundry carts, however, were a completely different story. They were always coming or going, always needing to be filled or emptied with clothing, or surgical drapes, or curtains, or anything else that might need to be washed from one of the hospital wards. But Beulah knew how to keep it all under control—she knew where each cart was at any point in time, she knew what was inside each cart, and she knew where each cart needed to go at any time during her shift. And she had learned long ago that the harder she worked, the less fearful the B-2 level became.

She only had eight minutes left before she could punch out her time card for another night of completed work. It was always more difficult to work on a Saturday night, but her four children were now grown, her husband had lost interest in any meaningful nighttime entertainment and, the truth of the matter was, there just wasn't much else to do on a Saturday night but work. She looked at her watch again. Seven minutes. Two minutes to collect the last carts for the next shift, one minute to walk slowly to the elevator, two minutes to wait for the elevator, and a final two minutes to amble to the time clock. Perfect.

She pushed the last two carts together in the direction of the laundry pickup, casting a quick look down the long corridor just to make sure there were none left. There never were, that was part of her expertise, but she always looked anyway.

And that is why she was surprised to see a lone cart, almost a hundred yards away at the far end of the north corridor. She shook her head, knowing her timing would now be off by at least three minutes. Her pace quickened as she strode toward the cart. It was the same as the rest: open at the top, canvas wrap around the outside, three wheels, and the large letters LAUNDRY stenciled on the side. She sighed and began to pull the cart in the direction of the others.

She jumped like she had been shot, her hand flying off the cart, her eyes opening wide with alarm. There was too much weight for a laundry cart. She walked slowly to the edge of the open cart and looked in. Laundry was inside, crumpled greens like the interns wear. She shifted the top layer of clothes to the side and discovered a white coat, with a name tag still attached. Damn! They were always telling the employees to take off their name tags before they sent their work clothes to the basement for washing. She looked closely at the tag.

RUSTY ESCH, PHARMACY TECH

She pulled on the white coat to remove the tag, and that was the moment when a layer of green cloth shifted away to expose the moonlike face of a young red-haired boy. His sightless eyes stared directly at her and didn't blink at the longest and loudest scream ever heard echoing down the B-2 corridors of L.A. County Hospital.

"Mr. Puuho? Mr. Puuho? Would you wake up, please?"

The prisoner stirred and rolled to his right side, staring into the dark. "Who is it? What do you want?"

"I'm sorry to wake you, sir." A penlight flashed on, shining light on a clipboard held by a young man standing at the bedside. A surgical mask was stretched across the lower half of his face and a surgical paper cap covered the top of his head. "Kekoa Puuho, right?"

"Almost right, goddamn it! It's 'Poo-*oo*-ho' not 'Poo-ho'! What do you want? And what are you doing with that mask on your face?"

"Oh, I'm sorry, sir, this is a surgical mask they require us to wear when we're on the wards—aerosolized bacteria risks they're trying to protect us from. Just last week, one of the aides was exposed to tubercu—"

"I don't care what your aide was exposed to! What do you want with me?"

"I'm really sorry to wake you up, sir, but your doctor wants your magnesium deficiency corrected before any arrhythmias develop. I'm from the phlebotomy branch of the lab downstairs, and the order just came in from Dr. Skeet—" The light popped on again for five seconds. "Sorry, Dr. Skeeters. He was worried about your magnesium that just surfaced on the SMAC panel, and he's ordered a stat infusion of 2 grams mag sulfate into your veins to straighten out the problem. Have to start it right now, sir. Should be all done by eight or nine o'clock in the morning."

"Can't it wait until later, for Christ sake? It's the middle of the night!"

"I'd be delighted to wait until the morning, although I'll probably catch hell from Dr. Skeeters, since magnesium arrhythmias often cause sudden seizures and death. Your level is only 0.7 milligrams per deciliter and it should be above 1.3 milligra—"

"Who cares what it is? It's probably been that way for years."

"Oh, no, sir, you would be having seizures and heart arrhythmias, and you would certainly be dead right now. Or, possibly, you would have developed brain destruction and vegetating—"

"Okay, okay! Run the damn stuff in. Just don't draw any more blood on me, and be damn sure you don't run any tests for AIDS!"

"Yes, sir. In fact, Dr. Skeeters has a standing order on your chart that no AIDS tests are to be drawn. Is that still your wish, sir?"

"Fuckin-A, no tests!"

A small exam light was rigged next to Kekoa Puuho's bed, shining on the upper surface of his extended right arm. A tourniquet was wrapped around his biceps, and a tiny needle with two plastic wings on either side was inserted into a ropy vein that ran down the front of his arm. As the needle popped into the vein, it was taped into place and dark red blood began to flow down the plastic tubing to a syringe held outside the field of light.

"What's that thing you got in my arm?" Puuho asked.

"That's a butterfly syringe," Mr. Puuho. We'll be able to give your mag sulfate through it, soon as I make sure the line is able to flow freely."

"Looks like it's flowing just fine, let's get this over with."

"Yes, sir, just a moment more and we'll be ready to do it." A dark band of sweat began to darken the front of the man's surgical cap as the syringe slowly filled to the 10-cc mark. *Anything less than 10 just wouldn't be enough—that fact had been made clear by the lab a thousand times.* The tourniquet was released and a line running from the plastic bag with $MgSO_4$ stamped on its side was connected to the needle that led into the prisoner's vein. The 10-cc syringe, filled with warm fresh blood, was capped and quickly pocketed in the greens and out of sight. A few seconds later, the tubing was taped to his arm and the magnesium began flowing into the patient.

"There you are, sir, all set now, you may go back to sleep now."

" 'Bout time," Puuho said as he rolled over and closed his eyes.

As the man stood and walked away from the bed, a needle was connected to the end of the blood-filled syringe and was quickly punched through the rubber cap of a red-topped vacuum tube. For the next minute, while he walked down the central corridor toward the Prep Room, the blood swirled from the syringe into the tube until it was completely filled. In the Prep Room, he carefully clipped off the needle and dropped the empty syringe into one of the large red plastic hazardous-waste containers. He took off his face mask, stuck the tube filled with blood into the pocket of his surgical greens, and took the elevator down to the first floor, where he followed the gray line to the main clinical laboratory.

"Have some blood for an HIV test," he said as he gave the tube to the clerk.

"This is an inpatient?"

"Yes, this is an inpatient."

"What ward?"

"You don't need to know what ward. Just run the test."

The clerk shrugged his shoulders. "Okay, all the same to me. Let me give you the number." He scrawled an eight-digit number across the white label on the side of the tube and an identical number on the top of the Human Immunodeficiency Virus Confidential Report Form. The information was entered into a Confidential HIV Log Book.

"Should have the report by next Wednesday," he said as he closed the book and handed a copy of the form to the intern. "Just call and give us this number, the date of the test, and we'll tell you the results, Doctor."

"Mission accomplished," Decker whispered as he climbed under the covers.

Katie Shields stirred from deep sleep and opened one eye just enough to see Decker lying next to her, his face barely visible in the dark room. "Mm-m-m, nice work, honey," she said sleepily, reaching out to embrace him. "Oh-h-h . . . you don't have anything on . . ."

"Didn't have time for pajamas," he replied innocently. He reached over to her and began caressing her thigh as she turned and moved closer to him.

"I guess that's okay," she said. "I won't let you get cold." As his warm hands reached under her nightgown and stroked her back, she closed her eyes with pleasure and pressed up against him. His hand traced a leisurely trail around to her breasts, where her nipples responded quickly to his light touch. "This is so early in the morning," she said, feeling a warm glow of desire spreading through her body. "Are you sure you're not too tired?"

"Oh, no . . ." he said softly. "Not too tired, just right. Besides, we don't have to do anything. Just think of this as kind of like a physical exam . . ."

" 'Kind of like a physical exam,' " she mimicked as she reached down to hold his hardness in her hands. "*My* exam indicates that you seem to have a big problem here."

"And, Doctor, what can you do for my big problem here?" he asked. "Is there a cure?"

"I have exactly the right medicine for you," she said with a smile as she pulled her nightgown over her head.

Chapter 9

By the time Blake Skeeters's open hand had slammed down to crush his alarm clock, Barbara already had a cup of hot coffee ready for him. Holding his cup, she sat down on the bed next to him as he stretched, blinked his eyes, and struggled to awaken. For Skeeters, the waking process had always been difficult, always requiring greater energy than for Barbara. It was like trying to clear away an impenetrable fog that seemed to cling to each brain cell until an extraordinary amount of time and effort forced his brain to start functioning. He glanced over at her and felt a warm contentment at her beauty that was enhanced by the morning light.

And then he remembered his right leg.

He looked down at his thigh. It still hurt a little, although the puncture wound had been healing nicely and was showing no signs of infection. Today, or tomorrow at the latest, he would learn the preliminary AIDS test results from the eight samples he had sent off. If any was positive, he would have to sweat seroconversion for the next three to six months. If they were all negative, he would still have to sweat, since the Aloha guy, the gay guy who had lost 43 pounds, hadn't allowed his blood to be tested.

"Waking up, honey?" Barbara asked as she handed him the coffee.

"Slowly, very slowly . . . as usual," he said.

"Take your time, the coffee will help."

They usually set the alarm to go off earlier than necessary to allow enough time for Skeeters to complete his awakening process. Whatever time the alarm was set for, Barbara always seemed to be already awake—it was one of her special talents.

He sat up in bed and took a sip of the freshly brewed coffee. He could understand her fear. She had tried not to show it, to accept the fact that there was now a risk—a small risk, according to all scientific evidence—that he might develop the AIDS disease, and that there was absolutely nothing that either of them could do about it.

But the fear of his possible contagious state was the additional terror that affected every gesture of affection between them.

He had tried to picture what it would be like to live with someone who had AIDS. How close could you get without thinking, again, once again, a thousand times a day, about the virus? And any thought of AIDS would be more emotional than scientific. The worry would affect every touch, every embrace. The question was always there: how intimate can I get without catching it? Sex was now out of the question, even with a condom, since condoms can fail, everyone knew that. Better not to take the risk. A kiss? Not without the chilling fear that the kiss would be the one in a million that would transmit the virus. How can you enjoy a kiss with someone who may have a fatal virus in their mouth? Just the thought of the virus kills the desire that allows for a satisfying intimate relationship.

And then there's the baby inside. The vulnerable baby . . .

Skeeters quickly sipped his coffee again as he thought about his life insurance policies.

The engine roared as the Corvette accelerated down the on-ramp onto the Glendale Freeway. As he merged with the traffic and eased into the fast lane, Decker glanced at Katie, checking to ensure that her seat belt was fastened. He had placed the top of the car behind the seats before they left, and the wind howled through the interior. He loved the excitement of being in control of such magnificent, high-performance machinery. With the thunder of the engine, the high-speed flashing of the center divider posts, and the howling of the wind through the open car, the feeling was something very close to orgasmic.

"Do you ever worry about the California Highway Patrol?" Katie hollered over the noise of the wind.

"Sure. I worry about them all the time," Decker answered. "But I'm only going seventy and I'm staying with the flow of traffic."

He studied the rearview mirror, looking for any ominous black-and-white silhouettes. *They always love to pull over Corvettes,* Decker thought. Not that Corvettes necessarily move so fast, it's just that they look like they are. The freeway behind them was relatively empty, and only a few cars could be seen, all moving along at about the same speed.

He was startled by the flash of a light from a car in the second lane, far behind them. On closer inspection in the mirror, though, Decker could see that it was just sunlight reflecting off the grille of an older gray car, some kind of a Ford, he thought. He smiled sheepishly and took one last look at the freeway behind them. No police cars in sight.

Eight minutes later, he was moving in and out of traffic on the Golden State Freeway, positioning him-

self for the Mission Road off-ramp that led to the
County Hospital. As he made the final lane change to
exit the freeway, there was another flash of light in
the rearview mirror.

The same gray Ford was about 60 yards behind
them, in the process of changing lanes into the exit
lane.

"What the hell . . ." Decker mumbled as he considered the odds. Eight minutes, two freeway changes,
at least six lane changes since he last saw the car.
Chances had to be close to zero that the same car
would just happen to be behind him—unless the driver
also happened to work at the County Hospital or at
the U.S.C. Medical School. That would explain it, and
it was approaching the eight o'clock starting time for
a few thousand employees.

Decker exited the freeway at Mission and watched
the Ford follow behind him. He waited at the stoplight
at the end of the off-ramp, and when the light turned
green, he powered his car into a left turn, through the
intersection, and abruptly back up the on-ramp and
onto the freeway again.

Katie looked around, confused. "Where are we
going?" she asked. "The hospital's back that way."

"I know. We're going back on the freeway, I'll explain in a moment," Decker answered as he studied
the rearview mirror. The Ford had been trapped behind several cars in the middle of the intersection. A
white cloud of burning rubber suddenly steamed out
of its rear tires and surrounded the car as it accelerated around the congestion and up the on-ramp behind them.

"There's somebody following us, Katie. Gray Ford.
Tighten your seat belt."

Katie looked behind them, searching for the car as
Decker stomped the pedal to the floor and passed

a cluster of vehicles behind a slow-moving eighteen-wheeler.

"Who is it?" Katie called out.

"I don't know, but he's a pretty good driver with a very hot car," Decker said as he watched the Ford moving down the emergency parking strip on the right side of the freeway, passing the traffic and finally moving to the fast lane, into position again a half mile behind their car.

"Why don't we just let him catch up? See what he wants," Katie asked innocently.

"I don't think he wants to just talk to us, Katie. I'm going to get off the freeway again," he said as he crossed four lanes and exited at Fourth Street. Closing the distance behind them, the Ford swerved around traffic to line up for the exit. Two hundred yards down the off-ramp, Decker lifted his foot from the brake, stomped the gas pedal to the floor, and jammed the steering wheel hard to the right. The Corvette immediately bounced off the pavement, and as Katie let out a shrill scream, they hit the roadside dirt and came to a halt after performing a perfect 180-degree turn in a cloud of dust and burning rubber.

"Steve! What are you doing!" Katie said.

"One last quick thing here and we'll be rid of this guy!" Decker yelled as they watched the Ford coming down the off-ramp, followed closely by a stream of cars and commercial trucks.

"What last thing are you talking about?"

"Hang on real tight!" Decker floored the gas pedal and accelerated his car up the off-ramp along the emergency parking strip, in the wrong direction. They caught a quick glimpse of the driver of the Ford as he passed: he was a large man with red hair who snapped his head to watch the Corvette flash by on his car's right side. Katie screamed, "Steve, look out! We're going the wrong way!"

"Not for long!" Decker shouted as he jammed the wheel to the right, squealed into another 180-degree turn in a cloud of burning rubber, and joined the flow of traffic again on the exit, three cars and one truck behind the Ford.

"He can't follow us when we're following him," Decker hollered with a big grin.

"I don't think this is so funny," Katie said indignantly. "In fact, this whole thing scares the hell out of me."

"Try to get his license number," Decker told Katie as they closed in behind the Ford and followed it for three blocks through the Boyle Heights residential area.

"I'm trying to. There's mud all over the back of his bumper, I can't see a thing."

As they approached the back of the car, the Ford suddenly squealed into a tight right turn and accelerated away from them, down an on-ramp onto the Santa Monica Freeway.

"Adios, amigos, we're off to work," Decker exclaimed as they watched the car disappear.

"It's about time," she responded. "My God, Steve."

At the next intersection, he made a left turn and headed for the hospital. Five minutes later, they pulled into the Pediatric Pavilion parking lot. Decker reached over and opened the door for her.

"Thank you, sir, and thank you for bringing me to work this morning. What a pleasant drive! Jesus!" She held out her hands. "Look at this . . . I'm still shaking!"

"You're shaking? I'm the one who had to do the driving. I'd just like to know who the character was."

"Next time, Steve, just stop and we'll find out."

* * *

"Dr. Marsh, there's a call for you on 3, a Mr. Bradshaw," the intercom squawked.

Dillon Marsh reached over and pressed down the intercom's lever. "Who is Mr. Bradshaw?"

"He says he has to talk to you right now, sir," the secretary said. "Says it's very important, something about Tyra Levy."

"Okay, I'll take it."

He released the intercom's lever and leaned back in his chair. He squeezed his eyes tightly shut and slowly massaged his temples.

A minute later, the intercom squawked again. "Dr. Marsh? The call's waiting."

He leaned forward and picked up the telephone.

"Dr. Marsh here."

"Dr. Marsh? This is Tom Bradshaw, Tyra Levy's fiancé." The man's voice was deep and strong but was spoken with anguish.

"Yes?"

"The police have just notified me that she—Tyra was just found dead in her apartment. She apparently overdosed on something. Some drug"—his voice cracked—"some drug that she took last night."

"This is terrible," Dr. Marsh said with distress. "I am very sorry to hear about this. She was a fine doctor and a very sensitive person." He took a deep breath and let it out slowly. "Has she been despondent lately?"

"No. Well, yes. Upset would be more like it. She was very upset about something, some incident that happened there several days ago. She didn't want to talk about it much . . . she tried to make a joke out of it, something about the 'barbecue case' or something like that, somebody—a patient—was ignited and burned to death."

"That was a very difficult case for everyone, all of the interns were upset. Did she leave a note?"

"I don't know. The police are looking all over her apartment. The county coroner is there too. They won't even let me in." His voice broke again. "I just wanted you to know. I'm going to call her family, her mother in Montana. If she left anything there at the hospital, would you send it to me?"

"Certainly, Mr. Bradshaw. My secretary will take your address, and I'll send you anything she has here. Again, I'm very sorry, she was a wonderful young lady."

"Thank you, sir."

Dr. Marsh placed the call on hold and pressed down the lever on his intercom.

"Mr. Bradshaw is holding," he said into the intercom. "Please take his address, and send Sergeant Grossman to my office."

"Good morning, Mr. Puuho," Skeeters said quietly as he walked into the prisoner dormitory.

" 'Morning, Doc," Kekoa Puuho answered sourly from his bed. "How's your leg, where that needle got you?"

"My leg's doing fine."

"No hard feelings about that AIDS test?"

"No hard feelings," Skeeters answered as he stood next to the bed and opened the man's chart, reviewing his blood pressure and temperature from the night before. The intern was wearing a fresh pair of surgical greens, starched and ironed that morning by Barbara. His pockets were jammed with sterile needles and syringes, a stethoscope and reflex hammer, and the ever-present *Washington Manual*.

Puuho was lying back against his pillow, his right arm connected by three feet of plastic tubing to a bottle with $MgSO_4$ stamped on the side. "When ya gonna take this thing out of my arm?" Puuho said, pointing to the intravenous line. "I'm right-handed, you know, real pain in the ass to have this stuck in my right arm. Had to drag this with me to take a piss this morning. Fuckin' pain in the ass," he repeated.

Skeeters looked at the bottle of intravenous fluid and, without saying a word, looked back at the chart. He flipped through several pages until the SMAC chemistry panel appeared.

"Magnesium level is . . ."

"I already know that, Doc. 'It's low Mr. Poo, gotta raise it above one point something,' like the man with the mask said at three fucking o'clock in the morning."

"Like who said?"

"Like that asshole from the flea-bottom division of the lab said."

Skeeters read the label on the bottle of intravenous fluid again and looked back at the chart. The orders had been neatly signed, and it *was* at three o'clock in the morning.

"The 'flea-bottom' division? Oh, from the *phlebotomy* division," he said. "Should be able to get it out in a few minutes, soon as the electrolytes have gone in."

"Well, I don't like—"

"How's your cough?" Skeeters interrupted.

"It's okay, Doc, not like it was on the plane yesterday. Christ, I thought I'd never stop."

Skeeters asked a few more questions and began to examine him. If anything, the prisoner looked skinnier than he had the day before, his ribs sticking out from his chest, his protruding hip bones covered with thin, tight skin. At the rate the man was losing weight, Skeeters estimated that he would become bed-bound within a week and would probably be dead within the next month, if some kind of treatment wasn't started pretty quickly. The best clue so far had been that 3-centimeter shadow on his chest X ray, looking like a malignant spider, sitting in the center of the upper lobe in his right lung.

"Blake?"

Skeeters looked up to see Dr. Eric O'Conner standing in front of him. "Eric, how's it going?" he said.

"It's going bad, real bad." His voice dropped to a whisper. "You know I'm paired up with Tyra Levy this month, right?"

"Of course."

"Well, I didn't see Tyra on Saturday, she didn't go to Marsh's party yesterday, she and I are supposed to be on call tonight, and there's no sign of her yet today. She has about three or four patients, and she hasn't seen any of them for the past two days.

"Did you try her at home?"

"About an hour ago, but there wasn't any answer. Another weird thing, I was just in the interns' sleeping quarters, and Tyra's locker was wide open and empty."

"We better report this to Dr. Marsh. Did you try to reach her fiancé?"

"Who knows where to find him? She never talked much about him . . ."

The loudspeaker abruptly blared out Gerald Brodie's loud, fingernails-on-the-blackboard voice, announcing that a general meeting of all interns would take place outside the Prep Room in twenty-two minutes, at "Zero Niner Fifteen hours."

"Guy thinks he's a combat pilot," O'Conner mumbled.

"In his world," Skeeters said dryly, "he *is* a combat pilot."

"I'll ask around and see if anyone else has seen her, and, if not, we'll talk to Dr. Marsh after the meeting, okay?"

"Okay, Eric. By the way, have you seen Steve Decker?"

"He just walked in, a few minutes ago, late for morning rounds. He doesn't know where Tyra is either . . ."

For the next fifteen minutes, Skeeters raced through his work on Kekoa Puuho. The intravenous line was removed, his skin was tattooed with tuberculosis and cocci skin tests, his sputum was collected for cultures and cell examination, and arrangements were made for a consult by a specialist in lung diseases.

The seven interns gathered in front of the Prep Room at 9:15 A.M. and talked quietly among themselves as they waited for Dr. Marsh. Skeeters spotted Decker and walked over to him.

"How's it going, Steve?" He tossed out a quick, self-conscious little wave.

"Not too good, my friend," Decker said. "Anybody been chasing you lately?"

Skeeters looked at him blankly. "Chasing me?"

"Like in a car, a Ford, to be specific."

"Not that I know of. What's going on?"

"Somebody tried to follow me this morning, when I was taking Katie to the Peds Pavilion—some guy, a tall guy with red hair who looked like he was about forty years old, stuck behind me for about ten minutes. Acted like he really didn't care if I knew he was there or not . . . really weird."

"So what did you do?"

"Did a couple of 180's, then I followed him. He didn't like that, so he bagged on out of there. It all wouldn't amount to much except that Katie was pretty shook up."

"Did you get a license number?"

"Couldn't, he had it concealed. Probably no big

thing, just keep an eye on who's behind you for the next few days . . ."

"Okay, thanks for the warning. Speaking of strange things, any idea who the masked bandit was last night who took care of my patient's magnesium deficiency?"

"Masked bandit?" Decker looked innocent.

"Mr. Puuho called him a masked 'anal sphincter', or something to that effect, but the rest of the description sounded like you."

"Ah, Mr. Pooho . . ."

"No, Mr. Puuho, like 'Poo' followed by 'oo,'" followed by 'ho' . . ."

Decker reached into his breast pocket. "You mean, Mr. 684–73–204?" He handed him the Confidential Human Immunodeficiency Virus Report Form. "Just call this number"—he pointed to the telephone number across the bottom of the page—"give them this identification number up at the top here, also known as Mr. Poo-oo-oh, and you will get a yes or a no regarding HIV." He looked at Skeeters's face. "I hope it's a no."

"Thank you, Steve, this is real nice of you to do this. I appreciate it very much. I thought you had been up to something when I found Puuho this morning with a liter of mag sulfate pouring into his veins."

"Fair exchange . . . he gets his magnesium and you get your results."

"Excellent, and everybody's happy. I'll let you know what happens."

Conversation died as Dr. Marsh walked briskly into the Jail Ward corridor and stopped in front of the interns, standing like a commanding officer ready to address his troops. His white eyebrows drew together and his voice was loud and strong in the enclosed space.

"I have received a call this morning that Dr. Tyra

Levy was found dead in her apartment. She appears to have died from an overdose of medication. The authorities are making every effort to precisely determine the cause of death."

Decker and Skeeters both looked at each other with disbelief as Decker whispered, "What the hell! Tyra is dead?"

"Jesus Christ!" Skeeters said through clenched teeth.

Dr. Marsh continued. "She was apparently despondent after the recent death of Theodore Hallbrook several days ago . . ."

"No way," Decker said quietly. "She was stressed, but she didn't kill herself. Not over Hallbrook."

"I can't believe this," Skeeters said. "Something else is going on."

"Marsh is trying to blame it on me. Hallbrook died from his hyperthermia, I did everything I could to save him. Marsh isn't going to drop *this* thing on me after everything else with Hallbrook. Damn!"

"That case and the stresses of internship apparently led to this unfortunate event," Marsh continued. "This is not the first time, and probably not the last time, an intern has struggled to deal with the psychological effects of excessive stress."

He looked around at the group of interns. "I want to encourage any of you who may be feeling excessive stress to let me know. I want to help any of you who need it. Dr. O'Conner, you'll be paired up with one of the minor trauma emergency room physicians for any admissions this final week. That is all. You may return to your work." He turned and briskly walked out of the Jail Ward.

"God, I hate the morgue. This is a terrible place," Skeeters said as he looked around and winced at the acrid formaldehyde fumes.

"Pretty nasty all right," Decker agreed. "Foster said they'd be through by now."

The room was gloomy and musty, with an old battered table covered with pathology magazines dominating the center. There was only one window, facing north, entirely covered with flat black acrylic paint that was peeling away in small dusty flakes. The walls were covered with deep shelves extending from the floor up to the ceiling, 10 feet overhead. Thousands of glass bottles were stacked on the shelves, each with a corroded cap, each with a label displaying a nine-digit number on the front, and each containing a formaldehyde-soaked tissue specimen from a human body.

The door behind them was shut and locked, its frosted glass giving only a blurred view of the activities within the adjacent room. And that was just fine for the interns, since at that moment the senior U.S.C./L.A. County Hospital pathologist and three pathology residents were conducting an autopsy on Dr. Tyra Levy. The interns could hear the occasional sound of muted conversation, intermittently punctuated by the chilling whine of the pathologist's Stryker saw, grinding its circular blade through the bones of the skull and the spine.

"You'd think they could ventilate this place a little," Skeeters said with a shudder. "Who is this guy Foster, and how do we know he is going to tell us anything?"

"Benjamin Foster is a first-year resident in pathology and I've known him since we started medical school four years ago. He's just going to tell us the preliminary pathological diagnosis on Tyra, that's all. He should be able to tell us in a few minutes."

"Couldn't he find a better place to talk to us than here?"

"Steve, this is Foster's home. This is where he does his work, and this is where he meets other docs who want to talk about a case. Besides, I think he likes to stress people with these bottles of body parts." Decker looked at the jars stacked on the shelves around the room.

"Well, it gives me the creeps," Skeeters said.

"You know, this thing with Tyra really pisses me off. She didn't do this to herself, something was done to her. She was spooked after the barbecue case, but she wasn't any worse off than the rest of us. She was getting stressed out but I don't think she was that depressed. Goddamn it, she just didn't look like someone thinking about suicide."

"Sometimes people look better once they make the decision," Skeeters observed.

"Fine, but it just doesn't fit for Tyra, not with her internship established and rolling along, not with a fiancé waiting to marry her, not with everyone liking her, not with good health . . . hell, she had everything going her way. It just doesn't fit."

The Stryker shrieked again, cutting through more bone. Both interns paused and stared at the glass that covered the upper half of the door.

"Christ," Decker muttered.

Skeeters gulped and said, "If your friend Foster isn't here in the next two minutes, I'm leaving. I can't stand this place."

"He'll be here shortly, Blake. Hang on, it'll be worth it to hear what he has to say."

"Okay, two minutes. Did the Julia Jackson story I wrote up sound okay?"

"Julia Jackson?"

"Trixie, Steve. Remember, the morphine she didn't get? I wrote it up in your black notebook."

"Ah, the gal who was stroked out from her carotid

injection. I did read it and had to work hard to suppress the desire to strangle Martel, the son of a bitch. Trixie's story is the best evidence we have so far about the narcotics diversion. The DEA will love it, I hope."

"Dr. Marsh will hate it," Skeeters said. "Especially the lab report showing zero morphine in her blood while the nurse is supposed to be pumping a continuous infusion into her."

"You know"—Decker brightened—"the hospital Pharmacy Committee would be very interested in that case—maybe we should send the results to them, too."

"Hell, Steve, that's the committee Tyra was going to report to. You know, she was going to report that event where she confiscated the narcotic cough medicine from the deputy sheriff."

"That's right, I forgot about that. Well," Decker said. "The committee might consider the death of an intern who was about to give them information about drug use more than just a little interesting."

"You know where she stashed that hydrocodone, that Hycomine syrup she took from Grossman's deputy? She stashed it in her locker on the Jail Ward. Her locker which is now empty, thanks to somebody."

"Thanks to the Sheriff's Department, you can bet," Decker said.

"No doubt."

"Hey, look at that, I thought I was being watched. One of the bottles has an eyeball in it. Look at that thing, isn't that the damnedest thing you ever saw?" He pointed to a smaller bottle in the corner holding an eyeball with four inches of pearly white optic nerve extending straight out behind it.

"I think I'm going to be sick," Skeeters said as he stood up to leave the room.

"Wait, just don't look at it, Blake, and it won't

bother you. Foster will be here any second." He grabbed Skeeters's arm and sat him in a chair at the end of the table. "By the way, I added another three pages of narcotic discrepancies I found in the nursing log to our black book," Decker said. "Martel doesn't seem to be able to add milligrams. The total amount of narcotics dispensed consistently adds up to more than the total per patient."

"Great, just like with Julia. Only he didn't give her anything, the bastard."

"And that's where the matter of the pharm tech, Rusty Esch, gets interesting," Decker observed, "since he delivers the narcotics from the first-floor pharmacy." Skeeters glanced at the bottle with the eyeball, then quickly looked back as Decker continued. "Something has happened to him, but nobody will talk about it. I asked the director of pharmacy and he just clammed up, not a word. I know for a fact that the little twerp hasn't worked since last Saturday. He was supposed to be at work today, but everybody says that he won't be coming in today. Or tomorrow, or apparently in the near future. It's really weird, and so I added it to the book."

"Where are you keeping it?"

Decker patted his side pocket. "Right here, it stays with me at all times. Hell, I have over twenty-five pages of hot stuff here."

Their attention was diverted to the door as a lanky man with a face like Abraham Lincoln entered the room. Skeeters caught a glimpse of a pair of legs at the end of a stainless-steel table in the autopsy room behind the man.

"Hello, Ben," Decker said. "This is Blake Skeeters, on the Jail Ward with me. We were both friends of Tyra Levy, and we really need your help on this one."

Foster solemnly nodded a greeting to Skeeters and

sat down as he pulled off his blood-stained gloves and tossed them into the trash can. "No problem, just keep whatever I say to yourselves for now. Anything specific you want to know?" he said as he looked at the two interns and crossed his arms across his chest, waiting.

"We just need to know the obvious, Ben—what was the cause of her death? It's very important to us, for several reasons."

Foster coughed once and wiped his hands on the sides of his trousers. "Don't know for sure, yet," he said. "It's very important to us, too, and to the county coroner as well. Suspect cardiac arrest, possibly secondary to sedation from an overdose of unknown drug or drugs. A couple of capsules had opened up in her duodenum, don't know what they are yet, sent them for analysis."

"Any signs of trauma, any injuries?" Decker asked as Skeeters watched from the end of the table.

"I can't remember when I have seen an autopsy of such a flawless human being. Tyra Levy was perfect, remarkably perfect. She had no marks, no injuries, normal brain, normal heart, normal kidneys, no atherosclerosis, perfect. I really mean that, she was perfect. Hell, everybody commented on that. Really unusual."

"No marks on her neck?"

"Nope, no marks anywhere. Nobody choked her, nobody injected her, that's for sure."

The room fell silent as Decker couldn't think of any more questions to ask. Finally, Skeeters said, "What was her potassium level, and what was her sugar level?"

"Her potassium was 13.2 meq's per liter and her—"

"Holy Christ," Decker exclaimed, "normal is about

4. Somebody must have given her an overdose of potassium."

"Actually, 10 to 20 is not too unusual after death," Foster said, "since potassium leaks out of the cells. Also, her sugar of 27 is not unusual—postmortem anaerobic glycolysis drops that down."

"Oh," Decker said quietly, "I forgot about that."

"What about levels of succinel choline, fentanyl citrate, and curare, will you be checking those?" Skeeters asked.

"Those are good thoughts, but they must be injected and we checked her closely for entrance sites of a needle. We checked her hair, her toenails, between her toes, and every other square inch of skin. Found nothing, nothing abnormal. Like I said, she was perfect. Never seen anything like it."

"Would you check the blood levels of those drugs anyway for us, and would you also check the insulin-connecting peptide—the C-peptide factor—just to make sure she wasn't given an overdose of insulin?" Skeeters asked. "It would really make us happy. Also, could you do a bioassay for botulinus toxin? And . . . sorry . . . could you please run a gas chromatography and mass spectrometer analysis on any designer amphetamines that might escape your usual tox screen? Just to be sure. It would really mean a lot to us."

Decker turned and looked at Skeeters with new respect. He looked back at Benjamin Foster. "We really would appreciate it," he said.

The repetitive honking of the Corvette's horn, an annoying blast that cycled about once a second, came blaring through the night out of the garage and carried across the parking lot, reverberating against the walls behind the building and into the open windows of the apartment. As the familiar sound from his car filled the bedroom, Decker's eyes abruptly opened and he looked around the dark room. The thought of Katie quickly flashed through his mind—she was far away in Glendale, as they had reluctantly agreed. For the working weeknights they needed sleep even more than they needed each other.

As he jumped out of bed, the noise abruptly stopped, leaving behind the sounds of dogs howling with a discordant cacophony across the southern half of Temple City. As usual, during the summer months, Decker had been sleeping in the nude—it had always seemed to be the natural thing to do. Within thirty seconds, he had climbed into his surgical green pants and was out the front door, tying the string across the front as he ran down the steps and across the dark parking lot.

Three cars were sitting side by side, facing the wall in the open garage, looking undisturbed. Decker stood in the dark behind them, searching the garage for any signs of human presence. Mr. Gallahan's black Lincoln dominated the garage with its haughty mass of steel, and a college kid's rusted Ford Pinto was next to it in humble contrast. The Corvette occupied the corner spot where swinging doors were least likely to impart the tiniest flaw to its gleaming sides. Decker leaned over and looked under the cars—nobody there, no movement. He scanned the driveway, scrutinizing the circles of lighted asphalt, looking for any movements.

The sharp sound of a bottle hitting the ground spun him around just in time to see a mongrel half-breed running in terror from his favorite trash can.

Decker walked slowly up to the Corvette, studying the car carefully for any signs of entry. The windows were up as he had left them, and he could see the glint of The Club spanning across his steering wheel, locked in position. A tiny image of the word SECURITY was flashing on the screen with the rhythm of a heartbeat.

He pulled the tiny transmitter from the pocket of his greens and pushed the button. The light on the dashboard blinked out. He turned the key in the lock and opened the driver's door. He cursed the fact that he had forgotten his flashlight as he climbed into the car, shut the door, and looked around. He reached down and turned on the parking lights.

The lid to the center console was shut; he opened it and inspected the collection of papers—a map of the San Gabriel Valley, a notepad, the owner's manual, and the registration papers. Nothing of significance had been in the console and nothing was missing. He placed everything back inside and swung the console door shut. He turned around and inspected the two locked compartments behind the seats; both had been locked with a key earlier in the day, preventing each lid from being opened. Without using his key, he pushed the button on the compartment behind the passenger's seat—it promptly opened. He reached around behind the driver's seat and pushed the button on the lid of the second compartment—its lid was locked.

So they had used a key, or at least some kind of a device to pick the lock, and they managed to open one of the compartments. He climbed out of the car and walked to the back, where he checked the scissor jack bag lying on top of the spare tire—it was sealed and its contents were intact.

He turned on the headlights and walked around to the passenger side. He inserted his key into the door and swung it wide open, the reflected headlights shining off the garage as he knelt down and inspected the window. Not a trace of any damage could be seen— the window was clean and without scratches. He stud-

ied the paint around the keyhole, moving his head to
catch the gleam of reflected light on the smooth red
Fiberglass. He gently ran his fingers across the paint,
searching for the tiniest imperfection.

He found a scratch in the paint directly below the
keyhole, not longer than a quarter inch. It had not
been there the day before, Decker was certain. Something metal had made it, something like a tool of some
kind or maybe even a key, slipping away from the
lock's entrance. The door was probably opened quickly,
Decker guessed, followed by an effort to ransack the
compartments as the Corvette's alarm tripped off.
And then the intruder, with no time left to open the
compartment behind the driver's seat and nothing to
show for his work, had fled into the night.

Decker turned off the lights, locked the car, and
pulled out his car cover from the trunk. He carefully
rolled the cover across the top of the car, attached the
cable with a padlock under the frame, and pressed his
transmitter to arm the alarm system again. He walked
slowly back to his apartment, locked his front door,
turned the deadbolt and, leaving on his green pants—
going to be ready for anything—he climbed between
the sheets. He lay back on his pillow, his eyes wide
open, and stared at the ceiling.

There were nine names on the folded sheet of paper
jammed into Skeeters's top pocket, each followed by
a series of numbers that matched those on the tubes
of blood in the lab. It had taken him thirty-five minutes on the telephone to connect with the correct lab
technician, including almost thirty minutes of waiting
"on hold" and it had taken another five minutes to
hear the AIDS result on each of the first eight patients
on his list.

It had reminded Skeeters of an old Perry Mason

rerun he and Barbara had seen one night, an episode that had shown a defendant, accused of multiple capital crimes, standing before the judge.

"Has the jury reached a verdict?" the judge had asked.

"We have, Your Honor," the foreman of the jury had responded.

"May I have the verdict, please?"

As the piece of paper had been passed from the jury to the judge, the defendant had waited, knowing that the next few seconds could bring to him a sentence of not guilty or a sentence of death. The camera had zoomed in on the defendant's sweating face as he had nervously awaited the reading of the final verdict.

"Negative for the HIV virus," the first decree was announced. Skeeters scratched a bold negative sign next to the first set of numbers.

The second set of digits was read and, ten sweating seconds later, another negative sign was marked onto the paper. The third was negative, as was the fourth. The fifth brought about some hesitation that set Skeeters's heart violently pounding—he remembered that the blood from the fifth man had belonged to the motorcyclist who liked to use intravenous drugs—before "Negative!" was finally called out. The sixth was negative, the seventh study required a backup study to confirm that it was negative. The eighth wasn't quite ready, "but will arrive in a few minutes if you would like to call back, Dr. Skeeters."

Five minutes later, when he called back, the irritated clerk told him that it still wasn't back. When Skeeters finally called again, ten very long minutes later, the verdict was, once again, "Negative for the HIV virus." Skeeters let out a mental cheer and placed another negative sign next to the string of numbers. Only one left now.

Mr. Puuho's blood sample had been inserted into the next batch of HIV tests, and it would take another twenty-four hours for the final report.

"Do you mind if I call you Spike?" Skeeters asked as Choo-Choo handed him the empty cup.

"Ha-a?" Spike Bond grunted as he stared down through the bars at the intern, his swollen black face confused as he struggled to comprehend the question.

"Would you like to be called Spike or would you like me to call you Mr. Bond?" Skeeters asked patiently.

"Uh-h-h . . ." Choo-Choo searched the Jail Ward corridor as if looking for help. He narrowed his eyes and looked back at Skeeters. "Spike," he said. "Call me Spike."

"Good, Spike it is. Thank you for taking your medicine so well this morning. You're doing much better now. How are you feeling?"

The prisoner grunted and turned away from Skeeters, walking the full length of the Cage to the far wall. His head hung low as he stood in front of the concrete blocks, his back to Skeeters, looking down at his bare feet, studying his toes. He leaned forward, tapping the top of his head lightly against the wall before finally turning around and looking directly at Skeeters.

He spoke in a slow rumble. "I'm doing much better now."

"I'm happy to hear that, Spike," Skeeters called out as he opened the man's chart and quickly scanned the vital signs and lab data. Choo-Choo was progressing, no doubt about it. He had been on the ward for just under two weeks now and already they were able to get him to take his medicine. Skeeters smiled. Real progress. He looked at the man again. Choo-Choo was still standing in front of the wall at the far corner of the Cage, his head hanging down, his shoulders slumping, his body looking fatigued. *Poor bastard doesn't even know why he's here.*

"Another couple of days, Spike, and we might be able to go ahead with that X ray we were talking about."

"X ray?" His head lifted and he turned to look at the intern. His eyes opened with new interest. "Then can I go home?"

"The CAT scan X ray, that special X ray of your head I was telling you about," Skeeters said, ignoring his question.

The prisoner reached up and rubbed the top of his head as if he was trying to feel what needed to be x-rayed. "No problem for me, Doc," he said slowly, "no problem for me at all." His head dropped again as he turned away from the wall and walked sluggishly back to his bunk.

Skeeters pulled up a chair in front of the Cage and wrote his progress note in Choo-Choo's chart, carefully following the highly organized format he had learned back at Harvard. It took a continuous and monumental effort to keep from just scribbling down the faster but almost unrecognizable standard physician's script. *Just like the Introduction to Clinical Medicine professor had preached back in the third year of medical school. "Simply cut down on the words and take a little more time—you will communicate better, you will document better, and you will care for your patients better."* Skeeters finished his note and looked over his neat writing before closing the chart—not bad, the prof would be proud. He stood up and walked down the central corridor, looking for Jack Diamond. If he hurried, he might finish his morning rounds before the Cursed Proboscis, as they liked to call the long-nose ward clerk, Gerald Brodie, called his name to admit the next patient.

Jack Diamond, sitting in his wheelchair at the center of the Jail Ward, spotted the approach of Skeeters and waved his crutch so vigorously that his wig fell off his head and onto his lap. He quickly grabbed the mass of purple hair and adjusted it back on his head as he flagged the intern to a halt.

"Dr. Skeeters! How is your leg?" He pulled a bright red shawl around his blue prisoner's shirt as he looked at Skeeters.

"My leg is doing fine, Mr. Diamond," Skeeters said as he walked up to the man.

Diamond pulled out a tissue from the box on his lap and blew his nose with a prolonged roar. "I hope so," he said. "I heard that guy from Hawaii hollering that he wasn't going to allow any AIDS tests . . . he sure isn't a very nice person."

Skeeters smiled at his patient. "You don't miss much from your vantage point out here in the hallway, do you?"

"Not much, Doctor." His voice dropped to a whisper. "I know about the little visits you and your friend are making to the Medication Room."

Skeeters looked surprised. "Nobody's supposed to know about that!"

He patted Skeeters's arm. "It's okay, I won't tell anyone. I know what you're doing in there, trying to track down where things are going, and I'll tell you, at great personal risk to myself, it is a good thing you are doing that. The problem is that Grossman knows you are doing it, too."

"Grossman knows? How the hell does he know?"

"He knows everything going on here. The officer of the watch, sitting half asleep at his desk"—Diamond pointed down the hall—"he reports everything he sees to Grossman. The nurse with the beard? He reports to him. Half the prisoners on the thirteenth floor are reporting to him. Grossman probably has a file on you an inch thick. And he has a line drawn somewhere— if you and your friend step over that line before you finish your month here, something awful might happen to you." Tears welled up and streamed down in black trails across his cheeks. "And I don't want anything to happen to you . . ."

His final comment was followed by silence, punctuated by an occasional quick sniff as Diamond blew his nose.

"Jack, why are the prisoners reporting to the sheriff?" Skeeters asked.

"Dr. Skeeters! Dr. Skeeters!" Gerald Brodie's loudspeaker voice sent a predictable flash of irritation up Skeeters's back. "Red blanket to Prep Room! Red blanket to Prep Room!"

Skeeters looked down the corridor at the entrance to the Jail Ward and spotted a four-wheeled gurney being accelerated out of the elevator. A red blanket covered the legs of a small man hunched over on the gurney, and a cluster of uniformed men trailed behind as it was pushed across the corridor and into the Prep Room.

"We'll finish talking later," Skeeters said as he shut Diamond's chart and began walking rapidly down the central corridor.

"Okay, Dr. Skeeters! I'll be here waiting for you! No place else to go!" Diamond eased into a more comfortable position in the wheelchair, adjusted his purple hairpiece, and resumed his corridor vigilance.

In his three weeks as an intern, Blake Skeeters had easily mastered the *accelerated walk* that allowed great distances to be covered in a fraction of the time normally required. This inherently unnatural means of locomotion is usually learned within the first week of the intern year, and is essential for survival—for both the patient as well as the intern. In less than ten seconds, he reached the Prep Room.

"Meet the Lone Ranger," Martel said, pointing to the man on the gurney.

The patient was desperately gasping for air. The front and back of his L.A. County Jail blue prisoner clothing was stained dark with sweat as he sat hunched over, gripping the sides of the gurney. He was remarkably thin and his skin was pasty white. He was making a strange strangling noise as he fought to breathe through a mouth that was wide open, showing badly stained teeth. His eyes were wide with terror as his head rotated back and forth in perfect timing with his labored breathing. Plastic oxygen tubing was connected to a pair of cannulae strapped under his nose and an intravenous line had been threaded by the emergency room doctors into a large vein deep in his right groin.

"What's his real name, Martel?" Skeeters quickly asked.

"His real name is Freddie Freeze and he's an asthmatic male prostitute who usually works in a cowboy outfit as a loner on Hollywood Boulevard—"

"I didn't ask about his life history!"

"I thought you might be interested," Martel said coolly.

Skeeters put his hand on the man's shoulder. "Mr. Freeze, did you get any medicines in the emergency room?"

Freeze shook his head rapidly, his eyes fixed on the intern as his gasping wheeze became louder and he began clawing the sheets.

"Are you taking any medicines?"

His head shook again, more vigorously.

Skeeters looked at Martel. "Are we ready to intu-bate him if we have to? We may have to put him on a respirator."

"We're ready anytime you give the order."

"Okay," Skeeters said as his thoughts raced through the most probable diagnoses. "Get the endotracheal kit to the bedside, we might need it in the next couple of minutes. Let's get him onto the exam table."

Ten seconds later, Freddie Freeze was sitting on the table, the oxygen flow was turned up to the maximum, and Skeeters began thumping his fingers up and down the patient's back, searching for any signs of fluid in his chest.

"Do you have any allergies?" Skeeters asked after listening to the man's rapid heartbeat.

"No!" Freeze gasped. "I can't breathe! Help me!"

"Martel, give him 275 milligrams of aminophylline intravenously and put him on a dextrose and water drip to deliver 50 milligrams per hour. Get respiratory therapy up here for some albuterol in the updraft neb-ulizer—have 'em give him 2.5 milligrams in 4 cc's nor-mal saline. Also throw some Solu-Medrol into the intravenous line . . . give him 200 milligrams stat! And open the line up to 150 cc's per hour!"

After Martel hollered out the door for Gerald Bro-die to get a respiratory therapist, the nurse began gathering up the medications for Freeze. Skeeters stuck a needle into an artery in the patient's left groin and pulled 10 cc's of bright red blood into a syringe that was quickly sent for gas analysis. He returned to his patient and conducted one of the fastest physical examinations of his life.

The man's body was a disaster. His muscles were scrawny and atrophic, looking like thin tendons stretch-ing across the bony joints. His skin was marked with long lines of needle tracks overlying what had been, at some distant and healthier time in the past, large underlying veins that were now clotted or withered away from repeated punctures of dirty needles. His emaciated and sickly forearms carried a scattering of coin sized punched-out indentations from years of poorly aimed cocaine injections. Freddie Freeze was a junkie, and the most amazing thing about his examination, Skeeters reflected, was that at the age of forty-two, the man was still alive.

"What ya got here, Blake?"

Skeeters turned to find Steve Decker, his eyes glassy and bloodshot, watching the examination from the corner of the room.

"My God, Steve, you look like hell, are you okay?"

"Thanks." Decker grimaced. "Didn't get much sleep last night. Somebody broke into my car about 2:30 this morning. I'll tell you about it when you've finished up with your friend here. By the way"—he pointed to Freeze's groin—"why did you plug the intravenous line into his femoral vein?"

"The ER docs put it there. I think it's the only vein he has left in his entire body. He's had some problems with drug abuse."

"Some major problems, I'd say," Decker said as he surveyed the man's skin.

Gerald Brodie walked up to the interns and handed Skeeters a page of computer-printed numbers. "Freeze's gases here, Doc," he said, handing the paper to Skeeters.

The two interns peered at the long column of numbers that summarized Freeze's blood levels of oxygen and carbon dioxide.

"Look at that," Decker said, looking over Skeeters's shoulder. "Ninety-nine percent saturated with oxygen."

"Should be, with his blood oxygen level over 300.

His carbon dioxide is normal . . . amazing, especially with a respiratory rate of about a thousand. His bicarb is normal, his base excess is normal, his pH is normal, everything's normal."

"Nice work, Dr. Skeeters," Decker said with a smile. "Don't let anyone say you don't know how to treat asthma."

"That would be great, Steve, but these values were measured *before* we started any treatment." He dropped the report sheet on the adjacent exam table. "This blood sample was sent when he was in dire straits, *in extremis*, when he first got here. Hell, this blood was sent when he was almost ready to be intubated!"

Peter Martel, listening from the other side of the room, interrupted their conversation with the observation, "Freddy Freeze usually responds to bronchodilator therapy. At least he did the last time he was here."

The two interns paused and looked at the nurse with open hostility. The room became silent except for Freeze's wheezing and the beeping of the machine pumping aminophylline into his veins. Decker briefly considered throwing Martel through the towering window behind them and felt a glowing surge of satisfaction at the thought. He glanced at Skeeters, cleared his throat, and looked back at Freeze. "Well, I have to get going on my rounds," he said. "See you later, Blake. Good luck with this one." He walked out of the Prep Room and down the hall, searching for his patients.

Skeeters politely asked Martel, "Why did you take so long to tell me that bit of historical data? How often does this man come in? When was Freddie Freeze last here?"

Martel thought for a moment and replied, "Sometime within the last three or four months. I think that was when it was."

Skeeters looked at Freeze who was breathing easier and looking more relaxed. "When were you last here, Mr. Freeze? Can you remember?"

The prisoner wiped his mouth with the back of his bony hand. "Shit, I don't know, Doc," he grumbled. "Few months ago . . . didn't do me no good, 'cause here I am again."

"Had you been taking any medicines while you were over at the County Jail?"

"Nope, nothing 'cept an occasional Proventil sprayer from time to time. Sure didn't work too good this morning."

"How much do you smoke?"

"Been doin' real good, cuttin' back, down to about a pack a day now."

"Ever think about quitting, considering the asthma and all?" *Not that it really matters, considering your intravenous drug habit . . .*

"I gonna quit, Doc, soon, I promise. Just not quite ready yet, been under a lot of stress with my parole hearing coming up. And don't give me any fuckin' lectures today, I don't think I could handle them."

"Okay, no lectures." Skeeters finished taking the man's medical history, which amounted to little more than a long story of smoking, breathing problems, and "some drug use" in the distant past. He put his notes away, poked his head into the corridor, and asked Gerald Brodie if he would be so kind as to get Freddie Freeze's chart from medical records.

Brodie's pointed nose sniffed twice as he conceded that it would not be too much of a burden to try. Returning to Freeze's bedside, Skeeters pulled up a chair and began writing a series of orders on the front sheet.

"Ya gonna let me on outta here, Doc?" Freeze asked.

"I'm going to see how you do tonight, and maybe tomorrow or the next day you will be ready to return."

"I feel pretty good now. Breathin's okay, I think you fixed me up real good."

Skeeters looked at the patient, then returned to the chart. "You are looking much better, Freeze. You sure did bounce back fast."

Another half page of orders was written before Freeze asked again, "So can I go back this afternoon?"

Skeeters looked at him again. "Are you serious? You want to go back? Isn't it better for you here than over at the County Jail?"

"Yeah, it would be if it weren't for all the sick patients around here. I hate to be around sick people, Doc. I'm afraid I'm gonna catch something like AIDS or tuberculosis. At least everybody back at the jail ain't sick like they are here."

"I think it would be better for you to stay here for a while. I'd rather send you out when I know you won't be coming right back with another asthmatic attack. A half hour ago, I thought I was going to have to put you on a respirator machine . . ."

"Okay, Doc, do what you have to do," Freeze said as he lay back and stared at the ceiling while the intravenous line carried the steroids and aminophylline into his bloodstream. Five minutes later, after the orders were finished and Skeeters stood up to leave, Peter Martel stopped him at the door.

"What's the plan, Dr. Skeeters?" he asked, standing in front of the physician.

"Read the orders, Martel, and the plan will become quite clear." Skeeters pulled himself up to the best height his stubby stature would allow and looked Martel straight in the eye. "Follow the orders, and the patient will benefit."

"Am I to assume that you are going to admit this patient?" Martel asked, a faint, almost mocking smile on his lips as he waved in the general direction of Freeze.

Skeeters handed the chart to the nurse. "Yes, you may assume that I am," he answered angrily. "Do you have a problem with that?" He stepped around the nurse and walked down the corridor toward the Dictation Room.

"Last time the doctor just sent him back to the County Jail after his wheezing cleared," Martel called after him.

"Last time, I wasn't the patient's doctor," Skeeters fired back over his shoulder as he felt a flush of heat spread across his face. *Goddamn drug addict nurse, goddamn drug addict patient, goddamn all drug addicts!*

"What's the problem here?" a deep voice boomed down the corridor.

Skeeters stopped in his tracks and turned around. Dr. Marsh was standing near the Jail Ward entrance, next to the duty sheriff's desk, his arms crossed across his chest with the usual stern authority. The director's eyes narrowed as he looked back and forth between Skeeters and Martel, waiting for an answer.

"Sir, the matter is quite simple," Skeeters said as he turned and walked back up the corridor. "This patient I just admitted, Mr. Freddie Freeze, was a red blanket in severe respiratory distress from asthmatic bronchospasm. I have treated him with some success, and I have decided to admit him for observation for the next day or so. Mr. Martel seems to feel that the patient doesn't need admission, and—"

"Okay, Dr. Skeeters, I got the picture." He turned

to the nurse. "Mr. Martel, what's your problem with this plan?"

"No problem, sir. I just suggested that this intern, who is new in the business"—Martel looked down at Skeeters—"needs to understand that you don't just keep everybody in here who happens to have been sick. The Jail Ward is almost full, the Lone Ranger is—"

"Who is this Lone Ranger? Are you referring to Mr. Freeze?" Marsh interrupted.

"Yes, sir, sorry . . ." Martel braced himself for the blast.

"Well, then, call him Mr. Freeze!" Marsh said heatedly.

"Yes, sir. As I was saying, Mr. Freeze can be given the same medicines back at the dispensary in the County Jail as he's getting here. The last doctor who pulled him out of it—"

"Is that doctor here now?" Marsh interrupted sarcastically.

"Is he here? Is the other doctor here now?"

"Mr. Martel, Dr. Skeeters is the treating physician and is therefore responsible if anything happens to the patient tonight. Do you understand what I am saying?"

Martel's eyes darted toward Skeeters, then looked at the floor. "Yes, sir," he said quietly.

"Good. I'd like you in my office in thirty minutes." He looked at his watch. "At 10:45 this morning."

"Yes, sir, I'll be there," Martel said as he turned to walk back into the Prep Room.

"You may return to your work," Dr. Marsh said to Skeeters.

"Yes, sir, thank you." Skeeters strolled back down the corridor, waved to an enthusiastic Jack Diamond, and thought about Dr. Marsh. *Maybe the crusty old man isn't such a bad guy after all . . .*

Twenty minutes later, Skeeters was in the basement of the hospital, standing at the medical records counter under a large sign that said RECORD REQUESTS. A thin woman of about forty stood on the other side of the counter, waiting for Skeeters to finish completing the small square of paper that requisitioned a chart. He signed his name on the bottom of the request and handed it across the counter.

"Here you are," Skeeters said pleasantly as he looked at the woman. Her face was a mosaic of deeply pigmented crevices with thousands of spiderweb-like lines running in all directions.

She stared at the paper, then pushed it back to him. "It would help if you would print your name under the signature here, like it says you're supposed to do."

"Oh, sorry." He quickly printed his name and handed the paper back.

She studied each letter, word, and number, until she was convinced that there was nothing further she could complain about. She picked up the paper and commanded him, "Wait here," as she turned and disappeared into the bowels of the medical records department.

With a face like that, no wonder she has a personality as bad as her skin—like some kind of lizard, Skeeters thought with irritation as he waited for her to return. *Another lizard, they're everywhere all over the West Coast. They never learn until it's too late. Tanning to achieve the "healthy look," the outdoor look, they begin to notice after ten or fifteen years that their skin looks worse—almost ugly—when the tan fades. Then at forty years of age they wake up one morning and discover they suddenly look like they're seventy.*

Five minutes later, the lizard returned and handed

the paper back to Skeeters. "Nothing on Freddie Freeze," she said.

"You must have some kind of record on the man. He's been here before, sometime earlier this year."

"Is he in the hospital now?" The wrinkled skin across her forehead developed new creases in what Skeeters presumed was an expression of concern.

"Yes, he is. I just admitted him to the Jail Ward."

"Well, why didn't you say so!" The crevices bunched up under her eyes, making her look hideous as she turned and stomped away. Less than a minute later, she grunted as she strained to place the huge chart on the countertop. "It was right there, in the thirteenth-floor delivery bin, just waiting to go up, just like Gerald Brodie requested. Next time—"

"I know, I know, next time let you know the patient has been admitted. Will do, and thank you, ma'am."

The chart was almost 4 inches thick, bound by steel brackets that penetrated the pages on the left side. Skeeters tucked it under his arm and returned to the Jail Ward, where he dropped it on the table of the Doctors' dictating room. He returned to the corridor, where Gerald Brodie handed him Freeze's order sheets and progress notes, with the observation, "You're going to admit him, hey?" Skeeters responded that, hey, he *was* going to admit him and that he hoped that would be okay with the ward clerk. He picked up a cup of coffee from the percolator on the watch officer's desk and returned to the dictating room.

He sat down in front of the desk and turned on the Dictaphone machine. He picked up the microphone and began to speak, rapidly and without pause:

"This is Dr. Blake Skeeters, dictating the admission history and physical on Freddie Freeze, chart #20349595767.

    "Chief Complaint: Shortness of Breath and Wheezing. Duration: One Day.

    "History of the Present Illness: The patient is a 37-year-old man transferred from the County Jail to the Jail Ward with progressively increasing dyspnea. This has not been associated with productive cough, chest pain, ankle edema, and there has been no hemoptosis. He has a history of previous similar events several months ago, on, on . . ."

Skeeters released the switch to the dictating microphone and reached over to open up the old chart. Like medical charts in most hospitals, it was arranged in chronological order, the most recent admissions on the top, the others in sequence below. He checked the date on the first page: June 27, 1992, Freddie Freeze brought to the Jail Ward for wheezing, not admitted. *That was last month.* He turned over several pages and came to the next previous visit: May 29, 1992. *Twice in the last two months.* Skeeters turned several more pages and found the next previous examination: April 29, 1991. *Three times in the past three months. Christ, the guy is a regular visitor here.*

The next visit showed that Freeze had come to the Jail Ward at the end of March . . . and at the end of February, and in January. Skeeters began turning the pages faster, skimming through all of 1991—Freeze had been brought to the Jail Ward twelve times, admitted zero times. He turned the pages in rapid flips, scanning back to 1988—regular visits each month, never admitted.

He turned through large sections of the chart, dating back through 1985 and found the monthly pattern continued. He had seen more than sixty different doctors in the past five years! The diagnosis always the same: "Emphysema with Bronchial Asthma, Acute Attack." No intern had ever seen the patient more than once—no way they could, since he never came twice in the same month. And no intern had ever reviewed the patient's chart. Freeze was always sent back to the County Jail before the chart could wind its way through the bureaucracy up to the Jail Ward for inspection.

He began thumbing through the pages again, searching for the handwriting and the signatures of the nurses who cared for the patient. For the past three years, the same name was scratched out on the nursing sheet with monotonous regularity—Peter Martel had been the nurse every time since his last vacation in 1988.

Skeeters put the chart off to the side and slowly sketched a little circle up in the corner of the progress note sheet. He reached over and picked up the microphone, holding the cold aluminum in his left hand.

He pressed the button and finished dictating Freddie Freeze's history and physical exam.

"I think you will have considerable interest in this notebook, sir," Decker said as he handed the black binder with the copies of their notes to Dr. Marsh.

"Good. I appreciate your work, gentlemen." The Jail Ward director smiled as he opened the binder and leaned back in his chair to study the contents. Decker and Skeeters sat quietly in front of his desk, watching him slowly turn the pages, soaking in the information. From time to time, he grunted a response to something he noted, but most of the time he remained silent. Two-thirds of the way through the binder, he abruptly frowned and looked up at the interns.

"What's all this about Rusty Esch?" he asked.

"He disappeared, sir," Skeeters said alertly. "We thought that since he was a pharmacy technician and since he was asking questions of Martel, and then, since he abruptly vanished, it could be a matter of some interest to you—and to those who may be involved in this matter."

"Well, where did he go?" Marsh asked.

"We can't find out, sir," Skeeters said. "We tried, but nobody will tell us whether he quit or what. He just seems to have disappeared. Somebody must have an interest in determining where he went, don't you think?"

"Oh, yes, certainly—although the turnover in employees here is quite high. Employees are always coming and going, and frequently nobody knows for sure where they've gone." A minute later, he looked up again. "Why did you put all this about Tyra Levy in here?"

"Tyra Levy died, Dr. Marsh," Decker said with more intensity in his voice than he had expected.

"I *know* she died, but it—"

"She died in the middle of this whole thing, and that seems more than a little unusual, doesn't it?" Decker said.

"While that may be true, I don't think she had anything to do with this. Have you seen the autopsy report?"

Skeeters flinched visibly. "Is it ready, sir? I was told it would be another two or three days."

Marsh ignored him. "I just think it detracts from the more important information to have anything about her in here."

"With all due respect, sir, you may take it out," Decker conceded. Marsh nodded and returned back to the binder. After thumbing through the final pages, he reached over and opened the right-hand drawer of his desk.

"You have done an exemplary job with this project, gentlemen. I'll be keeping your notes for safekeeping, while I review the records to determine which nurses were on duty during the shifts the drugs were taken. Frankly, I also want to review which *interns* were on duty during those same times. I can assure you that you will be receiving high marks for this month of your intern rotation."

He placed the book inside the drawer and closed it firmly. He pulled out a ring of keys from his pocket and locked the drawer.

"I have one other thing, Dr. Marsh," Skeeters said. He stood up, pulled a folded sheet of paper from his pocket, and laid it on the desk. He carefully opened it to reveal a large graph with a red line and a green line, moving together in jagged peaks and valleys across the page. Decker stood up and looked over Skeeters's shoulder at the graph.

"This, Dr. Marsh, is a graph"—he pointed to the green line—"showing the number of daily discharges of prisoners who originally came here from the County Jail and who were returned to the County Jail. And this red line, which closely—almost exactly—follows the green line, shows the milligrams of morphine that we calculated to be missing each day.

"Sir, they move up and down together, and we can therefore only assume that the missing morphine was not diverted for Peter Martel's personal use—at least not most of it. The missing morphine, sir, must be leaving the Jail Ward via another route, one that would seem to lead directly back to the County Jail. Dr. Decker and I believe that these prisoners, like Freddie Freeze with his little wheezing display yesterday and about ten others who have cycled through the Jail Ward so far this month, are supplying their friends at the County Jail with narcotics, compliments of the unsuspecting Central Pharmacy here and probably

with the blessing of, *and active assistance from,* Peter
Martel and Sergeant Grossman."

"Sergeant Grossman?" the director asked quietly as
he picked up the chart and stared at the interns. "Sergeant Grossman is a fine deputy sheriff with a superb
record of service to the Jail Ward for over nine years."

"Yes, sir," Skeeters said politely. "Sergeant Grossman *and company,* sir. Don't the deputy sheriffs on
the Jail Ward do the final frisking just before the prisoners leave here? We were wondering, are there any
records that show who examined the prisoners who
return to the County Jail?"

"We would be willing to bet, sir," Decker said,
"that all the prisoners engaged in this little narcotics
game were examined by one deputy, maybe Sergeant
Grossman, or perhaps by two deputies at the most."

Dr. Marsh leaned back in his chair and studied the
two interns. "You men have done a fine job, bringing
all this together here," he said, his face breaking out
in a broad smile. "This little operation has probably
been underway for some time now, from the pattern
you have identified, and if I can substantiate this in
the next two or three weeks, I'm going to bring in the
authorities for a complete investigation. At this point,
however, I would like to be very careful because of
the professional careers in law enforcement and nursing that are at stake here. I don't want to become a
loose cannon before all the facts have been collected."

"Sir, we have less than a week left on the Jail Ward,
and—" Skeeters started.

"Yes, I know that, gentlemen. However, you have
done as much as is necessary on this, and I'd like to
ask you to let me carry the ball from here. As I have
already said, your work has been excellent this month
and your marks will reflect the high quality of your
work."

Without another word, Dr. Marsh stood up and escorted them to the door.

At exactly 9 A.M., after making rounds on eleven patients, discharging three of the male patients back to the County Jail, and sending two of the female patients to the Sybil Brand Institute, Skeeters called the lab.

"May I have the HIV results on my patient, number 684-73-204?"

"What's the number again?" said a nasal male voice.

"684-73 . . ."

"Slower!"

"Sorry; 684-73-204. Given to you on Sunday morning."

"Hold!" And with an abrupt click, Skeeters was placed on hold. This would have annoyed him a few weeks ago, but now he hardly noticed. *The County Hospital is a government operation,* he reminded himself, *and rudeness is an inherent part of government business. Why should there be any courtesy? You're not going to use the lab across the street, are you?*

He pulled out the folded piece of paper from his pocket and looked over the list of names, eight of them with negative signs penned in next to them. He looked at the last name, Mr. Kekoa Puuho.

The voice returned. "What is the number of the patient with the HIV test?"

A small alarm went off in the back of Skeeters's mind. *Why ask again, when the number had already been confirmed?*

"It's 684-73-204," Skeeters said, his voice reduced to a whisper.

"The number is 684-73-204? You are Dr. Decker?"

The alarm became louder. He shifted his weight

nervously as he felt his heart beginning to pound again. "Yes, I'm Dr. Decker," Skeeters said.

"The result is positive for the AIDS virus, Western Blot confirmation will be completed in the next few days."

Chapter 10

Barbara Skeeters's eyes opened slowly, exactly on time.

The glow of dawn was beginning to brighten the bedroom as she stretched and sat upright, adjusted her pillow against the headboard, and finally leaned back to gather her energies. She pulled the covers high enough to enclose her six months of expanding abdomen; her muscles relaxed as she felt the warmth of the electric blanket penetrating through her body. Until the past week or so, she had always loved this time of the day. There were no interruptions, no problems, just the early sunlight that always seemed to carry a fresh optimism for the coming day.

Now it was difficult to enjoy the time before her husband awakened. Both of them had been sleeping poorly since he had been stuck with the needle. He reminded her regularly that he was trying as hard as he could to determine if any of the people he had admitted that night were positive for the AIDS virus, but all he would tell her was "The final results aren't in yet." And he would become angry, angry like she had never seen him before, if she asked any further questions on the subject.

She looked across the room at the framed picture of the two of them on the wall. It had been taken more than a year ago, a month after their wedding.

They had their arms around each other and they were both laughing at some long-forgotten joke. She turned and looked at her husband, lying on his side under the covers next to her. He was making small sputtering sounds with each breath, and every minute or two, he stirred restlessly as if he was having a bad dream.

Barbara Skeeters glanced at the clock on his nightstand, and that was when she saw the envelope.

It was a business envelope, gray in the dim light, and it had been propped up against the clock. She looked at it for a few seconds, trying to remember what he had needed to mail in the morning. Usually, envelopes with bills were placed on the counter near the front door, where they could grab them on their way out. It didn't make sense for him to place it next to his alarm clock. She finally decided to take a quick look at it before going to the kitchen for their morning coffee.

She climbed out of bed and walked around to her husband's side. She picked up the envelope and examined it closely. In the improving light, she could see there was no address or return address. There was no stamp. She turned it over. It was unsealed. She opened the flap and removed the enclosed sheet of paper. It was high-quality bond paper, tinted a light yellow color; she took it to the bedroom window where the light was better.

As she studied the tiny dot matrix computer print that was concentrated in the center of the page—it was difficult to see, the words were so small—and as she comprehended the meaning of the sentence, her eyes began to widen with horror.

"How did they do it?" Decker asked, pressing the telephone receiver against his ear. I don't see how they got into my apartment. The deadbolt was latched and locked."

"I don't know how they did it at our apartment either. We always lock the doors at night, and Barbara is almost hysterical," Skeeters said. "Nothing happens at our place without her knowing it, especially at night. She even pops awake when the electric coffee-pot in the kitchen clicks on. Somebody moving around our apartment without her knowing about it has put the fear of God in her. And in me too," he added.

"I think we should take this to the police, today, this morning, but first I'm going to go out and buy the biggest goddamn German shepherd I can find, and I'm going to keep it in my apartment."

"Your apartment manager allows dogs?"

"No, but there is a compelling need here. Maybe I'll have to sneak him in at night. Where can I meet you, Blake?"

"Where are you now?" Skeeters asked.

"I'm at a pay phone in Alhambra," Decker said. "I'm not going back to my apartment until I have a dog. Let's meet at the police station in Pasadena. Maybe they can find some fingerprints on the pages."

"The Pasadena police aren't going to care about the letter you have in Temple City. Don't you have to file a complaint with the Temple City police?"

"Temple City doesn't have a police department! The place is unincorporated, and all they have is a sheriff's department! I really don't think it's a good idea to take this thing to the sheriff's station. Grossman's brother might be the chief investigator."

"Good point," Skeeters said. "Pasadena has a police department near that big dome thing, the City Hall, just across from the courthouse, on the corner of Walnut and Garfield. Let's meet there in an hour."

"An hour. Why so long?" The rumbling sound of

a low-rider Buick with darkly tinted windows drew Decker's attention away from the telephone. There were three, maybe four men inside, and it scraped the driveway as it entered the gas station. The car pulled up to the gasoline pump nearest Decker's position.

"It's going to take an hour," Skeeters explained, "because I'm not going to leave Barbara here alone. I'm going to take her to a motel somewhere around here, at—"

"Don't say it," Decker interrupted. "There might be a tap on your telephone."

Skeeters hesitated, thinking. "This is enough to drive us to new heights of paranoia. Maybe we should get some kind of gun."

"Wouldn't have helped us much last night, but I was thinking we might need one in the future." He looked at the Buick as the driver, a large, dark-complected Hispanic man, got out of the car and began pumping gas. The other men stayed inside, all three sitting like statues, looking straight ahead.

"Okay, we'll think about it," Skeeters said. "I'll see you at the Pasadena Police Station in about an hour."

"Make sure nobody's following you," Decker tossed out just before hanging up.

Detective William Monroe looked up from the two letters the interns had given him and said, "I really don't think there is anything I can do about these notes."

The police detective was overweight and tired, looking like a man who had worked too many night shifts and heard too many stories of human savagery and aggression. His desk held a disorganized collection of reports and half-filled paper coffee cups, with a glowing computer screen on the far left side of the desk looking like a large green eye that surveyed the men. The sleeves of his crumpled white shirt were rolled up to the elbows, and his dark red necktie was loosely strung around his neck, the knot hanging just low enough to give the impression that Billy Monroe really didn't care about his appearance.

"You can't do anything about these?" Decker said incredulously. "These are threats, and we need to get some protection. Skeeters's wife here"—he pointed at the intern—"Skeeters's wife is almost seven months pregnant, and she needs protection."

"Wait a minute," Monroe commanded, holding up his hand. "I can see where you guys have a problem with this thing, but the letters don't say anything specific that could be considered a threat."

"How specific do you want it? Both messages say that the 'next message' will be under our bed and will not be so quiet," Decker said, his voice rising. "Doesn't that sound like a threat to you?"

"It might be a threat," Monroe said, staring directly at Decker, "or it might not be. An alarm clock under your beds could be—"

"You know damn well that this guy isn't referring to an alarm clock!" Decker said vehemently as he stood and glared at the detective. "It sounds to us like he's referring to a bomb. This man broke into our apartments, and—"

"Was anything taken?"

"No, but—"

"Was there any sign of forced entry?"

"No, and neither one of us know for sure how he got in," Decker exclaimed, looking at the other intern questioningly. Skeeters shrugged his shoulders. "But he sure as hell did get in. He got inside both our apartments, and that is, at the least, trespassing!"

Monroe reached over to turn off his computer screen. "I'm sorry, you gentlemen don't have enough here to indicate that a crime was committed," he said evenly. "We really can't do anything until you have more information," he said, "but I will analyze these for fingerprints and see if we come up with anything." He put the pages into a large manila envelope. "There is nothing to even confirm trespassing or an illegal entry. All you have is a couple pieces of paper, probably covered with fingerprints from wives or significant others and God knows who else, both saying that 'something not so quiet' will be under your beds next time, if you don't stop." He paused and looked at the men.

"If you don't stop what?" he asked.

"How thick do you want to slice his brain, Skeeters?" the radiologist asked. He was a tall man with an unusually flat face that reminded Skeeters of a pancake. He was peering through the radiology department's lead glass window at the black man who had been inserted, head first, into the doughnut-shaped CAT scanner.

"I'm not looking for some tiny tumor or anything like that, I'm looking for something big. Half-centimeter slices should show us everything we need to see," Skeeters said.

"Zero point five cm, you got it."

The radiologist tapped a couple of buttons on his console that controlled the expensive X-ray equipment in the adjacent room, and flipped a final switch to begin the scan sequence. The console beeped a couple of informative beeps, another final button was pushed, and the radiologist beamed—the equipment would do all the work from this point on. He turned to Skeeters and said, "Should take about an hour to complete the scan and have it ready for you. What kind of neurological signs does he have?"

"We aren't sure because nobody can get into the Cage to examine—"

"The Cage?"

"On the Jail Ward. Nobody can get inside without Mr. Bond reaching through the bars and trying to choke, claw, and commit mayhem. But his basic problem is acute psychosis, or, more accurately, a paranoid schizophrenic psychosis."

"I gathered from the double chains that he has not been a good little boy." The radiologist smiled, showing perfect teeth. "How did you quiet him down to get him out of the Cage and down here?"

"Just doubled his dose of Thorazine. He drank it right down and became very sleepy and cooperative, which was a very good thing, since he killed three people a few days ago, choked them to death," Skeeters said softly. "The Thorazine has been used to settle him down since he went into the Cage, but he's not nearly back to baseline yet. I think he's got something else going on. From the history I was given by his mother, the guy's mentation was normal right up until all this happened. He even had a decent job, doing repair work on diesel engines, and there is no history of any previous psychiatric problems."

"Okay, so we'll check out his frontal lobes."

"I think his temporal lobes will be the prime area of concern."

The pancake face looked at Skeeters. *Goddamn intern, has all the answers.* "Yeah, we'll check out everything." The radiologist looked through the window again. "Not much chance of his waking up, is there?"

"I hope not. One of the anesthesiologists squirted him with a little Versed; there's probably enough in his system to keep him out for another half hour. You might want to keep the deputy at the door, though, just in case."

The radiologist's perfect teeth showed again. "I

think the deputy will stay at the door regardless of what I want."

Five minutes later, Skeeters was back on the Jail Ward, standing at the bedside of Kekoa Puuho. If anything, the man looked skinnier, his face further shrunken, his hands bony and more atrophic.

AIDS, the son of a bitch has AIDS.

"Did the lung doctor get a chance to see you this morning, Mr. Puuho?" Skeeters asked as he thumbed through the chart, looking for the pulmonary consult.

"Yeah, he saw me," Puuho answered. "And he jammed that thing down my throat."

"Good. He checked out your lungs with a bronchoscope."

"He looked down there with something but I don't remember what." The patient looked up at Skeeters. "What's wrong with me, Doc, and when can I go back to Hawaii?"

Skeeters hesitated. "That's what the lung doctor is for, to find out what the problem in your right lung is." He scanned through the progress notes in the chart, reviewing the consultation comments. "You know, one of the concerns we have is that you may have developed an infectious disease, and that's why—"

Puuho held up his hands for Skeeters to stop. "Don't say it, Doc. I will not have any goddamn AIDS test done and that's that."

"Don't sweat the AIDS test, you've already made your opinion clear on the matter," Skeeters said calmly. "You'll be getting out of here after we have the biopsy and culture results from your lungs. We should know in about three days, from what the consulting doctor has said, okay?"

"No, it's not okay, but it will have to do," the prisoner replied unhappily.

Skeeters stared at the man for a penetrating five seconds, then turned and walked down the central corridor toward the ward clerk's desk.

Ungrateful, Skeeters fumed. *The man is probably going to kill me, just as if he had shot me during one of his abortive drug deals, and all he can do is whine that he doesn't want an AIDS test. He has the right to refuse a test on his blood, but what about my rights? Like my right to live?*

Gerald Brodie almost jumped out of his chair as Skeeters slammed Puuho's chart on his desk.

"Jesus, Doc! Getting a little violent, aren't you?"

Skeeters looked at the ward clerk's pinched face and thought about quickly flattening his long nose.

"Skip the commentary, Mr. Brodie, and let me have Frederick Freeze's chart."

"Right here, Dr. Skeeters," Brodie said politely as he pulled the man's chart from the slot behind him and slid it across his desk.

"Thank you," Skeeters said with a strained voice. He grabbed the chart and stormed down the corridor, eyes straight ahead, not even catching the friendly little wave from Jack Diamond.

Freddie Freeze was sitting on his bunk in one of the four-man rooms near the end of the central corridor. He was holding a magazine with colored pictures that looked like a gynecologic instructional manual for medical residents, and he looked up angrily as Skeeters arrived.

"I'm not wheezing, Doc, I feel just fine. Now, how about letting me get out of here and back to the County Jail, like now?"

Skeeters ignored the man's comments, pulled out his stethoscope and stuck it against the prisoner's back.

"Breathe deeply."

After making sure that Skeeters saw his look of contempt, Freeze breathed slightly deeper than usual.

Skeeters jammed his stethoscope back into his white coat pocket. "Lie down," he commanded. "Pull your pants down."

"Yes, sir," Freeze answered sarcastically.

Skeeters snipped the suture holding the prisoner's intravenous line in his right groin and pressed a small gauze pad over the skin to prevent bleeding. Then he quickly yanked out the 6 inches of tubing from the deep vein, including four strips of tape and about thirty hairs.

"Ouch! Goddamn, that hurt like hell!"

"Sorry."

"Like hell you are. Is my chest X ray they took this morning okay? That's why you wouldn't let me leave here sooner, isn't it?"

"Hold this gauze pad here for five minutes, then you can go back to the County Jail. I just reviewed your chest X ray fifteen minutes ago. It's normal, which is to be expected, isn't it, since you've never had any real problems with your lungs, have you?"

"Wrong, Doc, I almost died. You saw me when I came in. Remember, they made me a red blanket in the emergency room?"

"You fooled them, too. I'm going to write stat orders for you to be transferred, and you had better plan on not coming back here next month or—"

"Or what?" the prisoner bristled. "You're not going to be here next month, are you? I'll come back here whenever I get another asthmatic attack, and the next intern will send me back just like you should have done. And the next one will do the same thing, a month later. You don't belong on this Jail Ward, Doc. There's something wrong with you—you sweat the details too much."

Skeeters picked up the man's chart and left the room, walking down the corridor and back to the ward clerk's desk. "Mr. Brodie, this man is to leave stat for County Jail!" he said.

"Stat?"

"That's right, *stat*. See right there on the order sheet? The sooner he's gone, the better."

Brodie looked at the order sheet and said, "He'll be on his way as fast as the sheriff's wagon can get him out of here." He studied Skeeters's face and smiled. "Just don't slam the chart down, it makes me jumpy."

"Thank you," Skeeters said. *It was the first time the ward clerk has smiled since the Jail Ward rotation began.*

Ten minutes later, from his vantage point inside the Doctors' Dictation Room, Skeeters spotted Frederick Freeze being escorted down the central corridor by two sheriff's deputies. When he spotted Freeze's wiry frame pass by the door, he poked his head out and watched him being guided into the Search Room next to the elevator. Skeeters had once, out of curiosity, looked inside the room—it was little more than a small cubicle with bright overhead lights and a row of gray lockers lined up along the wall. There was no need for doctors to use the room, and it was usually kept locked.

He caught the Search Room door just before it swung shut.

"Do you need something here, Dr. Skeeters?" Grossman asked as he stepped inside the room.

Sergeant Grossman was towering over the prisoner as one of the deputies was busy opening a locker behind him. The third officer had stationed himself in the far corner of the room, to act as a backup during the search procedure, Skeeters presumed. Frederick

Freeze was standing in the middle of the room, his arms secured behind him with handcuffs.

"No, Sergeant, this prisoner just happens to have extremely unstable asthmatic airway disease, and I'd like to make sure he doesn't have another attack before he leaves."

Grossman's eyes narrowed as he pondered the answer. He stiffened slightly, slowly turned and looked at Freeze, then turned back to the intern.

"The prisoner looks okay to me," he said slowly.

Skeeters stared at the prisoner. "Thank you, Sergeant, I'd like to continue monitoring his respiratory status until he is off the floor."

"Bullshit," Freeze blurted out. "This is the guy that screwed up the—"

"Quiet!" Grossman roared. "Dr. Skeeters, you're welcome to stay and we appreciate your concern for this man's medical condition." He smiled tightly.

"Thank you, Sergeant." Skeeters continued to stare at the prisoner, his jaw muscles flexing.

"Take off your clothes," Grossman commanded to Freeze as the prisoner's handcuffs were removed.

After a methodical search of Frederick Freeze's body cavities with flashlights and rubber gloves, the prisoner was certified to be free of contraband, his handcuffs were replaced, and he was briskly escorted back to the County Jail.

The orderlies, two young black teenagers with shiny clean faces, were highly motivated to get Choo-Choo off the third floor and back up to the Jail Ward before he awoke. They normally moved patients up and down the corridors like all the other orderlies at County Hospital: at a leisurely pace designed to avoid tiring of the muscles or wearing of the feet. But when they saw the size of the patient they were directed to transport from the radiology CAT scanner, they endeavored to complete their assignment as quickly as possible. They were not reassured by the straps and chains that secured the man to the gurney, nor did they take comfort in his deeply somnolent state. They were also not reassured by the manner with which the third-floor guard walked slowly behind the gurney, County Style. The ride for the slumbering Choo-Choo from radiology to the Jail Ward elevator was, therefore, high speed. One orderly with his eyes wide open pulled from the front left side, the other with his eyes equally wide open pushed from behind.

They rushed Choo-Choo past the two deputy sheriffs standing in front of the open elevator doors, and quickly began hitting the buttons to shut the doors and to move them to the thirteenth floor. As the elevator began its slow and creaky journey up to the Jail Ward, the orderly near Choo-Choo's feet looked down and noticed that the prisoner's toes were beginning to slowly flex. *Well, look at that,* he thought, *isn't that amazing.* He rubbed his chin, trying to figure it out. *The man is deeply sedated with whatever powerful drug those anesthesia doctors use for these cases, and yet there were his toes—all ten of them—slowly contracting and relaxing like he was doing some kind of strange exercise in his sleep. Better check the connections of the chains to the underside of the gurney, just to be safe.* He leaned over to inspect the attachment site of the steel rings under the table.

And that was exactly the moment when the second orderly, standing attentively at the head of the bed, looked down at Choo-Choo's face and noticed that his eyes had, with no warning at all, popped wide open, revealing a pair of the wildest bloodshot eyes the orderly had ever seen.

When the elevator doors opened to the Jail Ward,

several things happened at once. The orderly nearest the door tried to squeeze out through the opening as fast as he could, while the orderly at the head of the gurney pushed violently to propel Choo-Choo out of the elevator. Choo-Choo began grunting and slamming his head on the back of the bed as he tried to lunge upward, straining against the leather straps holding his arms. The gurney jumped forward 3 feet until the wheels slammed against a 2-inch ridge of misaligned metal at the base of the elevator door.

As Gerald Brodie looked up from his desk across from the elevator, the gurney flipped to a vertical position, planting Choo-Choo's feet firmly on the Jail Ward floor, the gurney clinging to his back. Brodie immediately dropped his pen and jumped out of his chair, running down the hallway as fast as his legs could move. Choo-Choo spotted the fleeing figure and did the only thing someone with such size and power could do. He chased after Brodie, grunting with guttural gurgles, the gurney violently slapping against his back and legs.

It is not easy to run with a gurney strapped to the back, and it is even more difficult when the gurney is attached to straps that encircle the arms and legs. Choo-Choo therefore moved down the corridor more slowly than he otherwise could, his legs banging against the bed with a rhythm that matched his grunting. The squad of five sheriff deputies that ran after him had little problem intercepting the gurney and flipping it back so all four wheels were once again on the corridor and Choo-Choo was looking at the ceiling.

One of the deputies ran ahead of the gurney and swung the Cage door wide open. The other four men accelerated the gurney straight into the Cage, unlocked the chains from the underside of the gurney, and escaped before the snorting Choo-Choo could launch himself off the bed. They slammed the Cage door shut, congratulated themselves on the smooth operation, and slowly wandered back down the corridor to the deputies' desk where they began exchanging modified versions of the *Choo-Choo and the Gurney* story to all who would listen.

Let the doctor figure out how to get the gurney out of the Cage.

At ten minutes before five that afternoon, Gerald Brodie intercepted Skeeters as he walked in front of his desk, returning from one of Dr. Marsh's teaching conferences. This one had been about the damage bullets can do to human flesh, complete with full-color cadaver photographs. "There are two messages," Brodie told the intern. "One is from the radiologist who just read Choo-Choo's scan, and the second one is from one of the deputies. And which one would you like first?"

"The one from the radiologist," Skeeters mumbled.

"He wanted you to know"—Brodie looked at his notepad—"that your patient Spike Bond has a 5-centimeter tumor in his right temporal lobe that has recently hemorrhaged and has generated significant mass effect." He looked up at Skeeters. "Does that make sense?"

"It makes a great deal of sense," Skeeters answered, his shoulders straightening, his eyes brightening.

"And the sheriff deputy—"

"I don't want to know what the sheriff deputy has to say, Brodie, thank you."

"It's about your prisoner, Choo-Choo," Brodie said provocatively.

Skeeters ignored the ward clerk, turned, and walked to the telephone hanging outside the Prep Room doorway.

"They want you to give him more anesthesia next time he's transported off the floor," Brodie called after him.

"Department of Pathology," the woman or man—Skeeters couldn't tell which—answered his call with a strongly nasal inflection.

"Dr. Benjamin Foster, please."

"One moment, please." The voice was nasal almost to the level of being a handicap. A few seconds later, Foster came to the line.

"Bennie, this is Blake Skeeters—"

"Yes," Foster said, "Skeeters, I remember you. You and Steve Decker were asking about the Tyra Levy autopsy."

"Yes, that's right. Any news, yet?"

"We should have the final tox report in three or four days, probably by Monday. So far, however, all the histologic exams are normal, and the temazepam—Restoril—blood level came back low in the therapeutic range. Tyra Levy sure as hell didn't die from an overdose of Restoril."

"Thanks, Bennie. No ideas as to the cause of death at this point?"

"Lots of ideas but no facts yet. When the tox screen results arrive, we'll have more information."

"Good, thanks for the update. I also I wanted to ask about a patient who was stuck with a needle, a contaminated needle, from an inpatient with a positive preliminary HIV result."

"Oh, shit."

Skeeters winced. "I know. I haven't been able to dig out of the literature about the certainty of the positive HIV test, since the Western Blot confirmation is still pending, and—"

"Are you the one who was stuck with the needle, Blake?" Foster interrupted.

Skeeters tightened his grip on the receiver as he felt a hard knot develop in the pit of his stomach. "Yes, it was me," he finally answered, "with a needle from one of nine patients I drew that night. I'm not sure which one."

"Did you stick yourself soon after you drew their blood?"

"No, it was several minutes after the final blood draw."

"Good, that may decrease the risk, although I don't have any data on the subject—the HIV virus just doesn't do well outside the body. Now, back to your question. Let me see now, ah, yes, I've got it. The positive result is—you said the preliminary positive report?"

"Yes, that's correct."

"Okay, the test is done with the so-called enzyme immunoassay using the Virnostika anti-HIV viral lysate, which is 99.8 percent specific for the HIV 1 virus. What have you told the patient so far?"

"Nothing. He doesn't know we've tested him."

"He doesn't?" Foster asked, his voice sounding surprised. "Didn't he sign the consent for the test?"

"As a matter of fact, he refused to even look at the consent."

"Ah," Foster said slowly. "I think I'm beginning to get the big picture. Somehow I feel Steve Decker may have been involved with this event. Blake, give me that number on his blood and I'll make sure the Western Blot confirmation study is run through quickly. They're backed up several days in the lab, but I can speed it up and get the results a little quicker, maybe early next week. Levy's data should be back about the same time."

Skeeters gave him Kekoa Puuho's HIV test number and received a promise of a call in the near future.

* * *

The Corvette screeched into the parking spot next to the stairs and quickly turned off the headlights. Decker usually avoided the cramped visitors' parking area because of the high risk for door dings from those who didn't care about such things. However, it was the darkest part of the parking lot and so it was perfect for tonight. He climbed out of his car and walked around to the passenger side, furtively scanning the surrounding area for anyone who might be watching.

He opened the door and reached inside.

"Easy, boy, easy," he said as he enclosed the animal in the sheet from his bed and, with a grunt, lifted it from the car. He struggled up the stairs, his sheet undulating from the thrashing activities of the dog. Just before he reached the second level, a thin and wet black nose wiggled out of a fold in the sheet and two dark eyes looked up at Decker.

"Now, stay in there, boy," he said sternly as he quickly pulled the sheet back over its nose.

He set the animal on the floor at the foot of his bed and returned to his car for two boxes in the central console. They were both heavy. One had nothing but a packing number stamped on the side, the other was filled with fifty bullets. He pulled out a sack of dry dog food from behind the seats, locked the car doors and set the Corvette's alarm, and he finally returned to his apartment.

A plaintive whine greeted him as he walked through the door. After locking the chain and dead bolt, Decker turned around to face his new dog. The animal, a long, slender purebred greyhound, was standing in spite of the Kerlex gauze wrapped around his left hind leg. He was a graceful but fragile-looking animal. His eyes were large and dark, and at that moment he was looking at his new master, eagerly awaiting directions.

"Sit, boy, sit!" Decker commanded. The animal carefully folded its slender legs beneath him, letting out a quick yelp as his left leg stretched under the dressing, and gently placed his rump on the hardwood floor. "That's okay, you'll feel better in a week or two," Decker said. He patted the dog on his head, placed a bowl of water next to the bed, and began spreading newspapers on every available square foot of floor space.

He reached Katie at her apartment.

"Steve, I was getting worried. I tried to call you earlier, and when you weren't home, I tried the Jail Ward. They said you had left there hours ago. Why don't you get an answering machine for your telephone?"

"I'm sorry, honey, this has been a rather unusual day." He told her about the envelope at his bedside that morning and how Skeeters had moved Barbara to a motel somewhere in Pasadena, where he thought she would be safe. He told her about Sergeant Monroe and the problems trying to get police protection. And he finally told her that he had brought a new dog named Limpy.

"You brought a guard dog named *Limpy*?" She laughed. "They allow dogs in your apartment?"

"Actually, I didn't buy it and actually they don't."

"Somebody gave you the watchdog? What kind of dog is it?"

"A purebred greyhound."

"Somebody gave you a greyhound?" she exclaimed. "Those are valuable dogs."

"I paid twenty dollars for it."

"I see." She paused for a moment. "Steve, where did you find a purebred greyhound for twenty dollars?"

Decker smiled. "I wanted a big watchdog to guard

the apartment while I'm asleep. I left the Jail Ward an hour early and went to three pet stores to buy a good dog. All they sold were puppies. Turned out you have to go to a breeder if you want something in the watchdog line. And so I called the Humane Society and asked if they had anything bigger than a poodle. And they said yes, they had a racing dog that went lame during his last race."

"And so now you have a purebred lame greyhound racing guard dog to protect you—"

"Lame only for a few weeks. The Humane Society said they usually recover okay, but that they can't race anymore."

"You've done very well, Steve." Her voice became serious. "Honey, why don't you just quit the Jail Ward, get off the Jail Ward, and let the police do their thing up there? You're not a cop, you're a doctor. It isn't your business to nail those people. Let the police do it."

"I'm going to let the police do it. I'm just going to make sure they have enough information to do it right. Katie, those bastards have been stealing drugs from our patients all month long, from the patients who are in pain, and they have probably been doing the same thing for years."

"Okay, okay. When can I see you again?"

"Next Wednesday. On the first of August, when I finish with the Jail Ward and start my Urology rotation,"

"Next Wednesday!" she protested. "I haven't seen you all week, not since last Monday when that creep was chasing us!" Her voice softened. "I really miss you, Steve."

"I miss you, too, and I don't want anything to happen to you, Katie. I don't know how far these people will go to stop us, and I don't want them to know that we're . . . that we're together."

Katie was silent.

"Katie? Honey?"

After a few seconds, she finally answered, "Yes?"

"Katie, I don't want them to know how I feel about you. Do you understand how dangerous it would be for you if they knew . . . if they knew . . ." Decker stopped again, his mouth dry, his heart pounding in his chest.

"Steve? Are you okay?"

Might as well go ahead and say it like it is. "If they knew that I love you. I don't want anything to happen to you," he repeated gently. "They would come after you if they knew that, if they knew that I love you, and they would use you to stop me. Another five days, honey, and we can be together forever."

"How did you find this place?" Decker asked as the two interns sat down near the edge of the balcony. Their morning rounds on the Jail Ward were finished and they had estimated they would have about thirty minutes of free time before Gerald Brodie's whining voice would call them for the next admission.

"Found the balcony about a week ago, when I was carrying a syringe of arterial blood up to the pulmonary lab," Skeeters said. "First time since our orientation that I had been above the fourteenth floor. Came out of the elevator, went right instead of left, and popped out here. I think this part of the hospital is abandoned."

"Probably structurally unsafe, and here we are—stuck 'way out on the side of the building."

"Just don't look down," Skeeters cautioned with a shudder. "I almost lost my syringe over the side last week when I noticed it's a straight drop, nineteen stories to the emergency room parking lot. And the way the wind is blowing today, we better stay in our chairs."

It was a blistering "Santa Ana day" in Los Angeles. The hot and powerful Santa Ana wind had started the night before, howling in from the Mojave Desert, blowing over trees and signs while clearing the smog and spiking the temperature up to 103 degrees. The two men looked out at the unusually clear view of the sprawling city below, where the Golden State Freeway and the San Bernardino Freeway crossed in a swirl of circular on-ramps and off-ramps. Farther to the south, they could see cars racing back and forth across the Pomona and Santa Ana Freeway intersections before finally straightening out and heading for the horizon. A blend of warbling sounds from distant sirens carried up to the balcony, mixing with the whistling of the winds whirling around the side of the building.

Decker leaned back in his chair and looked over at Skeeters. "Did you get any sleep last night?" he asked.

"Skeeters stretched and rubbed his eyes. "Not much, Steve, not in that goddamn motel. And this whole thing has hit Barbara hard. She's afraid to go to sleep so long as those people are on the loose out there. I double-locked and latched the motel door, and nobody knows where we are."

"We could just drop the whole thing, Blake."

"Any other interns want to join with us?" Skeeters asked.

"They see about as much as the last twenty or thirty groups of interns have seen—nothing," Decker answered. "I think Tyra Levy was the only one who was really on to it, but she went at it too hard and fast. She pissed off Martel and pissed off that deputy with the Hycomine, and so they got her."

"We're still not sure about that, Steve. Remember how she looked the day before she died—she was pretty stressed out."

"Okay, that's still not definite, but damned suspicious. The other interns are just trying to survive the Jail Ward rotation. They're not even beginning to look at what's happening. I think this is up to you and me, whatever we decide."

"What do *you* want to do, Steve?" Skeeters asked in a strangely flattened voice as he studied his friend. "This thing has been getting really personal as far as I'm concerned."

"What do I want to do?" Decker sat up in his chair, his eyes narrowing. "Okay, Blake, I'll tell you what I want to do. I have become very pissed off during these last couple of weeks. I want to nail those bastards so hard that this big White Mama"—he slammed his hand against the wall next to his chair—"is shaking when we're through. Those guys are parasitic leeches, they have fucked up our patients, they have fucked up your marriage, they have fucked up my relationship with Katie, they have killed one of our colleagues, and I want to squash every goddamn one of them, right up to the top of their operation."

He took a short breath and let it out quickly as he sat back in his chair again. "There, that's how I feel. I just think we should both want to do this or we shouldn't do it at all, simple as that. If you want to get out of it, then we both get out."

Skeeters looked relieved and smiled as he said, "Believe it or not, I feel even more strongly about this than you do. Considering what they have done, there is no other choice for us, not now. The problem is that we're going to run out of time. I don't want to be rotating through Gastroenterology in one or two months and still be dealing with anybody attached to the Jail Ward. I want to get this over with before we start our new rotations, before next Wednesday."

"We have enough to warrant emergency meetings or ad hoc meetings, or whatever kind of meeting is appropriate with the hospital committees that deal with this sort of thing, don't we?" Decker asked.

"Hell, yes! We have enough to go ahead now. Since nobody seems to be running any drugs recently, or at least not since I screwed up Freddie Freeze's little mission a couple of days ago, we're not going to become any stronger than we are now. We need meetings with the chairmen of the Pharmacy and Therapeutics Committee, with the Ethics Committee, and with the Quality Assurance Committee, and we need to meet with somebody attached to the Drug Enforcement Administration."

"The DEA is a state of California deal, isn't it?"

"Yup, right out of Sacramento, where we send our money for the narcotics license."

"Think we can do it all on Monday?" Decker asked.

"Monday is perfect. We'll finish up our last night on call tomorrow, gather our ammunition on Sunday, and lay it all out for the DEA and committee chairmen bright and early Monday morning," Skeeters said.

"Like a show-and-tell operation." Decker smiled.

"Show them and tell them and then duck when the missiles start flying."

"I'll call the DEA, you call the chief of the medical staff this afternoon, and"—Decker snapped his fingers and grinned—"on Monday, we'll take care of this whole goddamn Jail Ward mess."

It had been a long afternoon on the Jail Ward for Steve Decker not only because of the surges of prisoners, delivered from all corners of the county, but also because of the whining voice of Gerald Brodie, broadcasting the admissions like he was handing out some kind of award to each intern. Decker had worked as fast as he could, scrawling admission orders and progress notes for each assigned patient, while he had tried to squeeze in a call to the Drug Enforcement Administration before Brodie's microphone could come to life again. On four occasions he had reached the DEA, and on all four, he had been put on hold for extended periods until Brodie's loudspeaker voice blasted out the announcement of yet another prisoner to be admitted.

In the middle of one of his calls, Skeeters walked by and announced that they would be meeting with the three chairmen of the medical staff committees, as well as the chief of staff at ten o'clock on Monday morning.

"Great, thanks, Blake. I'm still trying to get past the mechanical voice at the DEA that puts all calls on hold. *'Please do not hang up. Your call will be handled in the order received,'* " Decker mimicked.

"You still haven't completed your one call yet?"

Brodie's whining voice interrupted them, echoing up and down the walls of the thirteenth floor, calling for Decker to pick up his next patient, a red blanket en route to the Prep Room. Decker again slowly hung up the telephone, looking depressed as he mumbled some words that nobody could hear or understand, and wandered down the corridor to admit another prisoner to the Jail Ward.

By 4:30, he was finally able to contact a DEA agent with a deep rumbling voice and the unlikely name of Jeff Lord. To his immense surprise, Lord readily agreed to meet with the two interns first thing Monday morning, indicating that he would be more than happy to discuss the "little problem you say you have with drugs over there at the County Hospital." By the time Decker had finished his last admission and had dragged himself out of the hospital, it was after seven and he was exhausted.

He was halfway between the main hospital and the parking structure when he abruptly halted and looked at his watch.

It wouldn't hurt to give her a call, just a quickie call to hear her voice, he reasoned. *This is Friday night, for Christ's sake. Saturday will be another twenty-four hours of duty on the Jail Ward, and there won't be a chance to see her until the middle of next week.* He turned and walked toward a row of pay telephones.

Five minutes later, feeling that warm flush of having arranged for the evening's events—*We'll go somewhere quiet, Katie, out of the way. Nobody will see us, and I'll watch out for anyone following us. And I promise I won't even bring up the subject of the Jail Ward*—Decker walked briskly toward the parking structure with a new bounce in his step.

He had left his car in its usual place that morning, on the second floor of the dark concrete structure, in the corner, far enough from the other cars to avoid damage. When he walked out of the staircase on the second floor, the Rent-A-Cop guard who wandered up and down the lines of cars was nowhere to be seen. *No big deal,* Decker thought, the cars within the structure were well isolated from the high crime atmosphere that surrounded the County Hospital, and he had been told on several occasions that no intern had ever had a car stolen from the lot. He smiled to himself: the main reason for that was because few of the cars were desirable enough to steal. The money-making years for most of the physicians were still far away.

He spotted his gleaming red machine as he had left

it, backed into the corner spot 50 yards away, ready to accelerate away from this place! Away, and off to Katie's . . .

At the right side of the parking lot, across from the Corvette, brake lights flashed on briefly and an old engine rumbled to life. It was a Chrysler Cordoba, Decker noticed, a real gas-guzzling tank, and it looked like somebody had sprayed the side of it with rust-colored paint. As the car backed out of its spot, Decker could see that the rust color was from actual rust eating away at the side panels. It was the favorite kind of car for interns, he reflected, not pretty to look at maybe, but usually reliable and easy to pay for.

As Decker approached his car, he watched the Chrysler continue backing across the center of the parking structure, the white-coated woman behind the wheel trying to turn sharply to the left. From her struggle, Decker guessed the power steering was probably shot. As the driver struggled to finish the backing turn, it was apparent that its back bumper was heading directly for the low front end of Decker's car. "Stop!" he yelled, "you're going to hit my car!" He broke into a run, waving his arms. "Stop! Look out!" he yelled at the top of his lungs as the back corner of the Chrysler's rusted bumper rammed directly into the front of the Corvette.

Before he could say another word, the entire corner of the parking structure suddenly erupted into a blinding flash of orange flame, accompanied by a thunderous explosion. It felt like slow-motion, Decker later recalled, as he instinctively tried to shield his eyes with his arm. Almost before his eyes were closed, he felt himself lifted into the air, landing flat on his back and sliding another 3 feet. He lay on the concrete for a few seconds, looking up at shadows of flames dancing across the strips of concrete above him. He lifted his head slowly, trying to see his car. His chest was feeling some discomfort; he looked at it and discovered that his green intern's shirt had a round hole in the center, a round hole that was on fire. He lifted his head further and studied it closely; it was a ring of fire that was amazing for its perfection—the hole was perfectly round and expanding in a perfectly formed circle, the flames eating into the cloth, exposing his undershirt and forming a sooty black circle that grew with the beautiful orange flames.

His eyes lifted to scan the end of the parking structure. The Corvette was nowhere to be seen. That was strange—several cars were on fire and burning furiously, including the Chrysler, which was now back in its original parking space. Somehow that seemed hilariously funny, and Decker found himself beginning to laugh. As his laughter became louder, he suddenly realized with a profound shock that he could hear nothing.

Out of the corner of his eye, he saw people running. He felt a large hand slap his chest, killing the flames that were feeding his perfect circle. He felt tired and he finally settled his head back on the concrete to rest.

As his body metabolized the morphine, the sound of distant voices carried into Decker's mind. He felt as if he were suspended in space, with a peaceful vision—like a dream—of a hazy, rose-colored driveway sweeping down and away into the distance. He looked up and down the driveway, searching for his car.

His eyes shot open, and he was immediately blinded by brilliant lights shining down from the overhead of the emergency room cubicle. A large black man wearing the white uniform of a County Hospital nurse was standing next to his bed, staring down at him. The nurse turned his head to the left and spoke in a voice Decker could barely hear.

"He's coming around now."

Looking across the room, he squinted his eyes and could make out the shape of a man wearing a dark suit. The man answered, his voice sounding far away, like a bad telephone connection, his words barely decipherable. Decker squinted again. A police officer's badge was conspicuously displayed over his left front pocket.

The nurse spoke to the police officer again, his voice a strangely metallic sound. "His hearing will clear in the next few hours; the doctor has confirmed both his tympanic membranes . . . both his eardrums are intact and undamaged. Soon as we put a dressing on that burn and"—he looked at Decker's face—"as soon as the narcotics wear off, he should be cleared for discharge. He was just stunned by the concussion. His X rays are negative for any fractures."

The man with the badge watched as the nurse leaned over Decker.

"How do you feel, Dr. Decker?" he said as he shined a penlight into Decker's eyes.

The bright glare burned and Decker jerked his head away, immediately triggering a pounding headache. He took a deep breath and glared at the nurse. "I would feel better if you stopped shining that damn light in my eyes." He took another deep breath. His mouth felt as though it was full of cotton. "And I would appreciate it even more if you would stop talking like Mickey Mouse."

The nurse apologized and quickly put away his penlight. He walked to the side of the room and turned the overhead lights down to a soft glow.

"Thank you," Decker said, realizing that his voice

sounded as bad as the nurse's. "What's wrong with my voice?"

"Shock wave effect on your ears, from what the ER Doc said. Makes everyone sound like cartoon characters. Usually temporary, fortunately, and take it as a good sign that you can hear this well so soon. You've had a mild concussion and there's been some acoustic trauma to your tympanic membranes. A few more hours and you'll probably be back to normal."

He pointed to the police officer. "This is Detective Jeff Lord, from the DEA. He wants to talk with you. I'll be outside the door if you need anything."

The nurse left the cubicle, closing the door behind him.

Decker looked at the officer, trying to move his head slowly enough to avoid triggering another episode of pain. Lord's dark blue suit was immaculate, his colorful silk tie looked expensive and fashionable, and his gleaming gold badge looked brand-new. His face was square and solid, with dark blue eyes that studied Decker intently. *Looks like someone off a Canadian Royal Mounted Police poster,* Decker thought. The deep rumbling voice was unmistakable.

"How are you feeling, Decker?"

"I feel like hell. We were going to meet you on Monday."

"Right, change in plans, thanks to the . . ."

Decker missed the last half of the detective's sentence.

"Could you speak up? My hearing is all screwed up."

"Change in plans, thanks to the bad guys," Lord said, more loudly. "You are very lucky, Decker. If you had arrived at your car a couple of minutes sooner, you would have been inside that fireball instead of watching it from an almost safe distance."

Decker hesitated, absorbing the words. "What are you talking about, Lord?" he finally said, lifting his head off the pillow. His head pounded again, like a fist against the inside of his skull. "If I hadn't stopped to call my girlfriend, I could have moved my car before that rusted hulk plowed its gas tank into the front of my car!"

"Decker, it wasn't a gas tank that exploded. It was a bomb."

Decker's eyes opened wide. "What are you talking about? That was a bomb that went off out there?"

Lord nodded. "We think it was a bomb."

"Jesus . . . My Corvette is destroyed?"

"I'm sorry, yes, it is."

"Jesus," Decker repeated, turning away from Lord, looking up at the lights. "Katie saved . . . calling Katie saved my life. That call gave me the time. . . . Does she know what happened?"

"Nobody knows except the four or five people who put out the fire on your clothing and pulled the girl from the Chrysler. She's up in surgery right now, having some glass removed from the top of her head. The headrest on the back of her seat saved her . . . all the windows were blown out of her car. Nobody else was injured, but four other cars were completely destroyed. It was a powerful bomb."

"There's nothing left of my car?" he asked again, quietly. "I bought that car when it was brand-new."

"Decker, these guys are pros. Like I said, this was not an amateur pipe bomb. Your car was rigged for complete destruction, probably with two or three pounds of Composition-4 plastic explosives, triggered by a blasting cap and a motion-sensing device. From the way your engine was blown completely out of the area, they probably packed a pound or two of C-4 around the gas tank—the stuff is like putty—and a second glob under the engine, connected by a strand of explosive det cord. At least that's the theory of the guys on the bomb squad. They were definitely not trying to warn you with this, Decker, they were trying to *kill* you."

"Holy Christ . . ."

"The engine was blown completely out of the parking garage. It dropped two stories down and just missed three little kids and their mother coming out of your clinic. The rest of the car is gone. Nothing is left."

"Okay," Decker said as he closed his eyes and gritted his teeth. "That's the way it's going to be . . ."

"Dr. Decker?"

Decker said nothing and the room was quiet except for the distant sounds of crying women.

"Dr. Decker? I'm sorry, but I have to ask you. Was there anything in the car that might have helped us with our investigation?"

"Your investigation? Your investigation of what?"

Lord glanced at the door, making sure it was shut. "Our investigation of the drug problem on the Jail Ward."

Decker swung his legs over the side of the exam table and sat up, immediately feeling a wave of nausea. "What do you mean, *your* investigation? Skeeters and I have been working on this—"

"For three weeks, right? The DEA and the district attorney's office have been on this case for over a year now, Decker, and we're almost ready to turn the screws. We have a man undercover on the floor, collecting the last information needed to seal this thing up. The problem is, we haven't been able to get to the top. We don't know who's pulling the strings at the County Jail or here at County Hospital. We need a little more time to bring the loose ends together."

The room stopped spinning and Decker focused his eyes on the agent. "Nothing was in my car. I've got the information we accumulated in a safe place. We need to have it on Monday when we run it past the Ethics Committee chairman, the—"

"The QA Committee, and the PT & T Committee. We know all about your meetings. Where is Skeeters now? We haven't been able to find him."

"He's safe with his wife, and I can't tell you where. Hell, we both had a bomb threat placed in our rooms a couple of nights ago. Skeeters and his wife are really spooked out."

"I'm sorry, we didn't know about that."

"Well, it happened, and Skeeters doesn't want anybody to know where he or his wife is."

"Okay. It's important that Skeeters continues working on the Jail Ward for the rest of the rotation. Anything out of the ordinary will send them running before we can shut them down. They're already skittish as hell, and they're making mistakes."

"Like not blowing me up, right?" Decker asked ruefully.

"No, Decker, like even trying to blow you up. It was a bad decision for whoever made it. They probably assumed that if you weren't killed, you would be so thoroughly intimidated that you wouldn't even think about narcotics for the rest of your intern year. But a bomb generates a lot of attention and therefore works against them, especially when it doesn't even do its intended job."

"Well, it damn near did its job. . . . Skeeters and I are both on duty tomorrow, and you can talk to him then. Who's your undercover man on the floor?"

"I can't tell you that." The agent's face left no doubt about the futility of further questions on the subject. "I'm sorry, Decker, but you're going to have to stay out of the Jail Ward tomorrow. They won't expect you back after this thing, and your absence will give them a false sense of security. I've arranged for you to stay at the MacFarland Motel across the street, where you'll be under twenty-four-hour police protection until the arrests are made on Monday or Tuesday."

"Lord"—he looked up at the man—"look, I can't keep calling you Lord. Would you mind if I just call you Jeff?"

Lord smiled. "Sure, a lot of people have trouble with Lord. Go ahead and call me whatever you want."

"Thanks. Do you or your people know where the guard was, the one who was supposed to be guarding the cars in the parking structure?"

"Easy question. They paid him off, he's long gone. These people have a lot of money at their disposal. A couple thousand dollars to a minimum-wage high school flunkout is like winning the lottery." He looked at his watch. "I've got to go. Didn't want to spend this much time here, damn it. We'll see you on Monday." He turned and left the room.

Decker began pulling on his clothes, his muscles aching, especially across his back. The ringing in his ears had diminished, and he tested his hearing by trying to detect the ticking of his watch held up against his ear. Better, but not yet normal. He tied his shoes and pulled on his T-shirt, the front partially blackened from the fire. He rolled up his green shirt with the hole burned through the front—a little memento—and as he stood up, a harassed-looking man wearing a stained white coat walked into the room.

"Decker? Good, you're up and about. I'm Randy Bowman, ER doc tonight. I was going to check you out of here if you're back on the line again. Or we can keep you here tonight, if you want."

"Thanks, I think I'm doing all right. I need to get out of here."

"Okay with me. Helluva thing, explosion like that. That girl in the other car is going to be okay, they said. Fortunately, nobody else was injured—most victims of car fires are usually badly burned. Here, let me just check your dressing."

He lifted the T-shirt and examined Decker's chest, looking under the gauze pad at the burned skin. "It's superficial, won't be any scar, Steve. Just do the usual—keep it clean, wash it off with a little hydrogen peroxide, couple of times a day, put on some silver sulfadiazine, and it should heal up just fine." He dropped the shirt back down. "By the way, Dr. Marsh called to tell you he was sorry to hear about your accident. He's out of the county, giving a lecture in San Bernardino tonight, but he said for you to take a couple of days' rest from the Jail Ward. Said he'd arrange for one of the ER guys to cover with your partner, what's his name, Skipper?"

"Skeeters."

"Yeah, Skeeters. He'll arrange for someone to cover for you over the weekend. What did the DEA guy want?"

"Something about a drug screen in the girl driving the car that hit my Corvette," Decker said without hesitation.

"Good thought, the way she rammed your car. Must have hit it pretty hard for an explosion like that. Couple of more police of some sort are waiting for you right outside the room. Helluva way to get a vacation off the Jail Ward, my friend."

The sound of the switchboard telephone ringing startled her in the quiet of the evening. The lobby was empty and she was the only person available to cover the front desk. She put down the handful of reservation cards and walked over to the switchboard.

"Roundtree Best Western, may I help you?"

"Yes," the man's voice said. "Would you connect me to Mr. Anderson's room, please."

She looked at her watch. "It's a little late, sir. Are the Andersons expecting your call?"

"Yes, ma'am."

"All right, sir, I'll connect you." She sighed and pushed two buttons, dialed room 237, and pushed a third button. She hated to connect calls after nine o'clock. She was the person the guests always jumped on when they were interrupted from . . . she smiled. It wasn't her fault people called, after all.

The telephone rang loudly in the quiet room.

"Hello?" she answered softly.

"Mrs. Anderson?"

"Yes?"

"May I speak to Mr. Anderson, please? This is Steve."

"Yes, you may, here he is."

"Hello?" he said, taking the telephone from her.

Decker's voice cracked as he struggled to speak. "They're using bombs. They're trying to stop us with fucking bombs. My car's gone, they almost got me. Stay away from your apartment, stay away from your car."

"Steve, are you okay?"

"They're really trying to get us, buddy. They have gone way too far with this thing. They have now made this personal for me, too, Blake. They have now made this thing personal as hell."

Chapter 11

For the first time since they were married, Skeeters was out of bed and dressed before his wife awakened. His eyes opened abruptly at six sharp, his mind already racing, his body feeling charged and ready for the final twenty-four hours on the Jail Ward.

He searched through the cupboards next to the sink, looking for some food. They hadn't had time to grab more than a few boxes of cereal and some bread and cold cuts in the rush out of their apartment the day before. The motel ice bucket held a quart of milk in a bowl filled with ice water that had warmed during the night. Next to the sink was a small bottle of prenatal vitamins, prominently placed where Barbara would be sure to see it. He glanced over at the bed: she was still peacefully asleep. He took one of the pills from the bottle and placed it on a tissue next to the sink, filled a glass with water, and placed it next to the pill. He slipped a small note under the glass, wishing her a good morning and letting her know that he loved her.

Fifteen minutes later, after consuming a withered apple and a bowl of warm milk over Granola cereal, Skeeters dressed and pulled on a clean white coat— *might as well look nice for the last day*. He jammed his stethoscope into his pocket and walked over to the motel window. The Volkswagen was in the parking lot where he had left it the night before, the windows still up and the vehicle looking undisturbed.

He scanned the parking area and then looked back at his car.

After finding a number in the telephone directory, he walked into the bathroom and quietly shut the door. *Excellent idea, placing a telephone in the bathroom. Never know when you are going to need to use the telephone. . . .* He picked up the receiver and dialed the number.

"Yellow Cab," the voice answered.

"This is Mr. Anderson," Skeeters said, "at the Roundtree Best Western Motel, on Marengo Street. Would you send a cab as soon as possible."

"Yes, sir, we can have one there in about five or ten minutes."

"That will be fine, thank you."

Like a goddamn prisoner, he thought as he paced up and down the floor near the door. *Trapped in this miserable cockroach-infested place, guarded by police just like the drug addicts on the Jail Ward.*

He walked over and sat on the bed, fuming. Outside the room, the shape of a man walking down the corridor passed once again in front of the curtains; Decker raced across the room and pulled the curtain aside, watching as the man's avocado shape slowly ambled into the distance. It was the same man who had been there since 2 A.M. *Christ, the guy radiated police. Doesn't anybody around here have any brains? Just exactly how many Caucasian men do you see in this part of Los Angeles, strolling nonchalantly in front of a flea-bitten hole of a motel from 2 A.M. until God-knows-when?*

A rapid movement on the floor caught his eye. It was a cockroach, bigger than most of the creatures he had been watching throughout the night, racing in the direction of the bed, its antennae thrashing wildly as it searched for someplace to hide.

"Ah-ha!" Decker yelled as he pulled off his shoe and leaped halfway across the room, hammering the bug flat in less than a second. "Gotcha!"

As he looked around for something to clean up the remains, two more cockroaches crawled out from under the bed, and headed for a high-speed escape out the front door. "Nice try!" Decker yelled as he sprung across the room again and flattened one of them with another swift downward movement of his shoe. Before Decker could raise the shoe again, the remaining cockroach was under the front door and gone to the relative safety of the outdoors.

The avocado shape passed in front of the window again.

"Okay, that does it."

Decker picked up the telephone and called the number written across the back of the paper Jeff Lord had given him the night before.

"I'm sorry, the Drug Enforcement Administration is closed until nine Monday morning." The female voice recording was sweet and proper.

"Jeff Lord? This is Dr. Stephen Decker."

"If this is an emergency, please hang up and dial 911 now!"

"Thank you, Jeff, for leaving me some food and for the toothbrush and toothpaste. That was very thoughtful."

"If this is routine business, please hang up and dial this number again during routine business hours."

"However, Jeff, in spite of your courtesy and consideration, I find that I really cannot stay in this place any longer."

"If you would like to leave a brief message, please push 1 now."

Decker pushed 1 and hollered into the telephone, "This fucking place is crawling with cockroaches!"

He slammed down the receiver and stormed out the front door.

Pepe's Mexican Restaurant (Since 1937) was the only Hispanic dining facility in the Greater Los Angeles area to open its doors each morning at 6 A.M. Located within the shadow of the massive hospital one block to the north, the tiny restaurant catered to hordes of nurses, technicians, and doctors, all of whom regularly craved a quick snack before or after work. Whatever Pepe's food may have been lacking in flavor—and all agreed there was something lacking—was readily made up for by the low price and by the speed with which it was served. The owner, a large Mexican man whose size allowed the customers to see what they would look like if they ate his food for more than fifty years, took pride in the fact that his thirty-eight seats could allow meals to be served to over 200 health care workers per rush hour.

Decker walked through Pepe's front door at 6:55 and pulled up a chair near the far wall. *Sure enough,* he thought, *there they are, my protection, Mr. Avocado and Mr. Pockmark.* The only two men east of Beverly Hills with gray suits sat down on the other side of the restaurant, close to the door, and picked up a pair of menus. By 7:03, Decker's order had been taken by the undocumented worker for two tacos, one tamale, and skip those flatus-generating beans, *por favor.* By 7:07, a plate with food that closely resembled what he had ordered was dropped on the table in front of him. At 7:15, the usual surge of Saturday morning hospital workers pushed into the restaurant, taking every available seat and crowding around the counter, where many of them could informally gulp down a quick bite of Pepe's best.

At 7:25, as Pepe's customer load exceeded the Fire Department's occupancy limit by nearly 100 percent, Decker suddenly had to go to the bathroom.

Blake Skeeters arrived on the Jail Ward five minutes early for his morning rounds. Saturday morning was usually quiet, almost as if everyone on the thirteenth floor was bracing for the Saturday night crush of new patients. It was usually the busiest night of the week, and rarely did the on-call interns get more than a few minutes' sleep throughout.

Skeeters looked around the ward and discovered that Decker had not yet arrived. He hadn't said anything last night about not coming in today. Skeeters walked down the central corridor to the Cage, watched Choo-Choo pace for a couple of minutes, then began to hunt for his other seven patients scattered throughout the ward. Everyone was still alive, that was encouraging, and two of the patients were even doing well enough to be transferred back to the County Jail. By 7:51 the load of paperwork to accomplish that task was completed, and twenty minutes later, those prisoners were gone. Kekoa Puuho sourly announced that he had registered another 3 pounds' weight loss at his morning weigh-in, and Skeeters decided to start him on anti-tuberculosis medication while awaiting the cultures and lung tissue specimen report.

Just before eight o'clock, Skeeters wheeled Jack Diamond into the Prep Room to remove the cast from his right leg. A large, almost matronly woman in a white nurse's uniform walked into the room behind them and announced that she would help with the cast removal and anything else they might need.

"I don't recall having seen you here before," Dr. Skeeters said as she stood next to the exam table.

"I'm the nurse for the Jail Ward today. They transferred me here from the surgery floor."

Skeeters looked at her closely and asked, "Where's Peter Martel?"

"Oh, Peter quit yesterday. Just like that"—she snapped her fingers—"he quit."

"He quit?" Skeeters's jaw dropped.

"Just like that." She snapped her fingers again.

"Why did he quit?"

"Burned out, just like all the rest of us here. I'd quit if I had half the chance."

"Anybody know he was leaving?"

"I don't think even he knew he was leaving. Never did talk much about it to any of us."

"Where did he go?"

"Home probably, and if I were him, off to a good long vacation. The amount of time he worked here, without a break, good Lord, the man must have been a saint."

"Not exactly. And your name is . . ."

"Betty Miles. Just call me Betty. Anybody start calling me Ms. Miles and they can find themselves another nurse. I hate that woman's lib nonsense."

"Okay, Betty it is. This gentleman here with the cast on his leg is Mr. Jack Diamond. Had an osteomyelitis of his right femur that has been slowly healing. Need to x-ray the bone to check the structural integrity. If that looks okay, we're going to take the cast off."

"Nice to meet you, ma'am," Diamond said, reaching out to shake her hand.

Betty took a step back and put her hands on her hips as she surveyed Diamond. "Why, that is the wildest purple hairdo I have ever seen," she said, grinning broadly. "Fantastic, I love it!" She reached out and shook the patient's hand vigorously as Diamond smiled and pulled off his mass of hair, holding it out for inspection.

"Here you are, Betty, wanna try it on?" he said.

"Oh, my goodness! I've never seen anything like that. Why don't you keep it on your head where it looks so nice while I run and get the X ray for Doctor . . . Doctor . . ."

"Skeeters."

"For Dr. Skeeters."

A large man with dirty blond hair and puffy-looking pale skin abruptly walked into the Prep Room and interrupted Skeeters's examination of Diamond. "I am going to be taking Dr. Decker's place in the Jail Ward until the end of the month," he announced brusquely, "since he is no longer in the internship."

Skeeters straightened and looked at the man. He took his stethoscope from around his neck and handed it to Diamond. "Would you hold this for me for a minute, Jack?"

"I would be happy to, Dr. Skeeters."

"Thank you, I appreciate it."

Skeeters walked outside the Prep Room, motioning for the man to follow. They crossed the corridor and walked into the Doctors' On-Call Room. Skeeters closed the door behind them and turned around to face the man.

"Would you like to repeat what you just said?"

"I'm here to take Dr. Decker's place. I'm completing my residency in Emergency Medicine, and Dr. Marsh called me to fill in up here. Since Dr. Decker is no longer in the internship, here I am."

Skeeters fought to control himself. "I think you and Dr. Marsh are incorrect about Dr. Decker. He is still in the internship, he has been on call with me all month, he is on call with me today, and nobody is going to take his place. Do you understand that?"

"Sure, I was just—"

"Now, would you go back to the emergency room where they need you more than we do. Would you do that for me?"

Without a word, the man turned and walked off the Jail Ward.

Skeeters closed the door and sat down at the table. He could feel his body shaking and his heart pounding. He tried to force himself to relax. *What in the world is happening to me,* he thought. *I never used to talk to people like that. Maybe I'm going crazy. If Barbara ever heard me, my God, she would . . .*

A tapping at the door turned him around. He stood up and opened the door again to find Betty Miles standing in front of him. "I have some bad news, Dr. Skeeters."

"No reason to change the course of events. Go ahead, drop it on me, Betty."

"Sorry. Well, you know the X rays you wanted, the ones of Mr. Diamond's leg?"

"Yes?"

"They haven't been taken yet. He wasn't here when the X-ray techs came three days ago. Probably went to the bathroom or something. Anyway, he wasn't here and so they didn't take the X ray."

"Why didn't they come back and take the X ray another time? Like, when he wasn't going to the bathroom?"

Betty braced herself. "They tore up the requisition."

"They tore up my requisition for the X ray?"

"They tore it up, and they've been waiting for you to make out another requisition. Without telling you they had torn up your last requisition, they were waiting for you to fill out another requisition."

Skeeters didn't say anything for a moment as he looked down at the floor. Finally, he looked back up at the nurse. "Thank you, Betty," he said. "Would you take Mr. Diamond back to his place in the corridor and would you make out a new requisition for me? I really would appreciate it."

Steve Decker arrived on the Jail Ward at 8:05. It was Diamond who first saw him walking past the sheriff's watch station, and he almost flipped his wheelchair over as he quickly spun around and pointed his casted right leg in the general direction of the Cage.

"Dr. Skeeters!" he hollered.

Skeeters had been sitting in front of the Cage, writing orders for a new antipsychotic program for Choo-Choo when he heard the call. He turned around and saw Diamond pointing down the corridor.

Decker walked briskly down the central corridor, looking around at the various prisoners in the wards on either side. He nodded a quick greeting to Diamond as he passed by, and he flashed a big smile to Skeeters.

"On duty, ready to go, what's up?" he said enthusiastically as Skeeters pumped his arm and slapped his shoulder.

"I didn't think you were coming, my friend," Skeeters said with relief. "It is *very* good to see you, Steve. Dr. Marsh already had you replaced by some character from the emergency room. I thought I was going to go it alone today. And tonight . . ."

Decker looked around. "Replaced? I cannot be replaced. My car can be replaced, but I am irreplaceable."

"That's basically what I told the guy from the ER. I was real sorry to hear about your Corvette—the bastards."

"It was, in fact, a very close call. If I had not

stopped to call Katie, you'd definitely be on your own today." His voice dropped. "I thought you might not come in for your final call day, after that little extortion threat to you and Barbara."

"I thought about not coming in, believe me, but this is the last on-call day. I *have* to finish the rotation to get credit for the intern year. Besides, I have a batch of patients who need help until the next group of interns arrive. I think we should be fairly safe, in the hospital."

"Yeah, with all these deputy sheriffs around, I feel real safe. You know why I came back for the last on-call session, don't you?" Decker asked.

"No, why?"

"I came back here just to keep you from getting into trouble." Decker smiled, then looked around to ensure no one was listening. "Listen," he said quietly, "there is an investigation going on with the DEA. They grilled the hell out of me last night, and they tried to put me under some kind of police protection program. I'm supposed to be *in absentia,* hiding at the MacFarland Cockroach Motel. I don't know when it's going to come down, but I think they know about Grossman, Martel, and most of the prisoners from the County Jail, and I think they're going to take some action soon. The problem is, they don't know who's running the—"

"Steve . . ."

"They don't know who's—"

"Steve! Martel quit. Yesterday, he just quit."

Decker stared at Skeeters. "Peter Martel quit? You have to be kidding!"

"No reason given, no advance warning. Just went and quit."

"Holy shit. Most of the information we have is

about Martel's narcotics diversions." Decker thought for a moment.

"Do you think we should just turn everything over today," Skeeters said, "right now, everything we have, to the chief of the medical staff, to Marsh, or to the DEA guys?"

"We could, except the book with our documentation is still in my apartment, where I hid it. Thank God I didn't leave it in my car. I'm going to have to get it somehow, add anything we come up with today, and then we can turn it over to them . . . Monday's going to have to be the day, no way around it. Maybe I can get Katie to help us out."

"Does she know about the explosion and your car?"

"Yup. Last night I called her from the insect motel." Decker smiled. "Still loves me, she said. Even without my car. That's a good sign."

"Probably loves you more without the car, the way you drive it," Skeeters said dryly.

"Drove it, thanks, buddy. I'll give her a call again, later today. I want her to pick up my dog also, she's going to love doing that. . . . How's Barbara doing?"

"Still hiding at our motel. Scared." Skeeters looked away for a second, then looked straight at Decker. "We're just going to have to ride this thing out, Steve. We'll give them what we have on Monday, and the police will hopefully take them out of circulation, for a long time. And when it's all over, Barbara and I will pick ourselves up and get on with our lives. We'll make it okay."

"I think we'll all be okay. When do you get the word on that slimo Aloha's Western Blot confirmation study for AIDS?"

Skeeters grimaced. "Probably Monday. Your friend Bennie Foster is trying to speed it up—they take forever down there. Chances are over 90 percent that it will be positive and then we'll just do what we have to do."

"Well, even if it is positive, you don't know if he was the one who contaminated the needle that stuck you. And even if he is the one, you still probably won't catch it."

"Yeah." Skeeters felt depressed. "Try to tell that to Barbara."

"Difficult situation, for sure," Decker said sympathetically. "Well, I better get to work. I have nine patients on the ward, and I think I can send three or four of them out this morning." He hesitated for a moment, then leaned over to Skeeters's ear. "By the way, there's supposed to be a DEA undercover agent on the Jail Ward."

"Yeah?" Skeeters smiled. "A genuine DEA guy? One of the sheriffs, bet you anything . . ."

"Possible. But more likely it's the Purple Queen."

"Are you kidding? Jack Diamond? No way. Nobody from the DEA can act that well."

"Maybe so, but how do you know he broke his leg, Blake?"

"I saw the X rays."

"How do you know they were his X rays?"

"Nah, it wouldn't be Diamond. He doesn't have the personality for it."

"Okay, but keep an eye on him. Remember, he's been here for over a month now and he is perfectly positioned out there in the corridor to pick up everything going on around here. He's smart and he would be perfect for the job. At least the DEA knows about Martel leaving. Hopefully, they're trying to find him."

They were startled by a snarl behind them. Both men quickly jumped away and turned around as Choo-Choo slammed up against the inside of the Cage. His eyes were glassy and unfocused, and both of his arms were extending out between the bars as far as he could reach, clawing at the air at precisely the level of the interns' necks.

"Looks like he's decompensating, Blake," Decker observed.

"I think my patient needs a new medication program," Skeeters said.

The first new prisoner of the day, a thoroughly frightened seventeen-year-old boy, arrived on the Jail Ward just before nine o'clock. The youth had been found inside Sears, where he had spent most of the night trying to select which items he wanted to steal the most. The police would have taken him directly to Juvenile Hall if he hadn't cut himself trying to crawl through one of the ventilation ducts while Sears employees ran around below, investigating the scratching noises coming from the ceiling. Gerald Brodie, recognizing this as a surgical case, requiring the suturing of multiple arm and leg lacerations, naturally passed over Decker, the surgeon, and assigned the case to Skeeters, the internist. To maintain balance, the ward clerk assigned the next patient—a forty-three-year-old diabetic with a blood sugar of 873 and abnormal levels of potassium and bicarbonate—to Decker, the surgeon.

The two men worked on their patients as the other Jail Ward interns systematically finished their rounds before leaving for the day. At ten o'clock in the morning, while Decker and Skeeters were examining patients and suturing lacerations incurred during a recent Hawaiian Gardens gang battle, Gerald Brodie strolled into the Prep Room.

"Dr. Marsh would like to see both of you gentlemen in his office in five minutes," he said, his narrow eyes squinting at the men.

Marsh greeted the two interns at his office door and

politely escorted them to the chairs in front of his desk. They sat down and Decker glanced at the ruby eyes of the two caduceus snakes wrapping around the staff on the tapestry across the room. The snakes looked bigger and somehow more evil than he had remembered. He sat back in the chair and tried to relax.

"First of all, Dr. Decker, let me congratulate you for avoiding serious injury when that resident hit your car's gas tank. You are a damned lucky fellow." The gold on his front tooth gleamed as he smiled.

"Thank you, sir," Decker answered respectfully. "I understand the girl driving the car is also going to be okay."

"Good, good. After hearing about it, I didn't think you were going to be with us today, and so I brought up a man from the emergency room. Dr. Skeeters had more faith in you"—the gold on his front tooth glinted—"and sent him back where he came from. Are you sure you are up to a final run on the Jail Ward tonight, Dr. Decker?"

"Yes, sir, I feel just fine."

Decker and Skeeters both nodded simultaneously, showing just the right amount of enthusiasm.

"Just a little abrasion on my back," Decker continued, "some ringing in my ears and a burn on my chest, all healing and improving."

"Good. You finish tonight, and that will wrap it up for both of you here. You can spend Sunday and Monday just signing off your patients and preparing for your next rotation. I know it hasn't been an easy month on the Jail Ward, but I tried to do what I could to help; you both had some tough cases."

It was time to move away from the small talk, Skeeters decided. "Dr. Marsh?" he asked.

"Yes, Blake?" Marsh turned and looked pleasantly

at the intern. It was the first time the director had referred to Skeeters by his first name.

"Would you be able to join Steve and me on Monday, when we go to the Drug Enforcement Administration?"

Without hesitation, Marsh answered, "Of course, Blake, of course. I think you're right to move on this more quickly than we had planned, and it will be better for us to do it together. Why don't you both gather up what you have, including, Blake, those graphs you drew up showing the timing of the morphine losses, I'll add what I have with the nursing schedule information and the morphine inventory, and we'll set up a time to meet with the DEA on Monday. Do you have any more information to help put this nurse away?"

"Somebody's threatening us, sir, in letters about a bomb," Decker said. "We think it was probably somebody, like one of the nurses—probably Martel, who felt we were getting too close."

"We think they're trying to scare us off, sir," Skeeters added. "Steve and I have talked about it, and we took the letters to the police but they couldn't do anything very helpful. We've finally just decided to ignore the letters until after we meet the DEA authorities on Monday or Tuesday."

"Excellent idea." Marsh looked back and forth at his two interns as if he was admiring his two sons.

"And one more thing, sir," Skeeters said. "I just heard the prelim report on Tyra Levy's autopsy. She didn't die of an overdose of sleeping pills. They've done everything but the final comprehensive tox screen and the coroner people expect to have the report ready next Wednesday."

"So what do they think was the cause of death?"

"They won't say until the screen is ready."

"Well, then, I guess we'll just have to wait. They'll

be checking the usual OD substances like narcotics, potassium, insulin . . ."

"And designer amphetamines—"

"Of course."

"—botulinus toxin, and mass spectrometer analysis of any pills they find. It sounds like they're doing a thorough job."

Marsh's white eyebrows drew together for an instant. "I don't think they'll be checking all those things, Blake. The cost would be prohibitive."

"I asked them to, sir. And they said they would."

"I see . . . Well, good, that should take care of that. I'll be particularly interested in the blood narcotics level, since I think she was having a problem."

Decker bolted upright. "What kind of a problem?"

"A drug problem. I didn't want to mention it since we're not sure, but Sergeant Grossman found a bottle of hydrocodone when he cleaned out her locker after she was found dead."

"Sir, she took that bottle from one of the deputies. She was concerned that he didn't have a prescription—"

"I asked Sergeant Grossman about that, Steve, and he said he checked with all his men. None of them had seen the bottle before."

"He's lying, sir. Tyra Levy did not have a drug problem, that's for damn sure. And she sure as hell wasn't using any hydrocodone."

"Well, that may be, but Grossman has submitted a report about the bottle of narcotics in her locker, and I'll have to turn that information in, along with everything else we have."

Dr. Marsh stood up, smiled appreciatively, and reached across the desk to shake hands with his interns. He called each of them again by their first names, and he thanked them for their kindness in stopping by for the chat. He attentively escorted them to the door and asked his secretary to schedule one final meeting with the men, first thing on Monday morning.

Morgan Bacon was brought to the Jail Ward at 4:15 that afternoon, suffering from a Jacksonian seizure disorder. It was a curious case, Doc Barner had said to Decker over the telephone as he was preparing to transfer him from the County Jail. Of all the prisoners, this one was tough as nails, hadn't even lost consciousness when the King of the Exercise Yard had hit him over the head with the 10-pound barbell earlier that afternoon. He had just blinked twice, the other prisoners had reported, then he had hit the attacker in the face so hard that the man's nose was broken, and he was still bleeding, three hours later. Morgan had just walked away from that battle and was doing fine until a half hour later, when his right thumb began to twitch. The movement of the thumb continued in spite of yelling by the guards for him to control it. Within seconds the jerking began to move up his arm toward his shoulder, and within a half minute, the entire left side of his body was jerking violently. Finally, everybody in the north corner of the exercise yard witnessed a full-blown grand mal seizure, complete with staining of the pants and full amnesia of the event.

"It was classic Jacksonian," Barner said.

Decker listened carefully. It had become his policy to listen carefully to everything Doc Barner said.

"How long was he postictal?"

" 'Bout ten minutes, slowly woke up, standard seizure recovery."

"Having much of a headache?"

"Let me tell you, Dr. Decker, this guy doesn't complain.

Five minutes later, Morgan Bacon was quickly escorted out of the elevator and into the Prep Room by two sheriff's deputies. As he was marched across the corridor, he looked straight ahead, ignoring everyone around him. He appeared to be about thirty years of age, Decker estimated, although the deep lines that covered his face easily added another ten years. His large, heavily callused hands were handcuffed securely behind him and a deputy had a firm grip on the thick biceps of each arm. He was not as tall or as big as Decker had envisioned after talking with Barner, but he was thick and rock-hard solid.

After the deputies seated him on the end of the examination table, Decker walked up to the man. "How does your head feel?" he asked.

"Okay." The voice was a rasping loud whisper. His eyes moved slightly to the right, looked directly at Decker, then returned back to stare at the wall. In just that glancing eye contact, Decker felt an ice-cold chill run down his back.

"Your head feels okay? Didn't you get hit with a piece of metal this afternoon?"

"Yes."

"Do you have any pain?"

"No."

"What happened to you later in the afternoon?"

"I don't know."

"You had a seizure?"

"Yes."

"Do you remember it?"

"No."

"How does everything feel now?"

"Okay."

"You sure don't talk much, do you?"

Bacon stared at the wall.

"Are you always like this?"

Bacon continued to stare at the wall.

Decker looked behind the patient at Betty, who was gathering needles and other equipment to start an intravenous line. She caught his eye and shrugged her shoulders, briefly raising her right index finger to her temple in the time-honored circular gesture that suggests insanity. At that instant Bacon turned quickly and spotted the movement. Betty froze and slowly returned her hand to her side. He turned back and stared at the wall again while Betty scurried from the room.

"Have you ever had a seizure before?" Decker asked.

"No."

"Are you taking any medicines?"

"No."

"Have you ever had any surgery?"

"No."

"Any hospitalizations?"

"No."

"Do you have any allergies?"

"No."

"Do you want to go back to the County Jail tonight?"

After ten long seconds of silence, the voice rasped, "You tell me. You're the doctor." His eyes slowly fixated on Decker's face again. "You tell me," he repeated as Decker felt the chill again.

The exam was quick but thorough. The right side of his head had a linear bruise that extended from just above his hairline to the top of his head. It was an indented bruise, which gave some indication of the force of the blow, and the skin looked slightly reddened and tender. Decker pushed down on the area, asking if there was any tenderness. Bacon rasped out that *it really isn't a problem, Doc.* No pain, no tenderness, nothing at all. Apart from the scalp injury, the remainder of his exam was normal. Decker called Betty back into the room.

"If you can start his intravenous access, I'll order a couple of portable X rays of his head. If there's any evidence of a fracture or if there's any future Jacksonian seizure activity, I'll send him down for a CAT scan on his brain tonight. Otherwise, we'll just keep him at mandatory bed rest, watch him with neuro vital signs every two hours with seizure precautions, plug an intravenous line into him with a little D5W TKO, and I'll give you some contingency orders for seizure control."

"Okay, Dr. Decker, sounds good."

"We'll put him in that bed down the corridor, near the Cage, where we can keep an eye on him in case any more seizures develop."

That evening, as Decker had walked into the Jail Ward elevator to leave for the night, the call arrived at Gerald Brodie's desk.

"Dr. Decker!" Brodie called, after quickly putting the caller on hold. "Dr. Decker! Telephone!"

Decker's hand shot out and wedged between the closing elevator doors just before they slammed together. He wrestled with the doors, first cursing the elevator system, and finally the entire L.A. County Hospital as a loud buzzer began blasting. Finally, as several sheriffs stopped in front of the elevator to watch the show, he broke out into the hallway, cursed the doors, and tossed a "thanks for nothing" glare at the deputies. He stormed across the corridor to Gerald Brodie's desk.

"Line number four," Brodie whined as his face pointed to the telephone on the corner of his desk.

"Hello?" Decker said as he turned away from the ward clerk's distracting face.

"Is this Steve Decker?" a man's voice asked.

"Yes, this is Decker."

"This is Joel Peck, medical resident at Huntington Memorial Hospital. I'm sorry it took so long to get back to you. They take forever getting messages to us here, and I just found a crumpled note stuck in my locker saying that the paramedic, that fellow—Andy Blum—who was shot by the wife-beater down in L.A., asked me a couple of weeks ago to give you a call."

"Joel Peck? Ah, yes, Dr. Peck. Thank you for getting back," Decker said, his voice becoming hushed. "I picked up the patient you had last month, William MacFarland, on the Jail Ward and was—"

"Biting Billy?"

"Right, I picked up Biting Billy and continued your workup for his encephalopathy."

"Good! He didn't bite you, did he?"

"No, although he tried like hell. I was trying to confirm the guy's diagnosis, regarding the AIDS and all . . ."

"I was having the same problem. Really hard to get any blood studies or a decent examination on the guy. What did you finally come up with?"

Decker paused. "I couldn't come up with anything, since he was transferred back to the County Jail on the second day of my Jail Ward rotation."

"Transferred?" Peck asked, his voice incredulous. "He was transferred back to the County Jail, before the diagnosis was established? Who the hell transferred him?"

Decker hesitated. "Dr. Marsh told me that *you* transferred him."

There was a prolonged silence.

"What's going on over there, anyway? Since I sure

as hell didn't transfer that man out of the Jail Ward,"
Peck said angrily, "it would be a very good idea to
track down the chart . . ."

"I tried . . ."

". . . track down the chart in that archaic medical
records department and find out just exactly who decided to send that little psycho bastard back to the
County Jail without a diagnosis!"

Barbara Skeeters sat on the edge of her bed, staring
at the wall. She was wearing a new maternity outfit, a
white one with orange flowers her mother had sent a
week ago, hoping that the bright colors would make
her feel better. She had been depressed all day—all
week, for that matter—but much more today, since
Blake had already left their motel room for his last
twenty-four-hour shift on the Jail Ward. She hadn't
awakened until at least an hour after he had left, and
that was a disgrace. She had been drenched in sweat
from nightmares that had been terrorizing her during
the last hour of sleep, and when she saw that he was
gone and she found his note, she let loose with a good
fifteen minutes of open and unremitting crying—the
first time that had happened since she had been a
teenager. *And now he is going to be gone all night.*

There hadn't even been a good-night kiss last night.
Since he had been stuck by that needle, they had had
no sexual intimacy at all. Not because she had refused
his advances but because there had been no advances.
She knew that he was aware of her fear of the infectious diseases he could pick up at the County Hospital.
He had tried to protect her, not only from catching
anything that he may have been exposed to, but even
more important, to protect her from the embarrassment of being less responsive to arousal because

of her fear, the fear that now was becoming all-consuming.

Her day had been filled with boredom. There was simply nowhere to go and nothing to do. The maid cast a sideways questioning look when she arrived to make up the room. *Why would this pregnant young lady spend the entire day just sitting around in her motel bedroom?* After watching an endless number of soaps, sitcoms, and commercials on television, the day had finally passed. The sun set and she had another bowl of cereal with a glass of cold milk for dinner.

In the quiet of the evening, she made the decision. No matter what the result of Blake's search, even if one of his prisoners did have a positive AIDS test, she would bring to him all the intimacy and pleasure he could handle. She looked down at the growing expansion across her abdomen, covered by the orange flowers. She loved him and she would make him happy again.

She reached over and pulled her address book out of her purse. After calling the County Hospital's Pediatric Pavilion, the Jail Ward, and finally after obtaining the number from Steve Decker himself, she was able to reach Katie Shields at her apartment.

"Katie? This is Barbara Skeeters. I'm Blake Skeeters's wife, we met at Dr. Marsh's house."

"Yes, of course. How are you doing, Barbara?"

"I'm doing okay. I just called to say hello and to see how you're getting along."

They talked for a few minutes, exchanging observations about the Jail Ward and discussing their feelings about the events of the past week. In the middle of the conversation, Katie abruptly commented that since both of them were alone tonight, it might be fun to get together for a cup of coffee somewhere.

"I would really like to do that, Katie," Barbara

said. "I'm sort of stuck here, since Blake doesn't want me to drive our car until he has it checked out by the Pasadena police, probably tomorrow sometime. Especially after what happened to Steve's car."

"Steve said it's going to take the bomb squad a week or two to sort out that event, but considering what's going on at the Jail Ward, I think Blake is right. I have my car, and Steve wanted me to pick up his dog at his apartment after it got dark tonight. Why don't I just stop off there on my way back. You've already had dinner, right?"

"Well, in a manner of speaking, yes," Barbara said.

"In a manner of speaking?"

"I had a snack earlier."

"Okay, Barbara, this is how it's going to be, and I don't want any complaints. I'm going to get Steve's dog, I'm going to stop at Ming Loo's for take-out food—you like Chinese food?"

"Yes, I love Chinese food, but—"

"I'll pick up a decent dinner for both of us, and I'll be there at around 9:45. We'll have dinner together there, at your place. You're in a motel somewhere in Pasadena, aren't you? What's the address?"

Chapter 12

"Is Stoneface having any seizure activity so far tonight?" Skeeters asked as he sat down across from Decker in the Doctors' On-Call Room. It was the first time he had a chance to relax after treating fourteen new patients during the previous twelve hours. Although the number of prisoners was not a record, each patient seemed to have a problem that was so vague and so annoying that there had been little satisfaction trying to provide medical care. Maybe the problem was that he couldn't keep his mind on his work.

"Haven't seen anything resembling a seizure so far," Decker said. "He's just been lying out there in front of the Cage, staring at the ceiling with those cold eyes, with his intravenous line dripping away. That new nurse has been taking his neuro vital signs every couple of hours. His X ray was negative for any fractures, although he sure has an indentation on his skull—you can even see it on the X ray—but the underlying bone structure is intact."

"Good, maybe it'll be peaceful tonight. I think we're about due for a break around here."

"I'm going to run him through a CAT scan if his granite face even twitches tonight, but I'll probably just send him back to the County Jail tomorrow morning if nothing happens."

* * *

The brown Mustang eased into the right lane of the San Bernardino Freeway and exited at Rosemead Avenue. Two minutes later, Katie pulled into the Grand Palm Apartments, pulled out the key Decker had given her, and to the sound of excited barking from within, opened the door to the second-floor apartment.

The dog gave a couple more barks when she first walked in, but after soft words and stroking of his head, his tail began wagging hard enough to vibrate his entire thin hind end. Katie quickly picked up all the papers lying around and disposed of them—not much different from changing diapers at the Pediatric Pavilion, she told herself—washed her hands and gently slipped a collar over the dog's head. She checked his left hind leg—the dressing was in place but needed changing.

"There you are, boy, Limpy's a good dog," she said as she taped the fresh gauze to the leg. She poured out his water and emptied what was left of his dog food into the trash can. She led him to the front door and carefully instructed the dog to wait there.

She took the chair from the kitchen table and placed it just to the right of the main ventilation duct in the ceiling. She stood on the chair and pulled the corner of the duct away from the ceiling, opening a small space. She reached into the space and pulled out a black notebook with about 50 pages.

"Where's your leash, Limpy?" she asked as she put the chair away and began looking around the room. The greyhound perked up and wagged his tail again. "Hang on a second and we'll be on our way."

She found a leash hanging in the pantry cabinet next to the sink, and as she was removing it from its hook, she spotted a white box. It was tucked into the shelf at the top of the cabinet, almost out of sight, and it was surprisingly heavy for its small size. The top of the box simply said, "50 Cartridges, 380 automatic 95 gr, Made in USA." The seal across the end of the box hadn't been broken; she tore the seal and opened the flap. As she turned the box on its side, several thick bullets rolled out into the palm of her hand. She returned them to the box and reached as far as she could to the back of the shelf. She pushed aside a can of insecticide and several boxes of soup, until she felt it, next to the wall, right where she guessed it would be. The blue steel was cold and smooth, and it felt deadly as she grasped it and slid it off the cupboard shelf.

Ten minutes later, she pulled into the darkest corner of the Roundtree Best Western Motel parking lot. Balancing three containers of Ming Loo's best in her right hand, and holding a paper bag and a leash attached to the greyhound in the other, she thumped on the door of room 237.

"Who is it?" the female voice called from inside. It was a fragile voice, holding a mixture of hope with a trace of fear.

"It's me. Katie." She glanced at the dog. "And Limpy, with our dinner. Open up before somebody sees me dragging a dog into the motel."

The door swung open and Katie rushed in, pulling the greyhound behind her. "Hello. What a night. This is Steve's watchdog, Limpy. And this is our dinner," she said as she held out the containers of food. "Lock the door, latch the chain, and let's have something to eat!"

Jack Diamond had come to know the central corridor of the Jail Ward as he had known his own bedroom as a child. Every pipe coursing down the ward's overhead was familiar, every scar on the wall was locked into his mind, every defect in the floor tile was memorized. More important, every sound that passed by his bed was recognized and categorized into his almost automatic subconscious warning system. The sounds were the most important, for they provided the warnings that could affect his very survival.

And that is why the faint noise of a man walking quietly down the darkened, unusually silent central corridor in the direction of the Cage awakened Diamond before he had even passed his bed. The slight squeak of the shoe, the cadence of steps, the collection of noises so subtle that Diamond could not describe them if he tried, brought him out of his shallow sleep. With the techniques he had learned in jail, Diamond didn't alter his slow snoring or the rate of his respirations as he awakened. His eyes stayed shut and he didn't move any part of his body until exactly the right second when the man, whom he knew was Sergeant Mel Grossman, had passed.

Diamond's right eye opened so slightly that anyone looking straight down on his face in bright light would swear that both his eyes were closed. Sergeant Grossman was walking differently from normal—that was obvious, Diamond thought. He was lifting himself with each step to quiet the footsteps. That was not a good sign. There was no valid reason that the chief sheriff's deputy on the Jail Ward of Los Angeles County Hospital would be trying to move quietly to the Cage at the far end of the corridor. The contrast with his usual method of bulldozing and intimidating made his quiet walk that much more unsettling. Diamond's head turned slightly to the right to allow his eye to continue following the bulky sergeant.

Just before Grossman reached the Cage, he stopped and leaned down next to the bed the interns had stuck out in the hall earlier in the day. It was the cold-faced prisoner that Diamond had decided was psycho. What was Grossman doing? Diamond's eye opened an infinitesimal amount wider.

He was handing him something.

Grossman was giving him keys and something dark and small. From the way Stoneface took the object and handled it, from the way he placed it under his prisoner's pajamas, there was no question. No question that he had just been handed a gun.

As Grossman stood up and turned around, Diamond's eye snapped shut, while his snoring and slow breathing continued without pause. He felt a breathless feeling of pounding adrenaline as Grossman walked back down the corridor, paused briefly to observe the sleeping man with the purple wig, and finally disappeared into the sheriff's watch station at the far end of the Jail Ward.

The eye cracked open again. Stoneface was still lying there in the dim light, not moving. The Jail Ward was remaining curiously silent. Even the usual background noises of men talking had abated. In fact, Diamond reflected, it had been remarkably quiet ever since Stoneface had arrived. The eye opened wider, scanning the entire corridor. No prisoners were up and about, nobody else seems to have taken notice of a police officer giving a prisoner a gun. *No,* Diamond thought, *make that a police officer giving a psycho prisoner a gun.*

He felt himself beginning to tremble.

Diamond waited a minute until his nerves settled. With all the innocence of a man slowly awakening, he reached his hands over his head and stretched expansively. He placed his right hand over his mouth and yawned, long and satisfyingly. He sat up on the side of his bed, pulling his right leg—heavily enclosed within the plaster cast—off the sheets and down to the floor.

He was going to have to go to the bathroom—nothing wrong with that, it happened all the time. He looked down the passageway toward the Doctors' On-Call Room. The ward clerk was gone from his desk. That was strange but not entirely unusual. The Prep Room was dark—there weren't any patients being admitted, not right now, anyway. The light from the Doctors' On-Call Room shined out into the corridor—the interns must still be awake. There would have to be a warning for Dr. Skeeters, he would have to be told that a gun had just been passed to the worst prisoner of them all.

Diamond pulled his wheelchair up to the side of his bed. He took one more look toward Stoneface—there was no movement, *looks like he's gone back to sleep*, he thought. *Going to have to hurry*. He took the crutch from the seat of the wheelchair and boosted himself up from the bed and into the chair. He reached down and lifted his casted right leg to the wheelchair support, holding it off the floor. He quietly lay the crutch down on the bed and released the brakes on the wheelchair . . . he spun himself around and pointed his casted leg in the direction of the Doctors' On-Call Room. As he pushed the steel side-grips on the wheels, he heard the faint sound of a bedspring squeak behind him. He looked back quickly as he accelerated in the direction of the light shining from the room with Dr. Skeeters.

The bed holding Stoneface was empty, and a dark figure was moving rapidly down the corridor in his direction.

"By the way, Blake, I think we may have a problem, a real big problem, with Dr. Marsh," Decker said.

"With Marsh? You mean besides the fact that he worries more about careers than he does about patients who need medicine for their pain?" Skeeters asked.

"Right, something like that. Joel Peck called a couple of hours ago about the transfer of Biting Billy back to the County Jail. He says he didn't write any order to transfer him back there, but Marsh had told us that Peck did write the order. One of them is lying to us, and I can't think of any reason why Joel—"

A crash in the corridor turned both their heads toward the door just in time to see a purple wig sliding by.

"What is that?" Decker exclaimed as both interns jumped out of their seats and ran into the darkened corridor.

Twenty feet away, in the direction of the Cage, Jack Diamond's wheelchair was lying in the center of the corridor, upside down, wheels still spinning in the air. Diamond was facedown in front of the wheelchair, and a pool of blood—looking black in the dim light— was slowly expanding across the floor next to his head.

"Jack! What happened?" Skeeters said as he picked up the man's wig and both interns began walking rapidly up the corridor, scanning for signs of movement.

"Where's Brodie?" Decker asked. "He's supposed to be here until midnight. Where are all the deputies?"

"I don't know, I don't know where *anybody* is. Let's check Diamond," Skeeters said as they approached his motionless body.

"Oh, shit . . ." Decker said as he looked up and pointed down to the far end of the corridor—near the Cage, where Stoneface's bed was empty.

Limpy sat between the two women where he found he had the best chance to receive Chinese food scraps as they consumed their dinner. Barbara and Katie talked as they ate, bringing each other up to date about events during the past week. From time to time, one of them flipped a piece of meat or gristle in the direction of Limpy's head. His sharp eyes spotted each incoming morsel, and a quick movement with a snap of his jaws secured each bite.

"That was delicious, Katie. Are you sure you won't let me pay for at least half?" Barbara asked as she finished the last spoonful of rice and walked over to the sink to rinse her hands.

"Like I said, my treat, it's my pleasure. Ming Loo's is the place to go. Remind me to give you the address before I leave tonight. Have some more tea, and I brought some fortune cookies for dessert," Katie said.

"Sounds good." Barbara said. "What's in that other bag you have?"

Katie looked at the brown paper bag she had taken from Decker's apartment. "It's a gun Steve bought," she said nonchalantly. "He told me a couple of weeks ago, when a prisoner threatened him, that he had filled out the paperwork for it, but I don't think he even knows how to use it. I thought I should bring it, considering everything that's happening, although I don't know how to work it, either. Also, I have the notebook Steve and Blake put together on the narcotics problem. He wants to give it to some guy named Lord after the medical staff meetings on Monday. Thought I'd copy the pages tomorrow for Steve, so the original can be kept in a safe place."

"Don't point the gun in my direction. Those things scare me," Barbara said as she gathered up the containers from the restaurant.

Katie stood up and walked over to the window, moved the curtain aside and pulled down on the venetion blinds that had been tightly shut. The window looked down into the parking lot, and she could see her Mustang dimly in the far corner, parked next to another car, an older model, a Ford of some kind, she guessed. Closer to the motel building, and in better lighting, sat the battered Volkswagen Bug. Two men were standing next to it, looking inside.

Her eyes narrowed as she watched the men. One of them walked around to the back of the vehicle and shined a flashlight through the window.

"Barbara, isn't that your Volkswagen out there?"

"A Bug, sort of dark blue, all rusted-looking? That's the one," Barbara answered as she walked over and stood next to Katie, looking down at the parking area. "When Blake graduates from his internship, we're going to upgrade by about twenty years to— What are those men doing?"

"That's what I was going to ask you. They're starting to walk this way." Katie looked back toward her Mustang. The car next to her, the Ford, hadn't been there when she had driven in. No cars had been there, it was too far from the building. She studied the Ford again. It looked vaguely familiar.

The vision came to her in a flash.

"Barbara!" She released the venetian blind and pulled the curtain shut. "That's the car that was chasing us last week. They must have followed me here. Quick, check the lock on the door!"

"Who are they?"

"I don't know! I think they're with the drug runners on the Jail Ward!" Katie grabbed the paper bag from the bed and sat down next to the telephone. She jammed the receiver against her ear with her left shoulder, pushed 911, and dumped the contents of the bag on the bed. As she ripped open the box holding the bullets, a recording announced, "This call cannot be connected to the room number you have dialed. If you would like to make an outside call, please push 9 first, and—"

She slapped her hand down on the telephone and pushed 9; two seconds later, a dial tone hummed into her left ear and she tapped out 911. She turned the gun around, looking for where the bullets could be put in. There wasn't any opening! She looked for directions, an arrow, anything! The words "Walther PPK" were printed on the side. She grasped the black plastic handle, pulled back the hammer and looked for a way to insert a bullet. Nothing!

"911, may I help you?" the female voice was crisp and businesslike.

She began punching every lever and button on the gun as she rapidly fired out the words, "This is Katie Shields at the Roundtree Best Western Motel, on Marengo Street, room 237. We're having an emergency, somebody's trying to get in, send help fast!"

"What is the nature of the emergency?" the voice responded.

When she pushed in the small round button on the left side of the pistol, a slender metallic magazine popped out of the handle of the gun and fell on the floor.

"Like I said," Katie hollered, "two men want to get in to our room!" She grabbed the magazine, ignoring the fine sheen of oil that covered the metal, and tried to wedge a bullet into the end. It wouldn't fit. She turned the bullet around and tried again. A spring platform inside the magazine promptly slid away, allowing the bullet to neatly pop in.

"Are these men trying to break in right now?" the voice said.

"Don't you understand? There is going to be a shooting here in two minutes! Send all the police you can, Roundtree Motel. On Marengo!" She threw the receiver down on the bed, grabbed the gun, a handful of bullets and the magazine, and positioned herself 5 feet in front of the door. "Barbara! Get into the bathroom, take the dog with you!"

At that instant, there was a loud knock on the door.

The voice was unmistakable, a whispered growl from deep in the prisoner's throat.

"Both of you keep walking, straight ahead. I have a fully loaded pistol at the base of your skull, Skeeters, and I can empty eight rounds into both of you in less than five seconds if you don't do exactly as I say. Place your hands on top of your head where I can see them and keep walking, straight ahead."

Skeeters heard the sound of the pistol's·hammer being cocked as he felt the barrel jammed against the top of his neck. Both interns placed their hands on their heads and continued walking, moving around Diamond's motionless form.

"Any seizure problems this evening, Mr. Bacon?" Decker asked sarcastically.

"Steve, cool it, no point in getting him all pissed." Skeeters quickly said.

"I don't get pissed," Bacon hissed from behind the interns, "I just kill whatever annoys me. I'm very good at it. Now, both of you keep your mouths shut, and don't say another word or I might get annoyed."

They walked the full distance of the darkened corridor to the front of the Cage. Choo-Choo was asleep on his bunk, which protruded out from the far wall, snoring loudly. Bacon reached up to Decker's hand and gave him a ring of keys.

"Take these, Decker, and open the Cage," Bacon said. "One small error and your friend's brains go into the Cage."

"Open the Cage? The man inside is a psychotic

schizophrenic! He kills everybody he touches!" Decker said as he took the keys.

Bacon smiled. "It's the big key, the one next to the clip on the ring. You have ten seconds to open the Cage, Decker." He jammed the barrel of his gun hard against Skeeters's neck.

"What do you want?" Katie called out as she inserted a second bullet into the gun's magazine. It wedged halfway into the magazine as she worked to line it up properly.

"Open the door!" a man's voice called from the other side. "This is the motel manager. I have a complaint there is a dog in there. Open the door up!"

The bullet snapped into the magazine behind the first one. She grabbed a third bullet and popped it in behind the other two. "Come back tomorrow morning. Go away!" Katie said. She looked at the bathroom door, where Barbara was calling for the dog to come. Limpy sat on the floor next to the bed, his tail wagging, watching Katie. She motioned for the dog to go.

"I'm going to have to use the master key," the voice said.

"Go ahead, I'm keeping the chain locked. Come back tomorrow morning. There's no dog in here!" Katie yelled back. A clicking sound of metal against metal could be heard as the man began working with something to open the dead bolt. The greyhound's ears perked up at the sound, and he suddenly let out a low, rumbling growl that ended with a loud bark.

She was just able to get a fourth bullet into the magazine when the lock flipped open and the doorknob turned. The dog barked again, more loudly, as the door opened 2 inches, stretching against the chain. She looked quickly down at the gun, trying to figure out how to get the magazine back into the handle. She turned it around a couple of times and finally rammed it into the open base of the handle. It disappeared and locked with a satisfying click. She reached up with her thumb and pulled back on the hammer to cock the gun—it snapped back when she released it. She tried again and it snapped back again—the hammer wouldn't stay cocked!

The door rattled against the chain. "Open the chain or I'll have to get the police."

"Go get the police! I'll wait here for them!" she yelled.

She looked at the side of the gun—there was a lever, must be the safety, all guns have safeties. She pushed up, exposing a large red dot on the side of the gun. She pulled back on the hammer again. It clicked and held in the cocked position.

The door began to strain against the chain. "Open this door or I'm going to break the chain!"

I'll give him a warning shot, just one warning shot. That'll send them away . . . She aimed the gun high, at the top of the door, she closed her eyes and braced for the noise as she pulled the trigger.

The gun clicked. She pulled the trigger again and the gun clicked again.

The dog began barking as the door rattled and strained again against the chain.

"Get away from our room or I'll call the police!" she screamed as she frantically examined the gun. It wouldn't fire. She flipped the safety back and forth, squeezed the trigger again and heard another click.

Gerald Brodie flushed the toilet and walked out of the bathroom stall. He washed and dried his hands, and he studied his face in the mirror. *Should have done something about that nose when I was a kid,* he thought. *Damn thing keeps getting longer and skinnier every day.* He walked out of the bathroom and into the central corridor of the Jail Ward.

Within a second of seeing the three men in front of the Cage at the far end of the corridor, he was out of sight, crouched behind his desk. They hadn't seen him, he was sure of that. He still had the element of surprise on his side. He popped his head above the desk, then ducked down again. A man was lying on the floor in the center of the corridor, in front of a wheelchair, not moving. It looked like they were opening the Cage, and the man on the right was Bacon, no question. Bacon, the son of a bitch extortionist, Decker's patient, here from the County Jail. Of all the ones to go up against . . .

He reached down to his ankle with his right hand and pulled out his beloved Smith & Wesson .38 caliber stainless-steel revolver. Without looking at the weapon—he knew the five chambers of the cylinder were full, he had checked them twice this morning before coming to the hospital—he quietly pulled back on the hammer until he heard a satisfying click. His left hand reached up to his desk and he slid the telephone over to the edge of the desk. He lifted the receiver and placed it against his ear. *Just dial 3999, down to the backup crew on the first floor, that was all.*

There was no dial tone.

He reached around the telephone to the cord and pulled. It had been cut a couple of feet from the receiver. *Okay, no backup,* he thought, *going to have to move quickly. If he gets them into the Cage, they're gone.* He looked around the Jail Ward. *The nurse was down at the cafeteria, grabbing her evening snack, but Grossman had to be nearby. Where the hell is he? Gotta watch out for him, dangerous bastard.* He popped his head up again and saw the Cage door open. As both interns were pushed into the Cage, he jumped up and began running down the corridor, pointing his revolver straight at Bacon as he hollered, "Police! Drop the gun!"

During the next five seconds, a total of four shots were fired, the first three in rapid succession from Bacon as he turned and calmly—professionally—pumped the hollow point bullets from his 9mm HK semiautomatic at the figure racing in his direction. The first slug hit Brodie in the left thigh, spinning him around and away from the second and third slugs, which would have otherwise intersected directly with his throat. Brodie screamed and hit the floor of the corridor 10 feet beyond Jack Diamond. Before Bacon had a chance to lower the pistol and unload his remaining five shots, Brodie managed to give one vigorous squeeze to the trigger of his revolver. The slug hit Bacon just above his nose, precisely in the center of his face. His head slammed into the bars of the Cage. The brand-new black P7M8 Heckler Koch, with the assassin's convenient squeeze-cock feature, flew from his hand and slid 10 feet down the corridor. Morgan Bacon was dead before he hit the floor.

Prisoners up and down the corridor began yelling, creating a mayhem that was silenced only after Brodie pointed his gun straight up and fired a single shot. At the sound of the gunshot, silence immediately returned to the ward. The prisoners tried to shield themselves from further shots as they gaped at Bacon's body. There were twenty-seven pipes in the ceiling and the bullet penetrated the biggest one of all, the dark one in the center, with SEWAGE stenciled on its side. A dark fluid began to leak out of the hole and drip on the floor, leaving a puddle that began expanding in front of the sightless eyes of Morgan Bacon.

Inside the Cage, Choo-Choo was becoming agitated. At the sound of the shots, he climbed out of bed and lumbered over to the bars, ignoring the two interns who were crouching on the floor behind him, and not noticing that the door of the Cage was swinging wide open. He grabbed two of the bars and began shaking them with all his strength, vibrating the entire structure, as he roared his protest at being disturbed in such an abrupt manner.

When a loud shot rang out a few seconds later from a gun next to the Cage, making more noise than Choo-Choo had heard since his arrest, the prisoner went completely wild, jumping and hollering and pounding on the bars. And when he saw Sergeant Grossman standing in front of the Cage, having fired at the man with the long nose lying down in the corridor, now aiming and ready to make more noise, he became infuriated. He remembered clearly, this was the man who had kicked him and had fired the lightning bolts into him when he was on the street so long ago. This was the man who, like the others who looked exactly like him with that patch on their shoulder, had chained him, kicked him again and again, and then had thrown him into the back of that truck.

Choo-Choo jumped through the open Cage door and grabbed Sergeant Grossman around the neck. Before Grossman could even think about turning his gun against the prisoner, Choo-Choo snapped the man's right wrist with a loud crack, propelling the gun 20 feet down the corridor. The scream of pain from Grossman infuriated Choo-Choo even more as he dragged the man into the Cage and slammed the door shut.

"Pull back on the top of the gun, Katie. Pull back on the top!" Barbara called from the bathroom door.

Katie grabbed the top of her pistol and pulled back, immediately generating multiple internal clicking sounds as the first round was inserted into the barrel; the hammer stayed in the cocked position. She aimed the gun at the top of the door again and began to squeeze the trigger. A creak of pressure at the door was followed by two screws popping off the plate that held the chain. She quickly lowered the gun and aimed it straight in front of her, holding it with two hands the way she had seen it done on television. She waited and watched the door in front of her as the creaking sound became louder. Her arms began to ache and the gun began shaking violently; she had never seen that happening on television. She hoped she had loaded the pistol correctly . . . too late to change anything now . . . they really ought to include an instructional manual with these things.

Just as she began to wonder if they had made a mistake and it really *was* the motel manager outside, the door flew open with a crashing sound as the chain ripped off the wall. A large man holding a gun charged through the door.

Choo-Choo lifted Grossman high into the air, and with a grunt he heaved his body against the concrete wall at the back of the Cage. The deputy tried to break his fall with his injured right hand, which slammed against the wall with a loud crunch of further damage. He screamed and rolled on the floor, clutching his broken hand while trying to escape the enraged prisoner. Choo-Choo lumbered over to the man and reached down to grab him again.

"Stop him, Skeeters! He'll kill me!" Grossman yelled.

They all jumped at the sound of another gunshot into the ceiling from Gerald Brodie down the hall, accompanied by a shout for all prisoners to return to their beds immediately. Skeeters and Decker stood at the far side of the Cage, out of harm's way, watching Choo-Choo lift the deputy above his head again.

"Hold him there for a minute, Mr. Bond," Skeeters said calmly. Decker's jaw dropped as he looked back and forth at Choo-Choo and Skeeters. *Hold him, Mr. Bond?*

"He's not going to kill you yet, Grossman," Skeeters continued, "but you're the first one on his list. Right now, he's just playing with you. He's just having fun."

"You can control this monster?" Grossman roared as he struggled to free himself from the iron grip of the prisoner. "Jesus Christ, Skeeters, tell him to put me down before he kills me."

"Mr. Bond and I have an understanding. He trusts me, Grossman. He doesn't trust you, he doesn't even like you. If he wanted to kill you, he would have already done so. He's very good, just like you, Grossman. You were very good at taking narcotics from my patients, weren't you?"

"I never did that! I never had anything to do—"

Skeeters interrupted. "He looks heavy, Mr. Bond, why don't you drop him?" Choo-Choo grinned and quickly stepped away as he released the man; Grossman flailed wildly in the air as he fell to the tile floor, hitting the side of his hip and right shoulder.

"Jesus Christ, man! Tell him to stop!" Grossman cried as he tried to crawl away from Choo-Choo. "I think he broke my hip!" Choo-Choo grabbed the front of the man's shirt and pinned him against the wall, his right hand enclosing the front of the deputy's throat as he waited further directions.

"Her name was Julia Jackson, but we all knew her

as Trixie. Remember her, Grossman?" Skeeters said calmly.

"I . . . I. . . Yes! I remember her! Okay, we took some morphine sulfate from her. We had to do it for the quota. I didn't have any choice."

"Orders from above, huh? Orders from whom?"

"I don't know. We were just handed orders."

"Drop the bastard!" Skeeters hollered.

Choo-Choo immediately threw him to the floor with a vigorous downward thrust, causing his right knee and ankle to shatter with sounds of fragmenting bone. Choo-Choo grinned and hauled the man up into the air again, gripping his damaged right knee.

"Okay, okay! Jesus, let go of my knee! Okay, we took the drugs from the prisoners. Peter Martel did most of it."

"How did you get it out of the Jail Ward? Where did it go?"

Grossman hesitated and began moaning. Choo-Choo began rotating him in a circle over his head again, waiting in anticipation for the next command.

"Where did the narcotics go?" Skeeters repeated.

"It went to the Bloods at the County Jail. And it went to the Crips. And to the Panthers. And it went to every other fucking lowlife over there that had a delivery boy and that was willing to pay us for it."

"How did you deliver?"

"The prisoners carried it—they were the delivery boys. They get sick, they are brought to the Jail Ward, they get better, they return to the County Jail. Biting Billy, Knight, Lamb, Stark, all of them were delivery boys. They never search the returning prisoners back at the County Jail, since they have already been strip-searched here."

"How long have you been doing this?"

"I'm not sure."

"Drop him again, Mr. Bond!"

"No, no!" Grossman yelled as Choo-Choo tried to release him. The deputy managed to grip the thick wrist of Choo-Choo as he was dropped again. He fell halfway to the floor before he caught himself on Choo-Choo's arm with a desperate clutch. In an instant Choo-Choo violently thrust him against the back wall. As the deputy slid to the floor in a moaning crumpled heap, Choo-Choo ran over and eagerly hauled him upright, pinning him against the wall again.

"Six years . . ." Grossman moaned.

"Six years!" Skeeters exclaimed. "You've been running drugs out of the Jail Ward for six years?"

A voice came from down the corridor, the faint and wavering voice of a man in distress and having difficulty breathing. "What about Esch?"

Both interns spun around and saw Gerald Brodie lying on the floor in the center of the corridor, looking at the Cage.

"What about Esch?" he asked again.

Skeeters turned around and looked up at the deputy. "What about that little pharmacy tech, Esch? What did you do to him?"

"I don't know about Esch."

"Mr. Bond, are your arms—"

"All right. Red took him out. He was getting too close."

"Who is Red?"

"Red Malrooney, guard at the County Jail—he collects the money from the gangs outside the jail, so they can keep the stuff flowing."

"Who took out Tyra Levy, Grossman?" Decker hollered. "Did Red kill her?"

"She overdosed on pills—" Grossman started, then

abruptly clamped his jaw shut and glowered defiantly at the interns.

"Drop him, Mr. Bond," Skeeters quickly said.

Choo-Choo jerked him away from the wall and slammed him against the concrete again. "Stop him!" Grossman screamed. "Please stop him!"

"Who killed Tyra Levy? We would really like to know." Decker asked again.

"She killed herself! She took her own goddamn sleeping pills!"

"You bastard! Who else helped you run the drugs out of here? Who gave you the orders? Who ran the show?" Skeeters shouted.

Grossman clamped his jaw shut again, refusing to answer. Skeeters and Decker glared at the man as Choo-Choo's clutch around the deputy sheriff's neck tightened. Grossman's face developed a dusty blue color, his eyes bulged from their sockets, and his tongue protruded grotesquely as he began to make small strangling sounds. The interns waited and watched as Choo-Choo's grip tightened.

"We're going to watch you die, you son of a bitch," Decker said quietly.

Grossman's face became darker and he fought for breath for another ten seconds before finally gurgling out, "Okay, okay! It was Dr. Dillon Marsh. He's the one at the top. Dr. Dillon Marsh has been running the whole fucking operation since the beginning."

The man's shape was just a blur to Katie, and he seemed to be moving in slow motion as she repeatedly squeezed the trigger as fast as her finger could move. The gun fired rapidly, making deafening sounds and jumping wildly with each shot. She noticed through the smoke and the noise that the man had stopped his forward charge, and that he had, in fact, started moving backwards—right back out through the door.

The thought flashed through her mind that he had probably not expected a greeting like this from two refined and educated ladies. When her gun stopped jumping and all she could hear was a clicking sound with background barking noises from the dog, she dropped the gun and ran into the bathroom with Barbara.

"Come on, Limpy, come on!" they both called out through the open door as the dog stopped barking, looked in the direction of the women, and leaned forward to jump in their direction. A hand holding a thick black handgun suddenly reached through the front door and sprayed five shots into the room. The last shot triggered a painful yelp from the dog, who dropped to the floor next to the bed. The two women quickly slammed the bathroom door.

"Where's your gun?" Barbara asked as they crowded into the bathtub.

"It's empty! I think I got one of the guys, at least he went back out the door. It sounded like the other guy just got the dog," Katie said.

Three shots suddenly pierced the bathroom door and both women screamed as each bullet threw pieces of wood against the mirror. More fragments of plywood flew off as the man outside began violently kicking the door. A hole next to the doorknob finally popped open, and a white freckled hand extended into the bathroom and tried to grope for the inside doorknob.

Barbara reached over to the toilet, and with a powerful lurch, lifted the porcelain top from the tank. One of the shots had cracked off a large piece from the left side, but most of the original top was still in place.

"Stand back!" she yelled to Katie as she lifted her weapon and slammed it down against the man's hand.

They heard a piercing scream from outside, and a

moment later the entire door crashed open off its hinges, revealing a red-haired man holding a gun in his right hand, his face contorted with fury and his left hand bleeding profusely at his side. In an instant Barbara's porcelain weapon crashed down again, knocking the weapon to the floor. From behind the man, they suddenly heard a rumbling snarl, followed by another howl of pain as the greyhound sank his teeth deep into the intruder's left leg.

The man spun around and reached down to rip the dog away. Barbara lifted the piece of porcelain a final time and slammed it against the man's head as hard as she could. There was a faint groan as he fell to the floor and the dog attacked again, biting the man's right buttock with another solid chomp. Katie grabbed the gun while Barbara stood over him, her white porcelain weapon held ready to drop on his head if he started to move.

Katie aimed the gun at the man. She found herself out of breath and gasping for air as she turned to give Barbara a look of new admiration. "You can put your lethal toilet weapon down now, I have him, as they say, 'covered.' " She smiled. "That wasn't bad, Barbara, for a lady in your condition."

"I think he's out cold," Barbara observed, looking down at the still form. "You didn't do so bad yourself, getting the other one. Especially for a pediatrician. Where did you learn to shoot like that?"

"Are you kidding? I couldn't even figure out how to cock the gun until you told me to pull back on the top. How did you know you had to do that?"

"I once saw it in a movie." Barbara smiled.

"Well, I've never even held a gun, much less shot one. By the way, this character"—she waved the gun at the man—"is the driver of the Ford. Steve and I saw him last week."

A few seconds later, the apartment was swarming with news reporters and uniformed policemen. A tired man with rumpled hair and a loose tie, both of which were quickly restored to order after he spotted the television cameras, informed the women that the man outside their door was dead from four gunshot wounds in the chest, and there was nothing to worry about now that Detective Monroe of the Pasadena Police Department had taken over the investigation.

Dr. Dillon Marsh stood at his bedroom window looking out into the night. The expanse of ocean that stretched from the cliffs beneath his home to the distant horizon was completely black. There were no lights from the multiple ocean vessels that ply the waters off the Malibu hills, and there was no silver sheen of moonlight across the sea.

Marsh could feel and hear the pulsations of his heart in the silence around him. This had been a very bad day. He had lost control of the operation, that was obvious, and nobody listened to anything he had to say anymore. The disappearance of Peter Martel bothered him the most. He had worked with him, trusted him, and had shared the rewards with him to a larger extent than with any of the others.

Why did Martel have to leave!

Marsh clenched his fists and squeezed his eyes shut. Christ, the whole problem was Martel's fault! He had told him to stop diverting the morphine and Demerol if the interns had shown any interest in the narcotics their patients received. It was just too easy for them to track it down if they became suspicious. They were intelligent people, goddamn it. All Martel had to do was wait a week or two for a new batch of interns, and the money would start flowing again.

But greed, not common sense, had become the con

trolling force. Grossman didn't want to stop his stipend, the power lords in the County Jail wanted their drugs, and for Red Malrooney it wasn't even the money, it was the perverted pleasure of "taking people out."

I know they are coming after me, he thought as he strolled over to his desk and then turned to look out into the night again. *All the signs point that way. No further contact from Grossman after his nine o'clock report. And no call from Red as he had been told to do when he finished his work. No calls, the operation had failed, it was as simple as that. And on Monday, as soon as the medical staff and the DEA hears about the morphine, I'm gone. I will certainly lose my license, and I will be stripped of my professorship. I will probably go to jail, and if Red testifies against me about that little pharmacy creature, they'll hit me with the death sentence.* He felt his eyes become moist as his vision blurred from tears of self-pity.

Seven black and whites revved their engines as they turned onto Camino de Buena Drive and powered their way to the top of the hill. The first car abruptly made a right turn into a circular driveway in front of the two-story mansion. Detective Jeff Lord climbed out of the passenger side of the lead car as fifteen uniformed officers swarmed out of the others.

"Cover the back of the house!" Lord ordered as the men quickly spread out into the night to surround the structure. He reached into his shoulder holster and pulled out his black Sig Sauer 9mm semiautomatic pistol, quickly loading the first of the fifteen rounds into the chamber. He scanned the darkened windows at the front of the house. Marsh could easily be up there, looking down from any of the windows, preparing to resist with whatever weapons he may have. Lord draped his police badge over the front breast pocket of his suit as his right thumb automatically flipped off the safety.

He had just started walking to the front door when a window of the second floor lit up with a bright flash from the unmistakable detonation of a single gunshot.

Chapter 13

"Twenty-five minutes to go, baby. The end of the month is approaching," Decker said enthusiastically as he looked at his watch.

"The end is in sight," Skeeters acknowledged, looking around the Jail Ward at the clusters of patients in the central corridor. The two interns were standing in front of the empty Cage, both of them holding a stack of charts filled with the notes that would inform the new incoming interns about their patients' medical problems. "Going to miss this place," Skeeters said as he jammed his pen back into the front pocket of his white coat. "It's amazing, but I really am. Somehow my August rotation in Gastroenterology just won't be the same."

"Yep," Decker said, "that's the problem for you guys in Internal Medicine. It's boring. Like Gastroenterology, for example. Perfect example. If you have an ulcer, you give Zantac. If you don't have an ulcer, you give congratulations. Boring! Now, surgery, that's where things get exciting—like in the Urology rotation I start tomorrow." He smiled. "Prostates and testicles, day in and day out.

"Prostates and testicles, what excitement. Well, at least we didn't get stuck being on call here the final night," Skeeters said.

"Such a blessing. Five P.M. and it's 'Good-bye Jail Ward.' "

Skeeters looked at his watch and frowned. "Foster was supposed to call about the final results from that Western Blot AIDS backup test today. If it's positive, which it almost certainly is, I'll have to start the AZT today or tonight—until we find out if I am going to undergo seroconversion." It was getting easier to say the word.

"If he doesn't call before five, let's go track him down or you may never find out what's going on. Any word yet on Choo-Choo?" Decker looked into the empty Cage.

"None except that the surgery is going well so far. The tumor was big, lemon size, and they're trying to take the whole thing out. It's one of those oligodendrogliomas, so he has a fairly good chance for a cure. Damn thing hemorrhaged, probably a couple of hours before he attacked those people."

"So he really is going to be a nice guy?"

"You got me." Skeeters shrugged. "I don't know what his baseline is. He'll be whatever he was before the tumor started growing. His mother says he's a nice guy, so there's hope."

"His mother didn't see what he did to Grossman. Talk about an interrogation, Jesus!"

"He was definitely not a nice guy to Grossman," Skeeters agreed. "After the orthopods fix the bones Choo-Choo broke, he's off to trial and hopefully will spend a few decades in the state pen."

"Let's pray he doesn't cycle through the Jail Ward. Can you imagine having Mel Grossman for a patient?"

"Grossman and Red Malrooney, what a pair," Skeeters said. "They should be put away for a long, long time. Barbara's having nightmares about people breaking through the front door and the bathroom.

But at least we're back home now and settled into our apartment."

"Jeff Lord told me those two are going to be brought up on multiple murder charges," Decker said.

"I thought they only 'took out' one, that Esch character."

"Right, they are going after both of them for that little homicide, but they're also going to nail Grossman for the death of Bacon, and they're going to pin murder charges on Malrooney for the death of that guy with the gun who tried to charge through the motel front door. I want to know who's going to pay the price for killing Tyra."

"Everybody's still calling it a suicide," Skeeters said. "One thing they can't do, however. They can't hook Dr. Marsh's death on anyone."

"Except on Dr. Marsh himself," Skeeters said. "All that energy focused in the wrong direction, hell of a waste. The new temporary Jail Ward director was transferred from the emergency room—he looks pretty good, so far."

"At least we should get decent performance reports for our month on the Jail Ward," Decker said. "Hell, we ought to get an *award* of some kind, after what we went through. By the way, I finally found Biting Billy's chart yesterday and, sure as hell, it was Marsh who transferred him back to the County Jail."

"With narcotics, no doubt. Marsh probably had his mortgage payment coming due."

"And may his money-hungry soul rest in peace."

The interns walked down the central corridor, slowing to talk with Jack Diamond. His purple wig was gone and the upper two-thirds of his head was wrapped with several layers of thick white gauze.

"How are you feeling, Mr. Diamond?" Skeeters asked. "That was a bad blow to your head."

Diamond patted his bandage and looked up at the interns. "My headache isn't so bad now, and the emergency room doctor said the stitches can come out in another two or three days," he said with a smile. "I'm sorry again that I couldn't quite get to you in time for a warning, but at least my wig gave you some notice."

"You did the best you could," Decker said sympathetically as he spotted the wig folded and tucked neatly into a side pocket of the wheelchair. "We'll make sure the stitches come out on time. In fact, I will personally come up here and remove them for you, just to make sure it's done right."

The interns walked past the new ward clerk, a pleasant round-faced man with a cheerful smile and a manner that almost apologized for any burdens he might place on the Jail Ward interns. Even his name, Fred Flowers, evoked a happy feeling, with a sense of trust that he would not try to make life miserable. But then, he wasn't a DEA agent, either, the interns reminded themselves. They had both already visited Brodie twice, down on the fifth floor, and the thoracic surgeon had said that once his chest tubes were removed, he would likely recover without problems. The surgeon also confirmed that there had been no head injuries, no loss of consciousness, and no amnesic events. Yes, guys, he had told them, he will be fully recovered in plenty of time to testify against Sergeant Grossman.

Decker and Skeeters had told Brodie that they appreciated his remarkable bravery under fire and that for a masochistic, torturing, inherently evil son of a bitch, he was not a bad guy at all. They did suggest, however, that he stay with Drug Enforcement Administration and leave ward clerk assignments to nice people like Fred Flowers.

"Fifteen minutes to go," Decker said as the two interns settled into the chairs in the Doctors' On-Call Room.

"Fifteen minutes." Skeeters looked at his watch. "Fifteen minutes, and we're outta here. Seems like we've been on the Jail Ward for years. I'm not going to have Barbara cooking dinner tonight. We're going out somewhere, somewhere really nice to celebrate."

"My fiancée and I are going to drive off to a celebration dinner tonight in our new car," Decker said casually.

"Your new car? Your fiancée?" Skeeters stared at the intern. "You're getting married?"

"Yup," Decker said proudly. "Can't keep Limpy in my apartment, can't keep Limpy in Katie's apartment. Going to have to get a little house—"

"So you're getting married to solve Limpy's residence problem?"

Decker grinned. "Actually, anybody who can handle a gun like that—"

A knock on the door interrupted him as Fred Flowers called out, "Dr. Skeeters! Telephone call for you at the desk. A Dr. Foster wants to talk with you."

Skeeters bolted from his chair and picked up the receiver at the ward clerk's desk.

"This is Blake Skeeters," he said.

"Blake, this is Benjamin Foster, at the Pathology Department. I'll get right to the point—three points, actually. First of all, we just got Tyra Levy's results and the pathology department's in an uproar about the findings. Her blood level of the *Clostridium botulinum* toxin was about 10,000 times higher than the LD_{50}, the 50 percent lethal dose level.

"Botulinum? Tyra died from botulism poisoning?" Skeeters felt a cramping pain in the pit of his stomach.

"That's right, no doubt about it, almost 10,000

times higher than the usual lethal dose. I personally checked the results myself—injected a sample of her serum into two of our test mice, one protected with antibotulism antibodies, the other unprotected. The unprotected one was dead almost before I could remove the needle, the one with the antibodies was fine. There is no doubt the stuff was botulism, Blake. She must have gone fast, the toxin is one of the most potent poisons on the face of the earth, and at the dose she took, the muscular and respiratory paralysis must have been complete in no time at all."

"The goddamn bastards!"

"Also, we confirmed with gas chromatography that the toxin was in one of the two Restoril capsules recovered from her duodenum. The other capsule didn't have any traces of anything but Restoril inside, and all the capsules in the container at her bedside were normal."

"Somebody's going to pay for this, Bennie. Whoever it was must have slipped an extra pill into her pill container—she told us she was having the Central Pharmacy deliver the pills to the Jail Ward a few days ago, maybe the nurse here intercepted it."

"I don't know about those things, but botulinum toxin is what killed her. And we wouldn't have even tested for it if you hadn't mentioned it to us, Blake. Thank you. We don't often see death by botulism—it takes someone with medical savvy to pull that kind of a trick. All the information's been turned over to the DEA and the DA's office for whatever they want to do with it.

"Second thing, on a brighter note, they screwed up down here on that AIDS test they did, the one on sample 684-73-204?"

"Yes," Skeeters said, "the sample that was positive for the AIDS virus antibodies?"

"Right. Well, bottom line is that it should have been read out as negative. The Western Blot confirmation of the AIDS antibodies was negative, they repeated it twice, and so they went back to the original Virnostika anti-HIV viral lysate and found the technician had diluted the lysate on that one sample with an improper dilution ratio. He screwed up, one of the new guys here."

Skeeters's face lit up. "The technician screwed up?" he said. "Aloha's HIV test is negative? It's okay! Tell him it's okay! This is the best news I've had in years!"

"I thought you might be happy to hear about it—just found out a few minutes ago. I'm just really sorry you had to deal with this thing for so long. We double-checked the serum again five different ways. The sample just does not have any evidence of the HIV antibody or virus. The technician really feels bad about it."

"That is really great news," Skeeters said. "I really appreciate you tracking it down. My wife will appreciate it, too."

"I can imagine," he said sympathetically. "Finally, remember the bacterial testing we did on one of your patients up there, Mr. Puuho?"

"He's the same guy we did the AIDS test on—he's been losing weight."

"Okay, we were testing the sample of sputum the pulmonary Doc pulled out during that bronchoscopy? Well, it's 4+ positive for acid-fast bacilli. . . . Your man has tuberculosis, Blake. Better get him on triple antibiotics as fast as you can."

"Already did, several days ago, took a chance and did it."

"Already started him? On triple therapy?"

"Yup!"

"You're brilliant, Blake."

Skeeters thanked him and returned to the Doctors' On-Call Room where he brought Decker up to date about the news from the pathology department. Five minutes later, after Decker had stopped yelling and stomping around the room, the interns quietly made a solemn promise to each other that they would do whatever was necessary to identify and kill or otherwise bring to justice the person who had taken the life of Tyra Levy.

At four minutes before five o'clock, just as the interns were giving their lockers the final clean-out, Fred Flowers poked his head into the room.

"You interns are up for the next two cases," he said apologetically, "and there happens to be two patients on their way up from the emergency room. Since it is before five o'clock," he told them, "they are yours." His face radiated compassionate understanding as he told them that the prisoners were coming up in the elevator right now, so it would be helpful if they would come out to the Prep Room. He obligingly explained that the prisoners were red blanket emergencies. They were both bleeding badly from the wounds they received as they tried to take over the KTTV television station so they could warn the world of the upcoming nuclear holocaust.

Fred Flowers finally apologized for burdening Dr. Decker and Dr. Skeeters with more work at a time that was so *inconvenient*.

It was exactly six o'clock in the evening at the Mexicali border crossing when Tomasa Santos started his evening shift. At twenty-seven, Santos was already a veteran border guard at the crossing. His shoes were shined to a mirror finish, his green uniform was pressed and spotless, and his hat was square on his head, exactly as directed in the Immigration and Naturalization Service manual. He was a slender man who took pride in the lean profile that made him look crisp and professional to the drivers who slowed at his command. His eyes, concealed behind the Serengeti Drivers sunglasses, missed little as he studied each driver and passenger before finally snapping his right hand in the direction of the Sierra de Las Pintas highway that led down to the wastelands stretching across Baja California.

"Profile." The word was in his mind continuously, almost like a broken record. What is the profile that each driver exhibits, what are the subtle suggestions and clues that each automobile, each driver, each passenger has that warn of illegal activities?"

When the dusty Toyota Celica squeaked to a halt in front of Santos, the initial profile was that of a businessman. They were coming and going all the time, often in rental cars but for some of the younger men, in cars with a little extra flash. There was only one driver in this car, a tall man with a clean-shaven face who rolled down his window and looked up at the guard.

"Good afternoon, sir," Santos said.

"Good afternoon, Officer," the man said. Santos's eyes narrowed as he delayed passing the car into Mexico. The man's face looked vaguely familiar.

"Will you be staying in Mexico long?"

"Just a few days, on vacation."

"Where will you be staying, sir?"

"In San Felipe."

Santos's right hand twitched, almost ready to snap out the clearance to proceed. Businessmen were always going to San Felipe, trying to arrange for imports or exports of textiles and fruit. Nothing wrong with his story. But he did look slightly familiar . . .

"Do you have anything to declare?" Santos asked.

The bait question, the one that can fracture a profile that otherwise is perfect in all respects.

The man's eyes darted away from the guard's scrutiny for only a moment—just a quick glance away—before he answered, "Nothing. I have nothing to declare."

It was automatic from that point on. The right hand reached down and unsnapped the leather strap holding his pistol. The left hand pointed to a parking area next to the INS building. The right hand then rested lightly on top of the pistol as he said, "Would you pull your car over to the left here, sir, into that parking space for a routine check?"

Santos's suspicions jumped another notch when the man smiled nervously and asked, "Is there some kind of problem, Officer?"

When there is contraband, you ask if there is "some kind of problem." When there is no contraband, you become upset that you're going to be delayed for twenty or thirty minutes, that your business associate or your mistress in San Felipe will wonder why you're late, that you have to put up with all this bureaucratic bullshit. You never smile and ask if there's a problem.

Santos's hand gripped the handle of his pistol. It would only take three seconds to have it out and to empty all six cartridges into the car.

"No, sir, this is just routine. Would you pull your car forward to that parking space? You're holding up the cars behind you."

"Certainly, Officer." The man smiled again as he reached into his shirt pocket and pulled out a $100 bill. He smoothly rolled it up in his hand, just the denomination showing, as he held it out to the officer.

"Would this help clear up the need for a routine check?"

In an instant Santos's gun was out of the holster

and pointed at the driver's head as his left hand opened the door. "Put your hands on top of your head and get out of the car!" he barked loudly.

The man's face turned ashen as he placed his hands on his head and eased out of the car. "Lie down, facedown, right here!" Santos said as he kept his gun pointed at the man's head. Two officers ran out of the INS building with their guns drawn as Santos handcuffed the man's hands behind his back. One of the officers drove the car into the parking space and opened the trunk as the other officer helped frisk the man and escorted him to the holding area inside the INS building. Ten minutes later, they had logged as evidence the suitcase, packed with twenty-four stacks of small bills that totaled $237,480, and containing a tightly sealed container of granular crystals that looked just like sugar. The station commander congratulated Santos for remembering the fax picture of Peter Martel, and suggested that the border guard might be looking at an early promotion.

At 6:25 P.M., Detective Jeff Lord of the Los Angeles Drug Enforcement Administration received a call advising him that Peter Martel was waiting for him in the INS holding cell at the Mexicali crossing. The officers of the Immigration and Naturalization Service were thanked and then cautioned by Detective Lord to not open the container of crystals for any reason, until the U.S.C./L.A. County Public Health and Toxicology Department's specialist in botulism was ordered to proceed directly to Mexicali, without delay.

By 6:30 that evening, Decker and Skeeters had completed the repair work on the two World Saviors from KTTV and had endured over an hour of sermons that had told of the impending Armageddon that would finally settle the forces of Good and Evil. Fully educated on all matters pertaining to the Natural, the Supernatural, and the Future, they signed their final progress notes, said good-bye to all, and walked out of the U.S.C./L.A. County Hospital.

"Take care of yourself, Blake," Decker said as they shook hands. "Watch out for needles and Evil Forces, and good luck with your baby."

"Thanks, Steve, and good luck to you and Katie— she's a great gal and you deserve the best."

"Thank you, I appreciate that." Decker looked closely at Skeeters and smiled. "I've got to tell you something. When we started this month, I wasn't quite sure I wanted you as my partner on the Jail Ward. But considering your demonstrated ability to work well under pressure, could I invite you to be my best man at my wedding in a couple of months?"

"Of course, I would be honored, just let me know when," Skeeters said as he stuck out his hand. "Good luck the rest of the year, and please call me if any more of your patients develop problems with infra-mammary fungi."

They shook hands a final time and departed in opposite directions. Decker trotted down the steps to the wide emergency room driveway, searching for Katie. A brand-new 1991 Corvette pulled into the driveway, its wheels gleaming, its light-blue metallic paint shining with a flawless mirror finish; the beautiful dark-haired woman waved from the driver's seat as she pulled up to the curb. The passenger door popped open and a sleek greyhound dog with white gauze wrapped around both hind legs jumped out and ran unsteadily toward Decker. As the dog's tail wagged furiously, Decker patted him on the head and led him to the car.

"Hello, sweetheart, how does it drive?" he asked as she held the door open for him.

"Like a dream, and the stereo is fantastic!"

He gently lifted Limpy and climbed into the car, shutting the door just as the parking lot guard realized he had an opportunity to show his badge and exercise his authority.

"Let's get out of here," he said after giving her a quick kiss. As Limpy frantically licked Decker's face, Katie smoothly accelerated the car into a sweeping U-turn in front of the guard, the tires giving just the right amount of insolent squeal, and they accelerated up Zonal Avenue to the Golden State Freeway.

Skeeters wandered down the row of cars in the B level of the parking structure, searching for his Volkswagen. It was always hard to find because of its size and dark blue—almost camouflage—color. After the first couple of days at the hospital, when he had wandered around the parking structure searching for his car for prolonged periods of time, he had learned to note its position precisely. He found it in the far corner of the lot, and after several attempts he finally was able to start the engine and rumble out of the structure in the direction of Pasadena.

A half hour later, after avoiding several near-accidents among the surging masses of steel on the Pasadena Freeway, he opened his apartment door and announced his arrival. Barbara was wearing a white maternity dress with orange flowers. She smelled fresh and sweet as she kissed him and led him across the living room toward the sofa.

"You've got to be sitting down when you hear this!" she told him excitedly.

"When I hear what?"

He eased into the corner of the sofa as she sat next

to him and began telling him of the calls. The telephone had never stopped ringing all day. It had hit the AP wires like an explosion—the story of the search for the Jail Ward nurse, the arrest of the deputy sheriff, the drug possession and distribution charges against forty-seven prisoners at the County Jail, and the suicide of the director of the Jail Ward. Skeeters and Decker had become national figures almost overnight. *People* magazine had made the top offer, $45,000 to each doctor, including round-trip airfare to New York, and they had left the number to call "within the next twelve hours" when the decision about the offer had been made.

"Also"—her eyes lit up again—"fourteen internal medicine residency directors had called during the last six hours, including the one in charge of the UCLA Medical Center Training Program, asking if you would like to join the medicine residency at their facility. Somehow they all know of your record at Harvard, and about half of them, including the UCLA one, said you would be more 'in your element' with their programs than at the County Hospital."

"*People* will pay me $45,000 just to fly there and be interviewed?" Skeeters asked.

"That's what they said. They want to know about Choo-Choo and what he did to Grossman to get the confession, and they want to know about that fellow Diamond. You'll have to take a week off your next month rotation, and you have to agree to keep it an exclusive interview with *People*."

Skeeters leaned back on the sofa and stretched. "That $45,000 would help pay off the medical school debts, and we could buy a new car . . . it sure would help our future," he said. "But I start gastroenterology tomorrow, can't lose time from that."

"A little time away would be okay."

Skeeters looked into his wife's eyes and said softly, "Speaking of the future, you know all those prisoners I took care of that night I was stuck with the needle? They all were HIV negative. Just got the news this afternoon, straight from Ben Foster in Pathology. Even that one they thought was positive. So there is virtually zero risk of AIDS. One less thing to worry about."

Barbara had stiffened imperceptibly as he spoke, listening carefully to his words. When he finished, she let out a sigh of relief, leaned over, and gave him a tender kiss. "Thank God," she said so quietly that he could barely hear her. He put his arms around her and held her tightly as they savored the moment.

"What do you want me to do with this *People* offer and with the offers from the other medical centers?" he asked.

"I want what you want, honey, it's up to you. It is as simple as that."

"Okay," he said. Skeeters stood up and began pacing around the living room. "Okay! We politely decline offers from other medical centers—I have eleven more rotations at the White Mama, and I'm going to complete them. We'll be especially polite to UCLA and look at them again at the end of the year."

"And *People* magazine? We need to get back to them tonight—"

"*People* magazine! We'll tell 'em okay, but they will have to come out here—I'll do the interviews at night or whenever, so long as I don't miss any time in gastroenterology. They shouldn't have a problem with that; I'm sure they have a regional office in Los Angeles. And no medical information about the prisoners from me—none! They were my patients and I was their doctor, and they deserve the confidentiality; *People* will have to get what they can about the pa-

tients from other sources. But I'll tell them all they
want to know about Peter Martel and Mel Grossman
. . . about the deputy sheriffs and the director, they'll
love it."

"And we can get a new car?" Barbara asked.

"Yes, honey, we can get a new car."

"A station wagon?"

"A station wagon! Why do we want a station
wagon?"

She stood up and walked over to him, taking his
hands and looking into his eyes. "We're going to need
the room," she said. "Remember, I took the bus to
Huntington Memorial Hospital this morning, to see
Dr. Gracely for my seven-month OB checkup."

"Yes . . ." Skeeters said patiently. He knew that if
he interrupted, she would just start all over again.

"Well, Dr. Gracely thought I looked bigger than
she thought I should look, and so, next thing I knew,
she sent me for an ultrasound."

Skeeters's eyebrows raised as he watched her closely.
"And the ultrasound showed?"

"Well, the ultrasound showed that we're going to . . ."
She looked at her husband. "Are you ready for this?"

"You're going to have . . ."

"We're going to have twins!" she blurted out. "And
they look really healthy, too!"

He stared at his wife's abdomen. "You have twins
in there?"

"Isn't that exciting! Kind of scary, actually. Anyway, there's going to be four of us pretty soon, and
we're going to have to carry strollers and diaper bags,
and toys and all that sort of thing—"

"And diapers, tons of diapers . . . my God, twins!"

She pulled him to her and gave him a long kiss.
"Think of it as a reward," she said happily. "A reward

for both of us completing your Jail Ward rotation, a reward for being alive, and . . . most important . . ."

"Most important . . . a reward for our being in love."